# The Hornets' Nest of Our Desires

# Books by Ron Terpening

## Fiction

*In Light's Delay*

*The Turning*

*The Echoes of Our Two Hearts*

*Storm Track*

*League of Shadows*

*Tropic of Fear*

*Nine Days in October*

*Cloud Cover*

## Nonfiction

*Charon and the Crossing*

*Lodovico Dolce, Renaissance Man of Letters*

*Beautiful Italy, Beloved Shores. An Illustrated Cultural History of Italy*

## Edited Works

*Anthology of Italian Literature, Volume 1: Middle Ages and Renaissance*

*Anthology of Italian Literature, Volume 2: From the Seventeenth Through the Twentieth Century.*

# The Hornets' Nest of Our Desires

The Artie Crenshaw Trilogy

## Ron Terpening

Desert Bloom Press
Tucson, Arizona

For Vicki
"Nature has but little clay … like that of which she moulded you."
— VIRGINIA WOOLF, *To the Lighthouse*

This book is a work of fiction. Names, characters, places, and incidents are either the product of the author's imagination or are used fictitiously. Any resemblance to actual events or locales or persons, living or dead, is entirely coincidental.

Desert Bloom Press Trade Paperback Edition
© 2023 by Ron Terpening
All rights reserved.

For information please contact
Desert Bloom Press
6808 N Bobcat Ridge Trl
Tucson, AZ 85743-8351

Publisher's Cataloging-in-Publication Data
Names: Terpening, Ron, 1946-.
Title: The hornets' nest of our desires : the Artie Crenshaw trilogy / Ron Terpening.
Other titles: The turning. | In light's delay. | The echoes of our two hearts.
Description: Tucson, AZ : Desert Bloom Press, 2023. | The turning and In light's delay were previously published separately and are newly revised in this edition.
Identifiers: LCCN 2023942583 | ISBN 9780962145278 (pbk.) | ISBN 9780962145285 (ebook)
Subjects: LCSH: Man-woman relationships – Fiction. | Teenagers – Fiction. | College students – Fiction. | Travel – Fiction. | Marriage – Fiction. | Divorce – Fiction. | Oregon – Fiction. | Italy – Fiction. | Mexico – Fiction. | New York (N.Y.) – Fiction. | BISAC: FICTION / Coming of Age. | FICTION / Family Life / Marriage & Divorce. | FICTION / Historical / 20th Century / Post-World War II.
Classification: LCC PS3570.E6767 H67 2023 | DDC 813.54 T—dc23
LC record available at https://lccn.loc.gov/2023942583

*The Turning*. First Desert Bloom Press trade paperback printing February 2001. Revised edition © 2023 by Ron Terpening
*In Light's Delay*. First Desert Bloom Press trade paperback printing May 1988. Revised edition © 2023 by Ron Terpening
*The Echoes of Our Two Hearts*. Desert Bloom Press trade paperback printing July 2023. First edition © 2023 by Ron Terpening

ronterpening.com
desertbloompress.com

Printed in the United States. on acid-free paper

# Contents

... He has simply stepped into the quicksilver of a mirror as we all must—to leave our illnesses, our evil acts, the hornets' nest of our desires, still operative for good or evil in the real world—which is the memory of our friends.
— LAWRENCE DURELL, *Justine*

[Of narrow- and broad-gauge people]
He ... felt himself to be a giant whom life had made "broad gauge," and denied opportunity. Fecund nature begets and squanders thousands of these rich seeds in the wilderness of life.
— OWEN WISTER, *The Virginian*

... The shadows of our own desires stand between us and our better angels ...
— CHARLES DICKENS, *Barnaby Rudge*

# The Turning

## (1962)

Sixteen candles make a lovely light
but not as bright as your eyes tonight.
Blow out the candles
make your wish come true
for I'll be wishing
that you love me, too.

— Sixteen Candles
The Crests
(Dixon/Kent) © 1958

# one

I didn't mind being alone. I even left the radio off so I could hear the car as it whooshed its way through the warm night air, dark fields stretching away into nothingness at either side of the road. Not a car in sight at that hour. Nothing out there but ... what? Cows probably, all bunched up in the dark chewing their cud. Maybe a possum or two, a stray dog on the prowl. And somewhere farther back, well off the road at the end of dirt or gravel drives, there'd be families asleep in old farmhouses, ramshackle places surrounded by rickety wood sheds and big old barns with hay lofts that creaked as they cooled.

I didn't feel like going home. Too keyed-up for that. Too much of the night left.

*Come on, Artie, think of something.*

They'd let us go early at the cannery. It was the end of the season on blackberries, broccoli just starting, and one hour into the graveyard shift there was nothing left to do. Everywhere you looked, white lights blazed away, and then the machines—the feeder bins, washing tanks, grading lines, carton sealers—all rumbled to a stop, and the din faded away.

Strange—all those bright lights and no noise. Even the air, after so much clamor, seemed stunned by the lack of sound.

For a moment, just before punching the time clock, I thought about hiding out behind the stacks of empty crates on the loading dock so I could pick up a few extra hours, but the foreman was standing there eyeing us as we filed out and headed for the parking lot. Short paycheck this week and school about to start. It wouldn't make dad too happy if I came around later in the year asking *him* for money. Not that I'd get any.

In the parking lot, Eddy and Glenn were at it again—face to face, each waiting for the other to swing first. It was almost a nightly occurrence anymore. It started when Glenn took Eddy's girlfriend, Wendy. But that was never what they said; it was always something different if you listened to them. Glenn had scratched the side of Eddy's Impala or Eddy had stolen Glenn's lunch from the locker room and dumped it in the trash or … whatever. They had to work hard to hate each other, but it seemed to come natural—especially to Eddy.

I stopped about ten feet away and watched. There must have been about a dozen of us by then. The more of us there were, the less likely they'd actually fight. Most of the time it was threats. You had to watch out for Eddy though. He liked to kick. I saw him shift his weight, his knee bending, just so he could smirk when Glenn twitched.

I could see what Glenn was thinking: He'd started to lift his right leg and turn, ready to protect his crotch. But Eddy wouldn't aim for that; he'd go for a shin—a quick sharp kick before you saw it coming.

I listened to them cussing at each other for a while. Eddy, Glenn, and I had played on the basketball team last year and I thought about trying to say something to distract them. The only problem was, Eddy might take advantage of the distraction to get in a rabbit punch. Leave them alone and they might just shove each other. That way it wouldn't get too serious, and the rest of the guys could break it up if any blood started flowing. But you could see nothing was going to happen. I'd kind of hoped that Glenn would teach Eddy a lesson. He was big enough—but you had to fight dirty to have a chance against Eddy.

What a waste of time. I finally just walked off.

The Mercury was down at the other end of the dirt lot. On my way there, I kicked through the soft dust, thinking about how much I hated fighting. I never understood what Eddy got out of it. And I doubt he could've explained it either. I unlocked the car, knocked my feet on the door frame to clean my work boots, tossed my lunch sack in and slid behind the wheel. My stomach was churning like a washing machine and my skin felt tight as a drum—like all the moisture had been sucked out of the air. It wasn't hard to figure out why.

I'd had my share of fights with Eddy in grade school—most of the time when we were just supposed to be playing. Freshman year in high school I tried to avoid him. But last year, when we beat Centennial High in the last game of the season, and I'd made the winning basket with Eddy sitting on the bench, he'd rushed out yelling and screaming with the other guys and then raked me down the side with his fingernails. Like he was just celebrating and got carried away. It wiped the smile off my face. Thinking about it now made me feel bad again. I was sure he'd done it on purpose—and *why?* That's what I couldn't figure out. Everybody *else* was happy. Why couldn't Eddy join in?

I'd seen his dad one time, sitting in an armchair at their home, eyes open, never moving, metal plate in his head from when they cut out the tumor. But that was no excuse. Everybody had problems. Everyone was angry at the world over something. I mean, a father sitting there saying nothing was better than one who cuffed you on the head, called you a lazy, no-good bum, and beat you if you ever talked back.

I shook my head. I'd trade places any day.

But I didn't want to think about Eddy when the night was out there waiting.

Before shifting into reverse I looked at my watch in the light of the dash. It was just after eleven. Plenty early.

*Use your* head, *Artie.*

Maybe I could find somebody in town—guys hanging out around the Hood Theater after the late show or necking in the Piggly Wiggly parking lot after running the gut for an hour or two. If I went home, I'd wind up sitting in my room with nothing to do until I got sleepy. And besides, I had the car. Dad wouldn't need it until time for work in the morning. He'd have to be psychic to call the cannery and find out we'd been let go early. Psychic or his usual tricky self. Sometimes it seemed I had a knack for getting caught. That's what made it hard to decide where to go—and you couldn't just do what they said: When you come to the fork in the road, take the fork. No, you had to make a *choice.*

And that was when it started. That was when I took a chance. Leaving the parking lot, I turned left—away from home. I was betting that dad was sitting in his easy chair watching TV or working in the shop. Either way, he wouldn't be thinking about me. They didn't expect me to get off till six in the morning—and sometimes I put in an hour of overtime.

*Go left, Artie.*

That was what I said and it was like the steering wheel just turned on its own and my hand followed along.

Boy, the air was warm—especially after the cannery; they kept the place pretty cold so the berries wouldn't rot. I held the wheel between my knees, peeled out of my long-sleeved flannel shirt, and tossed it in the back. Couldn't help grinning at how good it felt to be free. I had the whole night ahead of me. It was just a question of filling it. Like I said, I didn't mind being alone but still ...

For some reason I thought of this girl. Sheryl Lynn. The prettiest girl in school. At least I thought so, though she wore an awful lot of makeup. But it was strange—I never saw her with anyone else. She didn't have any boyfriends—and none of the other girls used to hang around her either. Maybe because she was so quiet. I never saw her talk to anyone. That just goes to show you. Looks aren't everything. You gotta have a personality. If they don't run in your crowd, they might as well be dead.

I know I'd never talked to her. I never even thought about her maybe being a girlfriend. I don't know what you say to a beautiful girl when you don't know her. You can't just walk up and blurt out, "You're so beautiful it scares me." Which is pretty much the truth—but you can't just *say* it. And what would she do if you did?

Probably turn around and walk away.

I can't even *imagine* talking to a beautiful girl. I mean, some guys can joke. Just walk up to a girl, throw their arm around them and say something funny. Something to make them laugh and giggle and maybe even blush—but you can tell they like it.

For me, that'd be like trying to lasso a horse with a garland of dandelions. I just couldn't do it.

I can go home and think for an hour about what to say to someone I like— and it still doesn't come. It's like one of those story problems in math. You hear the question and your mind freezes. *Two trains start from stations twenty miles apart. Point A and Point B. One is going fifteen miles an hour and makes two fifteen minute stops. The other is going forty miles an hour and stops once for five minutes. Where do they meet? Point C.* You hear it and it's like a big wall in front of you. It's like all the cells in your brain just went dead. You go dumb. Same with a girl. You can't tell your tongue what to say. There's no connection between your brain and your mouth.

And if you could speak, you somehow know you couldn't pull it off. It would sound fake—like something you'd rehearsed at home.

Just thinking about it, my heart started thumping and my hands got sweaty. *Panic.*

I had to laugh. What an idiot. Eyes wide like a frightened horse's.

Yeah, that was bad. And it was worse if you were already in love. You're already in love and you haven't even said a word to her.

That was usually me, alright. In love and dumb.

Maybe it was time to turn on the radio!

But I didn't reach for the dial.

---

I came over a slight rise and the car sank down on its shocks like a flat pebble on its last skip across the pond. The smooth black surface of the road was slipping by below me and off in the distance I could see one lonely green dot—the last stoplight at the far end of town, all soft and hazy at the edges like a period at the end of a dark, moldy sentence. I stared at it for a while, listening to the tires whistle over the blacktop. The light didn't look like it'd ever go red.

Man, there had to be *something* better to do than drive halfway to Mt. Hood and back, just to be driving. Maybe take a run through town and see if I could scare up anyone I knew.

It was like I had to say it twice to convince myself; I don't know why it was so hard to decide—it wasn't like trying to choose between cherry pie and lemon meringue. It should have been easy: Stay out and have fun or go home and sit in a stuffy room. At this hour, it wasn't like I'd run into somebody who'd tell my dad in church—Hey, Pastor, saw Artie tooling around downtown the other night.

*Right?*

Before I could chicken out, I swung off the road onto the Loop Highway, passing just short of the spill of white light from the solitary pole at the intersection with Eastmont. Halfway around the curve, still going about forty-five, I slid the automatic into second. My foot eased off the gas and a grin broke out as the muffler went *pop-pop-pop-pop-pop* and then began its descent into a long throaty growl.

Man, that was loud. It sounded like a logging rig coming down a muddy pass in the Cascades. With a full load to boot. I was glad dad didn't have the money to fix the muffler. It had an old, rusty hole getting bigger all the time. I couldn't let it backfire in town was all. Cops would be only too happy to write me out a ticket. And then dad would wonder what I was doing in town at that time of night.

Coming out of the curve, the first thing I saw was the new bowling alley, sitting by itself in a field off to the right. Right then I knew what I wanted to do. Bowl! It wouldn't hurt to see if anybody was hanging around and maybe roll a line or two. It was something to do until I was tired enough to hit the sack.

When I pulled into the parking lot the tires crunched over the gravel with a sound that got me edgy with anticipation. To the left, half the lot was paved with fresh asphalt. You could smell the hot oil. A yellow steel-wheel roller sat at the end of the pavement. Swarms of moths fluttered around the light poles.

I saw right off there were only two other cars there, both parked up against the rough rock wall to the left of the double doors. Guys hanging around. The lights inside the bowling alley looked like they'd already been dimmed.

I hit the steering wheel.

*Closed.*

"Darn it, Artie, you're too late." And then I bit my lip.

That was a bad habit I'd fallen into over the course of the summer. Talking to myself. None of my friends worked at the cannery and I was pretty much a loner on the job. Sometimes I spoke out loud just to make sure I was awake and not dreaming. Still, I tried not to let other people see me doing it, especially in town. Like I didn't have friends or something.

It was too late to turn around without looking like an idiot. Have to play it cool, swing by the cars like I knew what I was doing. I didn't want to look desperate. I glanced at the guys as I got closer, foot light on the accelerator.

No one I knew. They looked like greasers, the guys in white T-shirts and jeans, the girls in cutoffs and skimpy blouses. Two guys leaned against the hood of a stripped-down '64 Chevelle, smoking and trying to look tough, with three girls hanging all over them. The other car was a white Ford Fairlane. It looked like it belonged to the owner of the bowling alley. No greaser'd be caught dead in that thing.

"Artie," I muttered, trying not to move my lips, "you made a mistake." They were eyeing me now, like I didn't belong there. Have to say something. I'd look like a dork, driving in and out by myself.

I tapped the brakes and stuck my head out the window. "You guys know Billy Deater?" Billy was my best friend. "Drives a two-tone Oldsmobile Eighty-Eight … green and white."

They stared at me without saying anything. I could feel my face flush. Stupid question. Billy didn't run around with greasers. They wouldn't know him if he was the president of the senior class. And Billy was pretty much of a nonentity; he sort of blended into the masses that occupied the middle tier at school between the rich, the intelligent, and the athletes—all at the top, and the poor kids, greasers and hoods at the bottom. And then there were some of us like me, stuck in the middle because we didn't fit into any of the categories—smart but not an egghead, poor but not a hood, an athlete but not a jock, someone who read books and wrote stories in his spare time—although I didn't let anyone except my English teacher know that. You would've thought I'd have a *lot* of friends, right? Only I didn't. Billy was the only one.

And that was because I'd known him since grade school.

I tried again. "You seen the car? It's a '58 two-door sedan."

They'd probably stolen and stripped a few in their time. You could tell just looking at their car that they knew how to work on them. Front shocks chopped, a blower sticking out of the hood, fiery pin striping down the sides.

One of the guys said something I couldn't hear and the girls laughed. No one looked too interested in me. I don't know why I even tried to talk to them. I didn't like feeling like a moron in front of greasers.

"Yeah, well, thanks anyway."

I turned the Mercury around and spun a little gravel in their direction. I looked at the cloud of dust in the rearview mirror, worried then that I'd overdone it and they'd come after me.

At the exit onto Eastmont, I hesitated. Another darn fork in the road. Same old decision—go right through town on my way home or head out into the countryside for a half-hour ride. I hated having to decide.

*One or the other?*

I guess having a choice was better than none. It was just that making a choice made you responsible for what happened. And if things went bad, Dad would be standing there with a switch in his hand when I got home. I shook my head and tapped the steering wheel.

*Make up your mind, Artie.*

But sometimes you don't even realize you have a choice—you just continue along the same old path like an ox heading for slaughter. And why? Because you're dumb and it's easier to do nothing. I didn't want to be like that. I had a chance for freedom and I was going to take it.

Anyway, a ride in the countryside was starting to sound better now. Out there under the black velvet sky with its tiny polka dots of mother-of-pearl, the car cutting through the night like an arrow, the only sound the *gre-gre* of thousands of frogs and the purring of the motor. And if I got lonely I could listen to KISN—"Ninety-One-derful on your radio dial," broadcasting strong from Portland, thirteen miles to the west. *Hey*, it was better than sitting in a little room going out of your mind with boredom.

"Don't want to go home yet, Artie," I said.

If dad was still up, he'd want me to come in and watch TV with the rest of the family. My older brother Richy and I were staying upstairs in a separate house on the property—a two-story fake-colonial mansion. The main floor was used as a church on Sunday and for Wednesday night prayer meetings.

But other than that, Richy and I had it to ourselves—and I hardly ever saw him because he was working days as a carpenter's assistant and I was working nights at the cannery. We each had a separate bedroom upstairs. Mom, dad, my younger brother Bobby and my sister Nancy were living in a smaller one-story frame house a stone's throw away from the church. The house used to be a chicken coop—no lie—and the church used to be an old folks' home. It had five big white Ionic columns on the front porch.

For all they knew, I was still at work. Why waste the chance for some fun? I was free!

Freedom—that was a double-edged sword! The night shift always got the worst of it, it seemed. None of us had any seniority. The day shift got most of the work.

And there was something else I didn't like. A lot of the farmers were switching from berries to broccoli. That didn't make me happy. You could snack on a good sweet berry—a nice, plump boysenberry, say, but who ever heard of munching on a sprig of broccoli? And if you were lucky and could swipe a whole can of something—like Grade-A Bel-Air raspberries—you had a real treat. And sweet, sticky syrup to dip your fingers in afterward. It made my mouth water to think of it. I had a can of strawberries in my lunch sack. Frozen solid an hour ago. I'd grabbed it off a damaged tray in the drive-in freezer when the foreman sent me in there to tell the Hyster driver we were shutting down.

I reached over, opened my lunch bag, and squeezed the can. The berries were already starting to thaw. It wouldn't be long before I could eat them.

"Artie, you should head in to Dea's before they close. Get some fries."

*Yeah, right.* Bounce from the greasers at the bowling alley to the rich kids at Dea's. They hung out there with their fancy cars, bought for them by their parents. They parked nose out along the sides near the drive-by window, then stood around in creased slacks and dress shirts, with their sweaters tied around their shoulders and their hair neatly trimmed. They probably went to the barbershop once a week and I'd only been once in my entire life. My dad cut my hair—when he got around to it, which, fortunately, wasn't more than once every four or five months. I *hate* short hair, just like I hated most of those guys.

Okay, it wasn't really hate, I didn't even know them, but I rarely stopped at Dea's In and Out. I didn't like looking like a country bumpkin while they talked about me behind my back.

But the hamburger stand was probably the only place open at that time of night.

*Shoot.*

Dea's was a weird place. They fixed their hamburgers on these strange rectangular buns, with the meat in the same shape. The rich always had to have things different. Made them feel special, I guess.

It's not that I have a chip on my shoulder, going on about those guys, it's just that me and my friends don't have money to throw around. And it's not even that Dea's is expensive, because it's about the same as anywhere else. Maybe a dime or two more on their hamburgers is all. It doesn't even look special—a square frame building with an overhanging roof on all four sides, a pole out front with a round Coca-Cola sign on it and at the top a big arrow pointing in with neon letters—SHAKES • BURGERS • FRIES—and on top that *Dea's In and Out*, and a yellow barrel for trash at one corner of the place.

I was still sitting at the exit from the bowling alley's parking lot and had just about made up my mind to go to Dea's when I looked up and died. It was like a bullet had gone straight through my belly.

*Our Chevy pickup was flashing by, barely twenty feet away!*

The second I saw it, my heart dropped about a foot, bounced into my stomach, burst into flames like a marshmallow on fire, ricocheted back to my throat, clanged like a horseshoe round an iron stake, and sucked the air right out of my lungs. *It was that bad.*

I knew right off I was done for. Dad had caught me. The son of a bum had done it again. I couldn't believe how sick I felt.

# two

There was no doubt about it. That was our pickup. I'd seen the busted-up fender on the right side, the lousy paint job—gray primer on light green, the wood stakes in the bed frame. It might as well have said *Crenshaw and Sons* on the side.

I couldn't breathe. I waited for the brake lights to go red and the tires to squeal. Dad had to have seen me. I couldn't move.

Caught again!

Why'd it always have to happen to me?

An excuse—there had to be something I could say. What was I doing? Taking somebody home after work? Dropping somebody off at the bowling alley? It'd be just like dad to go back to the place and check.

Another beating …

But the pickup kept going! I couldn't believe it. He'd gone right by me and been struck blind. *It was a miracle!* I almost laughed out loud.

I watched as the taillights moved away, then suddenly slouched down in the seat in case he looked in the rearview mirror. You could get thankful too quick around my dad—and then disaster would strike. Another week of bruises.

What was he doing out here at this hour of the night? I looked at my watch again. Eleven-twenty. There was a feed store in Boring out this way, but it would have closed hours ago. Had he gone to the cannery looking for me? If so, I didn't know how I was going to beat him home. Go a hundred miles an hour on some back route?

Not very likely.

I heard a girl yelling then.

I glanced to my left and saw the Chevelle had pulled up next to me. The driver gunned his motor and let the clutch in and out while keeping his foot on the brake. Big deal. I was still shaking and didn't feel like talking now. My hands gripped the wheel so tight they hurt.

"Hey, you wanna drag?"

I took a deep breath, loosened my fingers, and looked over at her. She had long stringy black hair, a saucy face. She looked like a Senior. Maybe a year or two older than me. Not anyone I'd consider cute.

I didn't say anything. I couldn't think straight. I was still trying to swallow—and at the moment that was hard enough.

I tapped the accelerator, left foot on the brake, and stared straight ahead. If dad was looking for me, I'd get whipped no matter when I went home. Scratch the car though and my butt would be sore for a month—and I'd have to pay to fix it.

Everywhere I looked, all I saw was trouble.

But it was tempting. A '57 Merc against a '64 Chevelle. A family car against a hot-rod. An automatic against stick shift. But I'd always thought the Mercury Monterey had good acceleration for its size. This was a chance to see how it would do. I'd never raced anyone before.

One of the guys in the back seat mouthed off, "Hell, he don't want to."

"Come on," the girl said. "You can see he wants to."

I looked over at her, she was popping the door, half out of the Chevy now. She bent over, her butt to me, tight pants cut mid-thigh, the bottom edge frayed. I could see her back where her blouse was riding up. She had white skin, which looked cool under the fluorescent lights in the parking lot. You could tell she didn't work in the sun. Probably slept all day and partied all night with these hoods.

"I'll ride with him," she told them. "He's by himself."

*Yeah, right. The loner dork.* How'd I get into these things?

I looked down at my work shirt. It was stained with berries and dirt. I'd been dumping crates on the grading lines until they let us go. I looked a mess, especially with the streetlight at the exit hitting me square in the face. I eased the Mercury forward, hoping to get into shadow. I still couldn't believe dad hadn't seen me.

"Hey, wait," the girl said. She opened the door and looked in. Her dark scraggly hair hung down over her chest. "I'll ride with you. Make the weight more even."

"I just got off work." Jeez, what a dumb thing to say.

She didn't seem interested. "Follow him," she said, rolling down the window on her side. The Chevy had turned left, out toward the Loop Highway. Away from dad and the pickup.

"Hey, what's this?" She had her hand on a paperback lying on the seat between us.

I swung out after the Chevelle. "A book." Gosh, now she probably thought I sat in the car and read for entertainment. The book was for break time in the lunch room.

"Oh, yeah? Whatcha readin'? This is big." Like all she read was comic books.

"*Of Human Bondage.*"

"You into kinky things?"

"What?"

"Bondage."

She got me with that one. I didn't say anything, just shook my head no, trying to figure out if she was joking or just dumb. I mean, we were in high school now, not kindergarten.

The other guy turned right at the intersection with the Loop Highway, and I had to step on the gas to keep up.

"So, you like reading?" She was thumbing through the book, head scrunched down to see in the dim light from the dashboard.

"Helps pass the time at work—during our breaks."

And, yeah, I liked it. That's one thing you'd think my dad would like, too, but he doesn't. He's always jumping on me, asking why I don't join the family and why I always lock myself away in my room in the other house and read.

I mean, he's the one who taught me. I could read before I was five. Sure, I talk dumb sometimes, but that's just for fun, to fit in. When I was growing up we had to read a chapter of the Bible every morning after chores before leaving for school. I could recite the names of all thirty-nine books of the Old Testament and all twenty-seven of the New. You know—hard names like Hosea, Joel, Amos, Obadiah, Jonah. Start me anywhere—Micah, Nahum, Habakkuk, Zephaniah—and I'd rattle them off like a pro—Haggai, Zechariah, Malachi. I bet by the time I was in the third or fourth grade, I'd read the whole thing at least five times.

Shortest chapter in the Bible? Psalms 117. Two verses.

Longest verse in the Bible? Esther 8:9.

Longest chapter in the Bible? Psalms 119.

Chapter with every letter of the alphabet except *j*? Ezra 7:21.

Don't ask me about "Jesus wept."

It's not a bad book really. Sure, there's parts that are boring but sometimes in church, when I got tired of listening to my dad preach, I'd let my Bible pop open wherever it wanted and just start reading. Usually it was better than listening to my dad. I liked the Old Testament best—Proverbs and the Song of Solomon and Job and Lamentations. Believe it or not, some of that stuff's actually interesting.

Well, compared to a dry sermon.

The girl dropped the book after a few minutes and swung around toward me.

"What's your name, anyway?"

"Artie."

"Not just Art or Arthur?"

I shook my head, then brushed the hair out of my eyes. "A. R. T. I. E. My parents named us all with nicknames. I got two brothers, Richy and Bobby, and a sister, Nancy."

"Nancy ... that's not a nickname."

She had me there. "Well, it ends with *y*," I said. But, anyway, we call her Robin. Don't ask me why.

"I'm Reta Jane."

Hey, what could you say about that? Pleased to meet you, I guess, but I didn't think of that in time.

We drove for about fifteen minutes without talking much then. I was lost for one thing—started paying attention when it was too late. Scrubby trees and saplings stalked through the darkness to each side, with big empty fields behind them. We were on a county road somewhere between Boring and Sandy—two small towns that were dead at night and didn't have much to see in the daytime.

The Chevelle slowed to a stop when we turned on to a straight stretch near some fresh-plowed fields with a stand of tall dark fir trees in the distance. At the last second, as I was coming up behind him, the driver pulled to the left into the oncoming lane. It was pitch black out, no cars in sight for miles, a long, straight road.

I eased up next to him.

"You ready?" the girl in the other car asked, her head and both arms hanging out the window.

I nodded. I'd thought the other guy might try to lay a bet on the outcome.

"Okay, I'll give a countdown." She paused, and I looked ahead at the road. I couldn't see very much. Four cones of light from the two cars illuminated the asphalt, with faded splotches of white showing where the lanes had been painted years ago. My foot caressed the accelerator.

"You know how to do this?" Reta Jane asked.

I nodded, concentrating on the other car. *Hey*, it wasn't like trying to hold a popsicle in your mouth with no hands.

The girl in the other car went through a *ready, set, go*, and I hit the pedal. For a few seconds we were side by side, although actually I thought I'd beaten him to the punch, and then he started to pull away.

Reta Jane had her right hand on the dash, tangled hair whipping around her face. "Wait a minute," she yelled. "Slow down."

I hit the brakes, fishtailed, and then managed to come to a stop. I looked over at her. She sounded impatient like she was angry at something.

"Pull up next to Carl," she said.

The other driver had come to a stop ahead of us, sitting off to my left still.

I didn't know what she wanted. When the cars were side by side again, she scooted over and leaned across me. I could feel her breast on my arm.

"Carl, he didn't even rev up. Give him another chance."

She turned to me. "Look, you ever done this before?"

I just stared at her.

---

"You gotta hold the brake down and accelerate. You took off from a dead stop with an automatic. Give it some gas. He's got a Holley four-barrel carb and over three hundred cubes under the hood."

I didn't know much about motors and less about cubic inches. A V8 was a V8, wasn't it? If I'd been smart, we'd have stopped right then, but I wasn't, so we tried again. This time, I held the brake and stepped on the accelerator, hearing the motor whine, hesitant to rev it up too much for fear it would throw a rod or whatever it is cars do when they blow up. If I ruined the motor I could forget a beating; dad would kill me.

When the countdown reached "Go," the other guy must have been ready because the Chevelle surged out ahead of me. I'd done better without trying so hard. This time I tried to keep up for a bit and then realized it was worthless. He was pulling away, red lights growing smaller by the second, and I was already up to seventy. He had to have hit a hundred.

I eased off the accelerator and started tapping the brakes, while the hood dipped and rose and my head started swaying like an old man's rocking chair. When the needle hit twenty-five I took a deep breath and glanced at Reta Jane. The wind was whipping her hair into an angry black mop. "Didn't help," I said, easing finally to a stop. I had to breathe through my mouth, short quick gasps, my heart thudding in my chest as loud as the car's pistons.

"He beat you fair and square."

*Like I needed to be told.*

I tried to swallow, my mouth as dry as a dusty cow path after a long hot summer. I was thinking about going home, starting to get anxious again like a bunch of heifers ready to hoof it that last fifty feet to the water trough. Only thing was, it might be a switch waiting for me.

"Listen," she said, pulling a strand of hair from the corner of her mouth. "Can you take me some place?"

It took me a moment to absorb what she said. I stared at her face, pale in the dim light from the dash, wondering what she meant. Around us all was dark, the only sound the quiet hum of the motor, at rest now, the soft rustling of the breeze. The other car had turned around and I could see its headlights coming toward us.

"I need to stop by my uncle Fred's house. It's not far from here. Just over the line in Clackamas County."

I wanted to ask what was wrong with her asking her friends for a ride, but she must have read my mind because she said they were going back into town for something to eat. She'd join them later if I didn't mind dropping her off at the Polar King on East Powell. Fine by me. I was thinking of going back through town anyway. I was still bored—in an antsy way, if that makes sense—and it didn't look like being with Reta Jane was going to change that.

Five minutes later she'd said her good-byes, arranged to meet her friends in an hour, and she was directing me down roads so dark I had no idea where we were. It looked like a time warp had picked us up in Oregon and set us down in Africa.

The terrain was uneven, the road rising and falling, and when we were at the crest of one slope she said, "There's a creek at the bottom. Turn right just beyond it."

I slowed when we were over the culvert, trying to find a cutoff, and then saw a break in the barbed-wire fence that ran alongside us, and just beyond that a gravel road with a cattle guard.

The tires shuddered on the cattle guard and then crunched over the gravel. Grass grew window-high to each side. When the gravel ran out, the road turned to dirt and the track grew more rutted. I could hear the dry stalks of grass swishing on the front bumper and smell fresh-cut hay. A moment later, just ahead and off to the right, I saw an arc lamp on a pole and then the lights of a trailer and a low, flat-roofed house.

"That's it," she said. "Stop there by the house."

I pulled up next to an old Plymouth. The car was set up on blocks. Its bare rims glinted in the Mercury's headlights. I cut the engine. In the silence, I could hear the motor ticking away. Somewhere in the distance, maybe in the trailer, a radio was playing. What now? I thought.

"Come on in," she said. "I won't be long."

# three

I used to raise pigs. We lived on a small, five-acre farm, just off Division street between Portland and Gresham, and rented another 15 acres from a neighbor. Dad was trying to raise Angus cattle and for some reason, when he went to buy some weaners to clean up the garbage and have a little pork some day, I forked over twenty-five bucks and bought an eight-week old female for myself.

Elsie turned out to be one great sow. Her second litter came in at seventeen, her third nineteen. The average for a Yorkshire was supposed to be eleven. I'd never heard of one doing better than mine, although I suppose if I looked it up I'd find it wasn't a record. I never did make much money off her though. Dad took his share and charged me for all the grain she got. But I learned a thing or two. Not that I'll ever use it. I don't ever plan on living on a farm, and it wasn't just because of the pigs. I hated the work. All we ever did were chores. I wanted a little fun in life.

When Elsie had her first litter I was out in the shed with her. We'd built a little shelf-like thing around the sides about a foot off the ground so she wouldn't crush the babies when she flopped over on her side. The first time she had piglets, I had to rescue one that she bit. I thought he'd die, she left a scar down his whole side. You have to be careful the sows don't eat them. If they develop a taste the first time, they're ruined forever. They think the babies are rats or something. Most people don't know pigs love meat.

I delivered the babies by myself the first few times. Dad was usually off at his weekday job in construction—or if he was home he'd be preparing a sermon and didn't want to be interrupted. He left most of the farm chores to Richy and me.

When the piglets popped out, the first thing I had to do was pull the mucus out of their mouths and get them to breathing. Once the sow had delivered them all, I tied and cut the umbilical cords, then took some clippers and snapped off their needle teeth so they wouldn't cut the sow's teats. That was the hardest thing I've ever done. Some of the teeth would snap, others would shatter. It wasn't pleasant but after one squeal, the second you set them down by a nipple, they seemed to forget it. And Elsie was happy. One sharp bite and she'd have kicked their heads off without even meaning to.

Anyway, you'll see why I was thinking about pigs.

Reta Jane had disappeared the minute we arrived at her uncle's place, telling me to sit down in the living room while she took care of something. I figured she had to go to the bathroom and I was going to ask if I could use it after her, but she didn't come back for a long time. The couch I was sitting on was a dilapidated old thing covered with a tattered bedspread. Probably came from Goodwill. It smelled musty. The shade on the lamp was a cheap red cardboard. It was dented and torn near one of the seams. Someone had turned that part to the wall but it was a feeble attempt to hide what the rest of the room couldn't. They looked *awful* darn poor.

Her uncle Fred, coming in from outside, didn't seem surprised when he saw me. He was a burly, unshaven fellow with red eyes, and the first thing he said was, "You Reta Jane's boyfriend?" I could smell the whiskey from where I sat.

"I just, uh, brought Reta Jane here," I said, choking on the words. I hoped he wasn't drunk. He looked mean as a cornered rat.

"Yeah, where is she?"

"I don't know. She said she had something to take care of."

He looked at my clothes. "You just get off work?"

I nodded. "At the cannery. Gresham Berry Growers."

"Maybe you can give me a hand. I got two hogs to get to the butcher tomorrow and if I wait till the morning it's going to be one pain in the ass to load them by myself. How about helping out?"

I shrugged. I didn't really want to, but what could you say? I got to my feet.

He said, "You like roast corn?"

"Roast corn?" I'd never heard of it, and coming out of the blue his question set me back.

"Yeah, leftover corn on the cob. We can have Reta Jane fix us some in the oven. You ain't never had roasted corn?"

I shook my head. "Don't think so."

"Well, come on. Let's get done and you can try it." Fred turned around and bellowed for Reta Jane, and she shouted something from a back room. "We're going out to load the hogs," he yelled back. "Fix us some roast corn for when we get back."

Jeez, it stank. Pig manure everywhere. A pen barely big enough.

Pigs are clean animals and if they've got the room they always crap off in one corner. Cleaner than cows. These were Yorkshires, just like mine, and should have been light white with a little pink skin showing through, but they were so dirty they looked like Spotted Swine or some other breed with a black hide. They just didn't have enough room.

"Been rooting in the mud," Fred said. He'd backed a Chevy pickup up against the ramp leading to the pen.

Yeah, right. He called it mud. It was more like a manure pile. I felt sorry for the hogs.

"You get in behind them and drive them my way," Fred said. "Then we'll see if we can shove them up the ramp."

---

He'd set a pan of corn meal just inside the tailgate but neither pig wanted to climb the ramp. They were big suckers, a barrow and an old stag, which is a castrated boar, not the best meat. Each one must have weighed close to three hundred pounds. Fred had penned them up and grained them for too long, but now was no time to tell him that.

I was glad I had work boots on. The mud was a good six inches deep.

Fred handed me a club, a sawed-off piece of broomstick for stirring slop buckets, and I got in and started swatting the barrow in the butt. It squealed and tried to get away, and before I could get it over to the chute I fell two or three times myself.

How was I going to explain that when I got home? Now I was going to have to do a quick load of laundry before falling asleep.

Fred was standing just outside the chute giving his pig call—"Here, suey suey, here, suey suey"—over and over again, but it didn't seem to do much good. I wondered if he was enjoying himself. Stoked up on liquor and giving his pig call.

I tried to push the barrow up the ramp, with him grunting and snorting, got him halfway and then he lurched forward, squealed like he was having a cavity drilled out without anesthetic, and leapt off the side. You'd have thought he was walking off the plank of a pirate ship or crossing a catwalk over the Grand Canyon. He just didn't want to go up that ramp. Finally, after about ten minutes of work and another three or four tries, we got the one hog loaded and tied down so it wouldn't get away while we tried for the other.

That stag was one mean son of a gun. He knocked me on my butt more than once. I could hear Fred grunting and swearing. He was down in the mud now, too, trying to help. When we got the hog to the ramp, each step was like pushing a ton of bricks. The stag huffed and fought and we worked like the dickens to keep him lined up. Suddenly he let out a piercing shriek and pitched forward onto his snout. He snorted once or twice in panic, keeled over on his side, and started bouncing like he'd bitten through an electric wire.

"Holy mackerel!" Fred said. "He's having a heart-attack."

I didn't say anything at first. I was breathing hard and trying to hold the shaking body on the ramp. I could smell his crap, even above the ripe stench of the pen, as his bowels loosened. I had to wipe some off my hand on the edge of the ramp.

"Here," Fred said, "help me slide him on up into the pickup."

The ramp had cross boards tacked on it and it wasn't easy to slide the hog but we finally got him into the bed. "Gonna have to bleed him," Fred said. "He's dying. Can't ruin the meat. You wait here."

He disappeared and five minutes later came running up with a big butcher knife. "Here," he said, handing it through the side slats. "I'll hold him down while you cut his throat."

"*What?*"

Fred came around to the back and made it up the ramp, his feet unsteady. "Just cut his throat."

I clenched the knife, feeling sick, and stared at the old hog. It was in its last throes now. Maybe it'd be a kindness to kill it quick. I started to saw at the bristly flesh, hoping I'd find the jugular before the stag felt much.

"Come on," Fred said. "Cut the dang thing. Put him out of his misery."

I started sawing hard then, and before I was through I'd slit its throat from ear to ear. Fred told me I'd just about decapitated the hog.

"Pew—ee," he said, as he was latching the tail gate. "We stink like the dickens. Come on, I'll hose you down."

I followed him into the back yard, stumbling over a saw horse in the darkness, and stood there while he turned the hose on. I started shaking when the cold water hit me. Blood, manure, and mud flew everywhere. It took a long time before I felt clean and then I did the same to him.

The warm breeze was starting to feel cold and Fred saw me shiver. "Come on inside," he said. "Roast corn'll warm you up."

"I'm all wet."

"Shucks, that don't matter."

"Maybe I should take off my clothes and wring them out."

"Suit yourself if you want, but like I said, it don't matter. Reta Jane can mop up after us. Earn her keep for once."

I caught a glimpse of myself in a mirror when we went into the house. I looked like a half-drowned rat. Reta Jane was nice enough not to laugh, and she had the best ears of corn waiting for us I think I've ever eaten. Boiled the day before and now roasted in the oven until the kernels were bursting with flavor. We slathered butter over them and dived in. Man, that was good. I finished three cobs all by myself and then said I oughta be going.

"Can you take me to the Polar King?" Reta Jane asked me, and I looked at Fred who didn't say anything. He was on his third beer in the last fifteen minutes.

I nodded. She'd already asked me before, so this must be for Fred's sake.

"It's on my way," I said. "If your—" And then I shut up. I was going to ask Fred for permission but it didn't look like he had much control. That surprised me. He had thick arms like a plumber and I could see him getting mean with her if he wanted to. But like I said, he didn't seem to care. And he was just her uncle, after all.

Outside, I started thinking about getting the car seats wet and what dad would say in the morning if he got in to go to work and got soaked.

"I'm too wet," I told Reta Jane. "This is my dad's car and he'll kill me if I soak the seat."

She touched me on the arm. "Want to walk a bit? The breeze'll dry you off before too long."

"Where to?"

"Just up the road," she said. "No place special. Come on. We can talk."

# *four*

A full moon was rising over the trees behind us as we started out down the road. The breeze puffed gently in our faces. I could smell the night scents—clover and vetch and fescue—and a hint of perfume on Reta Jane. She talked up a storm for the first five minutes or so, with me just listening and nodding in the dark. Boy, she was a talker—but I liked it. It made things easier for me. I could just walk along and listen and grunt every now and then and try to think of something to say if there was a gap—some question I could ask.

"Say," she said, poking me in the arm, "I don't think you've said a word since we left the house. You still thinking about the hog?"

"Uncle Fred?"

She laughed and I was glad she'd taken it as a joke, which was how I meant it. She'd already told me her parents were dead and that she lived with her uncle. We walked on a few steps before she said, "You go to Gresham High?"

"Yeah."

"What year?"

"I'll be a Junior."

"Jeez, jail bait."

I didn't quite know how to take that. Was she saying I was too young for her—or was she saying she was interested in me? She was somebody's girlfriend. She had a ring on a chain around her neck. And besides, I didn't even know if I liked her.

"I dropped out last year," Reta Jane said, breaking the silence which had lengthened while I thought about what she'd said.

She looked the type, but I didn't say that. Hanging around with greasers and hoods. Most of them didn't last through their senior year. I figured I'd better ask her something or she'd think I was a real dimwit. "You didn't like it?"

She shrugged. I could feel her brush up against me in the darkness. An owl hooted, and I imagined big wings sweeping down softly and carrying us away. We were walking down the middle of the road, trees, shrubs, and waist-high grass to each side, all rustling in the breeze like feet gliding in slippers. A quiet, steady shuffle. Lonely sounds. I wanted to put my arm around her but didn't.

And then, just when I thought she wasn't going to answer, she said, "I got pregnant."

I felt my head snap around before I could stop it. I was hoping she hadn't noticed in the dark. Her belly was as flat as a fence post. "You, ah, get, ah ..."

"An abortion?" She laughed. "No. Uncle Fred watches the kid when I'm out. He's a good guy."

I didn't know if she meant her uncle or her kid. "What is it? A boy or a girl?"

"A girl. Janice Ann. That's why I wanted you to take me there. She's just about eight months old. I'm breast-feeding her."

She said it so normal. I didn't know how to take that. For some reason, it made me feel awkward. I'd been a bit attracted to her, even though she was kind of plain—just because she was a girl and we were out together, I suppose—but now, thinking about her nursing a kid, I didn't know. It kind of ruined any fantasies I might have had.

After a minute, she asked me, "What's your last name?"

"Crenshaw."

"Crenshaw. I've heard that name. Is your daddy a minister?"

Rats! She knew. "Yeah," I said finally, plodding along.

"Evangelical Free Methodist, right?"

I nodded in the darkness. "Used to be just Free Methodist," I said. "Without the Evangelical. That church behind the Main Library. On the corner of Fourth and Roberts." I paused, but she didn't say anything. "We lived in the parsonage next door when I was in grade school. And then the church split up a couple years ago. Half the people went with my dad and half stayed with the new minister. We moved out to a place just off Division Street. How'd you know about it?"

She slipped an arm through mine. "You know Gail Sherman, right?"

"Uh huh." But I'd never told anybody at school about her.

"She told me about your dad's church. She's a friend of mine. She used to live out here but her parents moved to the west side. She goes to Centennial now."

"Yeah, I know."

Centennial was a new school, our biggest rival. Gail Sherman used to come to church with her older sister Beth. They were daughters of a hillbilly widower from Arkansas. My older brother Richy and I would take the girls home after Sunday evening church. I never really liked Gail, she always had baby burp on her shoulders from taking care of babies during the service, but it was a chance to make out. She and her sister always looked like they were desperate for some affection. It was kind of pathetic when you thought about it. Richy would find some place along the road where we could park and for ten minutes (no more or dad would start wondering what was going on), we'd make out. That was enough time to feel them up a bit and work on a few French kisses. It was better than smooching your arm for practice.

Reta Jane kicked at a pebble and it rattled off the pavement and into the brush at the side of the road. "What's it like working at the cannery?"

Her question came out of the darkness as if from miles away. It almost sounded like there was longing in her voice. Anyway, I was glad to get off the church and Gail.

"Oh, nothing special," I said. "Pay's good." But maybe she knew that.

She tucked her hair behind her ears. "I tried to get on once but they didn't need anybody."

"It's tight sometimes. This is my second summer and I almost thought I'd get cut."

"Is it hard?"

"The work?" I shrugged. "It can be. The women don't have it so good. They stand along these conveyor belts grading the fruit with their heads bent down the whole shift. At least I get to move around. Usually they have me dumping crates, but sometimes I drive a Hyster."

"You like that?"

"Sure. It's a lot better than dumping crates. But what I really like are the lights."

---

"The lights?"

"Yeah. It's real dark outside but inside it's like being in another world. All the bright lights and the machinery and the sounds. The rumble is almost hypnotic. I can dump a pallet of crates, that's four stacks over six feet tall, and be lost in thoughts and never notice the time. Or if I'm out on the loading docks where the empties are stacked, there's a kind of quiet above the hum. You get the feeling you're alone in the universe—one little spot of light in the vast darkness of space. The rest of the world's dead, everybody's asleep."

"Not everybody," she said. "People like me are up. I like it out here in the dark. I don't like bright lights."

I thought about that for a moment, then admitted, "The dark's nice, too." But it was funny, I almost thought of the cannery with pleasure. It was so much better than working on the farm for my dad, and better than most of the other paying jobs I'd had. Sometimes I got to go up alone into the attic where the number ten cans were stored, to feed the chutes leading to the bulk grading lines. Late at night, it was always warm there, a dusty smell in the air, mixing with the sweetness of the sugar machines on the second floor just below me. You could hear, off to one side, the clacking of the machines that wrapped and sealed green beans before they were stacked and hauled off to the freezers by electric hand carts. I just found all those sounds and smells soothing.

But, shoot, she was probably used to having her summers free and that was a lot nicer than working.

The moon had risen above the trees and hung at our backs like a gigantic gold disk. The breeze came soughing through the grasses, sowing a pollen of sighs in its wake—the smell of fresh-cut hay, drying in windrows before the next day's baling, the fragrance of wild flowers and thistle, occasionally a light hint of road tar to let you know you were still in the modern world.

"That don't seem real, does it?" she said, looking over her shoulder. "The moon. It looks so heavy you'd think it'd sink."

We stopped to turn around for a better view, and she slipped her hand around my back. I thought about doing the same to her, but she had my arm pinned to my side and it would have been awkward to lift it free—too obvious. She did everything like there was no thought behind it, just *natural*. I wished it came that easy to me.

I didn't know what to say for a bit then. I was absorbing her warmth and the pressure of her hand curled around my side. Not many girls had ever touched me like that and I could feel a stirring in my pants.

"You getting any dryer?" She patted me on the chest with her other hand, then let it drop down to my waist, her fingers finding my belt and easing inside the waistband of my jeans, as if she were trying to hang on. Her knuckles pressed into my belly and I felt a shiver run from there down to my groin. I started to turn away from her but she gently tugged me back around.

"My," she said, her voice playful, "I feel something."

I wished I'd liked her more. I'm a virgin and you know what that's like. When you're ready, the girl doesn't really matter—or at least that's what I'd always thought. I just wanted to lose my virginity and I didn't care who with. But now I wasn't sure. Oh, heck, maybe I was just a coward. I never did know what to do around girls. And she'd just had a baby. *She was a mother.* That made it hard to feel romantic. Every time I started to get aroused, I'd think of that and it'd pull me back to reality. The conflicting emotions were confusing. Back home with Uncle Fred she had a little girl.

A feeling of horror invaded me at the thought he might have—.

"Who's the father?" I said before I could help myself. "Of your baby?" I added, feeling like a moron now. Did I have to bring that up? What if she'd been raped by her uncle?

She dropped her hand. "You wouldn't know him." Her voice had changed, no longer cheerful, no emotion in the words at all. There was a moment of silence, while I pondered whether I should leave well enough alone. But the silence was worse than saying something stupid.

"He go to Gresham High?"

She shook her head, and we started walking again. "Used to. He's a mechanic. You ever go to Vic's Motors and Auto Parts?"

I breathed a sigh of relief. "Not really. They're on East Powell, right?"

"Yeah, he hangs out around there a lot. Working on the racing cars. We broke up before the baby came."

She wasn't touching me any longer. I felt bad for pulling away from her, but somehow it didn't seem right. I hadn't been comfortable. But my mind kept going back to what it had felt like when her fingers touched my stomach. Like an electric shock. And that reminded me of the dead hog jerking around. Which wasn't pleasant either. So everything she did left me up in the air, tossed one way and then the other. Attraction and repulsion. I didn't like how awkward it made me feel, so unsure of myself.

"Let's start back," I said finally. "I've got to be getting home."

She snorted. "Preacher's kid. I thought you guys were wilder than the rest of us."

I shrugged, pleased but uncertain. "I don't know about that. I always considered myself pretty dull."

She didn't say anything for a while and when she did, her voice had lightened again. "Hey, think I could come to your church?"

I glanced at her. The moon was highlighting her face in profile and with her long scraggly hair, she looked like the Gorgon. "Anybody can come."

"I don't go to church normally."

"Lucky you." I'd give anything to have my Sunday mornings free. Dressed up in a starchy white shirt and wool suit that drove me crazy with itching. And not only that. We also went to Sunday evening church services, though I didn't have to wear a suit then, and Wednesday evening prayer meetings. And like I said, every day before breakfast, after doing our chores, we had to read a chapter of the Bible out loud. She could have that, too.

And she could have my dad. If hers was like mine, she was *lucky* he was dead.

My dad was one of those hell-fire and damnation types. Not a holy roller, at least. No speaking in tongues. But one of those spare-the-rod-and-spoil-the-child types. If he caught me out bumming around I'd be in for it. I'd get my hide tanned. And like I said, he seemed to have a knack for catching me. But that's probably because I was always getting into trouble. At least it felt that way. I don't try—I mean, it's not intentional. Trouble just seems to find me.

Thinking about my dad spoiled any sense of freedom I might have felt out walking in the countryside with a girl I hardly knew.

Why did people always have to talk about religion? Like I said, my old man wasn't a holy roller but he could get going when he wanted to. Shoot, once he got so excited it kind of scared me. He was praying at the altar rail after this Sunday evening service, trying to convert this woman. There must have been ten or fifteen of us stretched out along the rail—sinners and converted alike—and my dad started praying louder and louder. I don't know if he didn't think the woman showed enough sorrow—no tears of repentance for her sins—or if somehow he thought she was a hard case, or didn't feel it deep enough, or what. But all of a sudden I hear this thumping in the church. Something hard hitting the floor. *Rat-ta-tat-tat. Rat-ta-tat-tat.* And I realized it was his toes—the toes of his shoes banging up and down while he was on his knees in front of her praying, his right hand on the woman's head, left hand on her shoulder.

It was scary at the time, because I hadn't ever seen him get so ... it wasn't just excited, it was like *filled* with the spirit. And I didn't know if he was faking or not—you know, acting for effect, but I don't think he was. I think he *meant* it. And that made it more scary.

I don't know why it was so hard for that woman to break down. Did he want her to cry or something? That was easy. Every Sunday before I was converted, back when I didn't know any better, I used to sit there in the hard pew and think about my soul winding up in hell, burning forever. Talk about guilt. It made my heart ache. Of course, that was something else my dad had a knack for doing to us kids. And if he wasn't doing that, he was whipping our butts or whacking us across the head. Always trying, as he said, to knock a little sense into us. Yeah, it was no fun being a preacher's kid, I can tell you that.

And he didn't treat the animals any better either. The pickup wouldn't have a dented fender if dad hadn't hit the bull. Our cows were always getting out. Sometimes, my mom would have to come in and get me out of class to track them down. One night the bull got out after one of the neighbor's heifers went into heat, and we spent over an hour trying to get him back where he belonged. Gorky just wouldn't leave. Dad finally got so mad he went for the pickup and started chasing the bull toward home—only every time Gorky stopped dad would bash into him with the bumper. He even knocked him down a few times. Richy and I were out in the field screaming that he was going to kill Gorky and dad was revving up the motor so loud he couldn't hear us. The bull finally swung around and hit the fender so hard it killed the motor. That was one time dad couldn't blame Richy and me for breaking something.

But I wasn't going to tell Reta Jane about that.

The last half mile of the return trip we held hands. It was Reta Jane who took mine, pulling me out of the way of a pothole.

"You walk with your eyes closed?" she said, her voice sarcastic.

I grinned. "Just thinking about my dad."

"There's gotta be better things to think about than that."

She was right there, but she was the one who brought up the church and got me to thinking about him.

"I'm always getting into trouble for something," I said, "and half the time it's not even my fault."

"But the other half it is, right?"

She had me there.

"Yeah, but I get beat all the time."

She laughed.

"Once my younger brother Bobby broke my tooth with a shovel—".

"Broke your tooth!"

I grinned. "Yeah, we were fighting. He was using the shovel to fill a pothole in the driveway and I needed it to dig out this caved-in septic tank. I grabbed for the shovel and Bobby swung it at my head." I laughed again. "And then he took off running, grabbed his bike and headed for the house. I knew he was going to whine to dad, so I threw a rock and hit him in the head."

"You guys ..."

"Yeah, well, he went bawling to dad and my dad made me stand in front of the shed while he threw rocks at me. See this scar?" I tried to show her a scar under the hair on my forehead but it was too dark. "And there's a smaller one on my upper lip, too."

Maybe I shouldn't have told her about that because it got me to thinking about another beating. I'd written it down once, hoping that would stop the hurt.

*It was just a story, but it had an air of truth.*

*The boy had gotten angry at his younger sister for getting into his stamp collection, so he'd grabbed her doll and flung it across the room and broke its ceramic head and now his dad was jerking him around and cuffing him on the back of the head while the boy held his puppy, Higgins, and tried to keep the dog from getting hurt.*

*"I'll teach you to pick on your sister," his dad said.*

*The blows stung and he couldn't keep from saying something, even though he knew talking back only made things worse. "I wasn't picking on her," he said. "I was picking on her doll."*

*His dad grabbed the puppy and held it by the neck. "Let's see how you like it when someone picks on your things."*

*His father raised his hand to swat the dog, which had started choking, and the boy yelled, "No, not Higgins." He was afraid his dad would crush its head.*

*"Well, what'll it be? You or Higgins?"*

*The boy didn't want to reply, didn't want to pick one or the other, but if he kept silent Higgins might get hurt worse, so he said, "Me."*

*His dad dropped the dog, which yelped and started whimpering, and when the boy bent over to see if it was okay his dad smacked him on the butt and knocked him down. "See what it's like," he said. He shoved the boy with his foot, then pulled his belt from its loops, and the blows started. The boy pushed the puppy away and put his hands over his head and curled into a ball. The blows started and he tried to think of something else—of running through the orchard with Higgins behind him—the dog trying to keep up, his ears flopping—and jumping the fence while Higgins squeezed under the barbed wire ... of clomping through the stubble of the wheat fields in search of pheasant, waiting for the thunder of wings and the puppy's vain leap ... of coming across the creek bed in the fir trees and lying down side by side, he and Higgins, to drink the clear cold water. He tried to think of the puppy's joy as it cavorted in the field, to see his clumsy gait, to laugh as Higgins bounded after the grasshoppers in the straw—but all he could feel, rising through the pain, welling up from deep within, was the all-consuming blackness of hate.*

*When the beating was over his father tossed the stamp collection and his sister's broken doll into the garbage can. "That'll teach you kids to fight over things," he said.*

*It had an air of truth, but it was just a story.*

*At least that's what he told himself.*

"You should've hit back."

"Are you crazy?" I took a deep breath to calm the quaver in my voice. "He'd have killed me."

"You don't do something, one of these days you're going to explode. *You'll* kill *him*."

She couldn't see me in the dark, but I nodded.

Maybe she was right.

We stopped talking for a while then and just walked.

When we got to the car, my shirt was pretty dry but my pants still felt wet. "Take them off," she said. "We can tie them on the antenna and let them dry in the breeze."

*"What?"* With her standing there watching?

"I've seen boys in underpants before," she said, reading my mind. "Don't worry. I won't bite."

I blushed. Thank God it was dark and she couldn't see my face. "I don't know," I said.

"Come on, it's no big deal. Do I have to take off my own?"

She put her hands on her cutoffs and my eyes widened. Before I could say anything, I heard the zipper going down. I swallowed hard. In one quick movement, she slipped her pants off and held them up in front of me. "It's easy."

Her white underpants stood out in the moonlight like a flag under a spotlight.

My breath caught in my throat. I was getting excited again. Embarrassing. I decided to act before it got worse. I unbuckled my belt, unzipped my pants, and tried to slip them off over my boots. That wasn't easy and I hopped around in the dirt at the side of the road, trying to keep my balance while Reta Jane whooped and laughed.

"Come on," I said, when I had them in my hands. "It's not funny. Besides, your uncle might hear." Just the thought was making me nervous, both of us standing there in white underpants.

"You worry too much," she said.

Yeah, right.

Before getting in the car I tied the legs of my jeans to the antenna and we started up the road.

Reta Jane had dropped her cutoffs on the seat between us. I wanted to look at her some more, but I had to keep my eyes on the road, which rose and dipped over a series of low wooded hills. Her cutoffs made me nervous. I shoved them toward her.

"What if the cops stop us?"

"I'll slip them on if they do." She sounded peeved.

"Yeah, but what about *me*?"

She snorted. "Well, I doubt they'll take you to jail for indecent exposure. Besides, there's never any cops out here."

I turned on the radio and we listened to that for a bit, while she directed me from road to road. We were running on flat ground by a dairy farm when Reta Jane grabbed my arm.

"Wait," she said. "The Johannsen's."

My foot hit the brake. "What's that?"

"See that house up ahead, just beyond the barn? Pull over before you get there. They have the best cherries anywhere."

I could see the tree in the darkness, sitting in their front yard all by itself, branches sweeping wide to all sides. The road leading in to the property had a spiked gate across it, and to each side stretched a four-strand, barbed-wire fence.

"I can't drive in there," I said. "They'll hear us if we open the gate. It's probably locked anyway. And that fence is hot. See the white insulators? The bottom and the top lines are electrified."

"We can go through the middle. You hold the wire for me and I'll hold it for you."

I didn't think that was a great idea, but she wouldn't give up. She *had* to have some of those cherries.

"I've been eyeing them every day for two weeks," she said. "Never had a chance until now to get some."

I pulled off the road into a grassy ditch just beyond the big house, a white two-story affair with a porch in front. With the lights extinguished and the motor dead, I could hear animals moving in the dark. "Horses," I said. They were standing under the cherry tree. "I don't think this is a good idea."

"Oh, come on, Artie. Don't be such a scaredy-cat. I want some cherries."

I came around to untie my pants from the antenna but she stopped me. "Forget them," she said. "It'll be easier in our underwear."

Easier. What in the world was she talking about?

"Come on. This'll be fun," she said, pulling me across the road with her.

I hoped no cars would come along. We stood out like the invisible man wearing a phosphorescent swimming suit.

To get to the fence, we had to slog through a ditch and I got water and mud in my work boots. I felt really weird. Shirt, underpants and work boots. *How'd I let myself get talked into this?* And I wasn't looking forward to getting shocked. We had electrified fences for the Angus and they were one pain in the neck. You try to jump them, especially with a scissors kick, and don't make it ... watch out. It didn't feel good to have your thigh whapped with current.

I held the two middle wires apart—they were barbed but not hot—and Reta Jane slipped through with no problem, but when she did the same for me, I caught my shirt and heard it rip. *Great*, now mom would wonder how that happened.

I shook my head. Couldn't something be easy for a change?

Oh well, there were plenty of excuses I could use with mom. I was always banging up against something at the cannery, including a machine that cut my head open and sent me to the emergency room for stitches one night. Maybe mom would just be happy I hadn't sliced myself to the bone.

It was only about a hundred feet to the cherry tree. The horses moved off without making much of a fuss and five minutes later we were up in the tree, furiously stuffing ripe Bing cherries into our mouths. Thick, huge clumps hung from every branch and twig—and, boy, were they good. I could see why she'd wanted to sneak in.

"We look funny," she said, laughing.

"Shh. Not so loud." She'd been giggling like a crazy girl ever since we climbed into the tree. But I had to admit she was right. Was there something in the laundry soap that made our underpants stand out so much in the moonlight? I felt like we were two spotlights calling attention to ourselves.

"Hope these don't have worms," she said, and then started laughing louder, shaking the branches so hard I thought she was going to fall. I could hear ripe cherries plopping on the ground.

A light went on inside the farmhouse.

"Oh, shoot," I said. "Someone's coming. Get down."

"Just a few more," she said, her words garbled. She spit out a mouthful of cherry pits.

"Come on, Reta Jane. I'm not waiting for you."

I was already scrambling down from branch to branch. I hit the ground with a thud, and then heard the front door swing open.

They were going to catch her. I couldn't wait. A flashlight beam stabbed out of the night and I heard a gruff voice yelling—something about a shotgun—and then the person charged back inside the house.

I swore.

Just what we needed—an angry farmer shooting in the dark.

# five

R eta Jane," I hissed. "Get down from there! He's going for a shotgun!" My heart had taken off like a frightened jack rabbit, skipping ten feet in each direction with every hop.

She'd heard him too and was really flying.

"Don't fall!"

With that note of warning, I took off running. I was going to have to hold the fence for her. Might as well be ready.

I didn't slow down when I got near the fence, just changed my angle and tried to scissors kick my way over the top, thinking that'd make my own getaway quicker. I wouldn't have to go through the barbed wire. But my boot caught on the top line as I tried to go over and I got shocked, a jolt all along my back and down one leg, and then I hit the ground hard on the other side. I couldn't move for a second. The wind was knocked flat out of me and my nerves were tingling.

Reta Jane was trying to get through the wire on her own. I could hear her swearing in panic.

"My hair," she cried. "I'm caught."

A man's voice from behind us shouted, "Where are you sons of bitches?"

A blast of buckshot ripped through the branches of the cherry tree and I heard the horses neigh and take off running.

Reta Jane's voice had died to a whimper but she was still tangled in the barbed wire. I grabbed a chunk of hair near the roots and pulled her away from the fence, while she yelled and slugged me in the side in a kind of reflex action.

Thanks a lot, I thought. Next time I'll leave you snagged. I could see the flashlight beam stabbing out of the darkness in our direction.

I grabbed Reta Jane's right hand and pulled her through the ditch. She was holding on to her head with the other hand. Little gasps of pain slipped out of her with each step.

I'd left the key in the ignition and the car started on the first try. I hit the gas with the lights still dark, leaning forward to make out the road in the moonlight. Behind us there was a sharp boom and I could hear buckshot pattering on the trunk.

Great. I hit the lights and floored it then, trying to watch the road and the rearview mirror at the same time.

When we hit sixty, there was a twang to my right and Reta Jane cried out and ducked away from the window.

"Your pants," she said. "The antenna broke."

I swore and hit the brakes.

"Keep going!"

"I can't go home without my pants." Was she crazy? And the antenna … I was in for it now. How was I going to explain that?

I started to back up, swerving from one side of the road to the other. It took about five minutes to backtrack and find the jeans off to the side of the pavement. At least no one appeared to be chasing us.

Reta Jane jumped out and came back with my jeans and the antenna. She showed me the rod. "It was still tied to the legs," she said. "Maybe we can fix it."

I reached up and flipped on the convenience light while accelerating. The antenna was bent all out of shape and one segment was missing. "It's busted," I said. "Darn it." I shut off the roof light and looked in the rearview mirror again, still worried about someone chasing us.

Reta Jane laid my jeans on the seat and then started tapping the antenna on the dashboard. "What are you going to do?"

I looked at the antenna in her hands. "I don't know." She held the end up to the dashboard so I could see it in the dim light. Ripped clean off all right. No way I could jam that back in the socket. I shook my head.

We drove without talking then. I shut off the radio, which was fuzzy with static, so I could concentrate. I tried to change routes, taking some country roads that she said would eventually lead back to town. It was going on twelve-thirty.

After a while, Reta Jane turned to me. "You park in the cannery lot, right? Just tell your dad somebody vandalized the thing."

"Yeah, and he'll make me pay for it, too." I hit the steering wheel. "Just what I needed."

"I could try to track down my old boyfriend. Like I told you, he works for a parts shop. Maybe we could get it replaced tonight."

I shook my head. "I don't have enough money on me."

"Dennis can get you one for free. Steal it if we have to."

I looked over at her but didn't say anything. She'd already gotten me in enough trouble. If I went to anyone, it'd be to my best friend Billy Deater. He was good with cars. Maybe he could do something. But I'd have to wake him up in the middle of the night and I'd have to do it without rousing his parents. Maybe Billy and I could break into the wrecking yard off Stark Street and find one on a junked Mercury. But I didn't know how hard they were to install and hadn't looked to see if the body was damaged when the antenna ripped loose.

Shoulda gone straight home when the cannery let us go at eleven. One thing had led to the other and look where it got me. Lie down with a dog and he's going to lick your face. *When are you ever going to learn?* That was what my dad would ask me in between whacks on the head.

"Put your pants on," I said to Reta Jane. We were still in our underwear. "I'll just drop you off at the Polar King."

"You'd better get yours on, too."

I pulled over where the road widened and we jumped out and got into our clothes. I could see by the convenience light that we'd tracked mud into the car. That'd take me an hour to get clean and I sure as heck couldn't do it at home. Couldn't risk getting caught. I'd have to ask Billy for help with that, too.

"Get in," I told her. She was standing with the passenger door open.

"I have to pee," she said.

She was facing me with the door open behind her when she dropped her pants. I gasped without wanting to when I saw her. And then she squatted out of sight, one hand on the seat, looking at me the whole time while she peed. I had to go, too, but I wasn't going to get out and try. Not even in the dark. I was pee-shy. Couldn't do it with other people around. I always had to go into the school toilets by myself, hoping no one else was at the urinals. And when the family was on a trip and we stopped to go in the woods, I always ran a hundred feet farther than the rest—and even then it took me five minutes before I could relax enough to go. There was no way I was going to relax now, not after having seen her body in the light.

She pulled up her underpants and cutoffs and jumped back in the car. She giggled. "Those cherries were worth it, weren't they?"

Yeah, only she didn't have to pay for an antenna—and maybe a new paint job on the trunk. I couldn't tell in the dark if the shotgun pellets had damaged it. And no one was going to box her around or cuff her ears until her head rang.

Reta Jane touched me on the leg. "Will you wait with me until we find Carl if he's not at the Polar King? He might be cruising the gut."

I pursed my cheeks, then muttered a yes. I had started thinking again about being a virgin and wondering if I shouldn't do something to change that. Forget liking the girl, forget if she was pretty or not, forget the fact she was a mother. She kept teasing me and it was starting to override my hesitance. But how easy would it be to do it in the car? And we were already close enough to town for there to be an occasional car or pickup on the road. I finally gave up on the idea.

Her friend Carl with the new Chevelle wasn't at the Polar King, which was shut down for the night. Some other kid hanging around a beat-up old Dodge told her Carl had been cruising up and down Powell and should be back soon.

The cherries had just made me hungrier, so I took Reta Jane to Dea's, pulling up at the drive-in window. I bought an order of fries and a strawberry milk-shake. They were just about to shut down and I lucked out getting the shake. Reta Jane said she wasn't hungry, but she had a few of the fries, after squirting ketchup over them. We drove back to the Polar King and ate in the car.

After a while, she asked me if I had a girlfriend and I told her about Laurie Snyder. I'd only had two girlfriends since the sixth grade. First Tracy Burkhart, who was kind of plump but was always laughing, and then Laurie Snyder. Tracy and I broke up in the eighth grade. Every Saturday night, I used to take her in to Youth for Christ at the Civic Auditorium on Clay Street in Portland.

We rode in the church bus, with Billy Deater's dad driving. Billy wasn't too happy that year because, before Tracy came along, he and I used to sit together, and if we wanted to have fun, we'd sneak out together—especially if they were holding the rally at Benson Polytechnic due to a scheduling conflict, which happened every now and then. We'd walk down to the Banfield freeway and cross the bridge to the new Lloyd Center Shopping mall where we fished for coins in the fountain. We usually found enough to buy a shake, burger, and fries—only forty-nine cents at Scottie's, back on Sandy Boulevard.

On the way home after the meetings, as soon as Billy's dad shut off the inside lights in the bus, Tracy and I would hold hands in the dark, but that's as far as it ever went. I was too young and inexperienced to do more. Usually, I was even too scared to grab her hand, so she'd have to do it, and once we started, I didn't know how to stop, not even when my hand went numb and started tingling. I don't know why I always froze up around girls, even ones who liked me.

And it was just as bad with Laurie Snyder. She'd been my girlfriend on and off for two years now. And it still seemed everything was awkward. I started to tell Reta Jane about the boat show.

"I can't ever take her anywhere fun because my dad won't let me go to the movies."

"Why not?" She spoke with her mouth full of fries.

"He thinks it's a sin. It was a wonder we ever got a TV. He used to say that was a sin, too—because you're paying to watch actors and actresses who smoke and drink—and then you have the commercials." I took a sip of the milkshake. "But then he got hooked on Bonanza—saw it one night at some friends' place—so now we've got a TV."

"So you never go to the show?"

"Not really. My older brother Richy and I snuck out one time when I was in the seventh grade. First time I ever saw a movie at a theater."

She took another clump of fries. "Where'd you go?"

"Here in town. The Hood Theater. We told my dad we were going to a baseball game in Portland. The Beavers. We had to leave the show early so we could catch the score on the radio and act like we'd been there."

"What'd you see at the movies?"

I wiped the shake off my mouth. "We got there in the middle of one show with Kim Novak. And then we saw most of *Wake Me When It's Over.*"

I sighed just thinking about it. Both movies had overwhelmed me. I must have fantasized about Kim Novak for a year—and the scenes in *Wake Me When It's Over* were a whole new world to me. A real eye-opener.

"So what happened at the boat show?" Reta Jane licked her fingers. She'd finished off the last of the fries. "Can I have a sip of your shake?"

"I've got a can of strawberries if you'd rather."

She shook her head, so I handed her the strawberry shake. "We went on a double-date with one of my friends." It wasn't Billy that time. He didn't have a real girlfriend. I had to go with his friend Dan. He had an old '52 Chevy that he'd bought cheap and customized, and at the time my dad wouldn't let me drive. But I didn't tell Reta Jane that.

"It was hard," I said, taking back the shake. "We walked around for a while, and I tried to hold hands every time we came off a boat, but she didn't seem to like it. Finally, she said she was tired of walking. She didn't want to see any more dumb boats. Dan and his girlfriend weren't ready to leave. There was a little auditorium there with a pool and some trained seals or something, and they said they were going to watch it for a while. Laurie asked me if I wanted to go sit in the car."

I paused, surprised I was telling anyone about what had happened that night. I'd been humiliated—and not because I'd tried to do something and failed. It was worse than that. I hadn't even told Billy about it, but I didn't really know Reta Jane and probably wouldn't ever see her again, and nothing seemed to embarrass her. Maybe she could tell me what I should have done—something to help in the future.

"I liked her too much," I said, "It's hard to explain."

Reta Jane nodded. She was licking the last of the salt off her fingers, making a kind of slurping sound. "I know what it's like. Everyone goes through that. You just got to get beyond it. The first kiss or whatever."

"I'd kissed her before," I said quickly, not wanting to seem a complete failure. "It's just, I never got over feeling ..." I didn't know how to put it. "Feeling too much. Awe almost."

"You guys still together?"

I pursed my cheeks while I thought about that. My heart felt heavy. I finally said, "I don't know. It's hard to tell. She's gone for the summer. I think she wants to meet other guys."

"So what happened in the car? You two make out?"

I shook my head. "She sat real close to me in the back seat but we just talked." I paused. "*She* talked. I couldn't think of anything to say. I wanted to kiss her, but … I was afraid, I guess. She seemed different that night. She'd dropped my hand every time she could."

I thought about that for a moment, reliving the scene in my mind. Horrible. I just hadn't been able to think of anything to say. I felt like a mute. This tremendous desire inside and nothing to push it out. My mind was locked up.

"So after a while the conversation died. We sat there not saying anything. Finally she scooted away and turned to me and she says, 'You never say anything. Why do you even ask me out? We never talk.'".

Reta Jane looked at me. "What'd you do?"

I shrugged. "Nothing. I didn't say a word. I couldn't at that point. I mean, when someone tells you you never talk, what do you say? I must've opened my mouth once or twice, but nothing came out."

We both laughed.

"I just couldn't think of anything to talk about. It was like there was this barrier between us—my desire … my wanting her so much."

I stopped. I'd never been able to express that before. I'd never been able to put it into words. It wasn't that it was hard. You just didn't talk about it like that. "I loved her too much."

"So what'd she do? Leave?"

I looked away for a second, embarrassed. "She hit the seat with her hand—in frustration, I guess—and got out of the car. I was going to follow, but she said I should stay there and think about our relationship. *By myself!* She said she didn't think we should go out together any more. I remember her last words. She said, 'Why do you even *like* me, Artie? We never carry on a conversation.' And she went back to the boat show and didn't show up until after Dan and his date returned. I had to pretend I was sick and had come out to the car by myself."

I tried to laugh again, but it hurt. "A week later, Dan's girlfriend Jackie told me Laurie had gone out with Gene Davis. He's this guy on the basketball team—a senior. Jackie said she saw them at a party and they were making out. I didn't want to hear about it. She said they were sitting on a bean bag … and kissing."

Reta Jane touched me on the arm. "Artie, you've got to pretend you don't like her—".

I took a deep breath. I'd almost started to cry!

"Easy for you to say. I feel too much to pretend."

"I meant, when you're on a date. You gotta tell yourself she's just another girl. You need to relax. You know, like now. We're talking."

"Now is different."

"Jeez." She slapped her forehead. "Then just tell her you love her and get it over with."

I looked out the window, feeling a constriction in my chest at the thought. "It's too hard."

"Artie, it's three little words. How old are you?"

"Sixteen."

She giggled. "I didn't mean that literally. I meant, you ought to be able to say three words without choking."

This time I smiled back. She had her leg up on the seat and poked at me with her foot. She was trying to help and I appreciated that. Maybe I needed more friends like Reta Jane—*girls* you could talk to, not just guys. Maybe it was easy. I just needed practice.

Shoot, what was I thinking? Here I'd just gone on about how hard it was to talk to my girlfriend and I was thinking girls were easy to talk to. It all depended on how much you liked them, I guess. But I felt better about it just talking; it made me want to start right in again with Laurie Snyder and see if I could get over the barrier. But who knew what would happen to her over the summer? Meeting again in the fall was always hard. Each time it took a week or two to feel like you knew the person—to realize they'd changed but not that much. That you still liked each other.

It reminded me of a girlfriend I had in grade school. At least I thought she was a girlfriend. Patty. I can't even remember her last name. Fourth grade I think that was. She went away for a month to summer camp and when she got back she was a different kid. She came back so tanned I didn't recognize her. But it wasn't just the skin. She was completely different. It was like she'd forgotten we'd even been friends.

That's why the summers scared me.

"There's Carl," Reta Jane said, sitting up. The Chevelle was pulling into the Polar King's lot. She opened the door and then looked back over her shoulder at me. "Remember what I said, Artie."

I nodded. "I'll try. Pretend you don't like them, right?"

"Yeah, but just to yourself. You don't have to act like you don't care." She paused. "And if you can't think of anything to say, turn the tables. Ask them a question—their opinion."

I hesitated—*opinion about what?* that was the hard part—and she said,

"Look, Artie, I gotta run. Maybe I'll see you around."

She slammed the door, started to walk away and then came around the front of the car and over to my window. "If you change your mind about tonight, I can talk to Carl about the antenna. We can look up my old boyfriend. Dennis is good with these things."

"Don't bother," I said. "But thanks."

"Okay." She reached out and tugged on my shirt sleeve. "If you decide not to go home right off, we'll be out at Hosner's Hole on the Sandy river. Come on out."

I grunted something noncommittal and she was gone.

I knew where Hosner's Hole was. It was a lover's lane about fifteen miles outside of town. I'd worked one summer in grade school as a kitchen boy at Camp Collins, a boy scout camp along the Sandy river just beyond Hosner's Hole. I used to sneak down there at night with the older counselors and we'd build a big fire and look at nudist magazines.

No time for that now.

I picked up the antenna and had another look at it. Dad was going to give me a licking if I went home with the car all busted up. It had been hard enough to convince him I was trustworthy enough to take it in to work at night. The only reason he let me was because we lived over two miles from the cannery and neither he nor mom wanted to take me in at night and pick me up early in the morning.

I guess one mistake wasn't enough for one night. On the way to Billy Deater's place to see if he could help with the antenna, I stopped and picked up a hitchhiker. I could see he was an older man, maybe in his forties, and a rough-looking guy to boot. But he was carrying a box in his arms and at that time of night, no one was going to help him if I didn't. I'd hitchhiked home from school after basketball practice on winter nights often enough to know what it felt like standing out there hoping someone would stop for you.

Even though I hesitated for a moment, my foot hit the brake before I could really think it all out. And by then it was too late. It would've been cruel to accelerate just as he got to the door. I'd had punks do that to me and I didn't like it.

So I let the man get in the car.

# *six*

Choice—that's what it all came down to. Hercules at the crossroads. Go left or right. Say yes or no. Course that was when things were simple—when it was one thing or the other. Like black or white. What did you do when it was gray? That was a lot harder. Choice was what made you what you were. And in my case I was beginning to think what it made me was stupid. But sometimes your mind told you one thing and your heart said something different. Or, if you weren't careful, if you were weak or slow or feeling stupid, someone else made the decision for you. You got pushed into doing something you shouldn't have. You knew it was wrong, but you couldn't think how to say no fast enough.

Only now I didn't have anybody to blame but myself. I'd made my choice and I was stuck with it.

Like earlier—back when I left the cannery. I had to say, *go left*, didn't I? I could have gone straight home. Instead, I'd headed out into the dark like a lost hiker whose last match had just been snuffed, letting fate take me where it would. And once you'd made up your mind to go one way, you were stuck. You couldn't go back and start over. Couldn't choose the other path—go right instead of left, say no instead of yes. And if you changed your mind and tried to get home, sometimes you found out the road back was a long, winding one with detours at every turn.

The first thing he did was pull out a pack of cigarettes. He'd set the box between his feet in the front seat. I couldn't tell what was in it, but it looked heavy. I'd also got a glimpse of his face as he was getting in. He hadn't shaved for a day or two and his clothes looked greasy. I hoped he wouldn't get the seat dirty.

"Hey, pal, care for a cig?" His voice was so raspy a cigarette was the last thing he needed.

"Uh … you can't smoke in the car," I said, shaking my head. "My dad will kill me."

"This your old man's car?"

I nodded. "Where you going?"

He cleared his throat. "I'm a carny. How about a lift to the fairgrounds?"

A carny. I'd never heard anyone actually say that word out loud. Those guys always looked rough, like they'd slit your throat in the dark if you had a few extra bucks on you. But like a fly with one leg already stuck I said, "Sure. It's on my way."

"What if I roll down the window, pal?" He had a cigarette half out of the pack.

This guy wouldn't give up. "My dad would smell it."

I was about to say I'd stop the car and let him out if he wanted, when he sighed and put the pack back in his shirt pocket.

A moment later his foot hit something. "Hey, kid, what you got down here?"

I looked over. I'd forgotten about the sack. "That's my lunch," I said. "There's a can of strawberries in there if you're hungry."

"Naw, I'd rather have a smoke."

I didn't say anything, just felt uncomfortable. I didn't want a confrontation. He reminded me of this red-haired guy at the cannery. The guy offered me a ride home one night when I didn't have the car and then tried to put his hand on my knee. I must have jumped a foot. I got out of there fast.

"So, kid. Going to the fair this year?"

I nodded. I couldn't wait to get there now and drop this guy off.

"I go every year," I said.

In fact, when I was in grade school and we lived downtown about two blocks from the fairgrounds, I used to go every day the fair was in town. I didn't tell him I usually snuck in. I'd go around to where they brought in the exhibits and the farm animals and climb the fence when no one was looking. I got chased by a guard once or twice but never got caught.

The Multnomah County Fair lasted for two weeks and was the only time all summer I had a chance for some fun. Sure, occasionally I'd get over to Blue Lake Park in the daytime—but that was about once a month and all I could do then was swim and jump off the high dive, and maybe order a cherry snowcone or some pink cotton candy.

The fair had a great midway with lots of fun rides, sideshows, and games. And I loved the hamburgers they sold in the food stands, big thick things slathered with fixins—and the corn dogs were great, too.

I usually went with Billy Deater and we tried to pick up girls—at least, that's what was on our mind most of the night. But about all we ever did was ogle them. Neither one of us had much guts when it came to going up to a group of girls. And they always seemed to come in a pack if they weren't with some guy. It might have helped if Billy wasn't so ugly—he was covered with boils and pimples—but I still doubt we'd have had much luck. We were always on the edge of asking and always backing off. We'd look at each other and then drop our eyes and scuff our feet. I felt the same way I did on the high dive at Blue Lake. From the ground it doesn't look too bad—but you get up there and out on the edge of the board and suddenly it looks like a mile-long drop. Whap, whap, whap—your heart starts thumping like a playing card clothes-pinned to a bike wheel. On the tallest board, I'd always backed away. And it was like that with the girls.

So every year at the fair we rode a few rides and played a few games of chance, spent all the money we had, which wasn't much more than five dollars, and then went to look at the exhibit halls or sat down to watch the stage show. And the next night we'd be back again, sometimes with money, sometimes not.

If I could, the week or two before the fair came to town, I'd go around knocking on doors and asking people if they needed anyone to do chores for a few bucks—weed their flower beds, cut the lawn, clean out the garage, anything to earn a dollar. Usually, if you knew where the old ladies lived, you could pick up something.

The money I earned at the cannery went straight to the bank, my dad saw to that. I had to buy all my own school clothes in the fall and if I had any left over, my dad usually made me pay rent. When we were working, me and Richy both paid ten bucks a week, which wasn't much, but it still bugged me. So I'd work extra doing yard chores when I was supposed to be sleeping, and wouldn't tell my dad about the money.

Anyway, I was thinking about asking this guy what he did with the carnival, when he asked what I was doing out that time of the night.

"Just got off work," I said. "At the cannery."

"Any place around here where a guy can find himself some fun?"

I shrugged. I didn't know about someone his age. "You gotta have a car."

"What about bars?"

"I'm not really sure. You're better off going in to Portland."

The second I said it I wished I hadn't. I was sure he was going to ask me to take him in to the city.

Instead he started talking about the Ferris wheel, about how some gear on one of the motors that drive the thing had gone out on them, and he'd had to find a machine shop in Boring to make a coupling sleeve and a gear shaft from scratch, which was one hell of a mess, and how some guy had worked all day and half the night on a forge to do it for him.

"Cost me a hundred bucks," he said. "But we'd lose more'n that if we was to shut down." He cleared his throat and spit out the window. "You ride the Ferris wheel?"

"Sure," I said. It wasn't the most exciting but you got a good view of the town.

I turned down Main Street. About five blocks now and we'd be at the fairgrounds.

"What's your favorite?"

I knew he meant ride, so I thought about that for a moment. "The roller coaster—if it's a good one. I can't take some of those rides that turn you upside down though. I get sick. I don't like getting dizzy."

He didn't appear to be listening because he said, "Yeah, pal, I wouldn't be out here walking except my truck broke down on the way back from the machine shop. You think you could hang around a while until I get the wheel fixed and then take me and a buddy back out with a tool kit? I think we can get it running."

I was afraid of something like that. I hesitated. "My dad's expecting me home soon."

"You work swing shift?"

I don't know why I couldn't just lie and say yes. But I told the truth. "Graveyard."

"Whatcha doing out here now?"

"They let us go early tonight. Not enough work."

"Your old man know?"

"No, but I can't hang around long." This guy was too sharp. "He might find out. I saw him driving through town about an hour ago." I paused, thinking about it. "If he stopped by the cannery, he's probably out looking for me now." The thought left a heavy feeling in my belly. I was going to get the crap beaten out of me when I got home.

"Hey, at your age, you could kick his butt."

He must have been reading my mind. I shook my head but didn't say anything. I'd thought about it, though. But I didn't have the guts—dad had us all tyrannized. You fight back and you might as well leave forever. Otherwise you'd lie awake all night waiting for him to come in and kill you. Something God told him to do.

Two, three years and I'd be gone. I just had to survive until then.

We'd reached the main entrance of the fairgrounds off Main Street and the carny told me to pull on in so he wouldn't have to carry the box so far.

"Damn heavy," he said. "Glad you picked me up, kid. I'd've been out there all night."

At the gate, he got out and unlocked a barrier and I drove on through. He pointed to the Ferris wheel in the distance, a looming structure barely visible in the darkness, and I drove to the right around the rides and down a back lane to where several trailers were parked. The only light came from an occasional bulb strung up on a line between trailers. Each light was a lonely glow in the dark, a fleeting glimmer splashed on the surface of the eye and then washed away in a flicker. The silence was eerie. The air suddenly felt cooler.

"I'll tell you what, pal," the carny said. "Wait here for five minutes and I'll see if I can't wrangle up my buddy. If he's around, maybe you could just take us back now and I'll fix the wheel in the morning. Give you some Jim Beam for your help."

"I really—".

"It'll just take a moment. The truck's back on the Loop Highway. It ain't far."

When he was gone, I shook my head. Why couldn't I just tell people no? I was always trying to help and getting myself into trouble.

Okay, I hadn't been trying to help when the guys in the Chevelle asked me if I wanted to drag. But I'd tried to help Reta Jane. And that's when my clothes got dirty.

If the carny wasn't back in five minutes I was leaving. But I wasn't sure he'd left the front gate unlocked. And if he was serious about the Jim Beam, I'd take it. Make a few bucks selling it to someone else.

I wasn't into drinking hard liquor much myself. The guys at the cannery, when they found out I'd never had alcohol, got together and bought me a bottle of cheap wine, which they gave me in the parking lot at the end of one shift. They shared a few swallows but you could tell they wanted me to guzzle the whole thing. I downed about half the bottle in one long swig and ten minutes later I was sick as a dog and puking in the parking lot while they stood around laughing. I barely made it home that morning. So I wasn't into hard stuff myself.

Ten minutes later, the carny materialized out of the darkness and startled me. Despite the broken antenna, I'd been trying to tune in a radio station, but all I could get was static. I flipped the knob to turn it down and leaned out the window, hoping I hadn't woke up anybody sleeping in the trucks or trailers.

The guy didn't seem to notice the radio. "Hey, pal, I couldn't find him. You think you could help me for a half hour?"

"With what?" I was getting worried about the time. I just couldn't get it out of my mind that somehow my dad knew we'd been let go early. If he found out and I wasn't home, there went my chance to drive the car for the rest of the summer.

"Getting this gear set in place. Might be able to pay you a few bucks."

I was too stupid to ask how much, just said, "I guess—if it doesn't take too long."

"Thanks, pal." He thunked a hand down on the door frame. "I'm going to need some light, so how about you drive down and line this car up so we can see?" He pointed out where he wanted me, and I drove over some heavy electrical lines and maneuvered the car until he was satisfied.

"Name's George," he said, offering me his hand. He had a grip like iron.

"Artie," I said.

"Good. Let's get this sucker in place, pal."

For the next twenty minutes I helped him, holding the gear in place while he hooked it up the way it was supposed to be.

"Some guy made this from scratch?" I asked, marveling.

"Not the whole thing," George said. "This piece here in the middle. Works like an axle. This is what they call a hypoid gear. It's got curved teeth, see? Teeth were fine."

I thought about asking him if he'd been to college, since he knew so much about gears, but thought better of it. He didn't look the type. For all I knew he was making up a name. Hypoid? Where'd that come from?

It took us a while to get the gear lined up correctly so it meshed with another above it at right angles, but finally George slid out from under the motor and wiped his hands on a rag. "That should do it," he said. "Let's see if it works."

He tossed the rag to me and I wiped the grease off my hands while he threw a few switches and warmed up the motor. And then he told me to stand back and plunked a handle and the wheel started moving, creaking in the night breeze. The seats glided past us like phantoms in the dark. "Want to see the lights?"

"Sure."

George hit another series of switches and the Ferris wheel blazed into life, colored neon tubes, segment by segment, gleaming against the night sky, pink, turquoise, yellow, emerald green, red, swirling around in the cool air like a kaleidoscope on fire. The moon had risen higher, turning pale and shrinking in size, but the colored lights still stood out like a Christmas tree in a dark room—no, better than that, it was magical. No one else there ... the sound of the seats rocking in their frames as the big wheel swung up and away from us ... the sense of onrushing power. I could have stood there watching all night if I wasn't worried about finding Billy and getting the antenna on the Merc replaced.

I thought about asking George for help but instead of shutting down the rig he turned to me and asked if I wanted to take a whirl.

I couldn't say no to that. "But just one," I said. "See what the town looks like in the dark."

George just grinned at me after the first turn and played like he was waving good-bye. The wheel didn't stop. I saw him laughing the whole time and figured it'd be just like him to walk off and leave me going around all night. But he was just having fun. He started slowing down the wheel, giving me one last smooth upward sweep. Near the top of the wheel I had my second shock of the night. Half a mile away, turning off Division right under a streetlight I saw the pickup again.

Talk about disbelief. I was in so much turmoil that when I came to the bottom I asked George if he'd mind one more slow turn. I couldn't tell him why and he didn't ask, just sent me up again, the carriage gently rocking back and forth in time with my stomach.

Sure enough. There was no mistaking the pickup.

The enormity of what dad was doing washed over me like a tidal wave. The old man was stopping by somebody's home.

My mind went numb.

The wheel was bringing me back down again.

Who lived along Division Street?

Was that where Mrs. Kolochny lived? She played the piano in church and her husband was still stuck off somewhere in Russia. She barely spoke English herself, had three kids, all little girls in grade school.

I couldn't believe it.

Maybe they were just talking about what music to play in church on Sunday. Sometimes she dropped by to talk to dad about that. That had to be it, didn't it?

At one-thirty in the morning? With mom home asleep in bed?

Yeah, real likely.

# *seven*

I don't know whether I was sick or angry or just too stunned to know what to think and feel.

When I stumbled off the Ferris wheel and George shut the rig down, I didn't hear the first few things he said. I must have been staring at him like I'd seen a ghost.

"Hey," he said. "It couldn't have been that scary." He laughed. "You thought it'd fall apart, didn't you? It ain't like a roller coaster, kid. You wouldn't have shot off the end."

I just shook my head and stood there like a dummy. I couldn't tell George what I'd seen.

He slapped me on the back, said he'd have to get busy and track down his buddy and get back to the truck, and if he was lucky maybe catch a wink or two before the fair opened at eleven that morning. I know he was waiting for me to say I'd take him back out, but I just stood there, shuffling my feet and stretching my neck to the side, and then I said I had to get going. I didn't know what to do. If I drove home, I'd have to go out Division. What if I ran into dad just as he was coming out? My eyes grew wide at the thought.

Hey, he'd be the one who was caught, not me.

That was a new thought.

But I'd probably get beat for that, too.

"I've got to be going," I finally said.

Almost as an afterthought, George pulled out his wallet. "Here's five bucks," he said. "Thanks for your help."

"Aw, that's okay," I said. I wasn't even going to ask for it. I was still dazed, I guess, by all the lights on the Ferris wheel—and what I'd seen from on top. "Keep it. I didn't do anything."

He didn't protest, just put the money away and shook hands again.

"I'll tell you what, good pal. You come with your girl tomorrow before you go to work and I'll give you as many free rides as you want."

"Thanks," I said, looking at my toes. I wanted to get out of there now. I didn't think I'd take him up on it. My girl, if you could call Laurie Snyder that, was out of town for the summer. Walking over to the car, I thought about Billy instead. "Is it okay if I come with a friend? A guy? I'll be wearing work clothes and ..." I stopped, like I was embarrassed to be seen this way in front of a girl—or at least that's what I hoped he thought.

He laughed. "Don't make me no nevermind, pal. You come and I give you a ride. You don't come and I won't."

I hesitated a moment. "What about the Jim Beam?"

He chuckled. "Got a memory like an elephant, don't you? You underage?"

I nodded reluctantly, like he was trying to cheat me out of something that was mine. It made me think for a second of the time I won a prize at the fair for dropping these gray metal disks on a red circle, covering the whole thing, and the guy tried to cheat me, pointing to a tiny dot of red in the middle, so small you could hardly see it. I started to raise a ruckus and the guy shut me down, gave me a stuffed bear, and started shouting about how he had another winner. But I didn't really have any right to complain. I told Billy later that I'd cheated anyway. I'd slid one of my disks when the guy was distracted by Billy, who was working on a red circle to my left at the same time and asking all kinds of questions.

The carny slapped me on the back. "Well, shoot, pal. I promised it to you, didn't I?" He gave me a look, maybe waiting for me to change my mind or just thinking it over some more himself, then told me to come along with him.

Let's make it fast, I thought, calling myself a dolt for wasting more time.

The carny was bunking in a trailer the size of a rabbit hutch. Things were jammed in every which way. The place was a mess. He poked around in a cupboard under the bed and then came out with a stubby rectangular bottle that was half full of amber liquid.

"This what you want?" He started to hand it to me and then drew it back just as I was about to grab it. I dropped my hand and he laughed, uncapped the bottle, wiped his mouth with the back of his hand, and took a big swig.

"Here, help yourself."

I couldn't tell him I wanted it to sell to the guys, so I took a swallow and gagged on the fumes. The liquor burnt its way straight down my throat and hit my stomach like a rock dropped in a stagnant puddle. Why'd people drink this stuff? It sure didn't taste like anything I liked.

He asked for another swig and I got to thinking he'd drink it all. He laughed again when he saw the expression on my face. "Hey, pal, don't ya want to drink with your good buddy here?" He tapped himself on the chest, then scratched and pulled at the hair sticking out of his shirt.

I shrugged, eyeing how much was left at the bottom of the bottle. Down close to a quarter now. "I was thinking of saving it," I said.

---

He laughed. "Get that girl of yours drunk, huh? See if it helps you get into her pants?"

I was starting to feel uncomfortable. Next he was going to ask me if I was still a virgin.

"Well, shoot, pal, don't stand around looking so scared. Here." He handed me the bottle and I could tell he hadn't meant any harm, just having a good time. "Get out there and raise Cain, pal, and don't forget what I said about the rides."

Fifteen minutes later, whisky bottle on the seat beside me, I'd driven to the area where Billy lived, just west of the Portland Traction Company's rail line. His family owned a home on a dead-end lane that led to a gravel pit about a half mile from where we lived. I drove by our own farm, looking to see if the lights were out, and breathed a sigh of relief when I saw they were. There was just the one arc lamp glowing, hanging from the fir tree near the shed. Both houses—the church where Richy and I had our rooms upstairs and the small place nearby where the rest of the family stayed—were dark. That calmed me down a little bit. Except the pickup was still gone. But I didn't think dad would be coming after me now.

This wasn't the first time I'd gone late to wake Billy. But the last time I'd done it, things had gone wrong. It was a work night, Wednesday or Thursday, I think, about midnight. I was standing outside his window tapping on the pane with a rock and whispering his name, when a figure stepped out a back door, shouted "Hey" real loud and clapped his hands.

I knew right off it was Billy's dad but I didn't have time to think. I tore out of there, running around the corner of the house and sprinting for the road in my heavy work boots. Thank God, I'd parked up on Division Street rather than right in front; I hadn't wanted his family to hear the motor. I hightailed it back to the car, dived in and roared off, going on in to Portland on my own to the Star theater, where I claimed to be twenty-one (they never asked for ID) and went on in to watch a few nudie movies—girls playing volleyball in a nudist camp and things like that. It always seemed weird seeing them nude and wearing a wristwatch. Like why didn't they take that off along with their clothes?

Later, Billy told me his dad didn't recognize me. They'd been scared for a week or two because someone had reported a Peeping Tom and they thought I was the guy. I had to swear Billy to secrecy because he wanted to tell his family it was just me. Besides, I said, it won't calm them down, not if there really is a Peeping Tom.

I think he wound up telling them anyway, but his dad was nice enough not to pass it on to mine.

This time I tried to be quieter but I couldn't rouse anybody. Both cars were parked in the back yard next to the tugboat on its trailer, so he had to be home. Billy's dad worked for Portland Electric and the Deater's had more money than we did. One of the reasons I like Billy was because when we were growing up he always had more toys than me. BB guns, motor scooters, electronic games, you name it. And always two. His dad even bought him two Mexican donkeys one time, little things with a stripe down their backs and across the shoulders. Billy was real proud of that, since it was supposed to be a sign they were purebreds. What they planned to do with them, I had no idea, since both donkeys were male.

I used to wonder if his dad was afraid Billy wouldn't have any friends if he didn't have something for them to play with. Billy was a short guy with red hair and boils all over his face and body. His skin was so bad he went swimming in a T-shirt. The only thing his family didn't have two of was the boat, an old tug that we used to take out into the Columbia river and on over to Government Island, where we could run wild.

I was just about to give up when the window slid to the side and Billy stuck his head out.

"What's up, Artie? What time is it?"

"I got off work early," I said. "I need some help. Broke an antenna on the Mercury. You think you can help me?"

"Give me a minute and I'll be out."

"Bring your tool kit and a good flashlight."

Billy's bedroom was located at the back of the garage, a little room his dad had added just for him, but the garage was attached to the house, so he had to be careful. A few minutes later, he eased out the side door, tool kit in hand, and asked where the car was.

"Back up on Division," I said. "Let's go."

"How'd you break the antenna?"

"Drag racing." We were whispering.

"Drag racing! You get in a wreck?"

I was too embarrassed to tell him about the pants. "Tree branch broke it off," I said. "It busted right off at the socket, and one of the segments is missing.

You think you can fix it?"

He shrugged. "Depends on the antenna mount. If it's damaged, where we gonna get a new mount this time of night? If that needs replacing, I'll have to go in under the fender. Which means jacking up the car, taking off the tire, and removing the splash shield. You're sure it didn't pull right out of the fender?"

"It didn't look like it. Just the mast came loose. I don't think there's anything wrong with the mount."

"You're lucky then. That should be easier to fix. Just find a new antenna that fits into the socket you got."

"I thought we could break into the wrecking yard."

Billy grimaced. "They got a night watchman now. Big guy with a baseball bat."

Billy'd be the one to know about that. He had an old '49 Ford Tudor sedan with white walls his dad had bought off a Marine for a hundred bucks. It quit running after about a week and ever since then Billy had been scavenging parts and rebuilding the thing. He never worked for pay during the summers like I did, and I guess he was afraid to ask his dad for money, so he stole the parts from junked cars in a wrecking yard just outside the city limits.

"What are we going to do then?"

Billy grinned. "Find a car in town."

"Not in town," I said. "Too risky. Maybe out here where the houses are farther apart."

I don't usually steal, but if I didn't get the antenna fixed ... I didn't want to think about what might happen.

"After we get the antenna replaced, you want to go in and roll drunks?"

When Billy said "roll" he didn't mean rob them. We'd taken the Mercury in to Portland one night with a bunch of other guys, not really friends of mine but Billy knew one or two of them from shop. I hadn't really wanted to take them, but it was too hard to say no. What they did was, we'd drive around the parks until we saw a bum sleeping on a bench. Two of the guys would jump out the back doors, dash across the grass, tip the bench over on the guy, and take off running for the car. I'd have to floor it then. After the third guy, I told them I'd seen a cop car and made them stop, but not before almost driving over the top of a street divider when I was trying to turn left to get away. Too darn risky—and besides, I was afraid they'd hurt the bums. What if one of them broke a leg and the cops caught us?

So I told Billy not tonight.

"What about the Star theater?"

I hesitated. Nude women were always an attraction. I'd seen in the paper they were showing a film clip of an interview with a stripper who had size 44 breasts.

I said, "Richy told me he went one night last week and saw Stan Weden there." Stan Weden was a deacon in the church. He was married and had two kids.

"You're kidding."

"Nope." We were driving back toward town, away from Portland. "Weden was sitting in the back and Richy thinks the deacon recognized him."

Billy whistled. "Still, Weden couldn't tell your dad, right? Not if he was there, too."

"I don't know, but I don't want to run into him. He could say he'd gone there to check for kids from the church."

Billy thought that one over, then asked, "Well, what'll we do for fun?"

I drummed my fingers on the steering wheel. "I don't know if we'll have much time, Billy. How long will it take to fix the antenna?"

Billy shrugged. "Not long—once we find one we can use." He thought for a second. "Dan told me Wendy Scoles was throwing a party tonight. You think they might still be there?"

"It's getting awful late." I sighed. Billy wouldn't be happy unless we did something for fun—and he was helping me out, after all. "We can check it out," I said. "Afterwards."

Billy sat up and pounded the dash. "I know what. Principal Thompson has a Mercury Montclair. That should have the same antenna as the Monterey. You know where he lives?"

"Not him," I said. "He'll kick us out of school." And then I realized school was already out. "Next year."

"Ah, hell, next year." Billy scoffed at the idea. He hated the principal. Two weeks before school let out, we got caught in the hall for something we didn't do. Some kid set off a firecracker in the hall when we were standing at the other end near the main office. Old Thompson ran out, nabbed us, and called us into his office for a lecture. It didn't do much good to say it wasn't us. He thought we were liars—in addition to being the culprits.

We got off with just a warning, but he said the next time he caught us doing something we'd be expelled. Stupid Billy. Right afterwards, we were walking outside Thompson's office near an open window when Billy made a threat about bombing the guy's home. He didn't mean nothing by it, he was just angry, but the principal called the cops and they stopped me and Billy at the ice cream shop across from the school. They took Billy down to the station and made his dad come pick him up. Ever since then, Billy hated the guy.

"Dan knows where he lives," Billy said. "Let's go crash that party at Wendy's place. If it's still going, Dan'll be hanging around and he can help us." He leaned over and punched me on the arm. "Be cool, Artie. We'll get you a new antenna in no time."

And then he chortled like a crazy man who'd just broke out of a straitjacket.

# eight

When we drove by Wendy's home, the lights were already out and the place was dark. The windows looked like puddles in snow.

"Dan's probably gone home," I said, disappointed but half-way relieved. I didn't think going after the principal's car was such a good idea.

"No way." Billy shook his head. "He stays up till three or four every night, tooling around with his girlfriend. Let's go to the high school. He and Jackie hang around in the parking lot there."

A cop car passed going in the opposite direction and I kept my eye on him in the mirror until he turned the corner on to Tenth Street. I was surprised he hadn't stopped us just to see what we were doing in the middle of the night.

There were three cars in the parking lot at the high school and a few kids standing around under the one streetlight.

"That's Dan's car," Billy said, pointing.

I knew it when I saw it, a customized '52 Chevy two-door sedan. Dan was Billy's friend, not mine, but, like I said, I'd double-dated with him once. He was a smooth, handsome guy, and his girlfriend, Jackie, was on the Junior Varsity rally squad and treasurer of the Student Council. She was one of the smartest kids in our class and I always wondered how she hooked up with Dan. He was no brain. In fact, about all I could see he did well was work on cars. He hung around in the shop at school most of the time.

Billy told him what we needed while I waited in the car. In a few minutes Billy was back. "Okay," he said. "We follow Dan."

Two of the cars were starting to back out of their slots.

"How many of us are going? We can't have three cars."

"Just Dan. Those guys are leaving for Hosner's Hole."

"Is Jackie with him?"

"Naw, he took her home after the party. But he's going to pick her up later. She has to sneak out. Wendy's out there. I guess she's depressed or something."

"What over?"

"Dan wouldn't say. Something about the party."

Dan turned north on Main Street and we followed him toward Wood Village. When we got to Halsey, we took a right and then another and drove into a subdivision with curved streets named after trees and with big new houses spread out on wide lots. I could hear the rumble of the muffler on Dan's car as he slowed down with the car in second gear. "He's going to wake them before we get there," I grumbled.

"We got a ways yet," Billy said. "He's just slowing down."

"I hope that cop didn't follow us out of town."

"What cop?"

"That one we passed near the high school."

"Going in the opposite direction? Don't be so paranoid, Artie. No one followed us."

Dan had his hand out the window and was gesturing for me to pull up alongside him. I eased around and Billy rolled down his window. "What is it?"

Dan pointed up ahead to the left. "See that house on the rise? That's his. We hit it with paint bombs one night."

I leaned over toward Billy so I could speak to Dan without shouting. "Where's the car?"

"In the garage, I guess. If they're home."

"I don't want us breaking into any garage," I said. "They'll hear us."

"Not me, they won't," Dan said. "If you're afraid, you can wait here."

Billy turned to me. "Come on, Artie. We're doing this for you."

I hesitated. "I don't want to get in any trouble, Billy. My dad ..."

We both knew what my dad could do. And Billy's dad for that matter. Billy's dad didn't even want us together anymore. They'd invited me over one Sunday for dinner and I was in Billy's room while he changed clothes. He happened to fall back on his bed and was scratching his balls when his dad walked into the room. His dad thought Billy was masturbating in front of me or something. That his kid was queer. He threw up his hands, shouted something about us going crazy, and stormed out of the room.

But Billy told me later his dad took him out in the countryside for a talk and then wound up kicking his butt—literally. Made him drop his pants and then started kicking him. Billy said he was scrambling through the brush, trying to pull up his pants so he could run, and his dad was chasing him and kicking him every other step. I had to laugh listening to him tell me about it. I told him if it was my dad and I tried to run, I'd get beaten so bad I'd wouldn't be able to sit down for a week. So, anyway, his family quit inviting me over, but they couldn't stop us from getting together at church or at school—or like now, late at night. We just couldn't afford to get caught.

"Look," Billy was saying. "We don't need you. Just stay in the car with the motor running. We'll be right back."

It made me feel like an idiot, but I decided to do what he said. I couldn't risk getting caught and I told Billy if the principal came out I was taking off. He could jump into Dan's car. He said okay, and if we got separated they'd meet me back at the parking lot. He shuffled around in the tool kit at his feet, put some things in his pocket and they slunk off into the darkness.

Principal Thompson's house had one small porch light in front and that was it. Nothing by the double car garage to the side of the house. I kept my eyes fixed on the white door to the side of the garage and after about five minutes, I saw what looked like shadows in front of it and then they disappeared inside. It seemed to take them forever. At least fifteen, twenty minutes.

It was funny about that masturbating thing. Billy's the one who taught me how when I was in the fifth grade. I always wondered how you found out if no one told you. Did it come natural? I don't remember touching myself before then. When I first started, Billy was always asking me had the stuff turned white yet. Another contest. It was like with pubic hair—who had it first?

At that time, my family still lived in town, in the parsonage between the Free Methodist Church at 4th and Roberts and the public library on Main. I spent most of my spare time in the library, reading kids' books and trying to get the librarian to let me over to the adult side. I was reading about three or four books a week and running out of things I liked. I always wanted to get into the stuff for older guys. More exciting novels. They finally let me when I was in the seventh grade.

That's one thing I did a lot of—reading. One time, Mrs. Dottle, my eighth-grade teacher, had a contest. She put our names on a chart, with a row of empty boxes after them, and every time we read a book and wrote a one-page book report on it, she'd add a star to one of the boxes. Well, when the term ended, most of the kids had somewhere around ten or fifteen stars and then there was this one long row for me where she'd run out of room. She'd had to go from gold to blue stars, which meant ten books each. I'd read seventy books all together. The other kids thought I was cheating, but I lived in that library—when me and Billy weren't out masturbating somewhere! Shoot, we'd climb the church belfry and do it by the bells; we'd hide out in the garage, or up in the attic, and once we even climbed one of the fir trees next to the church and did it near the top, with a view of the whole city. It was Billy who always came up with a picture or two of nude women, torn out of magazines.

Billy and Dan were still inside the principal's garage when I heard the siren coming from town. A light went on inside the Thompson's house and my heart jumped out of my chest. I almost killed the car trying to take off so fast. I laid a streak of rubber and hit the horn in case Dan and Billy couldn't hear the siren from inside.

The subdivision had circular roads and I tried to take a new turn whenever I could. Hawthorne to Cedar to Maple to Elm to Ash. Some were called lanes, others avenues and boulevards, but they were all small. I didn't know where in heck I was and how to get out of the place, but at least I couldn't see the red light, which meant the cops couldn't see me. It took me about five minutes to find Arata Road and then I really lit out for town, hoping I wouldn't run into a second cop car. Gresham had a small police department and I doubted they had more than one cop on duty. And he was back in the subdivision.

By the time I reached the parking lot at the high school, my heart had stopped pounding, but I was so worried I couldn't think. If the cops caught Dan or Billy, they'd probably talk. I didn't want to think about what my dad would do to me then.

I got out of the car and walked up and down the sidewalk, talking to myself, swearing at my stupidity. I shouldn't have let Billy talk me into this. We'd have done better to go to the junk yard and risk running into the guy with the baseball bat. That was better than getting caught by the cops.

I stopped suddenly, my eyes falling on a dark shadow off to the side of the walkway. Someone was sitting on the curb.

A girl said, "Is that you, Artie?"

"Yeah, who is it?" My voice was guarded.

"Wendy Scholes."

I was surprised she'd recognized me. We never really talked at school. She ran with a different crowd, even though I would have liked to have known her better. She was one of the shortest girls in our class and I was one of the taller guys, so I always felt awkward when she passed in the hall. We said "hi" to each other and that was about it. But I knew she was an assistant editor of the school paper, the Argus, and would take over next year when we were Juniors. No one had ever done that before; it was usually a Senior. And she wasn't bad looking. She had short dark hair, plucked eyebrows, and always wore dark clothes and black stockings.

"Miss Casterline says you've been writing poetry."

I nodded reluctantly, said, "Mostly short stories though," and then wondered if she could see me in the dark. This was a weird conversation to be having in the school parking lot at two in the morning. I hadn't told any of my friends about the stories and the poetry, just our English teacher.

"I did fifty-nine poems one weekend," I said. I don't know why I had to brag like that. As if quantity was all that mattered. "Most of them were short, though."

"Miss Casterline said it was because of your dad."

That was a shock. "What do you mean?"

"I was asking her why you never talked to me and she said something about your dad. How he repressed you. That you could pour out your feelings on paper, but it was hard to get you to talk to anyone, let alone girls."

I'd never thought about it like that. *I couldn't talk to girls because dad was looking over my shoulder!*

Hmm. I didn't know. Was that it?

"I'd like to read some of your poems."

I hesitated. "I'm not showing them to anyone." I hadn't even showed them to Miss Casterline and she was my favorite teacher. I wasn't sure they were good enough, and I didn't like other people seeing what I was thinking. It didn't have anything to do with dad or girls.

"Maybe we could publish one in the Argus."

I cleared my throat. I'd seen one or two of her poems in the school paper. They were different. Too literary for me. Mine were simple. Shoot, I'd even written a poem on the garden hose.

"I'm not very philosophical," I said, feeling the heat rise in my cheeks. "I don't have much to say. They're not very deep."

"Poetry doesn't have to be philosophical. Most of mine isn't. What's yours about?"

I shrugged. "Nothing in particular." She seemed to be waiting for more, so I said, "Just things about what I see or feel."

She sighed. "I feel like crap, tonight."

I was surprised at her language. Most of the girls didn't speak like that around us guys.

"What happened?"

"Why don't you sit down?" She patted the curb next to her.

I sat down, about three feet away, my work boots making me feel awkward. "I just got off work," I said, but she didn't seem to notice.

We were silent for a while. I didn't know if I should ask her again what had happened. Maybe I wasn't supposed to know she'd had a party that night. I thought about telling her what had happened to Dan and Billy and then thought better of it.

Wendy turned toward me and I could see her face in the light of the lamp in the parking lot at my back. She'd been crying. She had black streaks down her cheeks from her makeup.

She bit her lower lip, then looked into my eyes and said, "Would you turn a girl down if she wanted to make love?"

# nine

My heart flip-flopped. Was she going to ask me? She was a lot nicer than Reta Jane. I cleared my throat again. "I ... I don't know ... probably not ... No one's ever asked me that before."

"I asked Glenn tonight."

"You did?" I was surprised. Glenn and I played together on the basketball team. He and Eddy and I were the only Sophomores last year who made the varsity. I wondered if I should tell her about Glenn's confrontation with Eddy in the parking lot at the cannery. It was hard to believe Wendy used to be Eddy's girlfriend. He didn't seem her type.

Wendy wiped at her eyes. "He turned me down. I opened myself to him ... I made myself vulnerable ..."

She stopped talking and started to cry. I didn't know what to do. I felt like putting my arm around her but I didn't want her to think I was making a move. Not while she was crying over someone else.

"Why'd he say no?"

She wiped at her eyes. "He was with Cheryl. They kept hiding from me."

"Hiding?"

"I had a party at my home tonight. We were in the basement. Glenn and Cheryl kept trying to hide from me. I caught them in the back room playing with pennies and kissing."

Playing with pennies. I'd never heard of that before.

She must have seen I was surprised. "We had a casino night," she said. "They were playing Twenty-One, but they wouldn't do it with the rest of us. Cheryl kept …" She stopped again and I sat there feeling uncomfortable.

Cheryl was a new girl in school. She'd arrived just two months before we let out for the summer. I'd been attracted to her myself. She sat behind me in English class and was always passing me notes. She had long red hair and blue eyes, but always seemed too loud to me. I knew I'd never be able to talk to her. She was too witty and too bright.

"That's what happens when you love somebody too much," Wendy said. "They hurt you. Boys always do that."

I didn't know about that. I'd always wanted a girl to love me as much as I loved her. I could never tell with my girlfriend. Laurie seemed too controlled to me. But maybe poets like Wendy were different.

She looked at me and her voice turned earnest. "Are you like that? Why do boys turn away when you tell them you love them?"

I took a deep breath and let it out. "Not everyone does," I said, hoping she'd realize I meant myself.

"That's why I asked him to make love to me. I know he wanted to, but I've been saying no. He left with Cheryl and I don't know what they did. He might have made love to her."

Her lips started quivering and she dropped her head.

I had to say something to help, but all I could come up with was a weak "I doubt it."

I didn't know any of my friends who'd made it with a girl. Vernon Jenks bragged about it one time, but we all told him he was lying.

I was still in a bit of shock. In the back of my mind I was worried about Billy and the cops and I still couldn't believe that Wendy had asked Glenn to make love. None of the girls I knew ever talked about that.

I stood up for a second, brushing gravel from my pants, and when I sat down I moved over closer to her. "He was probably just trying to make you jealous." I know Laurie did that to me. She seemed friendly to everybody. That was something I never could understand. Did she do it to hurt me or was that just the way she was?

Wendy had started crying again and I put my arm around her shoulder to comfort her. It was a funny feeling. She was burning up. I could feel the heat radiating from her like an electric coil.

"Thanks," she said, after a moment, her voice broken. She laid her head on my shoulder for a second and I was trying to absorb the sensation when she suddenly sat up and turned so she could face me when she talked. "I wish I was still in grade school."

*Grade school.* I couldn't imagine anything worse. All I'd ever wanted was to be in high school—and after that ... Well, I hadn't thought much further.

"Things were simple then," she said. "You had a boyfriend or you didn't. You didn't have to worry about games."

I thought about the girlfriends I'd had. Tracy Burkhart again. She had fat, stubby fingers and the first time I tried to hold hands I couldn't get my fingers through hers. That was a shock. Hot sweaty pudgy little palms.

Wendy looked at me. "Did you play games? You used to like Patty Pane, right?"

Patty Pane! That was her name! I'd been trying to think of her earlier. Miss tanned-all-over and who-do-you-think-you-are?

"She moved away in the sixth grade," I said.

"No, she just switched schools. Her parents wanted her in West Gresham. Didn't you keep in touch?"

"I didn't know what happened. She was just gone one day."

But I was thinking that it might have ended before then anyway. Like I said earlier, Patty had come back to school after summer vacation one year and everything had changed. I didn't even recognize her. She'd gone somewhere—to some lake or summer resort, somewhere where the rich sent their kids, a campground in California maybe—and every square inch of her—what you could see at any rate—was tanned. *Chocolate.* And on the school bus, when I tried to sit beside her, she said she was saving the seat for someone else. It was like she'd forgotten over the summer that we were boyfriend, girlfriend.

Wendy said, "Did you ever kiss her?"

"Not really."

"Who's the first girl you ever kissed?"

"My mom."

Wendy laughed. "I didn't know you were so funny, Artie. Thanks."

I could tell I was blushing. I hadn't meant to be funny, just said the first thing that popped into my mind. But it was nice when she laughed. As long as she wasn't laughing at me.

"Jeff Kostas was the first boy I kissed," she said. "Fifth grade. He bought me some candies for Valentine's day and I saved him two pieces. Almond Roca in gold foil. When I handed them to him I kissed him and then ran. His friend Todd saw me."

She paused and I could see her lip start to quiver again.

"It was Todd who told me later that Jeff didn't like me anymore. I kept saying I wouldn't believe it until Jeff told me himself. So finally he came up to me in the hall and said he liked Sarah." She took a deep breath. "His exact words were, 'I don't like you anymore. Sarah's my new girlfriend.' I saw them together at the noon movie. He had his arm around her." She tried to laugh. "Remember the noon movie?"

"My parents wouldn't let me go," I said. "My dad says movies are a sin."

"You never came?" She sounded surprised. "I thought we all came after lunch. It was like a class period."

"I was excused. But they wouldn't let me go outside. I had to wait in the classroom. I thought everybody knew. I always figured you guys were talking about how *weird* I was. I never got to go to rhythms either."

Which wasn't quite true. My mom had written me a note but I didn't give it to a teacher. When the grade report came for that quarter, my dad saw a "satisfactory" by rhythms and asked me what that was. "Marching," I said.

I almost laughed thinking about it now—except at the time it got me a good whipping with a razor belt. The rest of the year I had to stand on the side of the gym while the other kids learned to dance. I always felt like an outsider at that school.

Wendy reached out and touched me on the arm. "Who you going with now?"

"Laurie Snyder ... I think. I haven't seen her all summer."

"She's working in California, right?"

I hadn't known that. I stumbled for a second and then said, "She just said she was staying with relatives."

"Yeah, her uncle runs a boat rental at Guerneville on the Russian River."

I looked off into the distance, where dark masses of trees stood against the night sky. Why hadn't Laurie told me that?

It wasn't important—but it made me feel like I'd never known her.

Wendy crossed her legs, her knees hanging over the curb, then plucked absentmindedly at one of the eyelets on her tennis shoe.

"I changed my mind," she said. "You know the best age? Three years old. You don't know you're going to die. You just *exist*."

I cleared my throat and shifted on the sidewalk. "Do you think about dying?" I was worried she was thinking about committing suicide, but she must have thought I meant it philosophically.

*"Don't you?"* she said. "How can you live without thinking about *death*. I think about it everyday. I have *panic attacks* thinking about it. Have you ever really *imagined* you're going to die?"

I couldn't respond for a moment. I was struck by the passion in her voice. The way she meant it—really *imagining* dying. I wasn't sure.

Finally I said, "My dad preaches about it all the time." I paused. "I'm afraid of dying and burning in hell forever." I'd never admitted that to anyone.

"You know what Miss Casterline would say about that?" Wendy raised her head and looked at me. "*Oh posh*. And she's right."

I shrugged. "You don't believe in hell?"

"I don't believe in an afterlife. This is it—except for one thing."

"What's that? Reincarnation?"

She shook her head. "The dead live only in our minds and memories ... Isn't that why you write?"

"What do you mean?"

She didn't say anything and I suddenly felt dumb. "Like I said, I'm not very philosophical ... That's what worries me sometimes. How can you write if you don't have deep thoughts?"

"I think you do, Artie. You just don't realize it."

People at school always thought I was smarter than I knew I really was. It was like a mask. No one knew how stupid I felt.

I tried to laugh, then decided to tell her. "My last poem was about a garden hose. We were reading Wordsworth and I wanted to use the expression 'tangled skein.'".

"That's deep," she said. "A metaphor for life."

I was sure I hadn't thought of that. I just liked the word skein.

"I think you write for the same reason I do," she said. "You write to live forever."

---

"I'm just writing simple poems and stories."

"That doesn't matter. You're writing. You're sensitive."

No one had ever called me sensitive before. I turned the word over in my mind. Was that good or bad?

"The better you write, the longer you'll live in the minds and memories of others."

I shrugged. "What good does that do if you're dead. You never know."

"You can imagine ahead of time," she said. "Don't you enjoy it when you read others? Don't you like the authors who give you pleasure?"

I nodded. "Sure." I was thinking, who doesn't?

"Then you know what I mean."

She fell silent, hunched over her shoes, not looking at me now. I was trying to figure out why she was so worried about dying. Was she just trying to show me she had an artistic temperament?

"I've never known anybody who's died," I said. "Except for my grandpa, I guess. But I was too young then to know what was going on. I've been lucky."

"Didn't you know David Keefe?"

"Oh, yeah." That set me back. Just a year ago. "I forgot about him."

David Keefe drowned at Rooster Rock State Park in the Columbia River. His girlfriend felt him grab her leg and said she thought he was just playing, just trying to scare her. They found him a day later, said it was probably a cramp. She never knew he was drowning when he grabbed for her or maybe she could've saved him.

Wendy was crying again and I suddenly felt confused. She had deep thoughts *and* deep feelings. I didn't have anything. *I'd even forgotten David Keefe!*

Somebody died and I didn't even remember him.

Jeez. Wendy had been *Eddy's* girlfriend. I just didn't understand that. He was so mean and angry. What'd she see in him? No way he was philosophical. I was beginning to feel like I didn't know anyone.

"You know," Wendy said, "everybody's always saying 'Mother Nature.' Nature's not a mother—she's a cruel stepmother!"

I thought about that for a moment. "I like nature. There's this woods out behind our house and sometimes I just go out there and listen to the creek."

"I don't mean nature like that."

I felt stupid again.

"Listen. You've got an apple tree, okay?"

I didn't follow her but I nodded.

"One day, an apple drops off the tree and hits Newton on the head and what happens?"

I shrugged.

"The universal law of gravity!"

Now I was really feeling stupid. It was so obvious and I was looking for something deeper.

"The next day," she went on, "another apple drops, right?"

I nodded, waiting.

"And what happens?" She paused.

"It falls on top of a hard-working, productive colony of social ants *and kills them all!* That's Mother Nature for you. She doesn't care. You're religious, right?"

I hesitated. "Not really. It's my dad."

"It's not Divine Providence—it's Divine Indifference."

Whew! I didn't have anything to say to that. She was too pessimistic for me. We sat in silence for a while. After a bit, I started to look around. I didn't want to just leave her but—.

Suddenly, Wendy jumped to her feet. "I've got to go," she said, sounding cold.

I got up, wondering if I'd done something wrong. Maybe I shouldn't have said I liked nature.

Wendy sighed and then stuck out her hand.

She wanted to shake hands! That was weird.

I shook her hand and she said, "Maybe we can talk some other time, Artie. I'd really like to read your poetry."

I stood there, feeling awkward. I'd meant to cheer her up and it didn't look like it had worked. "Do you need a ride home?"

She shook her head. "It's only three blocks. My parents are going to be wondering what happened to me." She paused. "Artie?"

"Yeah?"

"Don't tell anyone I told you about this, okay?"

I wasn't sure what she meant by *this*, but I nodded. "I don't have anyone to tell anyway."

"Thanks for talking."

"Sure."

I watched her walk away and then, when I almost couldn't see her, she stopped and turned back. "And, Artie?"

"Yeah?"

"I think you talk just fine. Your dad ... don't let him hold you back. Girls aren't bad."

Jeez. I don't think dad had put it like that—although he was always talking about sin and temptation. I just nodded and said thanks.

Boy what was happening to me? First Reta Jane peeing right outside the car door and now a girl leaning her head on my shoulder and then crying in front of me? I didn't like seeing Wendy sad but as she walked off I felt a current of electricity flowing through me and I was almost breathless. It was like all the words we'd said had swarmed inside me and there was no room for air.

But I'd talked to another girl! And it hadn't mattered that I'd felt like an idiot. I'd learned something about myself—if she was right.

Okay, it wasn't like parting the Red Sea or calling manna from heaven, but still ... I'd done something! I'd opened up. Talking to Reta Jane had helped. She was right. Just be yourself and let things happen.

Was it that easy?

The hard part was doing that with someone you really cared about.

I knew what Wendy meant about loving too much. That's what I'd told Reta Jane. That was what made it hard with Laurie. When she was around, love was like a dam, holding back everything I wanted to say.

I heard a whistle and jerked around. Two guys were walking around the corner of the shop and coming toward me.

"Hey, Crenshaw. What're you doing out here?"

I recognized the voice. Eddy Peterson. My heart fell. He was the last person I wanted to talk to. The last time I'd seen him he and Glenn were standing in the parking lot at the cannery, ready to fight. *Over Wendy!* That thought flabbergasted me again. Neither one—Glenn or Eddy—seemed her type. How could you ever figure girls out?

I turned to go and Eddy said, "Hang on, Crenshaw. What's the rush?"

I hesitated, frozen in my tracks. I felt just like I did one time in the eighth grade, playing football in practice. It was like a vision in my mind: *Running wide open through the gap, no one in front of me but Vernon Jenks down on his knees—and what did I do? Ran straight at him like iron toward a magnet.*

When he tackled me, he had the same big grin on his face as Eddy did now.

## *ten*

The short, stocky guy with him was Russ McKane. He played fullback on the football team. He'd never liked me either. I think it was because my older brother Richy broke up with his sister. I know she hated Richy now. And as for Eddy, he hated us both—me and my brother, although he always acted like we were friends.

Eddy and I had fought with each other on and off since the sixth grade. I think he had it in for me because I beat him out of a position on the basketball team in grade school. And when we got to high school and I grew four inches my Freshman summer and beat him out again, he sat on the bench for one year and then quit the team. Someone had told me he was going to transfer to Rockaway next year, a smaller school on the coast where his aunt lived, just so he could start on the basketball team. I'd be happy to see him go.

Russ McKane waved a magazine. "Want to look at some naked women?"

I hesitated. "I'm waiting for someone."

Where had Billy gone anyway? Had the cops caught him and Dan? I still didn't have an antenna for the car.

"It's got some great beavers."

The two of them had come up to me and all three of us were standing under the light in the parking lot. Eddy grabbed the magazine and flipped it open in front of my eyes, moving it so I couldn't get a good look. I'd never seen anything so graphic, although it was hard to tell for sure.

"Where'd you get the magazine?"

Eddy snorted. "From the mechanics at the dairy." I knew he worked a second job weekends, gassing and cleaning trucks at Fairview dairy. I'd been out there once and seen the shop. Every free surface on the wall was plastered with pictures of naked women.

"It'll only take a minute," Eddy said. He jerked his head over his shoulder. "Come on. We'll give you a better look."

"Where you going?" I didn't want to get too far from the car. If Billy came back and couldn't find me, I'd never get the antenna fixed. I was going to give him and Dan another half hour and if they didn't show up, that would mean the cops had them and I'd better get home. In my mind, I could already see the lights blazing in the little house and dad—wakened by the cop call—standing on the porch with a strap, waiting for me.

Eddy hit me on the shoulder and I flinched. It was too hard to be a friendly punch. "There's a ticket booth near the football stadium with a light," he said. "Come on. We're going there."

"What's wrong with here?"

"Light's too weak. Besides, somebody might see us. You want everyone looking?"

They started walking toward the football field and I found myself tagging along. I don't know why I did, I'd never liked Eddy Peterson. Not even when we were supposedly friends in grade school. He was always following me and wanting to do things together, but he always seemed to have a strange look on his face, a sneer almost, like he hated me even though he pretended to be my friend. He competed with me at everything. He was stronger than me, but he wasn't as smart—and I think it had really shocked him when the basketball coach picked me to start in the eighth grade and not Eddy. He didn't play *intelligent*, the coach said, and I think that was what made Eddy hate me. That's when I started really noticing his mean streak.

As we walked around the new wing at the school and headed toward the stadium, I was thinking about one time in the eighth grade when Eddy wanted to fight. He knew he could beat me, so he picked something to get mad about. We traded words a while in the cafeteria until finally one of his friends said why didn't we go out to the playground and settle it. I didn't want to, but there wasn't anything I could do with everybody staring at us and egging us on. So I said to Eddy, just you and me. No one else.

Recess was just ending and everyone was heading back to class anyway, so Eddy agreed. He wanted to fight bad. We walked out to the playing field and stood behind a storage shed. That was where I cried. The strangest thing. I cried a lot as a kid—mostly because my older brother always beat me up. But I never cried in front of my friends, even if I was hurt.

We stood facing each other for five, maybe ten minutes, with Eddy saying, come on, chicken, throw the first punch, and me, with my hands at my sides, saying, no, you throw the first punch, and him saying, come on, hit me.

But I couldn't. So we just stared at each other for a while and suddenly I felt this tear roll down my cheek.

I didn't say anything. More tears came but I didn't reach up to wipe them away. It was like I wasn't there, like I was someone else and those tears weren't mine. I hadn't wanted to cry.

"You're scared to fight, aren't you?" Eddy said.

I remember shaking my head but I couldn't talk. That wasn't why I was crying—not because I was scared. It was something I couldn't explain. It was like, why did we have to be there in the first place? Why did people have to be so *mean* to each other?

I could tell it bothered Eddy.

But not for the same reason.

It bothered him because he didn't know what to do. Maybe he could tell the tears came from something other than fear, some feeling deep inside that was strong enough to make me cry. After that, we never had much to do with each other.

And now I was following him like he was the Pied Piper.

*Explain that.*

When we got to the ticket booth, Eddy and Russ pried off a board over the top half of a double swinging door and then Eddy crawled inside and found the light. I was the last one inside. It looked to me like they'd been there before. Empty wine bottles were scattered about, gum wrappers, and other garbage.

At first Eddy and Russ wouldn't let me look at the pictures. Eddy kept shoving me away. "You kiss her boob and we'll let you look," he said, showing me the top half of one of the pages.

They were laughing like idiots.

"Come on, you guys. Just let me look."

"No way, Crenshaw. Kiss her titty and we'll let you look." Eddy mashed the magazine in my face and I jerked back, feeling blood on my lip. The bastard.

"Then I'm going," I said.

But Russ McKane pulled me back and knocked me off my feet before I could get my balance. The two guys crawled out the top half of the door and I tried to follow.

Eddy was there then, swinging his fists at my face. I backed away before he could hit me.

"Let me out."

"No way," he said, grinning. "Now you got to kiss the titty just to get out." He turned to Russ. "Come on, McKane, find the page, so he can kiss those big knockers. Then we can tell all the girls."

I tried to shove my way out the door and Eddy slugged me in the shoulder. "You try that again and I'll bash your face," he said. "And then Russ'll beat the crap out of you."

"Come on, Eddy, I gotta get home."

He shook his head, sneering. I knew if I kissed that picture that he'd tell everybody in school. Maybe even the teachers. He'd done something like that to me before. We'd stolen some candy bars together once, and every time he wanted to scare me, he'd start to say, "Let me tell you what Artie and I did in Piggly Wiggly." He even did it around teachers and when they'd say, "Go ahead, what'd you do?" I'd be there pulling on his arm and saying, "Come on, Eddy, shut up," which was almost as bad as him telling the truth. I knew he'd tell Laurie Snyder if I kissed the girl's boobs. I'd be ashamed to ever see her again.

"Hey, McKane," Eddy said, "let's roll the ticket booth."

"Come on, guys, this isn't funny."

The two of them started rocking the ticket booth and I stumbled around, trying to keep my balance while the light, which was hanging from a long cord, swung back and forth. There was a shower of hot glass when it broke and I shielded my face as I tumbled from one side to the other.

I could see the opening in the darkness. Why didn't I just charge it and slug my way on through? But something held me back. I didn't want the two of them to beat me up. Eddy might not stop until he knocked me out. I almost felt like crying I was so mad.

Eddy was at the opening again, yelling at me to kiss the titties. I got to my feet in the darkness, stumbling over the wine bottles. Sweat had broken out all over my body. I wasn't going to take any more.

Eddy didn't see me coming. I lunged for the window and ripped the magazine from his hands before he could pull it away.

He swore at me. "Get over here, Russ. He's got the magazine."

McKane tried to stick his leg in the window and I kicked at it, missing him on purpose and hitting the bottom half of the door. It was enough for him to jump back outside.

"He's kicking," I heard him say, surprise in his voice. I guess they didn't think I had it in me to fight back.

"Let me out of here or I'll tell the cops," I said, my voice breaking.

I could hear them laughing, and then Eddy said, "Let the crybaby out."

I didn't move. I was afraid to stick my head out the window for fear they'd hit me.

"Come on," Eddy said. "You wanted out, didn't you?"

I didn't move. They were talking quietly. I sat down on the floor and felt something wet. Darn it! Wine. I got up and wiped at my pants, then smelled my hands. They stunk like vomit.

I couldn't hear any noises from outside. What were the guys doing? For a second I thought I smelled smoke and got scared, but it was nothing. Just my imagination.

I waited another ten minutes or so, listening for voices, footsteps, some sign that they were lying in wait for me. I couldn't hear anything. Finally I dropped the magazine and crawled out of the ticket booth. I got to my feet and looked toward the parking lot. The Mercury was still there. It was the only car in the lot. Eddy and Russ were gone.

What had happened to Dan and Billy? I wanted them around in case Eddy and Russ tried to jump me.

The place was dead. Had everybody gone home to bed?

When I got back to the parking lot, I stared at the car in amazement. The antenna was fixed! I walked over and touched it to make sure. It was real all right, and there inside the car was the broken one. Billy and Dan had made it back okay!

I couldn't believe how happy I felt. I was back where I'd started!

I sat behind the wheel, turned on the dome light, and looked at my watch in the feeble glow from overhead. Three o'clock. An hour had gone by since I'd left Billy. I still didn't feel tired. If dad was home, he would be waking up in another three and a half hours or so. Until then maybe I was safe.

I laughed to myself. I'd been worried about the time all night and now with morning coming on I suddenly didn't care. I was either in trouble or I wasn't. I couldn't do anything about it now. And look at all the fun I'd had. If I hadn't stopped off at the bowling alley, I'd have never gone drag racing, wouldn't have met Reta Jane, wouldn't have wound up butchering a pig or getting shot at for picking cherries, wouldn't have broken the antenna, and wouldn't have stopped for the carny. Now I'd talked to two girls, my pants were finally dry (forget that damp patch from the wine), the antenna fixed, I'd gotten rid of Russ and Eddy, and I had a promise of free rides on the Ferris wheel if I wanted.

Hey, I thought, maybe I *should* go home. Quit while I was ahead.

But the night was calling me again—and its voice was like a Siren. I should've been tied down to the mast so I didn't jump overboard, but my desire for freedom got the better of me. I leapt at the call of the night and struck out swimming for the deep. It was risky, but everything had turned out okay so far. I was like a gambler who didn't know when to stop.

---

I put the car in reverse and backed up. Out at the blinking light at Main Street and Division, I hesitated. One last chance ...

If I turned right, I'd be home in five minutes. Turn left and ...

I turned left. This was getting easier!

Hosner's Hole. Lover's lane. I'd check there and if no one was around I'd go home. It was at least a twenty minute drive out to the Sandy River, but I knew the way well, and when I got out there, maybe I'd stop and pick a few blackberries by flashlight. They grew wild in all the fields out that way.

Or have a late-night picnic! I still had my lunch and those strawberries. They had to be thawed by now. I could sit on a riverbank and eat in peace and quiet.

And maybe scare somebody smooching in a car.

# *eleven*

I saw Billy had taken the bottle of Jim Beam, so I figured he and Dan had gone somewhere other than home.

As I drove through town, pretty much everything was dead. I checked the Hood Theater parking lot and a few other places along the way, but they were all deserted. I knew a lot of the kids stayed up most of the night in the summer. Those that didn't work, at least.

Party time—and, as usual, I was by myself.

But hey, loneliness can be comforting if you like yourself.

I shook my head. That was something Miss Casterline, our English teacher, was always saying.

Still, I didn't mind being alone—especially in the dark. It was like your head opened up to the whole night sky and you could breathe stars.

The air had cooled down, but I drove with the window open. The tires whistled over the pavement. It seemed time had been kept in a bag all night and now someone had untied it and time was starting all over again. I was back where I started. On the road.

After a while, I turned on the radio for company, listening to the disk jockey at KISN making his wisecracks. They seemed to talk more at night, maybe figuring anybody still up and listening would be lonely.

I wondered if Reta Jane and the guys in the Chevelle were still out at Hosner's Hole. Some people camped out there all night, even though technically it was illegal. The cops patrolled the area every now and then, since it was a lover's lane, but didn't really bother you unless you were drunk or fighting.

Fifteen minutes later, the road took a curve off the flat farmland and began dropping down a gentle slope through rolling hills dotted with clumps of blackberry bramble. Back when I worked at Camp Collins, which was this YMCA camp farther on along the Sandy river past Hosner's Hole, I used to wander these same fields, climbing over fences posted with no trespassing notices. I'd pick a bucket of blackberries, go back to the kitchen, and have the cooks bake me a couple of pies that I stored in one of the walk-in refrigerators. Then, late at night, I'd sneak down from my room on the second floor of the main lodge, get an ice cream sandwich, strip off the outer layers of chocolate, and have myself a piece of pie with a block of ice cream on top.

Just the thought made my mouth water. I was getting hungry. When I got to Hosner's Hole, I'd eat a sandwich and then polish off the can of strawberries before going home.

A half mile later, the curves tightened and then, without much warning, the road took a sudden plunge down a series of sharp twists and turns, riding the edge of a bluff that overlooked the river below. I slowed down and kept my eyes open for drunk drivers coming uphill. There'd been a lot of accidents along this stretch and if you went off the edge you were dead.

I'd seen enough cars in the ditch, even at the bottom where the road finally straightened out for its last slide to bottom land. Just before turning to gravel, the road took a sharp turn left and many drivers, brakes overheating, failed to see it in time and shot off the road and through the trees. When I was working at Camp Collins, we'd have to take the pickup out there at least once a month to try to pull a car out of the ravine.

I tapped the brakes for the turn at the bottom, moved on to the gravel road, and then came to a stop and doused the lights. I could hear crickets chirping and the pinging of the motor as it cooled, an occasional bird call. A fine layer of dust sifted by the open window and then settled back to the ground.

Several dirt roads cut through the scrub brush into Hosner's Hole, meandering around through the growth on their way to the river and the narrow strand where clumps of willowy grass held the sand together. The area was dense with thickets of bay, sandbar willows, alders, buckeye, and some taller trees scattered here and there—pine, mountain-ash, western hemlock, and cottonwood. I knew most of them from tagging along on the nature hikes when I worked at Camp Collins.

I could make out a few cars closer to the road, parked up against the brush. That meant a lot of kids were still out there, since the best spots were farther in, closer to the river. The river took a slow turn near Hosner's Hole, creating a swimming hole with deep pools and almost no current to contend with.

After a few moments of listening, I hit the lights again and moved on down the road, looking for a good place to head in. I took the third one along, passing a big, finned Chrysler with at least four kids in it. You could tell they didn't like my headlights, so after a bit I cut them again and sat for a few moments while my eyes adjusted to the darkness. The moon was high overhead now and cast an eerie pale sheen through the dappled trees.

I used to come down to the hole with the camp counselors late at night, and we'd sneak up to cars, get two or three guys on both sides, and then start rocking them—and then we'd scream with laughter and take off running. That usually shook up the lovers and they'd be out of there two minutes later. One night though, they were ready for us in one car, waiting with buckets of water. Must have been someone we'd scared before. That was a shock. Cold ice water in the face.

Thinking about it now brought to mind something my dad did once. I shook my head. Not a pleasant thought. You'd've thought I'd have forgotten by now, but some things just seem to stick with you like pitch from a pine cone. I don't know why I had to torture myself.

*"Get up."*

*I came awake slowly, felt someone yank me out of bed by the arm. What was I? Four? Five at most?*

*"You wet the bed yet?"*

*I reached down, touched my underpants.*

*Dry.*

*Whew. No whipping now. I shook my head, too sleepy to respond.*

*"Come on, we don't have all night. Get in the bathroom."*

*He followed me in, set me on the toilet. "I can't go," I said.*

*"You sit there until you do. Your mother's tired of washing sheets every day. You wet the bed again and you're going to sleep in it tomorrow." A cuff on the head. "You listening?" And with that he left the room.*

*Seconds ticked by ... minutes ... I tried to pee, but nothing would come. My head drooped ...*

---

*"You go yet?"*

*How much time had passed? A half-hour? Forty-five minutes? It seemed forever. I couldn't speak.*

*He yanked me off the toilet, looked at the water in the bowl, then cuffed me on the head again. "Get back on there. You're going to stay here all night if you have to."*

*He turned the water faucet on, let it drip, left the room again.*

*I could hear the clock ticking in the living room, the soft trickle of the water, every now and then a gurgle, but nothing would come ...*

*"What's taking you so long?" He'd jerked me off the toilet again. "I thought I told you not to fall asleep until you went to the bathroom."*

*"I can't go."*

*"You go in bed every night, why can't you go in here?"*

*I stared at him, couldn't think of an answer. Watched him as he turned and left the room.*

*Alone again. Was I going to have to sit on the toilet all night?*

*Suddenly the door flew open and he was in the bathroom, a pan in his hand. Was I going to get a spanking with it?*

*And then the shock as he poured the cold water over my head.*

*"Maybe that'll help you. You're wet now, aren't you?"*

*The cold night shirt stuck to my skin and water dripped from my hair and dribbled down my face.*

*I was glad he couldn't see my tears.*

Wow, what a bummer! I shook my head, trying to forget. I must have been what? Five years old? I had to do something to feel a little better. Man, that was heavy.

I eased off the road and parked the car. I needed some action. It'd be easier to walk around. I didn't want anyone seeing me by myself in the car.

Near the river, on foot, I came across the '64 Chevelle with what looked like Carl and Reta Jane. They were alone, making out in the front seat, and didn't see me.

Someone had a campfire near a sandy outcropping. I crept up on them, feeling better already, thinking it might have been counselors from Camp Collins, but it turned out to be Billy and Dan and some other guys from high school. They all had girls, even Billy, and that surprised me. He was with a mousy girl I'd never seen before, with buck teeth. No one I would have liked, but it still made me jealous. Dan had picked up his girlfriend Jackie and she said "hi," and that was when I noticed Eddy Peterson. He had his arm around Wendy, and she didn't look like she minded. When I'd left her earlier, she'd said she was going home. But she must have wandered around until Eddy found her.

What had happened to Glenn? Was she trying to get even? One fight over him and another girl and she was already back with Eddy?

I still didn't get that—her liking Eddy in the first place. Okay, maybe from a girl's point of view he was handsome, but he also had a perpetual sneer on his face and a chip on his shoulder. She was too sensitive for a guy like him. I mean, she'd said I was sensitive, but there was no way Eddy was.

"Sounds like you had a mess of problems tonight," Eddy said, like he hadn't seen me before. "Dan was telling me about fixing your antenna."

I was about to ask Dan and Billy how they'd got away from the cops, when Eddy's voice hardened. "And I told them about you and Russ in the ticket booth." Taunting me with an ugly smirk. "Kissing pictures of *nude* women."

I'd had enough from Eddy and called him something he didn't like, and before I knew it he was on his feet with his face in mine and we were jawing back and forth. I probably wouldn't have made anything of it, if Wendy hadn't been there—and Billy with another girl.

I shoved Eddy and I think it caught him by surprise. He usually tried to egg me on and I never responded. He stumbled back through the fire, kicking burning embers on the others. Jackie shrieked and there was a commotion around her.

The others were kicking sand on the sparks when Eddy came at me—*mean*. I could see it in his eyes, the fire glinting in them. He was going to get even for me beating him out on the basketball team and for everything else he hated about me—that I was smarter than him and had it easy in school while he struggled to get C's, that my dad didn't have a metal plate in his head.

Eddy flailed away with his fists, while I tried to parry the blows and strike a few of my own, but he was getting the better of me. I knew he was stronger, and he had what I lacked—the will to fight. For me, it was self-defense, even though I'd started it.

He caught me in the cheek with one punch and I was stunned for a moment. A second fist slammed into my gut.

I bent over, gasping for breath and trying to protect my stomach. He'd knocked the wind out of me and I felt like puking.

Eddy didn't stop fighting. Blows rained down on my head and shoulders.

I fell to my knees and tried to roll away, sand flying, and heard Billy saying,

"Come on, Eddy, he's down." But Eddy wouldn't listen. He kicked me in the side and I tried to twist away, my breath coming back in big gasps. And then he was on top of me and trying to shove my face in the sand so I couldn't breathe.

I jerked an elbow into his side and he grunted and tried to slug me in the face again, but Billy and Dan were on him then, pulling him away from me.

I got to my feet. I was shaking. Somehow my nose had started bleeding. I could feel tears ready to come. Wendy was holding my arm, asking if I was okay.

I didn't want sympathy. I pulled away from her and scrambled up an embankment, going for the car. But Eddy wasn't through. He came up after me and caught me by the arm, twisting me around and slugging me in the face again, a glancing blow this time but the same cheek as before.

Instinctively, I swung back just as Billy was coming up the bank on his hands and knees. Eddy dodged to avoid my fists, tripped over Billy and flipped backwards off the sandy embankment. Everyone heard his head hit the rock. It sounded like the snap of a breaking branch.

There was a moment of silence, and then we all scrambled to see what had happened.

A searchlight stabbed through the trees and I saw it was a cop car.

"The cops," I said.

"Come on, Billy," Dan said. He grabbed for Jackie's arm. "Eddy can take care of himself."

The mousy girl didn't want to leave. "Eddy's hurt," she said.

"I'll take care of him," I said. "He was fighting with me. You guys get out of here."

Wendy didn't say anything, but she left with the others and I lost a little respect for her. I hadn't asked her to stay, but I was hoping she would.

The cops hadn't seen us yet. I was trying to stay cool. I kicked sand on the fire, knowing that a bonfire would attract their attention. Camp fires were illegal in Hosner's Hole.

Eddy hadn't stirred. I reached behind his head and felt blood.

It was my fault and I didn't know what to do. The cop car was circling my way. The searchlight played through the trees, the sound of motors coming loud as car engines started and kids cut out of the hole, heading for the road to town.

I thought of dragging Eddy up against the embankment, hoping the cops would just move on past us, but it was too late. They'd seen the sparks of the fire and were getting out of their vehicle.

My heart sank. I should've known I couldn't luck out twice. They'd almost got me in the subdivision. And now this.

Why did I always have to be the one who got caught?

# twelve

Dad was going to tan my hide for this. I was almost too fed up to care. I was tired of worrying.

He'd knock me around while he asked questions and then I'd get a whipping that would last a month. One of those beatings that would make me feel like killing him.

Fine, that was just the way it'd have to be.

Both Richy and I were bigger than dad but—.

I shook my head. Raise a hand against him and … what?

I figured he'd kill us in our sleep. Come in with the thirty-ought-six and blow us away. He kept the rifle locked in a cabinet, probably afraid one of these days we'd do the same to him.

"What's the problem?"

I shielded my eyes from the glare. The cops had shut off the searchlight, but they'd come to a stop with their headlights focused on me and Eddy.

"What's going on here?"

"This guy's hurt," I said. "He hit his head on a rock." My mind was running in overdrive. "I was trying to help him."

"How'd he hit his head? You been drinking?"

"Not me. He tripped coming down this sandbank."

One of the cops, a big guy with a well-trimmed mustache, had joined me next to Eddy while the other went back to radio in. "He a friend of yours?"

"Not really. He was with some other guys who left when you came along." I paused. "They had the fire."

"What's your name?"

My heart went dead and then I surprised myself. "Billy Deater," I said.

Now I was really in trouble. The cops would find out who I was when they asked for ID. And my dad would beat me worse for lying.

The cop knelt by Eddy and I took a step away, wondering why he hadn't asked me about the blood dripping from my nose. My head felt like it was on fire, my cheek already puffy and sore.

"What are you doing down here this time of night? Your parents know you're out here?"

"Someone said there was a party." I didn't answer the second question. The cop was bending over Eddy.

I heard a groan. Eddy was regaining consciousness.

I edged away, trying to get into darkness.

"You hang around," the cop said, looking over his shoulder.

I must've gone crazy. I was more afraid of my dad than of the cops. All my life I'd done what I was told, but the second the cop looked back down at Eddy, I took off running.

Blindly.

I couldn't see a thing.

Behind me, both cops were shouting. Any second, I expected to hear a bullet come crashing through the brush after me. I tripped and fell and got up and kept going, scrambling away from the river. Branches slapped at me as I ran. I got whacked in the face and my eyes started tearing. I tried to protect myself but panic had taken over. I had to find the car and get out of there before they started looking for me. I didn't know how bad off Eddy was or how much he'd tell them—and I didn't care.

I slowed down after a while—trying to figure out where I was—and realized I was lost. At least I knew the area well enough to know that if I kept walking away from the river I'd come across the road leading to Camp Collins. And from there I could backtrack and find the car.

Maybe it was better not to go back. There'd be other cars there. Not everyone had left just because the cops pulled in. The older kids would stay. And just because the Mercury was sitting empty didn't mean it belonged to me. The cops wouldn't wait around forever to see. Especially if Eddy was hurt bad and needed a doctor. They'd have to take him in to the hospital. It'd take forever to get an ambulance out to Hosner's Hole.

I found a footpath and hurried along it, protecting my face with one arm. Ten minutes later, I stumbled out onto the road. I stopped and tried to catch my breath. My shirt was torn—worse than before— and I must have looked a mess. I could feel the blood caked on my lips and chin. My arms and face stung from what felt like a hundred scratches.

Jeez, I had to get home before dad got up, clean the car, and get to bed before anyone saw me. Maybe I could cover the scratches with Clearasil—or make up something about an accident at the cannery. A stack of crates had fallen on me— something like that. The same excuse I was going to use for my shirt, torn by the barbed-wire when Reta Jane and I were trying to get away from the cherry tree.

This wasn't my night. I felt betrayed by Wendy—and she wasn't even my girlfriend!

I tried to look at my watch under the moonlight. It looked like it was going on four o'clock. I still had two hours before I was supposed to be off work. And on top that, I had nearly a half-hour of leeway if I needed it. Dad wouldn't be up until six-thirty or so.

That calmed me down a bit. No rush.

My mom had a plaque on the wall in the kitchen at home: *In a rush? Relax!* I'd always thought that was for old folks.

Now that I was on the road, I wanted to get back to the river—wash up, find the car, make sure the cops weren't hiding somewhere nearby, and get the heck out of there. Had either of the cops got a good look at me? I was dressed like any other kid. I'd given a false name. If Eddy shut up I'd be okay. He'd looked pretty dazed when he was coming to.

I knew where I was, more or less. The summer I worked at Camp Collins I'd walked this road a hundred times in the dark. I wasn't far from the entrance to the campgrounds. I pondered going that way and then thought better of it. Too far from the car. I'd be better off going back toward Hosner's Hole along the road. At the first cutoff I could sneak back in, stick to the path and keep my eyes peeled for cops. If I was careful, I'd see them before they saw me. And once they left, I could wait five minutes and follow.

Fifteen minutes later, I was back at the river. I'd circled around the cops, who were still parked at the river bank, their headlights shining out over the water while they worked on Eddy. From a distance, it looked to me like he was on his feet. He had a shirt wrapped around his head to stop the bleeding.

When I got to the river, I moved along the bank, keeping to sand where I could, crossing pebbled areas if I couldn't. The clicking of slick stones under my feet sounded as loud as angry cowbirds but I knew it wouldn't carry far.

I almost ran square into the tent. I hit a guy wire and tripped, thudding into the ground with a gasp of surprise.

I heard a woman's voice, someone swearing, scrambled to my feet and scuttled over an embankment and into a little hollow, my heart pounding. I heard the hiss of a gas-jet lantern and the unzipping of a flap in the tent. I could see two of them now, side by side, in front of two small tents.

"What is it, Mom?"

A girl's voice, coming from the tent that was still dark.

"I don't know," the woman said. "I've got the gun. I'm going to shoot this time. I'm tired of being hassled."

My heart froze. I tried to bury my face in the sand. If she took five steps in my direction she'd be right on top me.

"Come on out," she shouted. "I see you."

I didn't move. I wasn't going to come out where she could shoot me. I thought about just getting up and running in the dark, but it'd be just my luck to catch a bullet in the back. Cops were trained not to shoot but this woman was a loose cannon as far as I was concerned. I could hear her muttering and swearing to herself.

"Go on back to bed, Colleen. They're gone. Stupid, goddamn kids."

"We shouldn't have camped her, Mom. I told you that."

"Just go back to sleep."

"I can't sleep," the girl said. "It's too hot in my tent."

"Open the flap."

"I did. I can't breathe. Do you have any more mosquito repellent."

"Colleen, I told you. There aren't any mosquitoes out here."

"Mom, there are, too. I can hear them."

"Honey, you've got bats in your belfry."

"You *know* mosquitoes like me more than you. I'm *hotter*."

I almost laughed. If I wasn't still pinned down, I would have. That's the way I was—mosquitoes loved me, too. I could be sleeping in the middle of ten kids and the mosquitoes would hone in on me and forget the rest.

The mother said, "Just go to sleep and you won't hear them."

I shook my head. She sounded just like my dad—only he'd threaten to cuff you in the head if you didn't do as you were told.

"They'll bite me when I'm sleeping."

"Colleen, I don't want to hear any more about it. Go to sleep."

"What are you going to do?"

"I'm going to sit here and wait for them dang kids to come back. I swear I'll shoot this time. That'll give us some peace."

"Can I go for a walk along the river?"

---

"What's got into you, honey? It's the middle of the night."

"No it's not. It's almost morning."

I peeked over the edge. The woman had shut down the gas lantern and I couldn't make out much in the tree-filtered moonlight. Then I saw the bright red dot. She was smoking.

"It'll be dawn soon," the girl said. She wasn't going to quit pestering her mother. "I'll walk downstream. I want to go swimming."

"You don't go swimming in the middle of the night. What's wrong with you?"

"I'll wait till dawn."

"I don't want you swimming by yourself. Now go back to bed."

They quit talking then. When the woman went back into her tent and zipped up the flapper, I waited another ten minutes, to give her time to fall asleep, and then moved around both tents and farther downstream where the river swept around a bend. I had blood on my shirt and I wanted to wash it out and clean myself up.

Not pig blood this time, I thought. My own. It had been a rough night. Time to call it quits.

Only good thing was I'd talked to two girls. Reta Jane and Wendy. How often had that happened?

Like never.

A few minutes later I found a pebbly beach and sat down just beyond the water line. I was starting to feel tired. I'd had too many adrenaline shocks in the last hour—and the fight with Eddy had taken it out of me, too. I still hadn't eaten my lunch. I wasn't going to go back for it now.

I took off my boots and socks and sat with my feet in the river.

The water felt good, nice and cool—but not too cold. Soothing.

I took off my shirt and washed my face and arms. It was hard to tell in the moonlight just how bloody the shirt was. I tried to wash a few spots and then let it go at that.

"Oh!"

I heard a gasp and sat up, swiveling around, heart kicking into high gear.

"You scared me," she said.

The girl from the tent. I recognized her voice. I hadn't heard her come up on me, and she must not have heard me washing.

"I thought you were a rock," she said.

I took a breath. "I'm just down here washing," I said.

She'd scared me, too. I slipped the shirt on, trying not to gasp as the cold spots hit my skin.

She laughed. "You're an early riser. Most people do their laundry in the daytime." She paused. "So, you must be camping out?"

I shook my head. She was standing right beside me and I looked up at her face, trying to get a glimpse in the moonlight.

"I work nights. I just came out here after work to see what was going on. Why? You camping out?" I was playing dumb.

She nodded. "With my mother."

"This isn't a very good place," I said. "Too many kids come out here to fool around."

"We're new here," she said. "Mom thought this would be safe." She sat down beside me, crossing her legs Indian-style. "Where do you work?"

"At the cannery," I said.

"With those boots, I thought you were a farm boy."

I was surprised she could see that well in the dark. The boots were sitting on the sand beside me. "You're right," I said. "I live on a small farm. My dad raises Angus."

"Those the black cows?"

"Right. We have a couple of polled Herefords and a Jersey, but I prefer the Angus."

"They're pretty in a green field."

She was right. I didn't like chores—trucking hay bales out to the cattle on a wheelbarrow, keeping the water troughs full, milking the Jersey twice a day, graining the steers we were fattening in a pen—but I did like to see the Angus clumped up together in the fields. "Where you from?" I asked.

"Seattle."

"I used to live there," I said. "Back in the third grade." Dad had started a church in West Seattle, not far from White Center. I flipped a pebble toward the water and heard it plop in. "Will you be going to Gresham High?"

"Yeah, I'll be a junior. What about you, farm boy?"

"Me, too." I liked how she said that, emphasizing the *farm boy*, as if she were making fun of me, but in a playful way. I heard her toss a rock after mine, another plop as if two frogs had jumped from the bank into a puddle. I cleared my throat. "What's your name?" Her mother had called her Colleen, but I didn't want her to know it had been me back at the tent.

"Colleen. That's my first name," she added. "My last name's Glover."

"Artie Crenshaw," I said. "Pleased to meet you."

She laughed. "It's kind of hard to meet in the dark. Do you mind if I look at you?"

I was floored. "Huh?"

"I have a flashlight."

"I'm kind of a mess," I said. "I got in a fight with this other guy."

"A fight? What over?"

"Oh, nothing, really. He started it. Old stuff. We don't like each other." I wasn't going to tell her about the magazine and getting stuck in the ticket booth.

Colleen reached out and touched me on the arm. "I'll tell you what, farm boy. Here's the flashlight. You can see me first."

"No, that's okay." I didn't want her looking at me. My face felt all puffy.

"You're too shy," she said.

And before I could do or say anything, she flicked on the light and held it to her face.

# *thirteen*

I didn't know if it was the darkness or what but I'd never seen a more beautiful girl. She had dark, curly hair hanging to her shoulders, bangs over her forehead, and dark eyes that even in the dim glow of the flashlight looked mischievous. Her complexion was so smooth her skin looked like a sheet of silk stretched over her cheeks. She had nice features, too—a perfect nose, and lips that were just the right fullness. Maybe too perfect. That kind of girl was usually stuck-up.

She smiled. "Had enough, farm boy? It's my turn now."

I started to protest, but she turned the light on me and I blinked and looked away, then back again.

"I know you!" she said. "I've seen you before."

That pleased me for some reason. It was better than her saying, *Jeez, you're a mess.*

"Where?"

She still had the light on me. In fact, she reached out and lifted my chin to see me better. It was just a quick touch but it made me feel good.

"I've been in to the high school a couple of times to swim," she said. "I'll be on the swim team next year. I saw you in the gym, right?"

"Yeah." I'd been in a few times … in the morning. Shooting baskets by myself and working on some new moves.

She shut off the flashlight and I waited a second for my eyes to readjust to the darkness. The moon was high and small and its pale beams cast a silvery sheen over the dark eddies of the river. I wanted to look at her again, but was afraid to ask for the light. Too obvious. And she might think I was trying to compliment her. I never did know how to do that right. It always sounded awkward if I tried.

But she was really nice looking, and that quick glimpse of a smile had made me go soft inside, a scary but good feeling like one of those jolts you get when you've got to jump across a chasm that's three feet wide and a thousand feet deep—you know you can do it but it still takes your breath away. This girl could have stepped out of a dream. Any minute now I expected her to get up and walk away.

I started to apologize again for being so grubby, and then stopped, remembering what Reta Jane had said. Just be yourself. Act natural. Tell yourself you don't care.

*Yeah, but I did.* I liked this girl. Even her voice was nice.

I ran a hand through my hair and felt sand. "Jeez," I said, "my hair's full of sand."

I started to ruffle it and she said, "Here, let me do that." She got to her knees. "Bend your head over."

She put one arm around my shoulder and fluffed my hair with her other hand. Tension drained from my scalp. I didn't want her to stop.

"You really believe in having fun, farm boy."

"Yeah, if you count fighting in the sand as fun. Did you see those cops? They spotted us. I got away but they caught the guy I was fighting with." I didn't want to tell her what had happened to Eddy.

"The cops came by yesterday, too." She stopped ruffling my hair. "There, I think all the sand's out." Her voice was like soft velvet.

"Thanks. That felt good." I sat back and moved my boots to the other side. I didn't want her smelling them. It was bad enough to be dressed for work.

She sat back on her heels, her knees digging into the sand.

There was a moment of silence and then we both started talking at the same time. She giggled. "You first," she said.

I hesitated. I didn't have any brilliant questions.

"I was just wondering how you liked Seattle," I finally said. "We only lived there the one year."

"Third grade you said, right? Maybe we went to the same school. Maybe you were the one who locked me in the coal bin." She laughed.

"Someone locked you in a coal bin?"

Colleen nodded. "It was one of the traumatic things that happened to me as a kid. That was the same year my father died."

I didn't know what to say. She seemed so cheerful.

"I miss him every day," she said.

"How'd he die?"

"In a car wreck. He was driving in the rain and a truck hit him from behind. He lost control and the car rolled."

That was horrible. *I was wishing it had happened to my dad!* "Does it make you sad?"

She shrugged. "It used to—when I was younger ... but then I decided there was only one thing I could do to make him happy."

I didn't know what to say to that. How could you do anything for someone who was dead? So finally I just said, "What was that?"

"Live. Be happy myself. The only time my mother really talked about him she told me how he was always talking about who was really the happy man. It wasn't the guy sitting in an office chair on the thirtieth floor of a skyscraper, making all the money in the world. It was the guy down at the shoreline sitting on a rock and wiggling his big toe in the sand, with his daughter beside him. She said he used to play with me all the time."

After a moment, I said, "That was nice." And I meant it, I couldn't remember my dad ever playing with me.

Colleen sat back and clasped her knees. "I have a confession. You know what I used to tell people about my father?"

I shook my head.

"I read about this guy in the paper when I was in the sixth grade. He was killed on a construction project—working on Grand Coulee Dam. So I borrowed what happened to him and told everyone that was how my father died. This guy was coming down a ladder on the side of the dam and didn't realize it had a missing rung—and he was carrying a dog in his arms. His Red Setter used to go to work with him. Just before falling he managed to shove the dog on to some scaffolding rather than grabbing it himself. He fell to his death."

She paused. "I don't know why I did that. Telling people that was how my father died. He was still a hero to me no matter how it happened."

She stopped talking for a moment but I could tell she wanted to say more.

"Have you read *The Cloister and the Hearth*?" She took a deep breath. "I memorized the first line. It goes, 'Not a day passes over the earth, but men and women of no note do great deeds, speak great words, and suffer noble sorrows.' That's what my father was—one of the obscure heroes. He was just a good man."

I thought about that for a bit, then said, "Well, he was the opposite of my dad, then."

We both laughed.

And I was glad to hear she'd read *The Cloister and the Hearth*. It was one of my favorite books when I first read it. One of those big ones that no one else ever reads. Yeah, some of it was slow and boring, but it was easy to skip those parts. I liked Gerard's escapes—the one from the tower prison with Margaret's help and then from the burning mill and the shipwreck near Rome. And you could see where Mark Twain learned the trick used to catch out Huck Finn when he disguised himself as a girl.

I hadn't said anything for a while so Colleen reached over and poked me in the thigh. "What's so bad about your father?"

I snorted. There was too much to tell—and I didn't want to get into the worst of it. I just told her about him being a preacher and that I'd be glad when I could leave home. "Two more years now."

She was thinking about that when I said, "You never told me why the kid locked you in the coal bin. What happened?" I wanted to change the subject.

She laughed. "I don't know why he did it. Just being a kid, I guess. I screamed so loud he got scared and let me out. That was my first traumatic experience with boys." She kicked sand in my direction. "So what was yours?"

"A traumatic experience?" I just about said every time I talked to a girl it was traumatic—but I didn't want her to think I meant her. She was too nice.

I stopped to think. Wendy had asked me about the first girl I'd kissed, and I'd never really answered her. I could tell Colleen about that.

I cleared my throat. "How's this? The first girl I kissed was in the second grade. We were living in Wenatchee at the time. There was this cute girl that all the boys chased at recess. I joined in one time and we pinned her against a fence. I kissed her on the cheek before we let her go."

Colleen laughed. "So what was so traumatic about that *for you*?"

---

I grinned. "Well, it wasn't easy to kiss her, but that wasn't it. Someone in our church was driving by and told my parents what I'd done." I shook my head. "My first kiss and my parents hear about it. How's that for luck?"

"It can only get better, farm boy. So tell me something else."

"Traumatic?"

She nodded. "The worst you can remember."

I couldn't think of anything like being locked in a coal bin. Finally I said, "There was this one girl when we lived in Seattle. She was a friend of my brother—he's two years older than me, so she must have been in the fifth grade. I remember her dad was in the penitentiary for something. Anyway, one time we were in the woods with her—this is in West Seattle, in the hills—and she tried to get us to unzip our pants."

Colleen laughed. "That would be traumatic. Did you?"

"I don't think so ... Maybe Richy did." I tried to remember. "There was this big, old stump in the woods that was cut like a chair. I remember this girl sitting on it and raising her skirt and talking dirty to us.

"Boy, you started young."

I grinned, feeling sheepish. "Do you know where Warden is?"

She shook her head. "I don't think I've heard of it."

"It's a small town near Moses Lake. On your way to Spokane. We lived there when I was five. Dad was always starting a new church somewhere."

"This is another traumatic experience you're telling me?"

I liked the playful sound in her voice.

I nodded. "Kind of. There was this neighbor girl who bet us a quarter she could wet her pants."

Colleen laughed. "That doesn't sound hard."

"She did, too. Richy and I got quarters out of mom's purse and this girl squatted down in front of us and peed her pants."

"She didn't take off her underpants?"

I shook my head, trying to keep from grinning. "Nope. She got 'em all wet and then went home fifty cents richer."

We were both laughing now.

A moment later I said, "Come to think of it, I must attract girls who do that." And I wasn't thinking about Reta Jane. I didn't want to tell Colleen about her. I was thinking about another girl. "I would've failed the first grade if a girl hadn't peed in the classroom."

"This I've got to hear, farm boy," Colleen said. "You're telling the truth now, right?"

"True as could be," I said. "I used to skip school a lot in the first grade—I think we were in Ferndale that year, up near Bellingham—and I remember walking into this Quonset hut where our class met and hearing the teacher say we had to recite the alphabet if we wanted to pass. I guess she'd warned everybody else one day when I wasn't there. I'd been reading the Bible for a couple of years, probably since I was four, but I'd never memorized the alphabet."

I shook my head. "Lucked out that time. The teacher had the alphabet posted over the blackboard. I started memorizing the letters while the other kids, one by one, recited it. They were just about to get to me. Boy, I was scared. I still hadn't learned it all. And then this girl right in front of me peed her pants. Scared, too, I guess. A big yellow puddle started forming under her seat." I laughed. "They had to go get a mop to clean it up and that saved me. By the time they finished and it was my turn, I had the alphabet memorized. So I passed first grade and here I am."

"We must be weird," she said. "Do you always talk like this with your friends?"

I liked how she said *we*. "You're the first one I've ever told that to. The guys don't even know."

We were both silent for a moment and I tried to figure out why I'd told her things I'd never mentioned to anyone else. There was just something about her that made you want to open up. Like you knew she wouldn't laugh—unless it was *with* you, not at you. She just seemed natural. She seemed to *absorb* what I was saying.

"So, farm boy, let's talk about something that's not traumatic. How long you been playing basketball?"

"In school?" I rubbed my chin. "Since at least the sixth grade. But I played at home before that. Richy and I nailed a backboard to a tree. That's what helped me make the Varsity last year. Me and two other guys made it our sophomore year. I'm hoping to start next year. The way I figure, I'll be the only junior on the starting five." I shut myself up. I didn't like people who bragged and here I was doing it. I took a breath. I wanted to know more about her. "So, you a good swimmer?"

Colleen laughed. "I've been like a duck on a pond since I was five. That's why I came out here now—to go swimming. I was going to walk downstream and find a place where I could swim across."

"You gotta be careful. The beach ends here. The river's cut the bank away."

---

I didn't want her to leave.

"I know. I was down here before it got dark. I swam across to that island. Lots of blackberries there."

"Yeah, the area's thick with them." I paused. "Doesn't your mother care about you being out here alone in the dark?"

"She's asleep. She's been up all night trying to scare off all the kids. I slept through most of it." She slapped at her arm. "Are you bothered by mosquitoes?"

"Yeah. But I don't think there're any out here now."

"Well, something's making me itch. You want to swim across?"

"The river?"

She laughed. "No, farm boy, the *ocean*."

I felt like an idiot for a second, but I liked the tone of affection in her voice. Was she this friendly with everybody? Just like Laurie Snyder, my old girlfriend.

I said, "I'm not a very good swimmer."

"It's easy. The only deep part's close to shore here and there's almost no current."

"What about in the middle? I've seen it in the daytime. It looks faster there."

"It is, but it's shallow. By the time you get where it's fast, you could probably stand up and walk across."

"I don't know." I hesitated. "A friend of mine drowned last year."

Colleen touched me on the arm. "Out here?"

I shook my head. "In the Columbia. They think he got a cramp." And actually David Keefe wasn't a friend. He'd just come to our church a few times. I hadn't even remembered him until Wendy brought him up. "Anyway, I don't have a swim suit with me."

She laughed. "Me neither. But no one's around at this hour. Haven't you ever gone skinny dipping?"

I swallowed. There was a lump in my throat. "In the bathtub," I managed to say.

Colleen laughed again, a clear ringing sound, and got to her feet, brushing the sand from her shorts. "Just kidding," she said. "I'm wearing what I got on. Go in your underwear. It's still dark." She sat the flashlight down by my boots.

I hesitated. Reta Jane had seen me in my underwear and I liked this girl a lot more. But twice in one night! I didn't know about that. The last time I'd gotten shot at.

"I'm going in, farm boy. You coming with me?" She held out a hand. "This is your last chance."

---

Sometimes in life you have a choice and you don't really make it for yourself—fate does. You know, you've been talking to a girl before an assembly and you walk into the auditorium and see rows of empty seats there. A few girls down at the front, a few guys at the back. She takes a row in the middle, heads for a seat. Do you pick another row? The same one? Do you sit two seats away or—who knows why?—plunk yourself down right next to her? If you thought about it, you could never do it—but you don't think. You let the hand of fate push you down and you find yourself right beside her. Right beside her and rubbing arms!

That was me.

Only now, instead of a nudge, fate locked my feet to the ground and I couldn't move.

# fourteen

She didn't turn around. Just backed away from me with her hand out until she reached the water. Then she seemed to give up on me and stepped into the river. She hesitated for just a second and then moved out until she was waist deep.

She turned around. "Aren't you coming, farm boy?"

From her shoulders down, she was bright with silver. The moonbeams danced off the water and illuminated her with a soft glow, a cool brilliance against the polished surface of the river. Pearl and pale ash against shiny obsidian. I thought of water orchids blossoming in the dark, in a still pool of lustrous shadow. It reminded me of the Lady of the Lake. I'd read it too long ago to remember for sure, but I had a vision of an enchantress rising out of the water's depths. The sight of Colleen filled me with the same awe and longing. She could have been a water nymph in a fairy tale.

She dipped down into the water, gasping before going under. Her dark hair floated for a second and then disappeared in the river like strands of jet dipped in black ink. I held my breath, eyes locked on the spot where she'd gone under. In a moment she reappeared.

"You scared me," I said. "Don't go under like that. It's too dark. I don't think you should swim across."

"Come on with me then. It'll be safer with two of us." Just her face showed now, coming out of the gloaming like a ghost. She seemed to create her own light, a luminescence of white flesh wavering on the surface as the river swirled darkly past.

I hesitated. I really didn't want her going across by herself, even if she was a good swimmer. But I had even more doubts about myself. I couldn't go fifty feet without tiring. "I don't like cold water," I said.

"It feels good once you get used to it."

"Yeah, but it's getting used to it I don't like." She laughed. I got up and moved my work boots and her flashlight over by the bank. I stuck the flashlight in one of the boots. "What if someone comes along and steals my clothes?"

"Put them back by that overhang," she said, pointing downstream. "No one will find them."

I picked up my boots and moved them down to where tangled roots of willow trees held the bank together.

After I took my shirt off, I thought about keeping my pants on. I don't know why I was suddenly embarrassed. It hadn't seemed to bother Colleen and I didn't want her to think I was a coward. There was no way I could get my pants dry if I swam in them. And I was afraid the weight would pull me under when I got tired. Finally I stripped down to my briefs, placed my clothes next to my work boots, and edged into the water. I went faster than I would have liked, gingerly making my way over slippery pebbles. It usually took me five minutes to get used to the cold.

She turned around when I was out to my waist and began to swim away.

I shoved off, adding my head-above-water stroke to her smooth crawl. In a few seconds, she was out ahead of me and I was afraid I'd lose sight of her in the darkness. I called her name and saw her treading water and waiting for me.

"You okay, farm boy?"

I was already breathing hard. I usually ran cross-country in the fall to get in shape for basketball, but I was bothered by asthma whenever we were haying. We'd put in the first cutting just the week before.

"How far before we can touch bottom?"

I could tell we were floating downstream while treading water.

"Not far now. I'll stay beside you. If you get too tired just flop over on your back. I'll hold you up."

"Sorry I'm not a better swimmer," I gasped. "Never did learn right."

"That's okay. I'll get you across."

---

A few moments later, when we finally touched bottom, we were farther downstream than I'd ever been before. The river had widened out and the current rippled—like fluid hands playing a piano—over rocks and isolated spits of pebbles and sand.

"We're lucky the breeze has died down," I said, coming out of the water. I could see her ahead of me in the dark. "It's getting cool. Too bad we don't have towels." I shivered.

"It won't take long to dry," Colleen said, looking back over her shoulder.

I looked down at myself casually to see how much she could see in the darkness. Being wet made me uncomfortable. Coming out of the water, I thought I'd caught a glimpse of a dark triangle behind the white cotton of her shorts. Up to now, the cold water and the swimming had kept me from getting aroused. But on land I didn't have those distractions. With her wet blouse clinging to her, her body was starting to get to me.

To get my mind on other things, I tried to think about the last basketball game of the season. We'd beaten our biggest rival Centennial by one point—fifty-two to fifty-one—and I'd scored the winning basket, a left-handed hook shot from the top of the key. Up to then in the game, I'd always faked left and gone right. This time I did the opposite and left the other center standing flat-footed and flabbergasted. I was lucky I'd made the shot. The coach would never have forgiven me if I hadn't. A hook shot from the foul line—and left-handed at that! But I'd always tried to claim I was ambidextrous.

Even with those thoughts—reliving the moment detail by detail in the back of my mind—it was hard to distract myself. I'd never been around a girl who was so desirable.

Colleen reached out for my hand. "Come on, farm boy. We have to walk upstream a ways. We can go beyond Hosner's hole before trying to cross back. That'll be easier at least. You can let the current help."

"I told you I didn't know how to swim well."

"We did fine together, right?"

"I guess."

We had to edge back into the water to get around a thicket of willow and I dropped her hand and led the way. Over my shoulder I said, "What about those blackberries?"

She laughed. "I know why you came. It wasn't to swim with me." She caught up with me and took my hand again and that made me feel good. "They're closer to Hosner's Hole. But we'll have to be careful in the dark. I scratched my arms even in the daytime."

"I know what blackberry brambles are like—especially these wild ones. I used to pick berries every summer. Even the ones in rows are rough."

We walked in silence for a while and then, out of the blue, she swung my hand and said, "So, farm boy, are you going to be my friend when school starts?"

"Sure." I tried to be light-hearted. Her voice had a coquettish tone and I didn't know quite how to take it. I wasn't very good at joking around. "You're a nice person."

"I know you better than you know me," she said. "I talked to Coach Miller about you."

Like mine, her voice had turned serious. Darlene Miller was a teacher and the girls' swim coach.

"She said she had you in Modern Problems. She said you were smart but shy. A nice person but very serious."

I had too many thoughts going through my mind to speak. I was still absorbing the fact that she'd been interested enough to ask the girls' swim coach about me. After just seeing me in the gym. How many people would do that? And to hear a teacher analyze my personality was a strange sensation. (How'd Coach Miller know I was shy? And what did she mean by "very serious"? Was that good or bad?) And then I didn't know if I liked being called shy.

Colleen pointed ahead to a dark mass off to the left and said, "There they are." I could feel her tug on my hand.

"Go slow," I said. "We step on a thorn and ..." I let her imagine what that would feel like.

"Coach Miller told me a little bit about your family, too."

"She did?" Now I was surprised. "She doesn't know my parents."

"She knows about them. About your dad being a minister. She said you were late for school sometimes because you have to help out on the farm."

"Sometimes the cattle get out," I said. "I've only been late a few times."

"She said your father made you burn a book."

That wasn't quite true and while we worked our way slowly into the blackberry bushes I told Colleen what had really happened.

*"Get up."*

*He was standing in the bedroom with a strap in his hand.*

*"You hear me? Quit playing with yourself."*

*I rubbed my eyes, then slid the covers back and sat on the edge of the bed.* What was it? Was I late again? *The strap flashed beside me and hit the bed with a whump. That woke me. I stood up and faced him. All I had on were my underpants.*

"Bobby said you told him to read a book."

"A book?" *I was playing dumb.*

"You heard me."

*I could feel my head begin to wobble as if the tendons had suddenly gone weak.* "The Catcher in the Rye," *I said.* "I thought it was good."

*It was a Modern Library edition that I'd bought myself. Bobby was younger than me, but I thought he'd like it, too.*

"Where is it?"

"Uh … I think I left it in my locker at school."

"Why isn't it with the rest of your books?"

*My books were stacked on the dresser. I looked around for my pants. If he was going to whip me—.*

"What have I told you about lying?" *He raised the strap.*

"Lie? I didn't say anything."

"I found the book in your dresser under your shirts. What's it doing in there?"

"I didn't have any more room on top."

"Don't lie to me." *He swung the strap and it wrapped around my back. The tip caught me in the stomach and I bent over and sat down, surprised by how much it stung.*

"Stand up when I'm talking to you."

*I got up and rubbed my belly. I could feel the welt. Tears started to form behind my eyes. I clenched my jaws to keep them from quivering. I wasn't going to let him see me cry.*

"You were hiding it, that's what you were doing. Filthy trash."

*I was angry enough then to ask him if he'd read it.*

*He poked me in the chest, hard.* "I saw the first page. That was enough. I don't want you giving any books to your younger brother without me saying so, you hear me?"

*He strode to the dresser and opened the top drawer.* "Here." *He tossed the book at me and I caught it with the pages splayed.* "Burn this filth."

*My mouth opened and for a second nothing came out.* "W—what?"

"I said, burn it. I don't want it in the house. Take it out to the shed and burn it with the other trash."

*He left the room and I looked down at the book through hot tears that welled up and wouldn't stop. I didn't care what he said or did to me, I wasn't going to burn it.*

---

*Books were the only thing I had that were my own.*

Modern Problems was a team-taught course and I'd asked Coach Miller and Mr. Norquist for advice the next day. I wound up keeping the book in my locker at school, and when summer came and we had to clear things out, Mr. Norquist promised to save it for me.

"So you had to lie about it to your dad?" Colleen had found a big, soft blackberry and held it out to me. I reached for it and she said, "No, open your mouth." She playfully tapped the berry on my nose and then stuck it in my mouth.

I grinned and looked for one to do the same to her. It was hard to see the berries in the darkness. I'd left my watch with my clothes and her flashlight on the other side of the river. I knew it would start to get light around five-thirty or so. But it was still dark, the only illumination that of the moon, which was slipping in and out of streaky clouds now.

She asked me again if I had to lie about burning the book. I shook my head. "He can always tell when I'm lying. But I didn't have to. He never asked me again. I guess, when the book disappeared, he just assumed I burned it." At least, that's what I'd always thought. But maybe he knew.

I'd finally found a juicy berry and I offered it to her. She laughed and ducked away. "Oh, no, you don't."

"What?"

"You want to squish it on me."

I laughed. I'd almost forgotten I was half undressed—and being natural felt nice. I really liked this girl, even though I'd just met her. She was fun. She knew how to make me feel close—special even—and that felt good. I hoped she felt the same. There weren't too many girls like her—at least I hadn't met any.

"You have to try this one," I said. "It's really ripe."

I moved toward her and she couldn't really run. We were surrounded by brambles. "Open your mouth."

"Uh huh." She said it in a low, soft tone—accepting but letting me know she knew what I would do—and I felt my insides melt like butter in a barbecue.

"Say that again."

"What? Oh, that." Her voice changed again, low then up a note. "Uh huh."

"You say that nice."

She laughed. "You like it, huh?"

I nodded. "I could listen to it all night."

---

"You're sweet, farm boy. Give me that berry."

I was amazed at myself. I'd paid a girl a compliment—sort of, anyway—and it had worked! It hadn't sounded artificial for once.

I thought about squashing the berry on her chin but for some reason I couldn't. I set it in her mouth. The touch of her lips on my fingers sent a shock through me.

"Maybe we should head back," I said. I didn't know how much more of this I could take.

She had a handful of berries. "Let me paint you," she said.

"What?"

"Let's go back to the beach. You'll be my warrior and I'll paint your face."

I was skeptical. "We're going on the warpath?"

She laughed. "If you don't let me paint you we are." She tossed a berry at me. "I have more than you."

I tossed one back, then looked around me for more. But she was already leaving. I followed her out to the sandy beach, avoiding the thorny streamers running to each side of the path.

"Kneel down," she said.

The moon had gone behind a thicker cloud and I could barely see her. I reached out for her hips and knelt in front of her. Even in the dark, her shape took my breath away. I wanted to kiss her on her stomach but I was afraid. Everything she'd done seemed innocent. She could have been a five-year old playing with her friends. Maybe I was presuming too much.

"Farm boy," she said, "I anoint you as my slave and guardian." She took a ripe blackberry and drew a line across my forehead.

"How can I be a slave *and* a guardian?"

I could see her teeth as she smiled. "You said you'd be my boyfriend, right?"

My heart took a jump. I'd caught the difference—from friend to boyfriend—or was it all the same to her?

"I already *am!*"

I said it with so much conviction that she laughed.

"Then you're my slave *and* guardian." She paused, then asked, "And you'll be faithful to me? You won't go back to your girlfriend?"

My eyes widened. How'd she know about Laurie Snyder?

"I like you better," I said, feeling sheepish.

"Ah, so you do have a girlfriend." She said it accusingly, but in a playful tone.

Shoot, she'd tricked me! I wanted to deny it. "I had one. We never really got along."

"Why not? You were too shy?"

I hesitated. I wished Coach Miller had never told her that. "I never thought it was shyness," I said. "I just couldn't talk to her. I loved her too much. Have you ever done that?"

She was silent for a moment. "Everybody does," she said finally. "If you love one person too much and they hurt you, you have to spread it around. Love many people. Share yourself—until you find someone who loves you back the same way and just as much." She laughed. "But don't listen to me. I'm no expert."

I was still on my knees. She put her hand on my shoulder, leaned over and kissed me on the forehead. Her lips were soft and warm and the air tingled around me. I wanted to take her in my arms but I was too scared to.

For a minute, I tried to dare myself. I have this thing I do. Every time I have to jump off the high dive at Blue Lake—or do something else scary—I say, *I'll kill myself if I don't do it before I get to ten*, and then I start counting. It had never failed yet because I believed it.

Before I could convince myself to start the countdown, Colleen stepped back and said, "I like you, Artie. You're nice."

I stood up. I felt dizzy. My ears were ringing. I could hear what sounded like a tremble in her voice and it left me breathless. Or was she just shivering with the cold?

I tried to speak, I wanted to tell her how much I liked her, but I didn't know how. Longing overwhelmed me. I felt like one of those dazed insects that's just been pounced on by a cat and is now too stunned to move even though the cat has already lost interest and walked away.

I took a deep breath. "Colleen …" All I could do was get her name out and I heard the same tremble in my voice. I didn't know what to do.

"It's like we belong together," she said.

I nodded. I was still shaky, tried to focus on the moment, on a sensation, something to ground myself. I settled on a taste at the back of my throat—or was it a smell?—I couldn't tell which, a mixture of blackberry juice and road dust, the scent of night winds that had roamed over fields ripe with hay and through woods bursting with summer growth, a hint of fir or cedar, and other aromas too subtle to identify.

"Yeah," I finally said. "It feels good."

We stood for a moment in silence, trying to look at each other in the dark.

---

I wanted to see her eyes. I thought about kissing her—she'd kissed me on the forehead!—but we'd been playing then. Now things were serious.

I reached out for her with both hands and she took mine in hers.

"We have a lot of time, Artie. It's going to be fun. I can't wait for school to start so I can see you every day."

I knew what she meant. I wanted to get to know more about her, too. I'd never felt so good with anyone. She was fun. It made me happy just to be with her.

"I liked you ever since I saw you in the gym," she said.

My eyes were wide. "I wish I'd seen you," I said. "You should've stopped and said 'hi.'" I paused and thought about that a second. If she had, I wouldn't have known what to do. Nothing might have happened. "But meeting like this was neat."

She laughed. "It was fate, that's what."

I grinned. "It had to be."

Fate. Boy, what a nice word. But I thought of all the choices and paths I'd taken tonight to get to this point.

"My stomach's all churned up," I said. "I guess that's what happens when fate hits you."

"Mine, too." Her voice had fallen to a whisper. She squeezed my hands and I squeezed back.

"This is like a dream," I said. My voice had choked up on me. "I'm afraid everything will change in the daytime. We'll go back to being normal. I'll just be another guy."

She swung my arms. "No, Artie. You said you'd be faithful to me, right? I'll be faithful to you." She paused. "I haven't ever felt like this with any other guy."

I swallowed hard. This was all so sudden. We'd just met and it was like we'd known each other since grade school. "Me neither," I managed to say, "with a girl, I mean."

She giggled and I liked the sound of it, I could tell she was happy.

"Colleen, let me tell you something." I stopped, searching for the right words. Our hands came apart. Too many thoughts were swirling through my mind, too many desires. "All my life, I've been searching—".

She laughed and pushed at me. "It hasn't been that long, Artie. We're only sixteen."

I couldn't help grinning back. "It seems like it's been forever," I said. But I liked how she included us together again. She had a knack of saying things that made me feel good. "Now that I'm talking to you—and feeling so different—it makes it seem longer ... the lack—" I stopped, knowing I was getting twisted up in my words. "I've been running—I don't know if away from something or toward something—but I've been running scared ..." I took a deep breath. "For the first time, I feel like I can stop. I've found what I want."

"And what's that?" she asked softly. I could tell she knew but wanted to hear it.

I took a deep breath and said it.

"Someone to love me like I love them."

"Someone, huh?"

Her voice had that nice lilt to it again and I couldn't help grinning. A flash of inspiration hit me. "Colleen, I've got a surprise for you."

"Uh huh. Like what?"

She was playing with me again and I said, "Stop that, Colleen. This is serious." But she could tell I liked it.

"So what's your surprise, farm boy?"

"Let's go back to the other side and I'll tell you."

She thought about that. "Okay," she said. "It's a deal."

She took my hand and we walked to the water's edge.

We waded out and the water felt almost warm now. The breeze had chilled us.

"You ready, farm boy?" Colleen placed her hand on my chest. "Just follow me—and scream if you need help."

I wished her touch could have lasted forever, but I just grinned and followed her.

# fifteen

Give me five minutes," she said, squeezing my hand. "I'll change clothes and leave a note for my mother."

I was dressed and we were standing near the two tents, whispering. It was just after five and the first faint hint of light was just beginning to seep into the sky, a thin strip of dark blue at the horizon. Sunrise was still forty-five minutes away. I was in a hurry. I wanted it to be dark for my surprise.

I watched as she disappeared, the flashlight picking out the path ahead of her. For a moment, waiting by myself, I wondered about the car. Had the cops found it and made a connection to me? Would it still be there? I hoped Eddy had been too spaced out to say anything. I didn't care if I got in trouble later. Finding Colleen was worth it. But I needed the car for the surprise. If it had been towed—I didn't want to think about that.

And then, even though I hated myself for thinking this, I wondered for a moment if meeting Colleen had been a trick. Something Eddie cooked up to make fun of me. She'd come back and tell me none of this was real. She'd been leading me on as a joke.

I did that accidentally once. A girl who sat one row away from me in class thought I'd been staring at her and started giving me the eye. I had to shut it down quick by frowning,didn't want to be mean, but I'd been looking at Laurie, another row over. It struck me that it wasn't so much how you looked—your appearance—but how you *looked* with your *eyes*. A gaze was enough.

Could Colleen even see my eyes in the dark? No, it had to be something else that attracted her. I was afraid to ask what.

Yeah, Artie, it be just like me—ask stupid questions and ruin something too good to be true.

But was it true? I wanted to believe everything she'd said, had no reason to doubt her, so like I said, I hated myself for even thinking this way.

Anyway, I'd told her I'd be taking her in to town. We had just enough time to do what I wanted. Get in to town, give her the surprise, get her back out to her tent, and drive home. If my dad said anything about the car being dirty, I'd just have to say it was dust from the parking lot at the cannery.

In a few moments, the flashlight poked its way back to me.

"I'm ready," she said. "Where's your car?"

"Follow me." She gave me the flashlight and I took a path that led away from the river and toward the road. When we were far enough away not to be heard, I asked her what she'd told her mother in the note.

"She's still sound asleep. I pinned the note to her tent where she'll see it when she gets up. If I'm back before she wakes up, I'll just take it down. I told her I was going to hike along the river till dawn, swim a bit, and that I'd see her later. Will that give us enough time?"

"Yeah. But we'll have to hurry. I need to be home by a little after six, and I have to get you back out here."

Wouldn't you know it? We saw these two guys just before leaving Hosner's

Hole. They were standing in the middle of the road, blocking our path. As soon as they saw the headlights, they started waving their arms.

"Something's wrong," Colleen said.

I thought about dousing the lights and putting the car in reverse, thinking maybe it was someone who wanted to rob us—or steal the car. I didn't have much money on me and Colleen hadn't brought anything. But then I saw the Pontiac just off the road at a crazy angle.

"They need help," Colleen said. She was sitting close beside me.

Shoot.

I rolled down the window and a kid I'd never seen before came over and asked if we could help. "Got high-centered on a log," he said. "We've got a rope but we need someone to pull us out."

I hesitated. We were short on time and I didn't want to damage the car. They were liable to rip the bumper off. Why did this have to happen *now*?

Colleen and I looked at each other.

"We could postpone the surprise," she said. "Do it another time."

"Tonight's my only chance," I said.

I stuck my head out the window. Their car was off to the side. I turned the headlights on bright to widen the beam. It looked like a new GTO or a stripped-down Tempest—a two-door muscle car, bright red. I knew something would go wrong if I tried to help. I'd stopped to help a guy jump start his car one time and what he said would take five minutes took over a half-hour.

"Come on," the guy was saying. "The radiator's okay. We just need someone to pull us off this log."

"Can't you find someone else?" I said. "I'm really in a rush."

"You're the first car that's come by. It's dead out here now."

He looked like a college-age guy, someone out from Portland. I didn't like them coming around the high school, always looking for girlfriends. They usually had more money and fancier cars. He looked too slick to me. I could see he was wearing pegged jeans, loafers and a dress shirt. In the summer?

"Someone's coming," Colleen said.

I looked toward the right, where the road turned into pavement. Whew, that was a relief. Let them help.

"Hey," I said to the college guy. But he was walking away. *Get them to help,* was what I was thinking.

I turned to Colleen. "Maybe the car that's coming can help. We need to get out of here."

---

"It's a pickup," Colleen said.

Good. Better yet. An easy excuse. That brightened me up. The pickup could do a better job than a family car!

And then I saw the pickup in our headlights as the vehicle hit the dirt road and started braking. A cloud of dust swirled up around it.

"I can't believe it," I said, my hands frozen on the wheel. "That's my dad." I felt sick. It was like a tub of lemon juice had been turned upside down in my stomach.

Neither one of us said a word after that.

I couldn't move. I stared at the headlights of the pickup, me frozen midroad like a possum caught in the glare and about to be run over. I heard the door on the pickup slam shut. Someone had gotten out. *Here it comes.* I'd been expecting it all night anyway. Like I said. Didn't I always get caught? Try to do something fun and I was doomed. It just wasn't fair. Not when I'd found Colleen.

"Maybe it's your older brother," she said.

I wanted to believe her so bad I almost said, "Richy, is that you? Where's dad?" and heard him say, "What do you mean, where's dad? At home. Where else would he be?" But imagination wasn't going to save me now. I had to face reality—and reality was that this was my dad and I'd been caught and everything was over. I'd made some choices, had been making them all night and now I had to accept the consequences. Still, I didn't like how sick I felt. Everything I'd planned for Colleen ... all down the drain. The nicest thing to happen all night and, like grit in spinach, my dad had to show up and spoil it. The beating I could take ... losing Colleen—I didn't want to think about that.

"Stay here," I said to her. "I'll see who it is."

I could see his shape haloed by the light behind him and I knew he could see my face in the pickup's high beams. Dad. Could he see the fear in my eyes? A dusty haze enveloped him, made him look twice as big. I could feel the same dusty light around me like an extension of nerves, feelers so sensitive they picked up the rustle of saplings in a breeze grown as soft as a breath on the cheek—a breath of terror, the last gasp of a rabbit dying in the jaws of a predator. I shivered. Our shadows flickered like those of giants, but I felt my heart shrivel up until it seemed the size of a peach pit. The smell of the pickup's exhaust reached me and I had an acrid taste in my mouth. Every inch of my skin came alive. Is this what it felt like to die?

His voice, when it came, pierced me like an ice pick, hard and cold.

"What're you doing out here? You're supposed to be working."

Massive brainlock. Atmospheric pressure weighing down like a lead blanket. I could forget taking Colleen anywhere.

I tried to catch my breath. I had to say something. "Just driving around." My voice barely above a whisper, as if I were trying out answers to get the right one.

"What? Do I have to knock you on the head to get you to speak up?"

"I couldn't sleep. I, ah …" Shoot, I'd have to get Billy in trouble. "Billy said he'd be out here, so I came out to see him."

"I thought I told you to stay away from Billy."

Darn, I'd forgotten. Billy's dad didn't want him seeing me and my dad didn't want me seeing Billy. Double trouble. But it was all I could think of.

"How many times do I have to thrash you before you learn to do what I tell you?"

What could I say to that?

Nothing.

The silence made my ears burn.

"Why aren't you at work?"

"They let us go early … ran out of berries."

"You get the shed cleaned out like I told you to?"

"At night?"

"Don't get smart with me." His voice had sharpened. "When else are you going to get it done? You'd sleep all day if your mother let you. I told you before—I want that shed cleaned out and ready for grain by the time school starts. If I have to hire someone else to do it, it's coming out of your hide."

I could feel the resentment eating away at my gut. Every summer he made Richy and me pay ten bucks a week for room and board, and now he was going to take my savings, too. And all because of a stupid chicken shed.

"I'll get it done."

He took a step closer. You could see he didn't like the tone of my voice.

"How many hours you put in on it this week?"

"I'll work on it this weekend."

"You can't get your work done at home, you can forget going in to the cannery."

He jabbed at my chest with his finger. It hurt and I could've knocked his hand away—if I wanted to get killed—but I braced my feet and let him jab.

---

I could tell he expected me to step back—just a quick glimpse of surprise on his face, a flash in his eyes from the glare of the Mercury's lights behind me and then anger in his jaw line. His forefinger changed to a fist and he started hitting me in the chest, punctuating his words. He was getting tired, he said, of me not doing what I was told. I'd never amount to a hill of beans. I could feel the thud all the way down to my boots, but I refused to flinch. In a minute I was going to explode, years of hatred building up in me. If he made me cry in front of Colleen, I'd—.

"Frank, what's going on?"

I froze. A woman's voice ... not mom's. It was like the air was sucked out and we were standing in a vacuum. I could feel the hairs on my arms, upright, waiting for the spark of static electricity, the space around us charged with atoms at war with each other.

*"Get back in the truck."*

You could hear the edge in his voice, harsh, like the scraping of boat hulls moored side by side at the dock.

She hesitated.

"Are you as deaf as this stupid kid?"

I heard the pickup door slam then, a shotgun bang loud enough to flush every lovebird from Hosner's Hole. He talked to her just like he would to mom.

And then I heard the Mercury's door open behind me and my heart jumped a little higher in my throat. *Please, God, don't let her say anything.*

"What're you staring at?" He'd hit me again.

"Nothing ... I was looking at you."

"Don't get any smart ideas in your head. That's Mary Jo's mother. We're out looking for Mary Jo. You seen her?"

Mary Jo—her mother was Helen Pearson ... divorced. She'd started to come to church about a month ago. Just last Saturday I'd been cleaning outside dad's study when I'd heard her voice inside. Mrs. Pearson. Coming over for prayer, I'd thought. Jeez ... they'd been locked in there for over an hour and when I'd knocked and asked if he wanted me to empty the wastebasket he'd gotten angry and said couldn't I see he was busy and to go help mom in the kitchen. And now ... here she was in the middle of the night. *Mrs. Pearson!*

Dad and I stared at each other. I hadn't seen Mary Jo. She didn't seem the type to be running around at night. But if I told him that—.

He jerked his head. "Who you got in the car?"

I could hear the change in his voice, higher, like a chainsaw biting into wood.

He didn't want me asking questions. He wanted to put me on the spot. *Why hadn't Colleen stayed inside?*

"Hi, Reverend Crenshaw. I'm Colleen Glover."

I started. She was right at my elbow. I hadn't heard her footsteps. She touched me in the back. I knew she was just trying to reassure me, but I was afraid she was going to put her arm around me in front of dad. My brain was the size of Kentucky. It was like every pore on my face was ready to absorb the shock. *Was there any way out?* I could barely breathe.

"I'm new in town," she said. Dad just stared at her. "Artie's been telling me about your church. My mom and I would like to come next Sunday."

"Your mother know you're out here this time of the night?"

"We're camped out at Hosner's Hole. We didn't know it was so busy."

"Hey, man—" It was the kid with the red sport's car again. "Can you give us a tow?"

Dad turned and I saw him hesitate.

"They're hung up on a log," I said.

He stood there a moment, then jerked his head. "You get out of here. When I come home I want to see you out in the shed getting some work done."

It was my turn to hesitate. Did I have to ask or could I just do it?

"Can I take Colleen in to town?"

He looked back and forth between the two of us. "What for?"

Colleen spoke up. "It's a surprise, Reverend Crenshaw. I'll tell you Sunday."

I could see him considering that. He wasn't used to people who didn't answer his questions. He turned to me then. "Well, what are you dawdling for? Make it snappy. I'll talk to you later."

I expected the next thing to be—*I don't like your attitude*—but he just turned around and walked away, almost like he couldn't wait to get out of there.

And my last thought was, *Holy criminy. Dad and Mrs. Pearson ... out looking for lost souls in the dark!*

Yeah, right.

## sixteen

**W**ow! That was all I could say for a while on the ride in to town. Wow!
*Wow!*

So ... when I'd seen the pickup from the top of the Ferris wheel—out on Division Street—it wasn't Mrs. Kolochny, with her husband stuck off in Russia. It was Mrs. Pearson! Did it matter? It wasn't mom. I thought about that while I drove. A divorcée. *Too much!*

After a bit, Colleen touched me on the arm. "We've got to do something about you and your dad."

I came back from miles away and then snorted when I realized what she'd said. "Yeah, like what?" You couldn't do anything about my dad.

"Well, he's a preacher, right?"

I didn't see how that was going to change anything.

"Do you have any youth meetings?"

It was hard to talk, hard to keep the despair out of my voice. Finally I said, "Sunday evening ... We divide up into age groups before the main service."

"Where's your dad go?"

I shrugged. "He's with a different group each week. Usually Mr. Deater goes with us teenagers. Billy's dad. Billy's my best friend."

Colleen thought for a moment. "But your dad's there sometimes, right? Maybe I can help. The next time we know he's going to be there, maybe we can convince Mr. Deater to make the topic father-son, mother-daughter relationships."

"What good's that gonna do?"

"You and I could prepare something."

I looked at her and then back out into the fading darkness. I still didn't see what we'd talk about that would make a difference.

"How's this?" she said. "I don't have a father ... I could talk about how much I miss him. We used to sit down and talk—just the two of us—about what was going on in our lives. I could try to make that an assignment. So you two would have to sit down and talk."

"Yeah, but what then? My father's never going to change. I'm just waiting until I'm old enough to get out of here."

"But you've got to live with him in the meantime, right, Artie? So we make the assignment something like responsibilities. You know, both ways—what parents owe kids and what kids owe parents. You can't be a slave all your life. We could talk about the need for some independence."

I laughed. "Yeah, and my dad will talk about the need for work—or discipline. A good beating to keep you in line."

"Well, if we all jump in, maybe we can get him to listen. It's worth a try."

A while later she said, "It won't work, will it?"

I grinned. I knew exactly what she meant. I shook my head. "Nope," I said. "He's too set in his ways. One of those spare-the-rod-and-spoil-the-child types. Everything he does is God's will; everything I do is the devil's."

"You know," she said. "I read somewhere that people misinterpret that line— about the rod. It doesn't mean you're supposed to beat your kids. The rod is a shepherd's crook. He uses it to guide the sheep. No shepherd beats his flock."

"Hmm—" I drummed my fingers on the steering wheel and considered that for a moment. "Maybe not, but if my dad was a shepherd you can bet that's exactly what he would be doing—beating the sheep until they went the way he wanted them to." I laughed. "And the sheep dogs would be out there cowering, wondering when it was their turn."

We weren't far from town when I noticed my stomach. Colleen heard it, too.

"Hey," she said, "was that my stomach or yours?"

"Mine, I think. You hungry?"

She was sitting beside me, our arms touching.

"I usually eat breakfast pretty early," she said. "My stomach was growling when you were talking to your father."

"I've still got my lunch from last night. And a carton of strawberries. You want some?"

"Strawberries! That sounds nice."

"Can you get my lunch sack? It's in the backseat somewhere." I reached up behind me. "Here, let me turn on the overhead light."

She scooted away while I found the light and then got on her knees in the front seat and leaned over the back. I had a hard time keeping my eyes on the road. She was wearing another pair of shorts, pink, with a white cotton top that had little triangles of red rosebuds on it.

"Found it," she said. "It was on the floor."

When she turned back around, she saw the title of the book I was reading.

It was on the floor in front.

"Somerset Maugham," she said. "I liked this book. You read anything else of his?"

I nodded. "Some short stories. And *The Razor's Edge*. You read it?"

"I don't think so. I just finished *The Tontine*."

"Gee, I thought I was the only one who'd ever read that."

"Both volumes," she said, and we laughed.

"So we both like long books," I said.

"Before that I read *Les Miserables*."

"I haven't got to that yet. I have a stack of books at home. Hemingway and Fitzgerald."

"I liked *This Side of Paradise* and *Tender is the Night*."

"Sounds like you read a lot."

"We don't have a TV," she said. "My mom teaches the fifth grade. That's why we moved here. She got a job at Powell Valley Grade School."

"Here, let me open that." I took the can of strawberries. "Can you hold the steering wheel?"

She held the wheel while I got the lid off the carton. It was always hard to do without spilling.

I handed her the opened container. "You take the first bite," I said. "We'll have to use our fingers."

She scooped out a big strawberry. "Here, this is your size." She put it in my mouth and then licked her fingers. "Mm, this is nice and sweet."

She ate a smaller berry while I waited for my second bite. "These are good," I said.

She gave a long slow sigh and then, like a whisper over the phone, said, "These are the best I've ever eaten."

By the time we reached the fairgrounds, the sky was turning a pale shade of blue, a slow almost imperceptible infusion of light into the atmosphere. I could tell the sun would be creeping over the horizon before long, splashing hot streaks of flame across the sky. It made me feel like writing a poem.

We had to leave the Mercury parked out on Main Street. The front gate to the fair was still locked, even though it looked like there might be some early activity back by the cow barns. I helped Colleen over the fence and clambered after her, hitting the ground on the far side with a thud. A soft layer of dust settled over my boots.

"It's back this way," I said, taking her hand and skirting the midway. We took the lane that led along the eastern edge of the fairgrounds. Ahead of us stretched the long tractor-trailer rigs that hauled the rides from site to site.

The light bulb outside George's trailer was still on when we got there. I didn't know if he'd be asleep or not, or would even remember me. I did see a pickup truck parked by the trailer, so he must have found someone to take him out and fix it.

I still hadn't told Colleen what we were going to do. I'd seen the smile playing on her lips every since we'd got to town. She liked surprises. She'd tried to get it out of me but I wouldn't tell.

I banged on the door for a minute or two before someone shouted, "Who the hell is it?"

"George, it's me. Artie. The guy who helped you with that gear."

The trailer door swung out and George appeared in the doorway, dressed only in a pair of boxer shorts. He had a fat, hairy belly and slouched there, eyes bleary, while he took us in.

"What is it?"

"That ride. Remember you promised?"

He spit off to the side and scratched his armpit, then yawned mightily. "Damn, pal, I didn't mean at five-thirty in the morning."

"It's a special occasion," I said. "This is my new girlfriend." I nodded toward Colleen.

"New? What happened to the old one?"

I cringed. Great. "We don't have a lot of time," I said. "This is my only chance. I can't come back before work tonight."

I stared at him, wondering if he could see the pleading in my eyes.

"Oh, all right. Wait there, pal. I'll be out in a minute."

Ten minutes later, we were sitting side by side in the Ferris wheel, grinning madly at each other. George started us up and then stopped the wheel after one revolution.

"What's wrong?" I said.

"Nothing. You want the lights on?"

My eyes widened. "That'd be nice."

He started us out again and as we rose into the air, the neon tubes of colored light switched on all around us. The effect was breathtaking. The same colors as before but in the growing light of dawn they were almost translucent. Frosty shades of pink and turquoise, bright red and yellow, deep green.

Below us stretched the midway, deserted and silent, the side shows dark, the mechanical rides waiting to come to life. Farther off, we could see the exhibit halls and beyond that the race track.

I put my arm around Colleen and she snuggled up to me.

"Thank you, farm boy. This is nice."

Simple words but said with so much warmth and affection that I almost couldn't breathe.

Suddenly, as we were on the upswing, the wheel started to slow. We came to a stop at the top, the gondola swinging gently.

I looked over the side, wondering what George was doing. For a brief moment, I was afraid he'd leave us up there and I'd get in trouble after all. And then I thought, who cares? I was tired of worrying about dad, tired of looking over my shoulder. That's all I'd done all night. I could imagine George down below saying, Jeez, kid, relax and enjoy life for once. You've been under your dad's thumb for too long. Stand up to him like a man.

Easier said than done. But all of a sudden I knew I was going to try.

George was looking up at us, surrounded by dark shadows. He cupped his hands around his mouth and said something.

"What?"

"I gotta take a leak," he shouted. "Be back in ten minutes."

I winced at his language, then watched as he picked his way over the thick electrical lines toward his trailer and waited until I saw him open the door and go inside. And then I turned and Colleen's mouth was right there and I kissed her. I think our teeth clacked at first but then I felt her lips and whatever I'd been thinking before that was another life ago.

After a moment she pulled away, and I wondered if I'd done something wrong. But then I saw what she was trying to do. My legs were bigger than hers, which gave her just enough room. She slipped her legs out from under the restraining bar and slid them across mine and I pulled her on to my lap. Her arms were around my shoulders and mine slid around her waist.

"Careful," I said, as the seat began to rock. "I don't want you to fall."

"I won't," she said. "Not with you holding me."

Like that guy with the Red Setter on the dam, I thought. I'd be her hero. Only he hadn't made it, had he? Saved the dog and lost his own life. Leave it to me to think of the wrong thing.

Colleen leaned away until she had my eyes locked on hers, wondering what she was going to do. "You know, Artie, back at the river? When I asked to see you with the flashlight?"

I nodded, unable to speak with her on my lap. I'd never felt anything so nice as the weight of her body. It was all I could do just to absorb the sensation. Her warmth was melting right through me.

"I knew who you were," she said. "I recognized you in the moonlight."

"You did?" I looked in her eyes. Deep dark pools. I felt like drowning in their sweetness. I didn't understand. "Then why'd you ask?"

"I wanted you to see *me*."

I absorbed that for a second, feeling my heart swelling. "Thanks," I whispered.

"Farm boy," she said. "I love you." And then, with the sun just about to come over the horizon, her soft lips closed over mine.

I was dizzy then and for a while I couldn't think, all I could do was feel. It was like her body was mine and mine was hers; I couldn't tell where one of us ended and the other began, and I didn't want to know, didn't want the moment to end, didn't want George to come back, didn't want the Ferris wheel to start turning again, didn't want ever to let go of Colleen.

A few minutes later, when we opened our eyes, we were both out of breath.

She put her hand on my chest. "Your heart's beating as hard as mine," she said, wonder in her voice.

I nodded. I couldn't speak, but this time no words were needed. I looked out at the eastern horizon. Far off in the distance, a pale yellow haze glowed behind a narrow band of dark fir trees. The thin green peaks looked like a picket fence cutting off from human view an unknown world beyond ... the future ... a new day ...

It was going to be a beautiful place to watch the sun rise.

*Just Colleen and me.*

Man, that had a nice sound.

And no matter how long it took, I planned to sit there with her in my arms until the last star faded from the sky and everything turned to gold.

# In Light's Delay

(1965-1968)

I wake and feel the fell of dark, not day.
What hours, O what black hours we have spent.
This night! what sights you, heart, saw; ways you went!
And more must, in yet longer light's delay.

— GERARD MANLEY HOPKINS

# — 1 —
## *Academe*

The evening breezes brushed against the ivy curling around the fir trees near Deady Hall. Sitting on the cold stone steps, indistinct in the growing darkness, Artie Crenshaw gazed absentmindedly as the ivy, awakened it seemed, clutched the bark tighter, pressing its flat leaves against the trees' roughness. Around him on the campus, the wide-leaved oak, the madrona, the thin fir and sharp pine began to rustle. The faint hint of a rainstorm breathed in the wind.

At his back, the windows of Deady Hall glowed through the shadows; the old history building still hummed with energy. Occasionally he could hear the doors of the examination room open and close, followed by the sound of muffled voices—and then a few tired students would walk down the steps and away into the darkness.

With a summer of work ahead, he tried to absorb the last impressions of freedom. His first year at the university in Eugene was like an escape from prison. Last night … last night was a silent farewell. He'd walked into this same darkness, down the tight asphalt alleys of the city. From haggard brick walls, from water seeping down garbage-strewn gutters, he'd slipped into newer, winding streets, lawns stretching indefinitely, houses large and white with windows like gray puddles. As the houses thinned, he'd felt his spirits rise and breathed deeper, taking the night into himself, and when he reached a field of last year's uncut hay, matted and bleached by spring rain, he sprawled out on the earth like a dog, while his mind ran free.

Youthful fantasies! Charging through trees, sylvan, hairy-hooved, he'd trumpeted and thundered, half man, half beast. Again he leapt, bounded like a startled deer, soared. Suddenly, he saw Spring slip off, naked, running through the forest—and he was after her, exuberant, excited by his quickened pulse, the crashing cascade of blood in his head. He chased nude flickerings (no aery costume of a Phrygian courtesan for this beauty), buttocks gleaming between tree trunks, and then she fell, gasping in the sand at the water's edge, melting away before him in the cool sea.

You've been reading too much D'Annunzio, he said to himself. And that brought to mind his honor's thesis and the grilling he'd received in his oral exam.

The Department Head started it. *By the way, where is Mount Verna?*

*Do you mean La Verna?*

*Of course.*

Hesitation. A stumble. *I'm not, ah, not really sure specifically* (the earth was now cold, wet, sucking). *I tried to find it on an Atlas but it wasn't there* (innumerable needles of dry grass now prickling). *I figured out it must be somewhere between Marradi ...* (the voice of a drunkard destroying) *Firenze ...* (destroying the immensity of the night like stars destroying the vast blackness of space) *Faenza* (pearls but also grit beneath the shell) *and Bagno di Romagna. Somewhere in the Falteronas, I guess."*

Man, channeling Dino Campana there.

The fat man with the bald head who always wore a blue silk suit and delicate gold spectacles chuckled. *It may not be on the physical map but you'll find it on the spiritual map, won't he professor?*

Professor Allisino, sitting forward like a broken straw, laughed but said nothing.

*Do you know what La Verna is noted for?* The department head again.

He shook his head, honest ignorance, shrugging. Wondered if Allisino with his puppet grin knew.

*Well, why did Campana go there? Why did he make this trek back into the mountains of Campigno and Falterona?*

*I never could find out.* (Remind yourself that this man humiliating you now, this man asking the most minor of questions, this man picking the smallest point where he sensed hesitancy in your thesis, this is the same man who...) *I knew there was a monastery there, but I couldn't find anything in dictionaries or other reference works about La Verna* (this is the man who told you to change your topic on the Fulbright application—yours was too specific, too detailed, too probing and difficult for a student your age, a Freshman. The problem you suggest has never really been studied by others and it's best at this stage for you to expand on what more advanced scholars have already put forward. Why don't you just put down that you want to go to Italy to study the language. Impress them with your love of Italian, its poetry. After all, no one really wants to go there at your age to study something like this. They'll think it was formulated by one of your professors.

So you had written a sentimental little piece on how you wished to develop your control of spoken and written Italian in order one day—maybe— to become a teacher. Later you found out the person the department head had really sponsored was a prize student of his own. The student who had taken the department head's course on Dante and his seminar on Ariosto and Tasso. You, unfortunately, as a Freshman, precocious as you might have seemed, had not weaseled your way into the good graces of this guy. After all, you'd been too busy studying. But ... pay attention. You're going to screw this up.)

*My dear fellow* (sarcasm now?), *La Verna is where Saint Francis received the stigmata* (he's making you feel sorry you didn't study medieval Italian lit, that you'd picked some minor poet of the early twentieth century for your honor's thesis). *This was a spiritual journey Campana took, not, as you imply, merely a journey to find himself at one with nature* (but what about my statement that this was an 'interior voyage'?).

And it went on like that for one miserable hour and now, when he finished going over it, his head burning, he could hear, louder than ever, the voice of a drunken student singing some unintelligible song.


The bad memory faded as Artie waited on the cold steps for his best friend, Phil Lockfall, to finish the history exam. Footsteps behind him announced the major horde of test takers. Scuffling by, some chattered and gleamed in glory for inspired essays; others drifted past, pale, but happy the torture was over, retreating with sighs of relief.

But still no Phil.

Instead, Artie's roommate came, short, fat Gordon Owens—pontificating as usual. Artie saw him make his way through what looked like disciples eager to know the answer to some unanswerable question.

Sliding over to let the chatterers pass, Artie thought of his latest attempt to ruffle Gordon. They were arguing about the existence of God and the afterlife. At one point, tired of the discussion, Artie interrupted to say there wouldn't be any Catholics in heaven, so Gordon might as well quit worrying about its existence. Thinking of how Gordon had flushed, Artie grinned. "For a preacher's son," Gordon had replied, "you argue like an idiot."

Undeterred, Artie shot back with something that had struck him during an Honor's College biology lecture. "You Christians *(it felt good to distance himself, the first time he'd ever thought that way)* have a hard time believing life could have started in the muck, right? A ray of light striking chemicals in water? But you have no trouble believing in the Virgin Birth. Life from nothing. God from nothing."

Gordon just shook his head as if Artie was a lost cause.

Leaning back into the steps of Deady Hall, wrinkling his nose to lift his glasses, Artie watched his roommate angle off up the sidewalk toward the dorm. Good old Gordy sure had been distant since then.

Good. If there was one thing he was tired of it was religion. He'd had enough of that at home.

After another ten minutes, with the cold stone steps beginning to prickle, he stood up and leaned against the concrete balustrade. He heard heels clicking on the steps and looked up, pulling his feet back as three girls—he knew one vaguely—walked by. And then she was turning toward him and asking, "How do you think you did?"

He remembered her name now. Patty. "Not too bad, I hope. Should have written longer though."

She hesitated as if she were waiting for more, then moved off with the others, who'd stopped to stare at him as if thinking, Why's she talking to this dork?

Their voices softened with distance, a memory of Colleen hitting him with a pang so strong he almost doubled over, No one's like Colleen, he thought. No one. One year ... that was all, and her mother had moved again. Back to West Virginia where she had family. He and Colleen wrote letters for at least a year, but then came graduation and college—Colleen at Columbia, Artie at Oregon—and their lives got so busy that everything just fell apart. He shook his head, wondering, and not for the first time, how that could happen.

Where in the hell was Phil? Had he somehow slipped by unnoticed? Go back inside looking for him or leave? He was just about to give up, had turned away, when he felt a clap on the back.

"Hey, man, didn't think you'd wait!"

Before Artie could reply, Phil took off running. "Let's go find some scantily dressed if not nude nymphs," he shouted over his shoulder.

Artie whooped, stumbled down the steps, shouted "or nymphomaniacs," and took off springing after him.

In the dorm, Artie stopped to get a warmer coat before joining Phil. The evening had turned cool, though it had been an unusually warm May for Eugene. Out above Robbins Hall, Artie could see the moon, small and pale; gray wisps of clouds, like veils of spider web, floated past her face.

On their way to the Dog House restaurant, riding bikes, Phil mentioned he'd met a new girl earlier in the day in the Student Union's bowling alley.

Artie swerved to miss a barely seen pothole. "What about her?"

"She knows you."

He sat up and looked back at Phil. "What's her name?"

"Patty Darr."

Artie turned back, saw a car coming, and pulled to the right to let it pass.

"Do you know anything about her?" Phil asked, nonchalant.

"Not much. Seen and said 'hi' a few times. She was in my biology lab. Sat two tables away. She went by just a few minutes ago."

"She thinks you're handsome."

Artie snorted. "Hey, no surprise." That, he knew, would irritate Phil. "Every girl in this school is dying over my bawd." Gave him a chance to get even. Phil liked to brag about all his conquests, always hinting that he'd taken so and so to bed. Artie thought he was probably a virgin. Like himself.

Phil paused for a moment, letting the silence emphasize his words. "I've got a date with her for Saturday night."

Artie forced a smile, aggravated he hadn't had the guts to ask her out himself. They crossed Franklin Boulevard in silence, the topic dropped while they parked their bikes at the entrance to the restaurant.

In the Dog House, over coffee, Phil said, "You know, Artie. I've found the secret to attracting girls."

Oh shit. Here we go with another hour of boasting. No one more irritating than Phil in his homiletic moments. What was that expression James Joyce used? He had a mouth big enough to whistle in his own ear. That was Phil.

"Self-confidence. All you gotta have is confidence."

Phil droned on for fifteen minutes, rambling on and on from the film *Lust for Life*-("That could've been a picture about me. Just don't let people get to you.")—to Faust—("You know what Mephisto tells Faust, right? Self-confidence is the key. Goethe knew. Everyone's got to find out for himself though").

Shit, what presumption. He's not only Van Gogh, he's Mephisto now.

"I mean, let me give you an example. I saw Sharon again last week—and you know how cool she's been to me recently. Anyway, I acted halfway indifferent to her and she started responding. I wound up taking her to the show with Ray. She kept playing kneesies with me, and toesies too, and even elbowsies."

Phil started to laugh and Artie joined him. "I think she had the hots," Phil said, as they were leaving the restaurant. "If we'd had the car to ourselves, we'd have made it on the way home."

The moon was hidden now by thicker clouds coming in from the coast, the air crisp, yet in the darkness the campus lay strangely more resplendent, golden lamps casting shadows and mysterious shapes along the paths.

"Why don't we ride over to Ray's house?" Phil said. "I have a bottle of sloe gin there—if he hasn't gotten to it yet."

From the dusky campus, they rode out to Broadway, nearly deserted now. It was as if they'd passed through a curtain. Bright colored lights cut the night, delineating every building with the sharpness of a scalpel. Only the all-night Eugene Bakery showed any sign of life; even the taverns were shut.

Ray Spencer lived out near 25th and Alder in a garage converted into a small apartment. There was only one room in the place with a small bathroom and pantry at the back. When they arrived, the windows were dark. "Is he asleep?" Artie wondered.

"Naw, I don't think so. His car's gone. Probably out with his girl."

Artie had seen Ray's girlfriend once. A beautiful, tall blonde, with a model's angular face. Phil had told him she liked Ray's brand new '65 Chevy. Was that what it took to get dates? No, Ray was better looking than Phil. That's why he had what Phil called "the hot chick."

The front door was locked, but Phil managed to get in through a cracked bathroom window. Inside, they found the sloe gin, washed a couple of dirty glasses, and made themselves at home with a deck of cards. Ray didn't return until after three.

Phil wanted to play cards but Ray said he was going to bed. "If you guys want, one of you can use the couch and one the other half of the bed."

Phil jumped to his feet and pulled a coin from his pocket. "Let's flip for the bed, Artie."

Phil promptly won the flip.

Minutes later, happy he'd lost the coin flip, Artie lay on the couch in darkness, thinking, wishing the summer wasn't so near. Phil intended to go to California to work in a resort near Guerneville, and Ray would go back home to Depoe Bay to work on his dad's salmon fleet. Both jobs sounded better to

Artie than working on the farm all summer.

On the farm, if you weren't picking up hay bales all night 'cause you were afraid of rain in the morning, or digging trenches 'cause you had a tall cow in heat and a short bull, you were sweating in the sun, feeding slop to the pigs, burning last winter's rotting hay, or cleaning chicken shit from beneath the wire coops. None too exciting. At least there was a chance he might get to do some construction work.

His dad, a construction superintendent since he'd left the ministry, back to the career he'd had before his "crazy conversion," as Artie thought of it, might put him on as a laborer. His older brother was already working for their dad as a carpenter.

Uncomfortable on the sofa, he longed for activity. The gin hadn't left any heaviness or desire for sleep. Ray was lightly snoring and Phil seemed pretty quiet.

"Phil," he whispered. "You awake?"

"Yeah." Phil responded instantly, as if he too had been waiting.

"Want to go out again? I'm not tired."

"Me neither. Let's go downtown."

They glided to their feet quietly, talking in whispers, picking their way in the dark around the table and scattered chairs. Ray didn't stir.

Outside in the cold, a new world appeared. It was nearly four o'clock, the clouds had sealed in—hermetic—and, except for the street lights, the world hunkered down solid black. Each block took on a new dimension in the chill electric light, the shadows now purple, the streets somehow narrower and longer. In the silence, the bicycle tires whistled plaintively. As they drew near the center of town, Artie wondered if there were any restaurants open that early and Phil mentioned the Greyhound Station. "The food's not great but they've got magazines we can look at."

Despite the hour, a few people were loitering on the barren streets in front of the station with its blue neon clock. After coffee and sweet rolls, Phil bought a magazine, the one with the most pictures of semi-nude women, and the two rode back toward campus, warmed and enlivened again.

When Artie suggested climbing venerable Friendly Hall, familiar home of Modern Languages, the site of his Italian classes, and said he knew a way, Phil yelled, "Shit, yes!" Parking their bikes on the west side, they found an old fire escape leading to the roof.

"We can't reach the bottom of that, can we?" Phil asked.

"Sure. It's not that high. It drops all the way to the ground. I saw it from a window of my Italian class. It's just hidden behind those shrubs."

Artie led the way and the two crawled along the stiff ground under the prickly shrubs, forcing their way through the lower branches. Next to the wall of the building, a cleared space left room to stand and when they did before them rose the magic beanstalk.

"I'll go first." Phil's feet clambered already on the lower rungs.

"Okay, but take it easy. They might be slippery."

Phil, halfway to the landing by the first floor window, stopped and whispered down to Artie. "Yeah. Be careful. There's a mist or something frozen on them."

They moved up slowly, climbing past the first and second floor windows. The building was higher than it seemed, the ground farther away than they'd thought possible. When they reached the fourth floor and looked down, both felt a clutch of fear.

"Hey Artie!" Artie looked up at Phil's tennis shoes, his friend's form fore-shortened above him. "There's a gable here we'll have to get by. The roof slants in, too, and there's no ladder. If we can climb up the eave without slipping, it's flat on top."

"Take it easy, okay?" Artie pleaded. "Don't go too fast, Phil. If you slip, we're in a hell of a mess."

"I won't. Come on."

Reaching the top of the roof, Artie paused for breath, his heart thudding in his chest. A stretch of the fire escape ladder climbed up in open air, and without the support of the wall beside him he was cautious and scared. He climbed without looking down, checking to make sure each time he gripped the cold iron that his hands held firm.

Level with the gable finally, he could see Phil bracing himself between the V of two sloping walls. "How'd you get up there?"

"I grabbed the gutter, kept one hand on the ladder and pulled myself on to the roof."

Artie did the same and for a moment felt the surge of adrenalin that came with the realization he was hanging on the edge of an icy roof. And then he clambered over the top, swearing at Phil because he was laughing.

"Now, dammit, we have to climb up that slant. We can't grab the edge of the shingles, can we?"

Phil tried it. "They might break." The two paused to think.

"Say," Artie exclaimed, "have you thought about getting down?"

Phil grinned. "Let's not think about it. Maybe I can shove you up the side, Artie, and once you get to the top you can give me a hand up."

"Will I be able to reach you when I'm on top?"

"I think so."

Slowly, Artie crept up the slant, Phil's hands on his heels.

"Hurry, Artie, it's hard to hold on here."

"My hands are there." Grasping the edge, with an extra shove from Phil, he pulled himself up, and soon both were standing on the roof, breathing heavily, excited at their conquest.

Phil slapped his legs, running along the roof. "God, what a view! You can see half the campus and the mill race." They strolled back and forth along the top, admiring the campus, glittering in early morning darkness, the dawn still delayed by a blanket of clouds. Just a hint of smoldering haze

"I know what," Phil said. "Let's take a leak off the side."

Shortly a warm cloud of steam rose from two arching waterfalls.

"Isn't this fantastic, Artie? It's great staying up all night."

"This is my first time," Artie said. "I wish we'd done it earlier in the term."

As they talked, still panting in excitement, small puffs of vapor rose about their heads and, with the elusiveness of morning fog, disappeared into the air. Below them lay thousands of sleeping dormitory students in dark, solemn buildings. Silence loomed over the campus, vast like an immense iceberg in a misty sea—and nothing except themselves seemed real. And then a knife blade slit the horizon and the rosy razor's edge of the sun slipped through, looking like a wound behind gauze.

Spurred by the growing light and the sight of a campus cop walking toward the building, they made a get-away back down the slippery fire escape and away into the night. But at the moment, when still on top, oblivious to the future, they felt masters of the world that stretched below them, masters of it and of the night.

# — 2 —
## Ceres

Though it was only late June, the creek flowed at a trickle, sluggish rivulets seeping mossy water between cracked and caked mud. What in past winters had filled the bottom of the slope so only the tractor could get through with hay for the cattle lay, in midsummer, nearly dry, and Artie could carry the bales across in a wheelbarrow. In the orchard, the pigs rooted their troughs over, spilling the water and wallowing in the mire. In the field behind the house, chalk-white dust floated in the air with each wisp of a breeze. Cottonwood poplars fluffed their confetti in the air and every now and then a calf snorted and broke into a spine-tingling run, a vain attempt to escape the bites of horse-flies.

Just now, as if awakened by the calf, the wind picked up strength, ruffling the brittle leaves of two dying ash trees. The leaves sounded and shone like a pinwheel done in sun-glare white and dark brown.

The small herd of black Angus lay clumped and heavy in the grass.

The building, caressed by the same indiscriminate breeze, creaked as it cooled. Upstairs in Artie's room, the heat lingered. He could hear crickets chirping outside, and several mosquitoes had flown in the open window and were buzzing around the bare light bulb. Occasional rasps of late returning bees—they'd made nests beneath the rotting shakes—added to the muted chorus of evening.

Artie's mom and dad, his two brothers Richy and Bobby, and his younger sister Robin (as she liked to be called, having abandoned Nancy when she started third grade) were watching TV in the small gray house a stone's throw away. In syncopated flashes Artie heard the faint sound of cowboy yells and gunfire bursting from the darkened living room, and then all was quiet again. Apparently a late-night movie.

His room was in a two-story erstwhile Colonial mansion—once a house, then a retired folks' home, later a church of which his father was minister, and now a storage shed below and empty rooms above. He'd appropriated one of these vacant Sunday School classrooms for his own.

The walls stood unpainted, for money and fervor had run out about the same time. The more carpenterial of the congregation, under the able direction of his father, converted construction man, had installed sheet rock to partition the larger convalescent rooms, had grouted the hammer marks, had laid strips of gauze over the cracks between panels, and had troweled plaster on to the ceiling, but that was as far as they got.

Artie's attempts to alter the atmosphere had been feeble. His desk stood to the left and beside it sat a makeshift easel constructed out of apple boxes. No carpenter he—unlike his father in this and so many other ways. In front of the one wall with windows, he'd placed a long oval table, covered now with books, tubes of paint, and drawing paper and at the head of his bed, as the room's only decorative note, he'd taped a reproduction of a painting of three Roman columns. Several texts of Italian grammar lay nearby.

Directly below his room, the now-scarred sanctuary, with its rows of old theater seats still schizoidally intact, protected a jumble of shabby furniture, assorted light fixtures, plumbing, plywood sheets, rusty stoves and refrigerators, baling twine, tools, a piano and a wooden pulpit—the latter built by his dad when Artie was in the second grade in Wenatchee, a mimeograph machine, bottles of chemicals for long-forgotten Sunday School object lessons, an old water heater they were burning in two with the torch to make more pig troughs, and more and more and yet more junk. Was it the preacher, or the farmer, or the construction superintendent in his dad who was the pack rat?

All three apparently.

Walking into the hall and down to the window facing north—Portland twelve miles to his left, Gresham a scant mile or two to his right—he pulled the two side pins out and with his knee shoved the glass upward, jamming the window at the top. He stuck his head out, looking over to his left under the fir trees, checking to see if the barn lights were out. His dad had left the Jersey in the barn after milking her, while she finished her grain. The milking had been put off until later than usual because of the haying. It was Artie's job before leaving for work to turn her out to pasture if his dad forgot, but the barn was dark.

Leaning out, Artie threw a beer can into the lilac hedge. I'd be in for it if that's found! At the moment he was almost angry enough not to care, his plans for the evening having been ruined by his dad in an all-too-familiar scenario.

For two weeks Artie had planned on meeting Phil Lockfall that Friday evening. Phil was up from his job in California, during a short midsummer break, to visit his parents in Portland. Artie had planned on showing Phil some of his latest paintings, mostly still lifes, but at six p.m. his mother had awakened him from a nap.

"Artie, your dad wants you to drive the truck for a couple hours."

"But we got all day tomorrow."

"He says it's going to rain, and you know your dad."

Shit! He knows I got asthma, the son of a bitch. Too cheap to pay someone five bucks an hour!

Artie had called Phil and canceled their get-together. Phil wanted to come over late, but Artie explained about his working nights. Damn! It wasn't enough to do chores in the morning and evening and then work all night. I can't even have three hours free in the evening! Now, thinking of the hours wasted, he burned again in fresh anger.

When Artie had gone down to the barn earlier, his dad was giving orders to Bobby, his curly-haired younger brother. "Hook up the baler and start at the west end. The windrows should be pretty dry there."

"The hay's a bit damp yet," Richy said, looking away from his father toward the pear tree in the orchard. He was the oldest. None of the kids dared talk back too openly to their dad. Years of severe discipline had seen to that.

"I thought we were going to finish it tomorrow," Artie put in, straightening his glasses.

"Don't worry about that," his dad said, turning to Richy. "This way we won't lose any leaves. This vetch'll go five dollars more a ton if it's leafy. We can stack the bales loose in the shed. It'll dry."

"Clouds might blow off before night," Richy had dared to suggest. "No use taking a chance on moldy bales."

"You heard what I said Bobby." The old man jerked his thumb back, ignoring the older boys. "Get a move on. You kids would wait till Christmas if you could." As Bobby passed—slowly—his dad cuffed him on the back of the head and then strode toward the house, muttering loudly enough for them all to hear. "Darn kids. Won't amount to a hill of beans."

When he reached the back door, he turned to Artie, who was following hesitantly, waiting to ask what he was supposed to do. Before he could say anything however, his dad spoke. "Did you get that shed straightened out like I told you to?" The shed he referred to was an old chicken coop. Long ago they had torn out the floor, then a foot deep with droppings, and had never put in a new one.

"I've been working on the pens for the steers. I thought we'd need them first."

"Well, get out there and lay down some two by twelves. In even rows. Use the old bricks under them. I want the bales kept off the ground. Your mother'll drive the truck."

At the back porch, his dad waited for Bobby to come around on the second row. He waved his arm and Bobby cut the engine. "Put it in third and get a move on," the old man yelled. "We ain't got all night."

When they were finally ready to do the haying, his dad climbed up on the truck bed, his mother at the wheel. The older boys were waiting. "I'll stack," he said. "Let's see if you two can keep up."

Turning to his wife he hollered, "Let her roll," and they were off, Richy and Artie running from bale to bale and half in spite, half to get the work done, trying to drown the old man in a pile of hay. Their dad worked like a horse to keep the bales stacked. Artie knew when the load got higher the old man could take it easier. He always went eight high. That would tire them out.

Artie hit him in the back with a bale thrown a little too hard, a little too high. His dad never said a word. Artie figured the guy would drop a few on them when they unloaded.

For the next few hours they'd worked silently. At the end of the third load, Artie was wheezing badly, his glasses clouded with sweat. Normally he could quit and take some cortisone pills but this time he worked on, driven by stubbornness and pride, hating his dad the while.

The sun fell when they were at the shed unloading the fifth load. They'd worked on in the dark, the lights of the truck picking out the bales up ahead. Far off across the field, Bobby rumbled along on the tractor, its two headlamps strong and white, the red taillights glowing. In the night air, all you could hear was the steady thump-thump of the baler and nearby the whine of the truck climbing over one furrow after the other. The field had been plowed the year before and never disked; the hay had grown on it before they could do anything about it.

His dad yelled at Richy. "Tell your mother to put it in second and speed this up. It's going to rain soon."

Richy ran up to the cab and passed the order on.

"What's wrong with your father, anyway?" his mother complained. "He must be off his rocker. This field's so full of gullies we'll lose a load if he's not careful."

"Guess who'll get blamed too," Richy said and left the cab window. It wasn't until ten that Artie was allowed to leave. Not a drop of rain had fallen. He had two hours until work. The rest would finish the evening chores, which had been postponed.

Having gulped down a warm beer from a six-pack he kept hidden in his room and having disposed of the empty can, he closed the window to keep the mosquitoes out and went back to his desk. He wanted to reread some of Phil's letters for a few minutes. In the last once he'd mentioned buying some new records—the Yardbirds and Them, adding something about how "groovy" "Gloria" was. Damn, I hate "groovy" about as much as "corny."

Phil was working at a boy's camp on the Russian River near Monte Rio. Bragged about how he was going to screw the cook's daughter, the only teen-age female around. And then he mentioned the kids.

*Last night my co-worker John and I took a rowboat out to where the kids were having a camp out. They asked us to participate in a skit. Luckily I didn't have long pants on. John did. They made him lie down on his back. Then they put a towel over his face, raised one leg, said, 'up peri-scope' and poured a can of water down his leg. I must admit was funny*

What was funny was Phil acting like he'd screw the only female around.

He put the letter back in its envelope. The beer had made him sleepy to read more. In a moment, his head dropped …

Was there someone walking in the hall? "Richy?" he called. No answer. Still dazed, he looked at the clock. Eleven fifteen. Have to make my lunch, he thought. Suddenly the curtain over the doorway to his room parted. Artie's hands grabbed the desk. Richy?

"Boo!" There was a scream of laughter and a blonde head appeared in the room. "Hi Artie. I brought your lunch over."

"Gee, thanks, Robin! Shouldn't you be in bed? It's after eleven."

"Dad let me stay up. They're eating dinner and watching a movie. What're you doing?" Her voice was so young and refreshing. Like a peal of bells.

"Just reading some letters." He took the sack lunch and set it near his hard hat.

"Gretchen's sick," Robin said.

"Oh, what's wrong?"

"I don't know. Dad gave her a shot. I took her back out."

"Weren't you afraid?"

"No, she's friendly to me. I talk to her."

"You do?" Artie turned toward her in his chair. "What's she say?"

Robin laughed. "Nothing."

"Nothing?"

"She just moos."

"She talked to me one day."

Robin smiled, her blue eyes shining. "Really?"

"Yep. It was after high school one day a couple of years ago when I was playing basketball and doing the chores late."

"What did she say?" Robin sat on her hands at the edge of the bed, her hair falling forward and over both shoulders.

"Well, I got mad at her because it was dark and she was scared to go by the hole outside the bathroom. 'You stupid beast,' I said. 'What in the world's the matter with you? Don't you have any sense? It's just the caved-in septic tank.' 'Sure,' she said, 'that's why I'm not going by the hole. It bothers me in the dark.'".

"Really?" Robin's eyes widened. "Why won't she talk to me? Bossy and Star don't either."

"Well, they only do it on rare occasions. Maybe only once or twice in their whole lives."

"Wow, that was neat!" She raised her voice on neat.

"Yeah," Artie went on, "she was really mad at me or she wouldn't have spoken."

"Did you hit her?"

"No, but I pulled her hard."

"Dad hit Bossy with the pitchfork."

"He did! When?"

"Tonight. She kicked the milk bucket. I was waving flies off but dad pinched her milk thing and she kicked. She stepped right in the bucket."

"Was there much milk?"

"It was half-full. She got manure in it so dad gave it to Wolf and Snowball."

"What's dad doing?"

"He's watching TV—but he fell asleep in the chair."

"Well, you'd better be getting back before he wakes up. I should be leaving for work by now." They both stood and Artie kissed her. "Thanks for bringing my lunch over," he called after her as she left, thinking how shy she was around him—now that he'd been gone a year at the university. Precocious kid, only 7 and already finished with third grade. So smart she was probably just pretending to be innocent and gullible.

Artie started work at midnight. It was an easy job. His father, no longer preaching, worked as a superintendent for the Henry J. Itis Construction Company, and was presently in charge of the new high school being built east of Portland. He'd given Artie the job of night watchman. Gangs of juveniles were making a habit of ruining the newly poured concrete, breaking windows, stripping electrical wiring, pulling down insulation, and carving up sheet rock. Artie's job was to keep them out of the project and to do as much cleaning up as he could under the moonlight or inside the building.

The main building ran in a long L-shape, at the end of which lay the foundations for a gym and for a cafeteria that would also serve as an auditorium. The walls of the gym had been raised just the week before. They were pre-poured on a series of long concrete slabs, a liquid rubber bonding agent having been laid down first so the walls wouldn't stick.

When it came time to lift the different sections, they'd used the largest, road-driven crane in the whole Pacific Northwest. Artie had seen it at night, a huge thing, like some ancient, Neolithic beast, its boom extending out over the tall walls braced in place for the pouring of the pilasters.

Now, with the pilasters poured, the gym was like a big box without a top. Artie had been forced to walk along the top of the sloped walls, eight inches thick, the first night they were all in place, watering the pilasters. He still walked them, not to work but to keep watch over the whole project. From that height, early in the morning, he could see Portland in the distance, Mount Hood fifty miles to the East and, up North, the crests of the Cascade range. At night only the city lights were visible.

Artie enjoyed certain aspects of his job, although it often frightened him. There was the knowledge that down below someone might be lying in wait to hit him over the head. And, in the dark, he saw a thousand shapes, heard a thousand sounds. All of them, unless he knew their origin, had to be investigated. Often it was only a piece of sheet metal the wind blew over or plastic snapping in the breeze.

When he drove into the site, a full moon was just rising above the picket-fence wood plot behind the project. He parked the car near a lift truck and locked it. In his back right pocket, he carried a flashlight, and through one of the belt loops on his right side he'd stuck a short length of heavy telephone line. This rubber-coated mass of metal fibers was wicked. Although he could bend it easily, it retained its shape under a sharp blow. He knew it was a good weapon, since a light but firm blow left a ridge across a wood plank.

The job had its good and its bad points. Once a huge, bare-chested man on a motorcycle disobeyed his orders to stay off the property and chased him on the cycle, threatening to kill him if he turned him in to the police.

"I've taken enough shit from punks like you," he'd shouted. "Call the cops and I'll be back."

Artie took his license number, but the threat was effective.

The good points were several, especially the freedom. Between his rounds, he could sit on the front porch of the superintendent's trailer, reading or drawing, or—now that the building had lights—he could draw inside. His only concern was that his dad would notice not much work was getting done and would sneak around to check up on him.

The night had turned cool and although Artie was supposed to be carrying some 2x6s into the gym, he sat in the car for an hour, listening to KISN radio and reading *Of Human Bondage*. Philip and Fanny Price! Jeez, I hope I don't turn out to be the type of artist who wonders if they have talent. He read with his flashlight although the moon was full.

At two, after working an hour, he made the rounds of the building on the outside, flashing his light in the windows. Someone had shut off the fuse box near the saw and the light there and those inside the building were out. Artie didn't know how to fix it, so the street light by the trailer was all he had.

Stopping in the entrance to the cafeteria, he sat down on a saw horse to rest. Earlier, he'd noticed that from the steps of the trailer, he could see a reflection of himself, the street light and the buildings in the hubcap of the car. The reflection, taking the round shape of the hubcap, intrigued him. Reminded him of those pictures taken with fish-eye lenses. I'll draw it later, he thought. With the dirt in the foreground, the trailer and cafeteria in a circle at the back and himself beneath the lamp, the scene seemed Mexican. His hard hat looked like a sombrero.

He was involved in these thoughts when something whistled from above and exploded behind him. Shit! He bounced to his feet and ran for a stack of pallets, hoping for cover. Sounded like someone was shooting. At him?

Hugging the ground and trying to keep in shadow, he crawled over to the car.

He lay there, heart thumping. An unseen object came whistling by. Had to come from the roof. What? Kids up there?

He moved to the front of the car and, from there, hoping no one could see him, crept behind a lift truck. From under it in shadow, he looked up at the building. There! Someone was moving on the roof. They must have climbed the bricks again.

---

Near the front entrance, following the architects' design, the masons had laid bricks indented in an elaborate design, and Artie knew the indentations were close enough to use for climbing. After a minute, he saw a dark form silhouetted against the sky. Then another.

Okay. Two of them.

He worked his way to where he could approach the building unseen.

Damn. Have to climb the bricks just like they did. Hope they don't catch me halfway up. Problem is, the second I raise my head above the roofline those guys will be less than five feet away. Might try to kick me off the edge.

He stopped, held on with one hand, took the cord whip from his belt loop and held it in his teeth. Suddenly, he heard a snicker and glancing up saw both heads looking down at him. He grabbed the whip in one hand.

"All right! Both of you. Hold it right there!" He spoke with authority but the heads disappeared. He scaled the last stretch and swung over the top, where he was greeted by a burst of giggling.

"Scared you, didn't we?"

"Phil, damn it all. What the hell are *you* doing up here?" And then he recognized the other guy. "Hey, Ray."

"Just came down to see you. How'd you like our little surprise greeting?"

"I thought someone was trying to kill me. What was it?"

"A shell. Me and Ray, we make them by filling an empty casing with gunpowder, then a few screws or nails and bits of metal. They explode when you throw them."

"Real funny. How'd you know where I worked?"

"I called your place about 11:30. Might have woke your mom. She told me where you work." Phil picked up and drop-kicked an empty milk carton left on the newly tarred surface by one of the roofers. "I should've asked you earlier myself but I didn't think of it."

For the next hour Artie led his two friends on a tour of the building from the roof down to the tunnels beneath the ground floor. After that, about three o'clock, they climbed to the roof of the cafeteria to rest. Artie had a surveyor's scope from the foreman's shack and they zeroed in on the houses about a mile away on the heights. No one seemed up, despite the fact that it was a Friday.

Ray Spencer stretched out on the cafeteria roof, hands behind his head. "What do you do all night here? Must be boring as shit."

Artie, arms resting on drawn-up knees, shook his head.

"Never. If I run out of work or feel like it I can always read or draw."

"What're you doing, studying architecture?"

Artie grinned. "No. I'd like to be a painter. I'm going to Italy to study next year." He pointed to the south. "See those trees in the moonlight ? Nice scene for an oil painting, right?"

"A painter! You're kidding." Ray sat up as Phil came back from his tour of the cafeteria roof. "I mean, I can see it as a hobby, but a career?" He laughed. "You'll wind up painting houses for a living."

"Yeah, right." Phil said, bounding around the two and then plopping down. "Why don't you screw for a career and paint clouds as a hobby?"

"Why not make a career of both?"

All three pondered the options in silence. "Hey," Phil said, "we have a six-pack of beer in the car.

"Did you drive in? I didn't hear you."

It's my car," Ray said. "We left it up on Stark Street and walked in. I'll go get the beer if you guys want to chat."

After Ray left, Phil and Artie lay back on the steeper slope of the cafeteria roof. The moon hung high in the sky to the south, a gigantic mother- of-pearl bright enough to blot out most of the stars—except Vega overhead. Artie could see there was no chance of rain. They'd worked their asses off in the hay for nothing.

"When do you go back to California?" he asked Phil.

"Next Monday. Some older guys'll be coming in to camp. I'm lucky to be going back at all though. I almost got fired last week."

"How come?" Artie stood so he could take off his flannel shirt. Climbing up the wall had raised a sweat.

"Oh, I got mad at the clean-up kids cause they were putting silverware in the wrong tubs. Threw a plastic plate and cracked one kid in the head." Phil broke out laughing. "He ran screaming like a stuck pig to his counselor. I got a good bawling out." He snorted. "Hey, did I tell you about the cook's daughter? I took her to a carnival in Santa Rosa last week. Had a bitchin' evening. She was hanging all over me. We rode the scrambler, the octopus, the Ferris wheel, necking the whole time. She let me feel her up. I'd of screwed if it hadn't started raining."

*Yeah, right.* Artie didn't say anything but the mention of a Ferris wheel made him think of Colleen. Man, sometimes that seemed like years ago. He'd sent her a letter just last month. It came back with "No longer at this address." Kind of like Elvis's "Return to Sender." Only he was sure she'd never seen the envelope. She was too nice. She'd have written back, even if it was to say he should forget her.

From down below they heard a yell. "It's Ray with the beer," Phil said. Artie crawled over to the lower edge of the roof. "Hey, keep it quieter, okay? The neighbors might hear us and call the cops."

Ray ignored him. "Do you have a rope to pull the beer up?"

"Just a second. You coming up the scaffold?"

"I'm on the first level but I'm afraid I'll drop the beer."

Artie found a carpenter's rope under some plywood and in a minute they had the beer on the roof. Phil ripped the flip-top off a can. "What took you so long, Ray?"

"Did you see that cop car driving around the place?"

"Hell no."

"Yeah. He followed that dirt road. Had his lights out. Didn't see me though."

"No sweat then," Artie said. "They check out the place every night or so. They know I'm here. First night they came though, we scared each other. I was inside, hauling scrap lumber in the wheelbarrow, when they must have seen the light and heard me. Anyway, one came in and I ran into him coming around a corner. We each thought the other was a prowler. He had his gun out so I guess he was ready for anything."

Ray handed Artie a beer and the three drank in silence. Artie felt a glow diffuse through his body.

"It sure is eerie around here?" Phil said, "but I like it."

Ray was lying on his side, shooting pebbles and chips of wood down the roof like marbles, one chasing the other. He'd already drunk three beers while Phil was on his second and Artie his first. "Just remember you got to get down that scaffold," Artie said. "I'd take you guys up on the gym walls but one of you'd wind up on the floor with a few pieces of rebar sticking through his guts."

Ray wanted to go immediately, of course, but Phil grabbed his arm. "Come on, Spencer, sit down. I want to tell Artie some more about my latest escapades in golden Cauliflower."

"Where in hell is the camp anyway?"

"Monte Rio's the closest town, about three miles away. Guerneville's about seven."

"So," Ray said, "tell us about these perverse sexual acts you perform with all the little kiddies."

Phil carefully retied a shoelace. His hair, getting longer, hung black and curly over his forehead. "Well, ruff! ruff! I already told Artie about the cook's daughter, Sheila. It's either her or St. Onan."

"What's she like?" Artie asked, taking off his hard hat and wiping his forehead with a handkerchief. "I'm already sweating and you haven't even described her!"

"She's seventeen and quite fine! Big butt and broad hips. But you know what that spells."

Ray jumped to his feet and like a cheerleader shouted out, "Gimme an S, gimme an E, gimme an X."

"You ought to see her mother though," Phil continued, when the three had quieted back down. "She's about three hundred pounds and the biggest, toughest, meanest looking woman I've ever laid—eyes on, that is." Artie grinned appreciation, while Ray encouraged Phil to "get to the juicy stuff."

"Anyway, I haven't had much time to work on Sheila since she was only visiting for two weeks, and I had to watch out for her mom who was on my back for a few other misdeeds of mine." As he talked, Phil stretched back, enjoying the audience.

"About the only time we had together was in the afternoon. After she'd been in camp a week, I convinced her to go boating with me a few times. I'd take her to a special spot I'd found across the river near a thicket of blackberry bushes. We'd pick enough to make a pie later, eating along the way until we were like giant purple people eaters. I'd lay down on the grass to bag a few rays and I noticed the more I ignored her the more she snuggled up to me. The first two times we went over, I just felt her up and was too dumb to try for more. Finally, I realized if I was going to do anything, I'd better do it fast because she was leaving to go back to her father in a few days."

Enough, Artie thought. Everything Phil said brought back visions of the night with Colleen. Blackberries along the Sandy River. But with her it was about love, not sex.

"When we went rowing the next day, I took the middle seat out of the rowboat and we spread a few blankets on the bottom. We rowed down the river past a curve where there're some nice pools below the trees and then started necking. Things were getting pretty hot and heavy. She was in the bottom of the boat and it wasn't too comfortable, but somehow I got the bottom of her swimsuit off."

Phil fell silent for a moment, as if enjoying the event once more. "Things were getting pretty wild by this time. I felt a few bumps and thought she was really getting turned on—but when they got wilder, I realized it wasn't Sheila but the boat. I raised up and looked around, afraid some of the kids had swum out and were rocking us, and I saw a swirl of white water. We'd floated five miles downstream to the rapids."

Ray whooped. "Let me sail her five miles and see how she responds to the rudder."

"Aw shit!" Phil said. "You wouldn't know an oar from an oarlock."

"Come on you guys." Artie stopped the banter, urging Phil to go on. "What'd you do then?"

"Well, Sheila kept pulling my head down and I kept looking up at the waves. She was getting off on the roller-coaster action and I was getting queasy from some of the wine we'd drunk on the beach! We went along like this with me struggling to get up, and getting pulled back down or falling on her every time the boat dipped or bounced off a rock. She must've orgasmed about the same time as I threw up because we were both moaning when the boat up and flipped on us. Talk about cold water. Shit! What a shock!"

Phil shook his head, pausing so the rest could share his marvel. "By the time we got the boat back we realized Sheila had lost the bottom of her two-piece suit. I laughed and she got real bitchy. Said it was all my fault. I loaned her my T-shirt, which was just long enough when she was standing to cover her bottom. I was facing her on the slow trip back up the river and she could see I was horny as hell. She was pissed by then though so I had to get rid of my frustration by rowing like a mad man. Can't wait till this fall at the old U of O. I'm go to lay a boatload of broads."

"Nice alliteration," Ray said.

"Too bad Artie's going to Italy to study." Phil hit him on the arm. "Course I guess some of those European gals ain't bad."

Artie had written Phil about his change in plans. Midway through June, he'd received a brochure from the university about the state's overseas program in Pavia. Usually only juniors were admitted but Artie had applied and was accepted, due to his having already taken a year of Italian and written an honor's thesis on an Italian poet. He'd been recommended by one of his teachers, Professor Kantubus, who was going over to direct the program.

"How are your savings doing anyway?" Phil knew from Artie's letters that his father never helped with Artie's school finances, other than by giving him a job. Which at least was something, he'd told Artie.

"Not too good. My dad's started asking for thirty bucks a month rent. I think he's irritated I didn't ask his permission to go. The only time I heard him say anything about it was when I told everyone at the dinner table that I was going, and he said he thought I was too young. He wants me to finish school and then go. But at worst I'm going to borrow a thousand from the government."

Ray, tired of the conversation, mentioned that they'd better call it a night and Artie agreed. He wanted them off the project before the foremen showed up around 7:30. Not too long now.

After they'd left, Artie stretched his cramped legs, yawned, and then headed off to make his final rounds. He hoped the night lasted a bit longer. Being on the job was better than being home doing chores. He'd gotten so he almost hated to see the sun rise.

"Sun of a bitch!" he exclaimed out loud and grinned, looking around sheepishly to make sure he was alone.

# — 3 —
## *Pastoral*

Artie had one more chance to talk to Phil that summer before leaving for Europe. It was in September, on a night when clouds, racing across the sky on rain-dimpled feet, not only hinted at storms to come but made sure they fulfilled their promise. The last cutting of hay was in, and what stubble of alfalfa remained to thrive in the showers would be grazed by the Angus, delighted as always at the green treat, although it invariably gave them diarrhea.

Phil, dressed in brown cords and a Levi jacket, arrived at eight and Artie ushered him through the jumble of theater seats they'd recycled for the congregation, by the pulpit his dad had built, and up to his bare cell. In the corner, a small green electric heater purred. Draughts of cold roamed down the hall and snuck under the curtain door into his room.

Artie sat at his desk, wearing over his clothes a checkered flannel bathrobe that had belonged to his late grandmother. Phil, for lack of a chair, had slipped out of his tennis shoes and was lounging on the small bed. Artie offered him some Cinnamon Bears, hoping the heat of the candy would help with the early chill.

The coming storm and a comment of Phil's about his own dad had reminded Artie of a childhood experience when his father was a minister of a small church in Wenatchee. "I must've been in the second or third grade then. We moved so much with my dad starting new churches that by the time I was in the fifth grade I'd been to six schools. Anyway, let me tell you what my dad—".

"Let's start a card game, okay?" Phil interrupted. "And then you can tell me." He sat up against the headboard, arranging the pillow behind his back, while Artie fetched the cards from a storage closet outside his room.

"How about Five Hundred?" Phil suggested, cutting the lower cards out of the deck and adding a Joker. Having shuffled and dealt the hand, he sat back to listen. "So what'd he do?"

"Well, we lived above a church there too, only it was in the basement of a big house with this huge orchard behind it. A guy named Kellogg ran a wrecking yard on the other side of the orchard and owned the place. He let us stay free since there wasn't much money coming in."

"Poor suckers as always, eh?"

"Yeah. In fact I used to go through the orchard and over a big board fence to get to his wrecking yard to look for money. I liked ransacking the smashed cars for loose change and whatever else I could find. I always figured if I got enough money I could buy a Dusty Burger. They were these fantastic hamburgers that we could only afford once or twice a year."

Artie stared at the cards in his hand, pondering which to play. "Anyway, I'd brought some loose change home one day and stacked it on the kitchen counter. I don't remember if I thought I had enough for the whole family or what. Well, when my dad saw it, he wanted to know where that came from. When I said from the glove compartment of the wrecked cars, he whacked me on the side of the head and informed me he was going to have to teach me not to steal. Shit, I didn't think anybody cared about what was in junked cars!

"He told me I was going to get a whipping but I'd better get a move on first, take the money back, and apologize to the Kelloggs. I trudged through the wet orchard, getting drenched. It was raining like crazy. I climbed on the porch, knocked, and no one answered at first. I remember I stood there and started to cry. I knew I couldn't go home until I gave the money back."

The isolation of his room, the rain drumming on the roof, the coziness lent themselves to melodrama. Both Artie and Phil had stopped playing cards, mulling over the vagaries of adults and the vulnerability of kids.

"Finally, I opened the screen door and knocked again. Someone finally opened the door. It was Mrs. Kellogg, this massive, matronly woman, must have weighed about 250 pounds. She stood there with her apron on. I couldn't even speak. I just stared up at her with my hand out, money lying there, feeling the warmth from behind her as it rushed out.

She took me inside, dried my head with a kitchen towel, and set me down beside her. She'd just baked some whole wheat bread and she gave me a slice, warm and moist with butter. When I told her about the money, she tried to get me to keep it."

"If you were slick," Phil joked, to lighten the mood, "you probably could have bummed an extra dollar out of her!"

"Yeah. She was even going to call my dad and tell him it was okay. I got scared then that if she did I'd really get my butt tanned. You know, the only reason he put off my punishment until I returned was to torture me. He knew the more I thought about it the worse it'd be."

Angered anew, Artie rose "Let me make sure the hall window is closed tight," he said and walked out of the room and down to the window, feeling emotions still raw after twelve years. At the top of the long hill on the other side of the creek, a string of street lights stretched small and unreal like a hazy string of pearls. Occasionally a car passed, first a funnel of white light and then a glow of red.

Phil stepped out into the hall. "It's lightning, huh?"

"Just flash lightning over the horizon. I can't hear much thunder."

The two stood at the window, waiting for the lightning to illuminate the valley. When it did, Artie could make out the three milk cows, standing with their muzzles to the fence, looking toward the shed. "I hope the electric fence doesn't conk out," Artie said. "I should've trimmed the grass under that bottom line last week."

"What'll the grass do?"

"Probably ground it out if it gets wet enough. The damn cows can sniff the wire and tell if it's electrified. Hate to chase them all night and then try to fix fence in the rain."

The door on the small gray house opened and a shaft of light illuminated the gravel driveway running around both buildings. "Shit!" Artie drew back from the window.

"That's my dad. Let's go back in my room."

On the bed, heart pounding as if he'd been caught stealing from the collection plate, Artie heard the back door slam downstairs and the footsteps of his father as he moved past the washer and dryer, then out near the shop, and finally into the bathroom.

"Thank God," he whispered. "I thought it was work."

"What's he doing?"

"He's using the bathroom over here. The septic tank for the other house caved in about two years ago. We haven't got it fixed yet. It used to be a well until an old lady who lived here filled it with cans. I had to dig it out down to about six feet. I don't think my dad will ever get around to fixing it."

They sat silent, waiting, until Artie's father finished and left. It seemed to take him forever. "Probably read the whole damn *Reader's Digest*," Artie said.

"Or," Phil cracked, "a *Playboy*."

"Does your dad read *Playboy*?"

"Shit, he's got a whole drawer full of nudie mags. You'll have to come over sometime. He's a little weird but you'll like him."

"Weird?"

"Real sensitive. Not much of an education. He works as a janitor, earns less than me. He's always trying to let me know how much he loves me."

"That's nice."

"Sometimes." Phil shrugged, flicking his arms to the side. "But I get bugged by it. You know what I did the other night?"

Artie shook his head.

"We were sitting there watching TV. He jumps up all of a sudden, scoots over and put his arm around me. I didn't say anything or pat him on the leg, so after a while he kisses me on the cheek. I jumped up about two feet, shouted 'You queer!' and moved over to another chair."

Phil laughed when he saw Artie's shocked look. "That's no big deal," he said. "One other night when we were sitting there, I kept hitting my shoes together like this."

Phil proceeded to demonstrate, putting his heels together and scissoring his stocking feet from a V to a closed position. "'That'd probably really hurt, wouldn't it,' my dad said, 'if a guy put his hand in there.' So I said, 'Go ahead, dad, try it.' 'No,' he said. 'You'd probably really smash hard.' 'No I won't,' I said. I spread the toes of my shoes apart. 'Go ahead. Don't you trust me? Come on, dad. Don't tell me you don't even trust your own son! I won't snap my toes.'".

Phil was enjoying himself, acting out the parts as he spoke.

"'Aw, I trust you,' he said, 'but I don't want to do it.' 'Aw, Dad, you don't trust me or you'd do it.'"

"Did he put his hand in?"

"Listen. 'Well,' he said, 'do you promise you won't swing your toes shut?' 'I promise,'" I said. So my dad stuck his finger in."

"What'd you do?"

"Smashed my feet together." Phil grinned.

"How could you!" Artie threw back his head, slapping his forehead. "Did you hurt him?"

Phil shrugged. "More emotionally than physically."

"You didn't plan on doing it, did you?"

"Sure! Why not?"

"If I'd done that to my dad, he'd knock me silly."

"Shit, you could pound your old man." Phil struck his fist in the other palm. "Cream him. Knock him on his ass."

Artie shook his head. "He's had all us kids terrorized for years. I should tell you about the night a year ago when I was a senior." Artie got up and looked down the hall to make sure no one was there. "I just want to make sure my older brother isn't home yet. He's out with some girl."

"Does he sleep here, too?"

"Yeah. His room's down next to the nursery." The nursery, still filled with old toys from its Sunday School days, perched to the left of Artie's room by the stairs.

"Anyway, we'd gone over to Aurora to a feedmill to haul some grain after school one day. I had to miss basketball practice. It was another one of these gray days and I've told you what the threat of rain does to my dad. There was already a light mist on the windows when we arrived, so we covered the oats with a tarp and set off for home. By the time we got the tractor and hammermill lined up it was about ten o'clock and pitch black."

"Black as a sick turd, eh?" Phil said, and Artie nodded.

"We worked all night in a light drizzle, me shoveling grain into the hammermill from under the tarp and Richy standing inside the barn shoveling the powder away from the mouth of the chute. When we finished about three that morning, we found Bossy, she's our Jersey, standing under an eave near the calf pen and we knew the fence had to be down. No way she could jump it."

"What's this got to do with your dad?"

"Well, we spent the rest of the night until chore time in the morning chasing the cows. You know how bleak a wet cloudy dawn is around here. We had an east wind blasting down the Columbia gorge that morning that about froze my hands off. Anyway, while it was still dark, I remember my dad in the pickup with the lights bouncing up and down. He's chasing our bull over this field that's rough as hell. My dad got so mad, he started hitting the bull with the bumper and knocking him around. I was hanging on to the mirror and standing on the running board on the passenger side, trying to yell at him to stop, but I don't think he heard a word with the truck rattling, the bull bellowing, and the rain drizzling down in sheets. Richy was out in the field, waving his arms like mad, afraid the bull would slip and we'd run him over. My dad wasn't satisfied until all the animals were as scared of him as all of us kids were."

Phil laughed. "So, you knock him down and he'll come at you with the pickup."

"Yeah, I'll have to duel him with the tractor! Can't you just imagine us some night out there in the field bashing into each other?"

Phil admitted as to how he could. "If it was me and my dad, he'd be on his knees with his arms spread telling me how sorry he was and thanking me for sharing my aggression with him."

"Didn't your dad ever whip you?"

"Nope. He knows I'd never be back."

"Well, I got whipped plenty, at least till I reached High School. After that, I was bigger than my dad and he just cuffed me on the head whenever he got angry."

"What's the worst he's done?"

Artie thought a moment. "The worst whipping was when I was in the third grade in Seattle. We lived in the west hills in a real poor area at the time. My best friend was a kid a year younger whose father was in the penitentiary. He had this sister in the seventh grade who was always trying to show her pussy to my older brother.

"Anyway, this kid and I started skipping school and going down to the Sound to look at the crabs and find shells. After one stretch, where I'd been out of school two weeks straight, we decided to run away.

"Right below our apartment there was this woods which always scared us a bit because someone had started a rumor about a witch who kept people in cages. We'd seen her shack from a distance. I was poking around in a garbage pit in the woods once and saw what looked like a bloody penis wrapped in napkins. It was probably just part of a hot dog or something but we were still scared shitless.

"Since we were running away, this kid and I decided to walk through the woods and on toward White Center. We went by this huge tree stump we'd seen before. His sister was always climbing on it since it was cut like a chair and would pull down her panties and sit there saying 'fuck me, fuck me,' all the while playing with herself. I was too dumb to do anything about it and so was my brother I think, even though he was in the fifth grade."

"Shit," Phil said, envious. "I was already jacking off by the fifth grade. I must of grown up around tame girls. The only one who ever did anything was this girl who'd squat in the playground and wet her pants for us." Phil grinned. "Exciting, huh?"

Artie smiled and continued his story. "We kept on going that day, past the witch's house, past a nettle patch we'd always been afraid to cross, and finally into this clearing with a pile of old rotting logs. It looked like some place where bums slept or guys brought girls, so we were feeling a few goose bumps. I was suddenly possessed with a desire to start a fire. Maybe the third grade is a fire-bug stage. I wanted to burn the whole damn forest down."

"Yeah, I'm familiar with the feeling. We all have a bit of the arson in us."

"Well, we tried with match after match to get a fire going, but when our pile of rubbish finally caught fire all it did was to scorch one tree about ten feet up the side.

"We walked for what seemed hours that afternoon and got as far as White Center but still hadn't found any watermelon patches to live off as we'd planned! We hadn't had much luck bumming dimes for fake phone calls so no treats. We did smoke any cigarette butts we found longer than half an inch!

"Oh wow, do I remember what happened when we gave up and went back home. My mom had called the school when I didn't show up by five. 'Was he in school today?' she asked and they say, 'Today! He hasn't been in school for two weeks!'

"The police had been looking for us all afternoon, and my older brother had been down to the Sound. I guess they were afraid I'd drowned. Anyway, I got home just before my dad did and begged my mom not to tell him. She did, of course, and he took me down to the basement, made me drop my pants and underpants and lie over a block of firewood.

"I was quivering before the leather strap ever hit me. Talk about a whipping! He took me upstairs afterward to show my back, bottom, and thighs to my two brothers as a warning to them. I remember walking by the clock on the stove and seeing I'd been down there fifteen minutes. It seemed forever. I had welts and bloody grooves all over my butt."

Phil shook his head. "Boy, I see why you've wanted to leave home. I don't see how you can stand it here in the summer."

"It's always a pleasure," Artie observed ironically, "to go from the groves of academe to the dales of pastoral wonderlands!"

Yeah," Phil added, exaggerating the countrified negatives, "only here there ain't no nude nymphs!"

"Well, if there were, my dad would have them out feeding slop to the pigs." Contemplating the scene, they laughed once more.

The next week, on a Monday at six a.m., Artie was to leave Portland with a group of forty-two other students. All would be going first by bus to Vancouver, British Columbia, then by train to Montreal, and finally by plane to Milan. When Monday came, Artie got up at four and finished his chores in a hurry. Just as he was preparing to go in and clean up, his father came out of the barn, carrying the milk pail.

"Take the cows out to pasture," he ordered. "And let the Angus into the north field."

Turning away, teeth clenched, Artie did as he was told without saying a word. Out in the field, by himself, he swore out loud. "Damn bastard!" Trying to make me as late as possible. Just to prove his authority. For a moment he felt like kicking and screaming at the Angus to get them to move faster, but he knew that wouldn't help. A few calm words and a little gentleness did better.

This is the last time I'll see the herd for some time, he thought. No use having a last memory of beating them. I'll leave that up to dad.

After closing the fence, he was called over to the back porch where his father was mixing milk with the pig feed. "Did you finish burning that hay I asked you to?" His father was referring to a pile of rotten, moldy hay by the barn, hay ruined by last winter's rain and then left to dry in the summer sun.

Artie was forced to say "no," his heart picking up a beat, fear rising in his throat.

"I thought I told you to get that done before you left?" His father hadn't raised his head from over the slop buckets. He continued to pour and stir.

Artie swallowed hard. "I, uh, I worked on it all week ... in the day ... before going to work but part of it's still pretty damp. It wouldn't burn."

"Did you paint any?"

The question struck doom in his heart. Artie was too scared to respond for a moment, thinking of lies.

"A little," he managed to mutter.

"Why weren't you working then? You'll have all year to paint and fool around. How are we supposed to get it burnt this fall with the rain?"

Artie stood there silent, unable to respond, hoping somehow he could ride this one out.

"Well?" his father said brusquely, standing and facing Artie, the mixing stick in his hand. Artie's eyes dropped from his dad's face to the stick, as if leery of a blow.

"I just painted a little at night when I couldn't see to work." He shifted uneasily while his father picked up the pails. Would it be sycophantic to offer to help? He didn't have much time and this was his dad's job, but guilt and fear had set him on edge.

"What are you standing there for?"

"I was listening to you. Can I go in now?" The question quiet, almost plaintive. Unable to show it, Artie burned with anger, while at the same time he was ashamed that he was forced to submit to his father's whims.

The old man didn't reply. He set the buckets on the edge of the porch and stepped back to pour some milk into one of the calves' pails. Artie stood on the porch for what seemed another eternity before asking again if he could go inside. It was as if permission to go in meant permission to go on the trip.

"Git," his father said grudgingly.

After washing, combing his hair, and shaving, Artie woke his mother and asked her to drive him in to the Greyhound station in Portland.

"Have you asked your father?"

*Oh, good God!* "Can't you just take me?"

"You know what he says if I do something without asking him first. Why didn't you ask him last night?"

"I didn't think of it."

Actually, Artie had been afraid to accost his father and broach so openly the question of his going. He could imagine the conversation: "Dad, can mom drive me in to Portland tomorrow morning?" "What for?" "I have to be there at six to catch the bus." "What bus?" "The one that's taking us up to Vancouver so we can get to Italy." "Who said you could go to Italy?" And there it would be. He'd never really asked his father for permission. His father had signed some papers for a loan but that was all. Artie had been hoping that it was just tacitly agreed he could go, since he'd gone ahead and paid the money and it was all his own.

Crap, he thought, heading reluctantly out to the fence by the pig pens to track down his dad. He's always talking about us kids using our own initiative and we have to ask to walk across the street!

He was so surprised his dad said yes that he added, "I'll pay for the gas."

When they were ready to leave, his father came out from the barn and prayed for his safety at the car window. "Guide his life, oh Lord," he said in closing, "so that through him thine own will might be accomplished. May he shine forth as a light for your glory. We ask all these things in Christ's name. Amen."

With that, Artie and his mother drove down the gravel road and out to the highway. There had been no saying "good-bye," no shaking of hands. Artie looked back over his shoulder at the farm buildings, the fields, the orchard, and the woods silent in the fading darkness of dawn. He shook his head as the car picked up speed on the paved road. Shit! he was thinking, what a way to begin a trip.

# — 4 —
## The Crossing

Howard Montrel stopped by the compartment around ten o'clock and in between puffs on his pipe asked Artie if he wanted to go up to the club car.

"I don't think I can, Howard. I'm only nineteen."

Howard pondered Artie's response for a moment, eyeing him as if to determine his age. "I don't think they'll even ask you for ID. I was up there earlier. They never asked me. I had a scotch with soda."

"Yeah, but you're of age."

"You look as old as I do though—".

"But not as ugly," Artie interjected.

Howard, instead of grinning, looked peeved. "They don't care how old we are." He shrugged. "As long as we pay."

Artie laid down his book—he was reading Barzini's *The Italians*—and rose. "Why don't we go back to the dome car first. I have some stuff I want to write in my diary."

"I guess. I can write a letter to my girl and then maybe we can get something. I'm supposed to meet Bruce Jenkins for a drink later."

The two walked through several cars, now dim. Most of the berths were already made up, but here and there a few people sat on the edge of their bunks, talking in whispers.

Howard, a year older than Artie, as were most of the students in the group, led the way. He was a tall youth, in truth not very handsome Artie thought, with a forehead that slanted back at an angle. His mother was of German origin and her stolidity was evident in Howard. When he walked, he plodded forward, heavy-footed and already a little fat in the belly like a married man.

They paused in the vestibule of each car and looked out into the night. The sky extended pitch black but occasionally as the train made a turn they could see the long line of cars, with the rotating white beam ahead of the engine. At other times, sporadic lights flashed by, houses dimly flickering.

When they reached the end of one car, Howard opened a window and stuck his head out. "Sure feels fresh," he said as if he were a foreigner practicing a strange language. Howard's hair, Artie noticed again when the wind hit it, appeared to be cut by his father. The sides were shaved high, and the front—stiff and close-cut also— jutted forward sharply over his slanting forehead. Weird guy. He's always wearing a sport coat. Makes his hair look worse.

Reaching the dome car, they found it nearly empty. At the back, an old gentleman and his wife sat napping. Artie and Howard picked a seat on the left near the front. While Artie opened his diary, Howard, methodical in all his actions, refilled his pipe and began to smoke. The two chatted for a half hour and then sat in silence writing.

Howard interrupted the stillness. "I think I'll move back a seat, Artie. I can't think with you writing beside me."

"Afraid I'll peek at your letter?"

He could tell by his frown that Howard hadn't caught the light tone. "It's just too hard to concentrate," he said, sliding into the seat behind.

Artie felt like asking him if he was writing a philosophical treatise to his girl. Be kind. Maybe the guy just wants to be alone to think about her. Wonder what she's like. Howard had mentioned her briefly but hadn't gone in to detail. Toni Walters, the name was all that stuck.

---

The monotonous clicking of the wheels on the rails warmed and relaxed Artie. He lay back in the seat, his pen gripped loosely, and thought back over the last few days.

He'd met Howard on the bus to Vancouver and when Artie learned he was from Orient an instant bond had formed. "We used to cut alfalfa and buy grain in that area!" United by geographical proximity, the two had spent most of their time together on first the bus and then the slow train trip across Canada.

Howard leaned forward. "How you coming?"

"Haven't written much yet. I was just thinking about the trip."

Howard cleaned his pipe in the ashtray and to the knocking of the pipe bowl Artie's mind returned to Vancouver. It was at the Central Station there that he'd first learned Patty Darr was in the group—the girl in his biology lab who thought he was cute. He'd stopped to buy a postcard and a little pin with a Canadian maple leaf for his sister, Robin, when he heard two girls talking behind him. He'd turned to see Patty and she'd smiled and stopped to talk.

"I saw you on the bus up front," she said, "but I didn't have a chance to say anything."

He grinned. "I'm kind of surprised to see you." He wondered if Phil had gotten along with her on his date, but didn't ask. Patty introduced the girl with her as Laura Torrelli. "Oh, are you Italian?"

"Kind of. My father is but I don't speak the language." She was an angular girl, tall and skinny, with long dark hair that looked as if it had never been cut. Her face was plain and the thought flashed across Artie's mind that she'd look better as a boy. By comparison, Patty was attractive, a little heavy perhaps, but pretty for a big-boned girl.

"What are you doing?" both girls asked in unison and giggled.

Artie showed them the pin and told them he was getting it for his younger sister. "Gee, it must be nice," Laura said, "to have an older brother like you." She took his arm and Artie laughed, a blush settling on his cheeks. He talked to them for about fifteen minutes and then excused himself to take care of his baggage.

On the train, he and Howard had sat down next to the two girls and they'd played cards until dinner time. Artie had eaten with Patty and after dinner, she'd suggested they go to the dome car for a while.

The car was dark except for a few footlights and Artie, feeling Patty's body beside his, was filled with longing. Reflections on the window blotted out everything so Patty had pressed her face against the glass to see out. Artie put his head next to hers, leaning across her, and felt the warmth and pressure send a tingle up his back.

"Oh look!" she said, jumping. "The engine's going into a tunnel!" Artie wanted to kiss her then but hesitated. He really didn't know her well. She might be offended. I'm just another guy on the train. Someone she met in a lab class. He couldn't tell if she felt the same attraction he did.

Going back to their berths, Patty stopped to talk to some friends, balancing herself with her hands on the seats, and Artie took advantage of the train's swaying to let his hand fall on and off hers. She probably didn't even notice, he thought now.

Howard leaned forward again, interrupting his thoughts. "I should be meeting Bruce Jenkins pretty soon," he said. "How about heading off in about fifteen minutes?"

"That's fine," Artie said, dating a page in his diary and then closing it. He still didn't feel like writing. It was easier in the darkness of the car to daydream.

He thought back to the second day on the train. In Edmonton, the conductor had announced a twenty-five minute stop. Getting off to mail a letter, Artie had seen Patty standing along the tracks.

"Hi," she yelled, pointing downtown, "let's walk up that way. We have enough time to see a bit of the city." They'd walked together up the street, looking at the storefronts. Artie thought of holding her hand but couldn't get the nerve. The most he dared was to brush hands every now and then as they walked.

"I think I'll buy some Lifesavers," he announced, to give purpose to their window gazing. "Let's see if they have them here."

They walked into two stores without any luck. Finally they spied a corner drugstore and Artie picked up a pack of Doublemint gum and a couple of rolls of Wint-O-Green Lifesavers.

Outside again, Patty looked at her watch and shrieked with dismay. "Come on," she cried, "we'll miss the train if we don't hurry and it'll be your fault. You and your darn Lifesavers."

When they dashed up, the train was already in motion, and, to make matters worse, as they clambered aboard the conductor said, "You kids is awful lucky. If we'd been on time, you'd never've made it." Patty gave Artie a dirty look and walked off without speaking.

Later, when he offered her a Lifesaver, she blurted out, "I don't want any of those Canadian Lifesavers. That's what made us late." Artie, uncertain if she were joking or serious, couldn't think of a reply, though he felt like saying, "Well, it was your stupid idea to go uptown in the first place."

That night, Howard, Artie, Laura, and Patty had gone to the dining car to play bingo. When they arrived, a crowd waited for the start of the game, but they managed to get four chairs around a small table. Patty, sitting next to Howard, jokingly promised the guys a kiss if either one won.

"I'll do the same for you," Howard had shouted.

Artie stared at him. Damn. The guy wasn't usually so exuberant.

Though embarrassed at not offering the same, he said nothing. He was beginning to wonder about Howard. Artie couldn't tell who Patty liked best. She was friendly to everyone—and that seemed strange to him.

After bingo—none of the four had won—they were returning to their car when Patty began to hang back with Howard. Artie could see she did it on purpose. She would wait until they started down a car and then would stop, with Howard behind her, while Artie walked ahead to open the door. The first time, he held it open for Laura and then waited for the other two to catch up. They were laughing and joking and Artie, not having heard what Patty had whispered, felt he was the object of their laughter.

When the two played the same trick in the second car, he left them and went ahead with Laura. For the rest of the evening he was angry at himself, first for not being more outgoing and then for liking someone as outgoing as Patty. It bothered him that even staid Howard with his clumsy pipe smoking and stodgy conversation was more sociable and more expansive with the girls than he.

Artie still hadn't written anything in his diary and Howard was talking. "I guess we'd better head off to find Bruce. He's probably waiting at the bar."

In the club car, after Howard had cautioned Artie not to act nervous or excited—to Artie's aggravation—they ordered their drinks, world-wise Howard a scotch and soda and Artie, after looking at a bar menu, a rye whisky with Coke. A few minutes later Bruce walked in.

"Hey, man! Where've you been?" he asked Howard, a large smile breaking out as he clapped him on the shoulder. "I've been all over this train."

Artie had seen Bruce once or twice but had never spoken to him. After they'd been introduced, Howard told him Bruce was majoring in medicine at Corvallis.

"Won't this year abroad drop you behind for med school?"

Bruce looked at him as if he were dumb. "No way. This is my last year of pre-med and they want me to acquire a little general culture. We have to learn how to spend those big bucks with class."

There was something about Bruce that made Artie dislike him at first acquaintance. Outwardly, he seemed pleasant, but Artie had noticed a haughty look. He had the air of some of the Easterners Artie had met at the university his Freshman year. Bruce, he'd observed, was the best dressed guy among them. He wore a clean, tailored shirt every day and Artie had never seen the same tie on him twice.

"Well," Howard said, "we have the night in Montreal to look forward to and in the morning the flight to Italy."

"Yeah." Bruce sipped his drink. "Some of us in the group—guys and gals," he winked, "are going to make arrangements to spend the night in a hotel near the airport. You want to come, Howard?"

"Sure."

"How 'bout you, Dave?" Bruce added, constrained by the silence.

"Artie, you mean."

"Ah," he raised his hands, as if in a sign of benediction. "That's right … "

Artie felt his face flush. "Thanks for asking, but I guess I'll just look around the city."

The other two stared at him.

Can they tell why I turned down the offer? No money for such a luxury. He'd never in his life slept in a hotel. He planned on walking until dawn. "I thought I might as well see the city while I can."

"Actually, that sounds like fun," Howard said. "If you don't mind, Bruce, I think I'll cancel and go with Artie."

Bruce shrugged. "Suit yourself. You'll be pretty tired though on the flight tomorrow."

To change the subject, Artie brought up an idea he'd had for a painting. Earlier in the day he'd shown Howard an illustration from the text he would be using in his art history class in Pavia—Janson's *History of Art*. The work was Pollaiuolo's bronze statue of "Hercules and Antaeus," which showed the two nude men locked in combat. Telling Bruce about the work, he said, "Now, I want to see what you think. I already know Howard's response."

Artie asked because, when he'd told Howard about his idea earlier, Howard's reaction had been to look him coldly in the eyes and say "crude," putting into the one world all the disgust of an old Puritan discovering his son beating off in the wood shed.

---

"My idea is to paint two people in the same position making love. It'll be called 'Ecstasy.' So, what d'you think?"

Bruce pounded the table. "Pure pornography," he hooted, "I love it! Give me more!"

Artie pursed his lips. "It's supposed to represent pure love." He was aggravated that Howard had joined Bruce in laughing.

"Kid," Bruce said, "you got a lot to learn. One good fuck and that'll cure your romanticism."

"You guys are both screwed up," Artie said, rising. "I'm going back to my berth."

To Artie it seemed he'd just fallen asleep when the train came squeaking to a stop in Montreal. It was nearly three in the morning and outside, the air stretched cool as a tight sheet. Puffs of steam rose along the track where the engine had dripped water.

Taking leave of Bruce and a group of girls, Howard and Artie left the station, walking through a tunnel built to protect passersby from a construction project. Howard, who'd asked directions in French, led the way into the French quarter, where they stopped at an all-night grocery store to buy some seedless grapes.

In the distance, the tall spire of a church rose as if to do battle with evil spirits. As they drew near, passing tenement houses leaning against each other for support in rough old age, the cathedral, etched in black against dark blue, loomed above them. At the entrance, they heard muffled voices and stopped on the steps.

"Where are they coming from?" Artie whispered.

"It's hard to tell," Howard said. He grabbed Artie's arm. "Look! Over there."

Beneath a large oak tree Artie made out a bench and two dark shapes.

"Come join us, my good fellows," they heard someone call. "We're merry thespians having a drop to quench our thirst."

Neither Artie nor Howard moved. The two figures seemed to ignore them, as if not expecting an answer.

Arms around each other's shoulders, the self-styled actors moved off up the street, shouting lines histrionically into the night air.

Howard sneered. "Talk about drunks."

"They're just improvising. Let's see where they go."

They followed the two men, now just shadows in the distance. Under the street lamps, set far apart, the air tingled like colored confetti.

When they came up within hearing distance, the squeaky-voiced little shadow was gesticulating. "No, but King Christ, this world is all aleak."

"You know what they say, don't you?" the big fellow cried, turning his head slightly as if he'd seen or heard them following.

There was a moment of silence. "What's that?" his companion finally asked.

"I read in the paper yesterday …" He raised his hands as if in benediction. "That the U. S. of A. is going to declare peace on the world."

Suddenly it seemed to Artie as if they'd come to a vast gulf and the forms halted at the edge and then disappeared. No street lights any longer.

Howard put his arm out. "It looks like an old sand pit."

"Do you know where we are, Howard?"

"Don't worry. We'll find our way back. We've got several hours yet."

"A couple of hours, you mean. We should be back by six or seven at latest."

The two scrambled down an incline and found a series of steps leading in stages farther down the hill.

"Maybe it's a park," Artie said.

In the distance, as they stopped on a landing, they heard the thin squeaky voice again, "But see how these Christians love one another?" The two figures were now so far away that the voice of the larger fellow was indistinct.

Standing there, uncertain whether to go on or head back, they listened in the darkness. Occasionally they heard what sounded like small showers of rock and sand. They'd made up their minds to return, when all of a sudden Howard jerked, let out a blood curdling yell, and started dancing up and down, running in place like a madman.

Artie jumped away, his hair on end. "Oh Lordy," he let out. An old man with no legs had grabbed Howard around the knees. A grizzled wino with fiery eyes, he slobbered over his beard as he gummed some indecipherable words.

Howard's dance freed him from the fellow's grasp and took off. He jumped down three steps, tripped, rolled down a few more, landed in some gravel, got up and tore off with Artie hard on his heels. The old wino looked after them with his arms raised. "Up the stairs," he croaked, "the stairs."

"No way I'm turning back." Howard had finally slowed down.

Artie agree. After a moment, he said, "I got a feeling this is going to be one hell of a trip."


When Artie and Howard came out of the gloom to a street with lights, they were lost. Drawing near a railroad trestle, they decided to follow the tracks, hoping the way led back to the main station. They found themselves near a canal and what appeared to be a series of locks. A freight train rumbled up from behind and curved off on a side track. After the train passed, the wind picked up and they were showered with the brittle, autumn leaves of an ancient tree.

Going through an industrial district, the streets barren and stiff, and then by a small, brick Methodist church, Howard, out of the blue, said, "You hear what that guy said? About Christianity? I hate all religions."

Damn! Never heard anybody so adamant.

"It's used to exploit people," Howard said. "I'm an atheist."

"Really." Howard was the first person he'd ever heard admit that. "My father was a minister, along with a few other occupations. I pretty much rebel against everything he stood for." But he'd never had the courage to say he was an atheist. "But maybe there's a cosmic consciousness."

"Bullshit. Let me tell you why."

And off Howard went, talking about how religions were man-made and if you had to be religious, well then, maybe the oldest one was best. You know, paganism.

Walking through the train station to the restrooms, Artie stopped listening. "Will we ever get to Italy?" he said, to change the subject. "I can't wait."

"Yeah, I won't believe it till we get there."


Later, while Howard napped on a bench in the train station, Artie wandered over to a large glassed-in area and gazed absentmindedly at the window. It was impossible to see through it. Outside, the night, still impenetrable, paused, on the edge of dawn and activity. Though Artie didn't notice it, in fact hadn't yet even begun to look for it, on the inside of the window lay a pale, distorted, almost imperceptible form. His reflection.

# — 5 —
# *Venus*

D ripping wet and chilled from the November night, Artie slipped in the big front door of the *Foresteria Universitaria* in Venice and made his way up two flights of marble stairs, down a long high corridor with gray lockers on each side and finally around a corner and into a small cubicle. Behind him his soggy shoes left a trail of large pointed footprints.

The room, which he'd rented for a week with the regular student inhabitant on break, was simple and bare. Inside the door, to the right, squatted a dwarfish table, books running its meager length against the wall. The back wall, also gray, was bare except for a chair and, to the left, a miniature steam heater to which he now rushed. Along the left wall stood a small bed, leaving just enough room at the head for a fragile lamp stand and the door.

Having opened the heater valve, Artie sat on the edge of the bed, too tired at the moment to remove his wet clothes. The heater, clanking, began to send out some warmth, which set him instantly to shivering. Taking off his flannel shirt, he ran his fingers through his hair in front of the heater, listening to the hungry sputtering as the drops of water hit the hot metal.

He'd spent the last two hours struggling to find his way back to the hostel. It had taken him almost an hour in the maze of canals to find San Marco—the island of San Giorgio Maggiore covered in mist—and then to make his way to the Wooden Bridge. From there, lost in a plethora of smaller waterways, it had taken another hour to wind his way out of the maze, crossing small footbridges here, larger ones there, watching the canals become tight and dark, listening to the scrape of tarp-covered dinghies tied up along the quay.

It had been a disastrous night, "climaxed"—the pun was involuntary—by a hasty leap out a second story window into a canal.

How'd I ever get involved with Gina Bargutto?

The heater was already too hot so Artie removed his soaking pants and hung them over the chair to dry. At the small desk, he opened his diary and reread the entry for the trip to Rome. Hettie Whitney had asked him to accompany her in a group outing late one evening—and he'd accepted, since she was one of the prettier girls in the program. He held hands with her and enjoyed the evening but was surprised that night when Howard told him Hettie was engaged. A strange girl, Howard said. He told Artie about the weekend when he and Hettie had hitchhiked to Perugia together. They'd slept in the same room, he said, the same bed even, to save money. He'd turned his back when Hettie undressed and they'd slept back to back.

Poor Howard, Artie thought. He's such a clumsy oaf. He'll never make it with a girl—not that I'm doing much better.

He got up from the table and looked through his flight bag for a roll. He'd skipped dinner. He felt a little lonely for Pavia although he knew he would miss Venice when he left.

In Pavia, he'd been allowed by Professor Kantubus to take an advanced art class even though he had no previous course work in painting. Talk about pressure. He'd never painted the human body before. In the first session, when they worked with charcoal, Artie had felt like dying. With only seven students, each received personal attention. When the instructor, Talori, came by his easel, he erased everything Artie had done and in a minute had redrawn it.

At the rest period, he told Artie to turn his sheet over and start fresh. During the long second half of class, Talori said nothing. He would come and stand behind Artie's back, watching, and then go on to another student. Artie was still trying to get the basic form and the others were already shading and working on the facial features.

The model was a bleached blonde in her thirties, flabby in the legs and rear, with sagging breasts. Before the class began, Artie had been jittery, wondering what his reaction would be to a nude model. He was disappointed when she wasn't as pretty as he'd imagined.

After class the first day, the model, wearing just a tight pair of black panties, had stopped him in the anteroom. "You have trouble?" she asked in broken English. He nodded. "A little." "You come visit me sometime," she said. He'd been a little embarrassed and didn't respond. In the days that followed, Gina Bargutto would stop by his easel after a sitting to see how Artie was progressing. She seemed to take an interest in him because he struggled so hard and was obviously frustrated with the results.

Talori, who said "Coraggio" every time he looked at Artie's work, seemed to like him too. Perhaps because Artie was the only student to talk to the model during the break, when the rest rushed out for a Coke and fresh air. For Artie it was a chance to practice his Italian since Gina knew very little English, and Talori was grateful the model was not entirely left out of the students' activity.

In the hall after class once, Gina invited him again to visit her in Milan, but somehow he never stopped by, despite the fact that he and Howard took regular trips to the city. Thinking about it now, he recalled one trip with particular chagrin. He'd decided to visit the Brera museum alone, since Howard was going to Pisa with some of the others in the group. It was only Artie's second time in Milan.

Arriving early, Artie walked from the train station to the cathedral, coming into the piazza from the Galleria. As before, the sight was magnificent and his heart soared, his senses exulting in the vastness of space, the myriad spires, the forests of clustered pillars.

After such strong, heady emotions, he couldn't help but feel that everything and everyone in the world were filled with goodness. Walking among the pigeons, unable to leave the splendor, Artie watched a young man with a black bag of corn throwing kernels in a sweeping motion to the pigeons flocking about him. He thought the guy was employed by the city, since he'd seen several other fellows doing the same.

One of the men walked up to Artie and put some corn in his hand. Artie's eyes opened with pleasure, and, thinking to help the fellow, he began sprinkling the kernels about.

"No, no, no," the man said. Artie stopped. What did he want? The fellow motioned for him to hold his hand higher. Artie did so and began scattering the corn again.

"No, no, no," the Italian repeated. "Stop!" Walking up to Artie, he placed more corn in his hand.

"You English?" he asked.

"American," Artie said.

"Okay," the fellow replied, lifting Artie's hand. "Hold high. Flat, okay. No move." He placed a few more kernels on Artie's palm and backed away. In a moment, pigeons had landed all over him and were scrambling to eat from his hand.

The fellow snapped several shots at different angles, first with the Galleria as a backdrop and then the cathedral. Suddenly another man rushed up. "Follow me," he said.

Still uncomprehending, Artie followed him obediently, wondering what he was getting into but not knowing how to get out of it, whatever it was.

He was led below the piazza to some shops. In one narrow room, the photographers had set up an office and for the first time, he realized what had happened. He was irritated at himself for falling into such a trap but, at nineteen and still green behind the ears, too afraid to realize he could still back out. They might make trouble. I did let them take my picture, after all.

"How many?" a clerk asked him.

"Two or three?" Artie hesitated. .

"Two's the minimum," the clerk said brusquely.

"Two then."

"4,900 lire."

Artie's eyes widened. That was eight dollars! He'd expected maybe four hundred lire. Sick inside, he handed over the money. He had so little to spare. For the rest of the day, though famished, he bought no food.

After visiting the museum, he was exhausted. Already he missed Pavia and the sense of home. He'd planned to stay overnight in Milan, but the expense of the photos and his loneliness made him change his mind. Stopping on a corner to study his map, he looked up into the eyes of a dark-haired woman of about twenty-five. She was staring at him without smiling. Taken aback at first, he felt his cheeks flush and lowered his head. After she walked off, it took him another minute to realize she must have been a prostitute, the first he'd ever met. "God," he thought, "I'm such a fool."

In his room in Venice, he smiled at the memory, shaking his head. How can I be such an idiot sometimes? This present trip was no exception.

Just before mid-semester break, Gina had told Artie she was going to Venice for the week to visit her folks. She invited him to stop by in the day and left him her parents' full name and address. He was pondering the idea after class when she pinched him on the chest, asking him if he wasn't cold with such a thin shirt. Though she stood there half-undressed herself, she said in Italian, "You never wear an undershirt."

"You must get cold, too," he said, "posing nude."

She laughed. "No, I have too much fat. You're thin." And she pinched him again. Looking at her, Artie had wished she were prettier. She wore a lot of blue eye shadow and he thought she would be nicer without it. The idea of trying to seduce a young beautiful model was exciting, but Gina somehow didn't live up to the part. It was hard to imagine her in bed. She had to be middle-aged.

Still, her invitation more persuasive than normal, Artie had decided to stop in at her folks' place if he got the chance.

He left Pavia on a Friday evening, making his way down Viale Libertà toward the train station. In the twilight the street lamps shone blue-green, creating an atmosphere for a movie or a painting. Fog hung in the trees in patches like balls of cotton. In his mind he titled the painting "The Fog-Drinker"—a long street, hazy in the evening fog, with a gray figure walking alone. Then, just before he reached the station, the wind picked up and it began to rain lightly, dispersing the fog. He'd been about a half hour early for the eight-thirty *diretto* and spent the time watching an old steam locomotive move in and out of the station on some mysterious errand.

On the trip to Milan for his connection to Venice, the sky, despite the late hour, lightened imperceptibly as the clouds were driven off. He could see the flat fields with occasional groves of poplars standing tall in even rows. Small canals and irrigation ditches crisscrossed the land. Some of the fields were flooded and a passenger told him they were rice paddies and that the area was famous for it.

Stepping off the train in Milan, he was surprised to see two other American students from the program. He stopped to talk.

"What are you two doing here? Were you on the train?"

Steve Saltzman, the more talkative of the two, spoke. "We're going up to Lugano for the week to see about getting a camera. They have some good German ones. I don't think we'll have to pay any duty on them."

Bud Rogers, a red-cheeked, brown-haired fellow, turned to Artie. "You're just coming in to Milan?"

"No, I'm going on to Venice. I've been through Milan a lot."

"I was here last week," Bud said. "I can't stand the place. You can't walk a block without having your face caked with soot."

Steve and Bud, Artie knew, had a reputation in the group for being eccentric. Bud was always washing his hands and showering once or twice a day. He thought everything was too dirty. Steve, a gangly kid, wrote poetry all the time, but he was also a business student. He raised daffodils on a small farm south of Roseburg, Oregon, and had told Howard he'd kill himself if he wasn't a millionaire by the time he was thirty.

The two had said goodbye and Artie was off for Venice. He'd arrived in the city at dawn and spent the first day and night in ecstasy. This was a city, he felt, made for him. The waterways, melancholic under a late November mist, enchanted him. At night, the lights of a host of little shops slivered the water into a crystalline kaleidoscope. In the day, the reflections in the canals, shattered sometimes by mist, sent up waves of glowing light, pastel in the shadows, of prismatic brilliance in the open.

With the weekend behind him, Artie had thought of visiting Gina. She should've arrived at her folks' place by now. The address she'd given him was quite distant from his place, out past St. Mark's near the Arsenale, Venice's ancient shipyards, and San Giovanni in Bragora.

Crossing the wooden bridge near the Accademia, he made his way along the Grand Canal to St. Marks. The piazza, quiet though not deserted, stretched out in the late afternoon shadows of a weak November sun. Here and there a couple wandered arm in arm or a lone walker crossed at a fast pace—obviously with a destination in mind, spurred on perhaps by the thought of warmth. Artie hurried on with his own thoughts of a different kind of heat. He recalled how Gina had patted her fat rear when she invited him to visit, throwing out her chest at the same time. He'd wondered if that was a signal.

When he found the apartment, room 27A in a dilapidated old palace, she opened the door dressed in a short bathrobe. There was no sign of her parents. She seemed slightly embarrassed, saying she'd just finished showering. While she mixed them drinks, Artie sat on the sofa, looking around the cluttered apartment.

She sat opposite him, still in the robe, and they talked of art and of Gina's place in Milan. After pouring Artie another drink, she left the room and returned in a loose shift. This time she sat on the sofa. After their third drink, Artie was feeling a little dizzy. Gina excused herself and went into the bathroom, leaving the door open. He could hear the trickle of water. When she came out, she was dropping her shift and he caught a quick glimpse of black hair between her thighs.

She sat closer to him and laid her head back. He could see her nipples were extended and felt the heat radiating from both their bodies. He was surprised to find himself aroused by such an unattractive woman.

Gina stretched out on the sofa with a sigh. "I get so tired, modeling," she said. He didn't know if she meant as a living or momentarily from posing. "I need something to take the tension from my body."

Unable to think of a response, he muttered agreement. Why am I so dumb? he thought, wishing he were less awkward and more sure of himself. The first step was always hard. He never did know if he was going too fast or too slow with girls. He thought of putting his arm around Gina, but it seemed suddenly absurd, like a high school act.

Somehow he got past the first kiss. He didn't enjoy it but feeling the pressure of her breasts against his chest, he was aroused again. She put her hand on his pants and pulled at him. As an afterthought almost, he began to touch her breasts. She had the shift off in an instant and her chubbiness, rather than repel him, suddenly made her seem the epitome of sexual attraction. She was fumbling with his belt, without too much success, while he continued to kiss her.

"Come," she said, standing up and leading him into the bedroom. He looked down as she walked ahead of him, noticing the way her flabby rear bounced. Hers was the first nude female body he'd ever seen.

In the bedroom, she lay on her back, touching herself with both hands, as he undressed quickly. He wanted to penetrate her immediately, but she slowed him down. "You're too young." She laughed. "You'd finish in two minutes."

He lay beside her on the bed, his socks still on, and began to caress her body. It seemed to him he would only last two minutes as it was. Suddenly Gina sat up, a shocked look on her face. "Did I hurt you?" Artie asked, and then he too heard it. Someone was knocking on the door and yelling.

"Oh God!" he said softly, sitting upright. "Who is it? Your parents?"

"My husband," she said. "He's supposed to be at work till ten."

Artie felt like sinking through the floor. Could it be that late? He looked at his watch. "It's only nine o'clock," he said.

Why didn't you tell me you were married, he wanted to ask, but by then both were grabbing for their clothes. As if reading his mind, Gina said, "We're separated but I visit him on vacations. He must have asked to leave early." She shoved Artie into a tall wardrobe, handing him his flannel shirt.

The knocking had grown more insistent. "Gina! Why is this door locked?" someone bellowed in dialect, but Artie understood only too well.

With a quaking heart, he slid the wardrobe door shut and pulled some dresses down on top of his body. He was half-dressed but he'd managed to get all his clothes in with him. *Or had he?*

Oh my God! *My shoes!*

He could hear an angry voice and Gina's responses and then what sounded like kissing. He hoped they didn't come straight to the bedroom. Could she get the guy out of the house?

A moment later the wardrobe door opened and Gina handed him his shoes. "He's in the bathroom," she whispered, "but he'll see you if you try to go out the front door."

She ran to a window and opened the casement.

"What are you doing, Gina?" a voice bellowed from the bathroom.

"Getting some fresh air," she shouted, motioning to Artie, who was pulling his shoes on.

He looked out the window. "That's too high. I'll kill myself." Gina was shoving him, frightened now at his delay.

Artie heard a noise behind him and turned to see the hairy back of a short but stocky Italian. The guy was drying his face with a towel and looking toward the kitchen.

The fear created by this sight was greater than that caused by the height. Artie, on the sill in a flash, closed his eyes and jumped as far out as he could—to clear a boat tied up at the side of the building. On the way down, the thought flashed through his mind that he would hit so hard he might stick in the mud and drown. He surfaced without touching bottom, however, and drove for the side of the canal where he could hide behind the boat. Looking up from the shadows by a piling, he could see the guy, an ugly fellow with a thick mustache, staring out the window. "Gina, it's too cold in here," the man said, leaning out and looking in both directions before closing the shutters.

Artie stayed in the water, though it felt like ice, for another minute or two—he was afraid the fellow might be peeking through the slats—and then swam down to a landing where he pulled himself out and crept off, dripping wet, into the darkness.

Hot toddy! he thought, still able to laugh at himself. Since I *did* have only two minutes, I might as well have used them while I could! No more waiting next time. Damn. Still a virgin.

In his room, ardor cooled by the late night dip, Artie felt suddenly isolated and alone. No one to talk to, no one to laugh at his experience and raise his spirits. Most of his friends seemed to travel in groups but Artie, unwilling to impose on anyone, had heard no one say they were going to Venice for the break.

Falling asleep with no clothes on, he spent a fitful night and in the morning, homesick, walked to the train station and left for Pavia.

Coming into Pavia in the evening was an experience he would never forget. Although he'd been gone only three days, it seemed forever. Seeing the dome of the cathedral rising above a mass of tile roofs, he felt so much pleasure that tears came to his eyes.

On the platform, he was surprised to see Steve and Bud. They'd planned on being gone the whole week too. Both grinned sheepishly, and Bud just said, "We decided to come back once we bought cameras. We didn't feel like staying in Lugano."

"Have you guys eaten?" Artie asked.

"No," Steve said. "And it's too late to catch dinner at the hotel."

Steve and Bud were staying in the Hotel Palace, overlooking the new bridge, whereas Artie had been placed in the Collegio Fraccaro, one of the dormitories for Italian scholarship students.

"How about eating at the Casa dello Studente?" Bud asked. "That's not far from the hotel."

They walked to the Student House near the Ticino River, dined on pasta, drank wine, and laughed while recounting equally horrendous travel experiences.

Virgin or not, Artie thought, it was nice to be home.

# — 6 —
## The Gold Fleeced

Damn Giovanni Pivelli! More than two hours had passed and he hadn't shown up yet."

"What'd you do then?" Gary Norling asked, walking over to the window to open the shutters. The room was full of smoke but a night breeze swept in to clean the air. Not a star showed in the Umbrian sky.

"Well, about that time I started thinking about the advantages of him never showing up."

"But what about your money, Artie?"

"The thing is, I needed the money but, if I didn't make contact with him that night, I'd have all the cloth at only half-price. I wouldn't feel any moral obligation about it either because that's all I'd promised to do. If he didn't keep his half of the bargain, I was free."

"But what about the Turk?"

"Hell, Gary, he was clean out of the picture. He'd been paid off in full by both of us."

"Pivelli would've lost out there, too, wouldn't he?"

"Yeah. About 40,000 lire."

Gary grinned. "Wouldn't you be worried about Pivelli? You know, him getting the police after you?"

"Sure. I realized, though, that he didn't know where I'd be. I was heading back up to Catania the next morning. But I planed on being there just long enough to catch a train out to Agrigento. I was moving fast by then, anyway. Spending less than a day in each city. I thought it out and figured, if the police were after me, I'd keep one step ahead of them—Agrigento, Selinunte, Segesta, Palermo, Cefalù, Messina, and then the mainland.

"Anyway, I was hungry. I went to a rosticceria and ate a pizza until about seven o'clock. From there I went back to the shop thinking Pivelli would be there. I had decided in the end that I was obligated to wait at least until midnight. If he wasn't there then, I could assume he'd never make it."

While he talked, Artie went to the window and leaned out. The Perugian night was peaceful but very cold in January. In the moonless night he could barely make out the tile roofs of a cluster of houses clinging on the side of the hill. He wondered if it would snow before morning.

He turned back. "I waited another hour and a half at the shop. The shutters were locked. I pounded on the door anyway, thinking he might be asleep inside. No one answered. Most of the time I spent sitting on a bench up a side street where I could see the door and still be hidden. I didn't want people to notice me and make any trouble. Finally, I decided I'd at least walk down to the harbor and enjoy myself. What a way to spend Christmas night, huh?"

"Yeah." Gary shook his head. He walked over to the bed and arranged a small dirty pillow before sitting and leaning back against the headboard.

"What were you thinking all this time?"

Artie shrugged. "I don't know. A bunch of thoughts. I was worried for a while that the guy was going to double-cross me. Wait for me to leave so he could catch me and try to get everything for himself.

"I didn't plan on letting him get away with it, but he could've made things rough, right? I don't think he would've gone to the police, because neither of us had receipts and the stuff was in my possession. All he'd need, though, was a few friends. Follow me up some dark street and that'd be the end. I was carrying the suitcase all this time because I expected to turn it over to him—after he paid me my commission and the money I'd put in on it."

Artie shook his head, marveling at his own blind stupidity. "He still hadn't shown up at the shop by ten. So I tore a sheet off my expense pad and left him a note. Said I'd return at midnight and then headed back to my hotel."

Gary held up a finger to stop him. "Hey, want a cig? It's a Muratti Ambassador."

Artie took the cigarette and leaned back in a rickety chair. "Can you close those shutters, Gary? It's damn cold out tonight."

He took a drag on the cigarette. Whew, too strong.

"I had a horrible hotel room. Half of the wallpaper was shredding loose. One weak lamp and a light bulb hanging from a cord in the middle of the room. I tried to keep busy by reading an old comic book I'd stolen from a hotel in Naples. I left a postcard of the Virgin in its place."

They both laughed.

"It didn't take long to read the comic book, so I sat there going over everything I'd done since leaving Pavia."

Artie had left Pavia on a Friday morning. Christmas vacation had just started and he had twenty-three days to travel. Howard was going to Yugoslavia and Greece, but Artie decided he wanted to see all of Italy first. On the trip south he'd seen many beautiful cities and sights, had undergone his usual humiliating scenes trying to bargain for cheap rooms and avoid tips, had enjoyed the mild weather after the cold in the North—trucks rolling through the dank streets of Naples, laden with oranges, lemons, tangerines, and melons—and had witnessed as well the usual oddities of human behavior, including a confrontation in Naples between the driver of an Alfa Romeo and the motorcyclist he'd hit. The clash evolved into a fight, for Artie an occasion to pick up a few new and useful swear words!

Artie arrived in Sicily a week after his departure from Pavia. It was in Catania, two days before Christmas, that he first met Giovanni Pivelli. Artie had been walking from the train station toward the cathedral when he was approached by a weather-beaten man asking in broken English for the Turkish Consulate. Artie tried to explain that he'd just arrived in the city, but the man misunderstood and launched into a long explanation of his problem. He was a Turkish sailor, coming from England. He'd be in port for just a day. He needed *lire* to buy medicine for a sick shipmate. He had English wool to sell.

"I'm sorry." Artie raised both hands. "I don't know where the consulate is. You should ask an Italian or go to the information booth in the railroad station.

"But I no speak Italian," the sailor protested. "You ask for me?"

Artie was looking around for someone when the sailor grabbed his arm, pointing to a fellow walking by. "Ask him."

Artie hesitated, but the Turk had stopped the guy.

"Scusi, signore," Artie began, "sa dove si trova il consolato turchese?"

"È chiuso oggi. Natale."

"He said it's closed today. Because of Christmas."

The Turk launched into his problem again, holding on to Artie's arm to keep him from leaving. He translated what he could, his vocabulary lacking.

"Is it good cloth—*lana?*" the Italian asked.

"He says it's wool from England."

The Italian asked to see it and the three headed toward the cathedral, talking. Suddenly the Turk disappeared, returning just as quickly with a small brown suitcase.

"Can we go to your house?" the Turk asked the Italian.

Artie translated.

"Well, we could walk there, but it's quite a ways," the Italian said. "I'm staying with my sister for the holiday. My home's in Siracusa. Let's find a bar."

As they continued to walk up the street, the Italian turned to Artie. "I don't know if his stuff is any good or not," he said. "We'll give it a look. If it's good wool and cheap, I'll buy it. *Ho uno zio che è sarto.*"

Artie wasn't sure he understood but thought the guy was saying his uncle was a tailor. Not something to tell a guy selling wool. A secret shared.

The Turk spied an open door leading into a pension. "Pst. Here."

The three ducked inside, leaving the door ajar so only a thin streak of sunlight entered behind them.

By this time, Artie figured the cloth was stolen. All the precautionary measures, the Turk's not having the cloth with him at first, his furtive watchful eyes, the secrecy.

The Italian, as if sensing his discomfort, said, "It's better not to look at the stuff on the street or in a bar, anyway. Too many people gather round."

Okay, the Italian was eager to get something cheap. Fine. He'd help.

Opening the suitcase, the Turk showed them four rolls of cloth, each three meters long. "Each of those is enough for a suit," the Italian said.

He laid the cloth over Artie's arm, snapped it sharply, gathered it in a bunch, matted it in his hands, and then let it spring loose. The cloth fell back to its original shape, wrinkle-free.

"Don't tell him," the Italian said, "but that's damn good cloth." He scratched his head. "Let's see what he wants for it."

"How much do you want?" Artie asked.

The Turk took out a piece of paper and wrote, "120,000 lire."

"No," said the Italian, shaking his head. "Tell him I won't give more than

80,000 for it. I'd make a small profit at 120,000 but not enough. Tell him the cloth isn't worth more than 80,000."

Artie wrote out the figure for the Turk. He grimaced.

"You won't get that much for it anywhere else."

Though clearly reluctant, the Turk gave in.

The Italian pulled several 10,000 lire notes from his billfold.

"I want American money," the Turk said to Artie.

"You can go to any bank in the city," Artie replied, "and cash this into American money tomorrow. Besides, you said you needed lire."

"Is his money good?" the sailor asked.

"Sure!" Artie showed him the 10,000 lire on the note and the name of the *Banca d'Italia*.

The Turk nodded. "Okay."

The Italian counted out four ten-thousand lire bills and said that was all he had at the moment. "I don't carry too much when I'm traveling," he said. "Tell him I'll buy two of the four rolls."

The Turk protested. He would sell all four or none.

Turning to Artie, the Italian proposed that he put up the other 40,000 lire. "You can take all the cloth to Siracusa," he said. "I'll leave you my address and meet you there tonight. You can have your money back, I'll take the cloth, and I'll give you 10,000 lire for helping me."

That was sixteen bucks. Great.

The Italian wrote out his name and address: "Giovanni Pivelli, Via Roma 92, Siracusa."

"Don't you want to take part of the cloth for security?"

"No, I can't be bothered by it. I trust you." The Italian smiled and they shook hands. Artie felt a warmth of brotherhood steal over him at the thought that a foreigner would trust him. It always made him feel good to help someone, too, especially when he was rewarded. The money he'd get for carrying the suitcase to Syracuse would help cover his expenses. He was barely scraping by.

After visiting the cathedral in Catania, he took the train for Syracuse. On the train, he thought of cheating the Italian. If he sold the cloth for what the Turk initially wanted—say, 120,000 lire—he'd have a profit of 80,000, about $128. A lot, but ... no, the guy trusted him, right? He wasn't going to be the Ugly American.

I'll keep my side of the bargain, but I'll ask him for the suitcase after I hand over the wool. My flight bag is getting ripped to pieces.

---

That evening, sitting in his room in the Albergo Milano, he wrote a postcard to his parents. At the end, he added:

"Today doesn't seem like Christmas weather-wise, but in a few minutes I'm going to receive 10,000 lire for doing a man a favor. So I guess it's Christmas after all."

Gary turned to him. "Did you go back to the shop?"

Artie nodded. "When I went back, it was eleven o'clock so I waited until twelve watching the place. The note was still on the door. Finally I wrote another one and said, if he wanted his cloth, to be down at the central railroad station at five the next morning.

"I made it early hoping he wouldn't come. If he'd missed the train the night before, he couldn't make it to Syracuse until after I'd left. We'd cross because I had to go back to Catania to catch a train to Agrigento.

"At the bottom of the note I added that if he didn't show up, I would sell the cloth and mail him his 40,000 lire. That way I'd make the profit, but I figured that would keep him from calling the police.

"The next morning, I was at the station an hour early. It was still dark and no one was around. I was so greedy by then to make the extra money that when my train came in I got on board and closed the window blind so Pivelli wouldn't see me—if he did come. I hoped he'd wait out on the platform until departure time and only then realize I might be on the train."

"Did he find you?" Gary asked.

"Nope. I don't even know if he came to the station. I didn't dare lift the blind to peek. I was a little worried in Catania, too, but my train for Agrigento was leaving immediately so I figured I was safe. And I was."

Gary offered Artie another cigarette and he took it and looked around for an ashtray. "I guess I dropped the ashes from the first on your floor," he said. "You got an ashtray?"

"There aren't any," Gary said, picking up a magazine. He opened it in the middle and they dropped their ashes into the crease.

"You know, Gary," Artie said, "when I left Sicily, I traveled to Lecce in the heel of Italy to visit two of my friends from the collegio. They told me I probably got tricked into buying that cloth. Both men were Italian. There was no Turk. It was all a scam. They said it's probably worth just what I paid for it."

"Wow, you're kidding."

Artie shook his head. "That sixty-four dollars hurt." He pondered the loss in silence, while Gary leaned back yawning. It was nearly three a.m. Artie had met Gary earlier in the evening in the Trattoria Da Primo, a small restaurant in Perugia, around the corner from the cathedral on the narrow, sloping Via Ulisse Rocchi.

At the time, Artie was eating his best meal of the trip—a first course of *pasta al forno*, some Frascati wine and bread, a beef steak with salad, and then a tangerine and Pecorino cheese for desert—when Gary entered. He'd told Artie he was spending the entire Christmas vacation in Perugia. It seemed he didn't want to say why, but when Artie raised his eyebrows, he said, "Rosa's here."

Artie's eyes widened. "You staying with her?"

"Her parents made sure she stays with some cousins. They wouldn't let her travel with me. I wanted to take her to Greece."

Gary was one of the few Americans in the group with an Italian girl friend. Artie had met Rosa the first month in Pavia and had been surprised later to learn she liked Gary.

Apparently Gary's long red hair attracted her. Artie had always thought him too quiet to have much personality. He was stocky, powerfully built but with a tendency to go fat at the waist.

"Maybe when we're back in Pavia I'll tell you about Rosa."

Artie nodded. "Okay. You going to bed now?"

"Yeah. Aren't you tired? It's three."

"I don't feel it at the moment but I probably am. I'll be leaving early for my train so I won't see you in the morning."

"Okay." Gary spread a couple of blankets on the floor for Artie. "I have a little heater so I don't think you'll be cold. Help yourself to some rolls when you get up.

"Thanks," Artie said. "See you back home in Pavia."

He fell asleep almost immediately, but it was a light sleep, broken finally by a nightmare. Afraid he might miss his train, he got up at five, left Gary a note of thanks, and was gone.

# — 7 —
# Feudal Knights

Following two cold months of winter, spring had come early and by April the nights were warm and summer-like. One weekend, near the end of the month and his stay in Italy, Artie was returning from his last visit to Milan.

It was easy to sleep on the train, especially following an exhausting three day excursion, but Artie was afraid of missing the Pavia stop and ending up somewhere down the line. Instead he stood in the end compartment of his car, in the wind, the top of the door open, breathing in the sweet smell of the first cutting of new-mown hay. With imaginary fingers he traced the slow unwinding of the irrigation canals through fields of stubby green and along rice paddies, blue-silver with the evening sky on water. The poplars, standing sternly in rows as far as one could see, were waving their aspiring branches in the evening breeze.

Pavia was always different from the train. Sometimes he saw the Duomo resting on the tile roofs of the apartment houses that stood around the outskirts of the city and sometimes all he could see was the smudgy, red-brick factories clustered near the station.

That particular Saturday in April, the train, as usual, braked to a stop in a long, seemingly interminable, dwindling slide. When they passed the old coal-burning engines on the sidings, he knew they were nearly there.

The wooden platform appeared, the red glow of the coal-burning engines fading behind.

He stood on the lowest steps, waiting to open the door for his car, suitcases piled high behind him. When the squeaking began, he clutched his twenty-four hour flight bag in his left hand and with his right pressed the handle down, swinging to the platform a second later and running a few steps to catch himself as his forward motion pulled him off balance.

He was later than usual getting to the platform. Already the passageway was jammed with the businessmen from the first-class car near the engine and with the people from the first three second-class cars. Unwilling and unready to face the tripping and shoving of the anxious-for-a-taxi crowd, Artie sat down on an empty baggage cart that for some reason was removed from the surge.

A sigh eased from his lips. He was exhausted. In his mind he pictured the farm in Oregon, imagined himself jumping over an electric fence and walking down the cow path that led to the woods and the creek. He'd always liked the quietness of the woods, the tall motionless firs, the ground soft with ages of fallen needles. Deeper in the woods, near the edge of their property, stood a meadow with patches of wild blackberries.

In the midst of his reverie he heard someone call and looked up, green grass fading to a brown wooden platform, the fir now heavy beams rising to an evening sky of dirty gray. Coming down the tracks, a thick black case in hand, a camera hanging from his shoulder, the caller waved.

Artie stood, smiling. "Hi, Howard. Didn't know you were on the train."

"I got on late. I'm coming back from Verona."

The two joined the thinned-out crowd, trickling through the underground passageway to the station and the street.

The air was heavy with the dusky twilight that only a provincial Italian city exudes.

Setting off up a narrow tree-lined street toward the Piazza Minerva and the city, the two slipped from one patch of mottled light to another. Overhead the deformed cottonwood scattered the streetlights into shadows that never stopped dancing.

The two students ate together—a quick dinner of pizza and Peroni beer—and then headed over to the Collegio Fraccaro and Artie's room, looking out on the three impressive towers in Piazza Leonardo da Vinci.

Howard lay down on Artie's bed while Artie leaned out the window, watching several gray pigeons settle down for the night in the tower arrow loops. Though tired both boys felt a nervous energy.

Five minutes later they were on their feet in the square below, enthusiastically considering the possibility of scaling the Visconti castle.

They found a bus to the Piazza of the Lion near the castle.

*"Mi dispiace ragazzi, ma il castello è chiuso,"* the bus driver said, as they stepped down.

"What'd he say?" Howard asked, unable to hear from the sidewalk.

"He says the castle's closed."

They laughed. Crossing the street, they made their way through the deserted, fog-shrouded park to the bridge over the dry moat that led to the large front doors.

It was Howard who mentioned the back of the castle— how it was crumbling away and they might have better luck there, if they could get down into the moat and walk back. They found a rickety wooden staircase at the far side of the bridge near the big central doors. The staircase was boarded off, but they kicked some boards loose and made their way down two flights of damp, slippery, moldy stairs.

At each step they cringed. In the stillness, the creaking of the steps was loud. It seemed each one was going to break.

The castle, lit by two strong arc lamps at the front corners, rose above them in golden light, but in the dry moat it was dark. Wisps of fog floated at irregular levels in long thin sheets across its facade.

"I saw a watchdog here one day," Howard whispered.

"Where?" Artie whispered back.

"Up above. Inside."

"I hope they don't leave him there all night."

They moved around to the back, straining to catch a glimpse of what lay ahead. Behind them, the arc lamps now far away and hazy, the darkness closed in.

"Shh." Howard grabbed his arm. "Did you hear something up ahead?"

Artie stopped, ears straining to hear, eyes squinting to distinguish solid forms in the shadows.

"What was it?"

"Don't know. It sounded as if someone stumbled into a stack of bricks."

Dimly through the fog, they could see a pile of jumbled construction materials, close up against the castle.

"The ruts lead away from the castle here," Artie said.

"Let's stick to them, anyway."

Artie nodded unseen agreement. Neither wanted to forge his way through the pile of bricks, lumber, sand, and whatever else lurked there.

"Howard, I think if we don't cut off now, this path'll lead us too far away from the castle."

"Maybe we should."

The fog thickened, the air heavy with its mist. A faint smell of rotting hay and manure reached Artie's nostrils.

"I didn't expect the fog to be so damn thick this low down, did you Howard?"

"It's warmer here in the moat. Maybe it will rise in a bit."

Around them stretched tangled masses of vine.

"Hey, Howard, I think the canal's up ahead. I didn't realize it swung by the back of the castle."

"I can't even tell where the castle is now."

"Isn't that it?" Artie pointed to a dim mass, looming on their left and nearly behind them.

"Let's follow the canal back until we're further around," Howard said, "and then maybe we can cut into the back easier."

They walked along the cement wall of the canal until the brush thinned out, and then a fence, a small garden, and the crumbling wall of the castle appeared. The back had never been repaired and showed the results of innumerable assaults of wars and time. Vines clung in its crevices and a mass of shrubbery quilted parts of the wall. The fog hung, like giant fruit, in and around the leaves.

Howard, leading the way, climbed the fence and jumped down. "Be careful, Artie," he cautioned. "It's wet here. The ground's awfully soft."

"Wait for me, okay? I can't even see you. Wish we had a flashlight."

"A rope with a hook, too." Howard took a few steps toward the wall. Suddenly Artie heard a muffled yell.

"Hey, Howard, *Howard*! What happened?"

"Hold it, Artie. There's water here and the bank drops off. You'll have to jump. I jumped just as I started to slide, but I didn't make it all the way."

Artie crouched at the sloping ditch and felt his shoes sliding.

"Jump!"

"I can't see."

"You've got to or you'll be in water."

Artie bent his legs and leapt into the darkness. He fell longer than he expected and hit with a jolt, sprawling forward into mud.

Howard stooped beside him, smothering a laugh. "You should see me," he said. "My pants are wet to the hips. I thought I was in quicksand."

"It's a good thing you didn't lose your shoes."

Howard surveyed the way before them. "Hey Artie," he said, turning to find him. "I don't think this wall leads into the courtyard. It's a wall slanting straight back from the castle."

"I wonder what it is? If we can get to the top, I think we can walk along it to the main wall and get up there."

"It looks pretty old to me, Artie. I'll climb it first. Wait until I'm up before you start, okay?"

"Yeah. Don't fall."

Howard moved forward slowly until the vines were in front of him and then grasped a few which pulled loose when he applied his weight. A pile of crumbled brick and dirt followed in a soft whoosh. Digging his toes into the thicker vines, he worked his way slowly up the high wall.

Artie sensed his progress but Howard himself was soon lost in the fog. Faintly, Artie heard labored breathing.

"Artie?" Howard's voice drifted down softly.

"Yeah?"

"I made it but you'll have to be really careful. It's tricky."

Several minutes later, after a near fall when a large surface of the wall caved off below his left foot, he felt Howard's hand and found himself lying on top the wall.

"I hope no one heard that rumble," Howard said. "What'd you do? Kick a hole in the wall?"

Artie sat up and looked around. The air seemed clearer. Beyond the dark thread that was the canal, he made out a string of poplars bordering a road whose dim streetlights cast a hazy glow every hundred feet or so. Across the road glimmered the lights of a row of tall apartments.

"We're going to have to climb more when we get to the main wall, aren't we, Howard?"

"Yeah. It'll probably be harder there, too. I don't think there'll be any vines. It'd be nice to have a rope."

The wall was a little over a foot thick, but in places it had crumbled, leaving the top pitted and rough. The two made their way along it, straddling it, then pulling themselves forward in small sliding movements. Once, when Artie sat up to judge the distance, he lost his sense of balance and for a moment had to cling dizzily to the wall.

Howard had moved on. Struggling to regain his equilibrium, Artie pulled himself forward just as another part of the wall slid off—and he felt himself about to go with it. He grabbed blindly at the stones, as he listened to the clatter of rocks and dirt crashing through the thick vines below. Clutching the crumbling stone projections, he managed to scramble forward where the wall seemed firmer, wondering the whole time why they had ever decided to scale the castle in the first place.

"Damn, Howard!" I

"I've reached the back of the castle. Come on."

In a few moments, happy the stone was now firmer, Artie reached Howard's position.

"We should've come around the moat from the opposite side," Howard said. "All we would've had to do is climb those trees and then follow the main wall back to the main building."

"You're right. How in the hell are we supposed to climb now? There's nothing to hang on to."

"I was thinking you might push me up. I think I could reach the top, don't you? And then give you a hand up."

"I don't know." Artie hesitated. "It's kind of hard standing on this wall. We both might fall. It's going to be harder getting down."

"I thought maybe coming out we could open the front doors from the inside. Don't the locks just slide open?"

"Those big doors! Hell, we'd never be able to budge them, and if we did, I'd be afraid some policeman or someone else would see us. We'd be in for it then."

Howard frowned. "There's a small door for the caretaker. Come on, we'll get out. Can you cup your hands?"

Artie got to his feet gingerly, making sure that that part of the wall was solid. Bracing himself against the main wall, Howard put his foot in Artie's clasped hands and slowly stood up.

"I can't reach it, Artie. There's another foot yet. Can you lift me higher?"

"You're hurting my hands," Artie gasped. "Just a minute." Straining his arms, he lifted Howard a little higher.

"Howard," he wheezed, "I can't do any more. Put your left foot on my shoulder."

Howard kicked him in the head, found the shoulder, and stepped down as Artie winced and gritted his teeth. Howard's shoe was cutting into his flesh. And then the weight was lifted, he heard a scrambling, the scrape of a shoe, and small flecks of sand fell into his eyes.

"Made it, Artie!" Howard whooped with joy. "It's the courtyard. Just a second. I'll look for a rope or a ladder. It'll make it easier."

"Hurry," Artie whispered, but Howard was gone already.

Minutes passed that seemed hours.

Damn. What in the hell is he doing?

Artie was nearly above the fog, though occasional wisps drifted by. Out on the highway, he could hear the click-clop of a horse and the creaking of cart wheels. Downright early for someone to be going to market.

"Artie! I found a ladder, but it was tied down. No sign of the dog. He'd wake the whole town."

Howard lowered one half of the extension ladder, and Artie placed the ends securely on each side of the wall.

"Make sure you hold the top," he cautioned Howard. "I don't want to slide off the side."

It was darker in the courtyard. Around them walls rose on three sides, the back having collapsed in the Renaissance during the Franco-Spanish conflict of 1525. In his mind Artie imagined jousts, the thunder of iron-clad steeds, the breaking of lances, a pavilion for him, inside a maiden waiting.

"Do you think we can get into the museum?"

His maiden turned into Howard. "Damn wizard," he muttered.

"What?"

"Nothing. Just talking to myself."

The door to the museum in the left wing, firmly locked, resisted however, and nothing succeeded in opening it.

Disappointed, the two sat on a stone bench to enjoy their conquest. After a moment of silence, Howard asked Artie if he missed his family.

"Not much," Artie said. "How about you?"

Howard, lighting his pipe, didn't respond. When he finished, he reached for his billfold and pulled out a picture. "I just received this. It's a photo of my girlfriend with two of her housemates. She lives in a co-op."

To Artie, Howard's girlfriend had too round a face. "I like this one," he said, pointing to a thin one in the middle.

Howard grunted. "That's funny. She knows you. Toni— that's my girlfriend's name—said this other girl remembers you as being smart, tall, dark, and handsome—the old line. I wrote Toni about you once."

Artie grinned. "Really? Her friend's not that bad herself, but I don't remember ever seeing her."

"I think her face is too long," Howard said.

"Too long! I like it. Your girl's is too round."

Howard stared at him. "That's the way a face should be."

"Hell, most people have faces longer than round."

"Well, you do," Howard said, "but that doesn't mean everyone does."

Artie grinned, contemplating what to him was good news, and then asked about Toni. Howard told him how he met her and about her mental problems. Apparently her folks were pretty religious. "I even went to church with her," Howard said. "She was really hung-up though. Anytime I tried to touch her she would get hysterical. She always talked about making love, but then couldn't stand to have me touch her."

Howard took several small puffs from his pipe.

"I've always needed a goddess."

"A goddess?"

"Someone who's smart *and* beautiful."

"Isn't Toni?"

Howard nodded. "She has both qualities."

Artie remained silent, hoping Howard would go on, knowing that he usually didn't like to talk about personal things.

"We used to be open with each other, but now I keep sensing a mood of evasion. She wants to tell me something, but she's reluctant-—maybe afraid. She said she was seeing another guy ... but I don't know what's going on."

Howard paused, drawing on his pipe and looking off across the dark courtyard. After a while, feeling awkward in the silence, Artie mentioned a letter from Phil Lockfall.

Phil had written about his own amorous escapades, bragging about wild parties and hinting at sexual encounters. Artie brought up the letter because Phil had also written about Ray Spencer's problems.

"He's this friend of Phil's who's quiet, but nice once you get to know him. He was split from his girlfriend, just like you, and things were kinda hairy for a while but I guess they got back together."

Artie couldn't tell if Howard was interested, but he told him the story as written by Phil. While he talked, Howard cleaned his pipe and then stood.

"We'd better be going, Artie, before it gets light. Help me tie this ladder back where I found it and then maybe we can stop off at the Caffè Cavour for some coffee."

Having replaced the ladder, the two slipped to the front of the castle and eased out of the small side door used by the caretaker. Once outside, Artie gasped and pointed to the big front doors. Howard turned and his eyes widened.

One portal stood open about a foot. Clambering over a barrier, they set off running across the footbridge. A turmoil of shouts and barking dogs broke out behind them. The shouts of *"Alt! Alt!"* added lightning to Artie's feet and he shot by Howard and out into the park in front of the castle.

When he reached the cobblestone street, he took off up an alley, having lost Howard somewhere in the park. The alley was lined by dark, barred windows and smooth gray stone walls. A Fiat passed him as he ran, the driver blinking his lights as a warning.

At the corner of Corso Cavour and Strada Nuova, Artie sat on the curb, gasping for breath. There was no sign of Howard, but Artie could still hear dogs barking in the distance. A half hour passed and he was about to return to the collegio when Howard came into sight, limping, one foot missing its shoe.

"What'n the hell happened?" Artie asked, laughing. "Did they catch you?"

Howard looked back the way he'd come. "We'd better get off the street in case any cop cars are out. I thought I was going to lose a leg."

"So, where's your shoe?"

"Some dog's enjoying it somewhere."

"At least it's not you he's chewing on."

"He had me cornered in a doorway! The damn dog was barking so much this guy on the second floor opened his shutters—he couldn't see me in the doorway—and tossed an empty bottle at the dog. That drove him back a bit. I took off but the dog caught up and kept biting at my heels, so finally I started kicking at him. He grabbed my foot and wouldn't let go. I knew if I hung around much longer the watchman would get there. At least with his mouth full the dog wasn't barking."

Artie was laughing so hard tears came to his eyes.

"Finally, the dog tore off my shoe, shook it around, and ran off the way he'd come so I gave it up and hightailed it."

"Fair exchange for your life."

They were glad the caffè was almost deserted. It was still dark and too early for many people to be in the streets.

Howard's pants were muddy to the crotch, and with one shoe missing, he looked like a poor peasant coming in from the barnyard. "Didn't lose my pipe at least," he said, patting his coat pocket.

Service was slow. The waiter lingered in the midst of an animated conversation with the only man at the bar. When the coffee came, Artie gave his cup a generous dose of sugar and sat back. It cost more to drink at a table, but both were too tired to stand at the counter.

Bolstered by a second cup of espresso, Howard, as if to lessen his own loss, changed the subject to the misfortunes of Gary Norling. "He got in a fight the other day, didn't he?"

"It wasn't really a fight. I talked to him later and he said he just hit this Italian once, and gave him a black eye. He and Rosa were making out in an empty classroom and some Italian guys saw them through the window.

"They don't like Gary because he's got an Italian girl, so one of them walked into the classroom and made a few dirty remarks. Gary walked down to the front, socked him in the eye, and the guy ran off."

Howard slapped the table. "Good! He's so damn shy. Nice to see him do something. I know he hates most of them. How's he get along with Rosa?"

"She loves him," Artie said. "He's made love to her, you know."

"You sure?"

"Yeah. He can't take her to a hotel so they go across the bridge and do it in the fields. He says all the cheap prostitutes go there, too."

They were silent for a moment, both envying Gary's luck at finding a girl who'd sleep with him. Artie accepted a cigarette and went on talking. "The next day, after Gary hit this fellow, everybody knew about it. They were mad, too. The Rector of the university heard about it, because all the Italian students were asking for an apology.

"They caught Gary outside the classroom the next day. From the way Gary told it, he kind of liked the excitement. Anyway, the Rector heard the commotion, came out, and they asked his permission to give Gary the *lucido*."

The *lucido*, familiar to all the Americans living in Italian dorms, was a rite in which black shoe polish was applied to the rear end of unlucky first-year students. Artie had always managed to avoid it.

"The Rector told them they could do it, and he himself personally held one of Gary's hands. Some other official had the other. I guess Gary resisted and said he wouldn't drop his pants. They compromised and unbuttoned his shirt and gave it to him on the chest. He must have been scared or maybe just nervous—you know how he is when he has to speak in front of the class—because he told me the sweat started running from his armpits all the way to his hands."

Artie laughed. "He said he liked it because it ran into the Rector's hand, and the Rector kept moving it trying to avoid Gary's sweat. Now, whenever he's in the collegio, he locks himself in his room and doesn't speak to any of them."

"He's probably glad the year's about over. I know I am."

The two lapsed into thought, Howard calmly smoking his pipe and staring at the tablecloth, Artie leaning back with a gaze that didn't see the coffee cup in front of him.

Intent on his own thoughts, Artie didn't notice that Howard had ordered more coffee for both and was adding fresh tobacco to his pipe.

"What are you thinking?" Howard asked.

Artie looked up, saw the coffee and began to add sugar.

"Oh, just about this coming summer. How about you?"

"Nothing much." Howard was often taciturn. Probably dreaming of his girlfriend.

"What time is it?" Artie asked.

He was surprised that it was nearly six. They had been in the caffè for over an hour.

"I think I'll go back to the apartment," Howard said, finishing his coffee. "Want to come along? We have some canned peaches."

"Sounds great, but I should get back to the collegio. I have a letter to write and some other stuff to do. Shall we go rowing again tomorrow?"

Howard nodded. "Yeah. How about three o'clock or so?"

"Fine."

The two had gotten into the habit of renting a boat every Sunday and rowing up the Ticino river. They got a good workout fighting the strong spring current. Both enjoyed rowing up past the two bridges to the Lido and running barefoot in the sand. One the way back they dove off the floating boat and swam a bit in the icy water. It was a good way to get an early tan.

Having settled the bill, the two separated. Howard headed for his apartment and Artie, on an impulse, walked toward the covered bridge. The coffee had keyed him up and he wasn't ready to go in yet. Though it hadn't rained, the cobblestones were slippery and black.

On the bridge, he walked to an abutment and watched the water rush by the pilings. Overhead, from the dark recesses of stone, he heard the cooing of pigeons. "You should be asleep," he said, and then, as a cyclist pedaled by, turned and headed for home.

— 8 —

# Trisoctahedron Trips

Slowly, the light began to diffuse over the meadow as the sun, near the horizon, sank below the clouds. Not a blade of grass moved. Around the meadow on three sides hung a tapestry of trees, dark green but turning to black as the sun set. Coming up from the creek through the trees, he stopped at the edge of the meadow and lost himself in the stillness.

From the far left—it seemed to stretch from here to the horizon—the figure of a girl floated into the meadow, stopped, and began to dance in the silence, a slow dance, a gentle swirling of gossamer. He felt a quickening in his blood, a dizziness of senses. The first sound came as it grew darker. Castanets began to click with light—red and green, orange and black, scarlet, white, and blue. To the clicking of the castanets the meadow began to dissolve, and the music grew until she stood on a wooden platform.

"Artie! Hst! Hey, Artie?"

"Where are you, Gary?"

"Right here. Beside you."

He felt Gary's hand tighten on his arm.

"Where have you been?" he whispered. Eyes like stars, fractured and refracting.

"Just walking." The highway's pretty close. There're some shrubs straight ahead."

"What time is it?"

"About three o'clock." Gary lit a cigarette, his face burning.

"Don't, Gary!"

Gary dropped the match, whirling around. "What?"

"Nothing. I was ... afraid."

Gary cupped the cigarette in his hand. "Let's go over there." He pointed to his left. "There's a bench."

On the bench, beside a winding asphalt path, Gary pulled out a small dope pipe and stuffed it from the matchbox where he stored his weed, taping the box back up and putting it in his coat pocket. "Want to light it?"

"No. Go ahead. Do the honors."

Gary threw the cigarette butt into a black puddle reflecting yet more blackness. "Man, this night is dark. Where's the fucking moon? He lit the pipe, inhaled, and passed it to Artie.

As he inhaled, he could feel it pull him back, further back than the dream girl in the meadow.

The apartment had one lamp on in the corner. A miniature phonograph, battery powered, rotated slowly on the coffee table. Six eyes stared at him. Gary Norling, Phil Lockfall, Ray Spencer. To avoid them, he lay down on the floor, his eyes finding the ceiling, feeling the others watching him.

———

"Who's jerking the coffee table?" He sat up and looked around.

They seemed embarrassed. Gary's face was turned away.

"No one," Phil said. Gary flipped through a Playboy.

Ray sat in the corner, motionless.

Artie felt a twist of nausea, but Gary said that happened the first time. "Nerves. Just relax. It'll be okay."

"I didn't get enough sleep last night," Artie said. "It would've been better if I'd come rested."

Gary looked over at Phil. Phil hadn't turned on.

Artie began to feel cold. "I'm shivering," he said, "Must be a draft on the floor."

Phil burst out laughing. "He sure is *logical*, isn't he?"

Artie lay back again. Maybe I'm searching too hard. Am I high? He could see his mind working. He really did want to get high.

"I'm hungry," Gary said.

"Me, too." Artie got to his feet. The room swayed around him.

"You know what that is, right? Hunger? Guilt feelings."

"Bullshit." Artie looked around. "What time is it?"

"Eleven-thirty," Ray said.

"Let's go get something to eat."

He saw Gary hiding a small green bottle that once held pills and now contained grass. All four left the apartment.

Across from the Dairy Queen on 13th Street in Eugene, they met Gary's roommate with a girl. Gary had already told Artie the guy was straight.

But the roommate made a big deal of staring at them, walking back and forth in front of them, peering with his head tipped to the side.

"High, right?"

"No," Artie blurted, then felt like an idiot. He shuffled his feet. Come on, Gary, get rid of the guy.

"Well, we're off to the Student Union. See you later, Gary."

When the guy and his girlfriend were out of hearing range, Artie turned to Gary. "Why's he act so queer? He always seems to be trying to tell if you're turned on or not."

Gary looked at Phil. They smiled. "You're paranoid," Phil said.

"No, I'm not." He looked from one to the other. "You're joking, right?"

Gary hedged a bit.

"It's not paranoia," Artie said. "I thought the same thing earlier in the week—when I wasn't turned on."

"Don't start getting hostile now," Gary said.

Artie stopped. "I'm not getting hostile. I'm just trying to prove that what I said was normal. You're only trying to make me hostile by suggestion. Quit it, okay."

"Ho, ho," Gary danced away. "You're afraid I'll talk you into it, aren't you?"

"No. Go ahead. It doesn't bother me. I'm peaceful by nature."

The rest laughed, but Artie felt a tightness in his throat.

In the New World coffee house, they ordered peach pie and a cappuccino, and ate without speaking, watching the people around them.

Then they were at Gary's place again, smoking. This time Artie fell asleep. Sometime in the middle of the night he awoke to find Gary standing by him, poking him in the shoulder. Howard Montrel was there. Artie found himself no longer at Gary's place but in his own bed, in the house he shared with Howard.

"He's dead," Gary said, poking him again. "He's dead."

Artie sat up, irritated. "The hell I am."

He stopped. Damn, dreaming or hallucinating. It was San Francisco again, Golden Gate Park, not Eugene. The night before the big peace march. Walking to Kezar Stadium in Golden Gate Park. They'd come out a day ahead of time to see what it was like.

"Maybe we should move somewhere else," Gary said.

Artie stood and looked around. "Is anyone coming?"

"I don't like being on this path. Let's go back to those taller trees."

They made their way across the park lawn, their feet leaving wet swaths behind them. Artie could see one of the streets now, and cars. They sat down on an embankment.

The Saturday after he first turned on, Artie went into Portland with Ray Spencer, married now, with his wife working as a nurse to put him through school. Ray had become an architecture major, but he was interested in all the arts. The first few weeks they talked together, Artie listened in awe but later came to realize Ray just repeated the same things over and over—the human spirit, values, philosophy, architecture, art, literature. Vague words, half of which, in the abstract, were meaningless to Artie.

They were going to Portland for two reasons and Artie for a third as well. They wanted to take pictures of Portland's older areas, especially near the river, check the Portland State library for works on or by Italian poets and Artie was to meet Gary Norling later in an attempt to score some acid.

Walking near the rows of concrete pillars that supported the overhanging freeway routes, Artie and Ray turned off into a metal dump near a wrecking yard for old freighters.

They were talking about art.

"I just wish I knew the techniques," Artie said. "I have so many ideas but I lack the skill to fulfill them. About the only thing I can do beside paint is take photos, I guess."

"Then study photography."

Artie laughed. "Okay. But this steel crap here reminds me of an idea I got in Italy for a sculpture. There's this archeological museum in Florence. I was there looking at some pottery and saw this long narrow rod with a small figure on top of it. What I'd like to do is make several round disks all the same diameter but each one a little smoother than the other."

"Yeah. That's not so hard."

"Then I'd put them on a long rod about a foot apart or so. The disks couldn't be very big, I guess. As the rod got higher I'd bend it out to the side as if the weight of the disks was getting too heavy for it. The disks are supposed to look as if they are balanced on the rod. Finally, the smoothest disk—I'd like it to be like glass—would be perpendicular to the ground. I want to have a little figure in clay on his hands and knees, trying to hang on to the top edge of the disk to keep from sliding off."

Ray shrugged and turned to take a photo of the freeways intersecting overhead.

"I'd call it 'Progress,'" Artie went on, ignoring Ray's lack of enthusiasm. "The roughest disk at the bottom stands for the world before man starts to deal with it. I want to show that if we're not careful enough all our science and technology—you know, the smoothness of the disks-—will be turned against us."

"I'll have to take you down to the metal shop sometime," Ray said. "Maybe we can see if someone can help you. You know, Dostoyevsky says something in his Notes From Underground about how the only gain of civilization for mankind is a greater capacity for a variety of sensations."

"Maybe that's why so many people take drugs."

Ray shrugged. "Might be. I know quite a few of my friends smoke pot."

"You ever try it?"

"I'm not into that. You thinking about it?"

Artie hesitated, wondering whether to play dumb or tell the truth. "Well

... actually ... I tried it a couple of times this last week."

"You like it?"

"I didn't feel too much the first time. Might not have smoked enough. The second time, though, whew, that was heavy."

"Don't know if I'm stable enough."

"Didn't bother me. Hell, you could take it. Half the crap you read is just that."

"My wife's been talking about taking acid."

"Shit! That's ten times stronger than grass. From what I've read at least."

"Would you ever take it?"

He didn't want to admit now that he was planning to that very night. "Depends. I've read a lot about it."


That evening, after Ray left for Eugene, Artie waited for Gary Norling in a restaurant near Portland State. Night had fallen when Gary finally appeared, walking alone up Fourth Avenue toward the college.

From the college, Gary led Artie down a side street, across a bridge, through a park and up into some hills. They were in an area of run-down shacks, once expensive Victorian mansions. Psychedelic signs and paintings decorated the windows along the street.

Gary stopped. "Maybe you should wait here," he said. "These guys don't know you. They uptight if a stranger shows up."

"Damn. Just be quick then, okay. This area's a skuzz bucket."

"Hey, man, don't come unglued. This is hippieville. A little grungy. Nothing to worry about."

A few minutes later he reappeared with a small paper sack. "Let's go."

"Hadn't you better carry that in your pocket?"

"What? My lunch?"

"Yeah, right. Is that what you'll tell the cops?"

The two walked toward the Ross Island bridge and finally turned down Corbet Avenue, where Gary was looking for a friend's house. "He has a car. Maybe we can get him to drop us off at my parents' home."

When they found his place, no one answered the door. Going around to the back, they found a rickety stairway leading to the top apartment. There was a dead bird on the upstairs landing, lying in a pile of old newspapers and wine bottles.

"He lives up here," Gary said. "A couple of girls rent the downstairs, I think."

They broke open the nailed door and went inside where Gary left a note on the bed, saying they would be at the Black Forest Coffee House.

The Black Forest Coffee House sat at the corner of Second and Grant, two streets down from the old Civic Auditorium. After Artie's eyes adjusted to the dark, a new world appeared. Scattered through the crowded main room a few candles flickered inside red, green, or blue jars. In the middle of the room, a square area was marked off by counters, behind which two women sold coffee, tea, cake, rolls, pie, sodas, and a variety of exotic foods and drinks.

"Hey, that's him," Gary said. "Bill Brooks."

"So, 'Ace' Norling wants to score again?" the guy said, emphasizing the jargon. Artie liked him. Making fun of wanting to be "in."

"We got grass, man, but we want acid. "Can you get it for us."

"You sure you want something that'll ruin your brain? Something evil?" He sneered. "I don't think kids your age ought to take such potent stuff. The next thing you know, you'll be wanting to shoot it, right? Stuck on it, aren't you? A doper."

"Come on, Brooks, let's get out of here," Gary said heavily, scooting back his chair. Bill didn't move.

"Who's this friend with you, Ace? Someone you're going to turn on and corrupt?"

Artie grinned.

"What do you go by, man?"

"Artie Crenshaw. Just call me Flash."

"Kid's got a real sense of humor. Flash! How do you like that, Ace?"

Gary grabbed his head as the two laughed. "Let's split the scene," Bill said.

Outside the café the three stood on the corner waiting for the light to change.

"Hate to get you busted, Gary. Walking against the lights. Cops search guys like you." He smirked. "By the way, how about a toke?"

"I don't have any joints rolled, man. Let's wait till we get to your place."

"You expect to score acid and you can't share your grass?"

"I'll give you some later," Gary said.

"Greedy dope addict wants to keep it all to himself."

If it were not for the intricacy of design, the Victorian house would have been shabby. Even then, paint-flaky and dilapidated, it shed an air of gloom on the outside. From the second story, a dim light showed, and they could hear one of Donovan's records playing. "Season of the witch."

The two forms on the veranda didn't see the three fellows coming up the walk. "Let's scare the shit out of them," Bill said. "It's Dana and Tammy."

They crept closer to the porch, hiding beneath a large weeping willow in the front yard. They could hear the girls giggling.

"Quick," Dana was saying, "let me have another drag."

A thin, hand-rolled cigarette was passed in cupped hands.

Artie heard a long, slow sound of breath being released.

"That must be Tammy," Bill whispered. "Yeah," Gary answered, lecherously, "Tammy with the long black hair. You don't like her though, do you Bill?"

"She's Connor's woman now, but I've got plans. She and I and Dana and Gill are going to the beach tomorrow morning. How'll that look, Gary? All that naked flesh on the sand!"

On the porch an impatient voice spoke, "Hurry, Tammy. I want a toke."

"Hold it there," Bill commanded in a stern voice. "This is Officer Hanson, Portland police."

There was a shriek and Bill burst out laughing.

"Oh God, Bill," Dana gasped. "You scared the shit out of me."

Bill stepped forward and took the cigarette between the nails of his thumb and forefinger. "Down to the roach already." He turned to Gary, offered the joint to him, and then pulled it back, grinning, and took a deep drag. "Ahh. That's okay." He inhaled again, pulling the sweet smoke deep into his lungs, holding it and then exhaling it slowly.

"'S good stuff," he said, handing it to Gary. "Nice and mellow. Not like yours, huh?"

Climbing the front stairs, the five stood outside, while Bill found his key. The house opened into one long room divided by curtains, which were now open. At the street end, the dumpy bed where Gary had left the note earlier was occupied by two couples, all sharing the same joint.

From there on down the length of the room, people stood talking or sat on cushions along the wall. At the back, a group of musicians from one of the local rock bands sat around a stereo.

Half-way down the room, a Christmas tree bubbled with lights. Artie and Gary joined some girls, sitting in front of the tree like wide-eyed children. After a couple of bowls of grass provided by Gary, Artie felt his mind expanding. It seemed to be half in and half out of his head, floating in the room with the smoke. He lay down beneath the Christmas tree, shutting his eyes.

"I wonder where Phil and Howard are?" Gary said. Artie opened his eyes. In the distance, car lights flashed between the trees. He exhaled deeply. "Whew,

I don't know. I'm really stoned, Gary. Where are we?"

Gary grinned. "In the park. Don't want to move, huh?"

"Maybe we should. Maybe Phil and Howard are back at the park entrance. Should we walk up Haight Street again?"

"Naw. Let's stay here. I don't like all the people."

Artie looked around him. Wary. "Did you fill the pipe with tobacco?"

Gary nodded. That was just one of their precautions in case they saw cops. Artie felt for the two matchboxes in his pocket. They were still there.

"Gary, who was with us the first time I turned on to grass? I was thinking it was Bill Brooks, but it couldn't have been because he didn't know me the time we met him in the Black Forest."

Gary thought a while. "It's too deep for me, man."

"Yeah … You're right. Let's walk a little."

They followed a circular, concrete path deeper into the park. "Sure hate to get lost in here," Artie said. "Fucking, pitch black!"

He thought about Howard Montrel. A week or so after Artie first turned on, Howard—his roommate, now that they were back at the university in Eugene—found out about it. Artie expected him to get all self-righteous. Instead, he wanted to try it too.

In the following weeks during Fall term they turned on most nights. Eventually they made a few trips to Portland without Gary, and Artie made contacts on his own. They bought about half a kilo of grass in a brick and Artie divided his share into lids and then into matchboxes. He could pay for his share selling a few matchboxes to friends, five bucks each, fifteen for the lid, and still keep quite a bit for himself.

Gradually the circle grew and the small two-bedroom house he and Howard rented became the gathering place of Phil Lockfall and Ray Spencer, rooming together in a dorm. The four, sometimes joined by Gary Norling, turned on several nights a week.

In the middle of the term, they heard more often about police raids, but the most frightening experience occurred the evening Phil telephoned from the dorm.

"Artie?"

"Yes?"

"Listen, one of my chicks was telling me about this list."

"Yeah?"

"Well, an informer took a list of forty-some people over to the dean's office.

They think he's going to pass it on to the cops. This chick says your address is on it."

Artie's heart jumped. "How'n hell did they get that?"

"Not sure. Remember the time I brought that kid by with the tapes and electronic music? Might have been him. Anyway, you'd better make sure you don't have the stuff where they can find it."

Artie hung up. "Howard, hey Howard!"

Howard came plodding out of his bedroom, an unlit pipe in his mouth. "Yeah?"

"Cops are on to us. We've got to get the grass out of here!"

Howard cuddled the pipe bowl in his right hand while chewing on the mouthpiece. "Who told you that?"

"Phil."

"I don't believe it."

"Howard, don't be so damn sceptical. We've got to hide the stuff better."

At first they had kept the grass in their rooms, but later Howard had removed the plate on an old stove flue that was no longer in use and had hung the marijuana in sacks from a straightened coat hanger down inside the duct. Anyone opening the plate would see a stretch of pipe going back and nothing more.

Still, ingenious as it was, Artie finally convinced Howard to hide the grass outside the house. Artie tried an old stump in the back yard—then under a rock—but finally gave up. He was sure it could be found there, too.

In the end, they wound up driving out Fox Hollow Road into the country and hiding it alongside the road in a rotten stump by some dead blackberry brambles. The stump was near a bend in the road. They were sure they could find it again.

Eventually the scare died down, but Artie and Howard continued making the drive into the country whenever they needed grass, and the only close call they had was a false one. Howard and Ray Spencer had driven out for the grass one evening, since Phil and Artie were playing cards.

They returned a half-hour later, bursting into the house with the news that the grass was gone.

Artie couldn't believe it. "Then we must have been seen there by someone. We've been ripped off!"

"Remember that farm house just before the bend?" Howard said.

"Yeah."

"Maybe someone there saw us."

"But dammit! We've been so careful!"

"Let's check again," Phil said. "The stuff's buried. Maybe you missed it."

The four climbed into Rich's Barracuda and drove out to Fox Hollow. In the night, with all the twists in the road, it was hard to find the right bend. Parking the car past the spot, they back-tracked quietly.

"Stay off the road," Artie warned them as a car passed, and they dove into the underbrush until its taillights disappeared. Finding the stump was difficult. They stumbled from blackberry patch to blackberry patch. The wild brambles were everywhere. It was Phil who finally found the stump with his flashlight.

Howard dug again at its base and there, below a short piece of wood, they found the plastic sacks.

The first time Artie dropped an acid tab he took it at Gary's place, since Howard didn't yet know of his activities. Phil and Ray were present, turned on, but not with acid. Phil was eating speed—a little methadrine and some DMT. Gary and Artie split a capsule of LSD, separating the white powder with a knife and then eating it. They smoked some pot to heighten the effect.

An hour passed. Artie moved around the apartment, uneasy. "You feel anything, Gary?"

He nodded.

"I don't feel it yet." He turned to Phil. "How will I know when I'm high? Is it at all like grass?"

"Man, you'll know. That's when you'll be high—when you know. This stuff ain't grass."

"Let's split the scene," Gary said.

The four of them got their coats and headed from Ferry Street to the university. On the corner of 13th and Patterson, they entered a small store.

"God!" Gary grabbed Phil's arm. "Look at the brains!"

Phil opened his eyes wide and hit his head. Gary swung his eyes and staggered theatrically.

What'n hell are they so wild about? It just looked like meat to Artie.

"Do you have a match?" Ray was at his elbow, a cigarette in his lips.

"Yeah ... sure." Artie found a book and lit one for him. There was a fan overhead and they moved back a step.

Suddenly Artie was gone. That was all there was to it.

He stood there with the match burning, lost. The fan blew the match out and Artie moved his hand. A sigh eased from him. "Wow! Let's get out of here."

Outside, he and Ray waited for Phil and Gary. Artie could feel the air about him, the particles brushing over his body. "I was sure entranced by that flame! It would've burnt me except for the fan. Time seems so unreal! It seemed forever I was standing there and I couldn't break away until the light went out." He felt suddenly effusive.

Ray laughed.

"It's funny though ... I never thought about breaking away until I was already freed. Before that I just wasn't there ... " He closed his mouth. It was rapidly becoming difficult to talk. His mouth belonged to someone else.

When Gary came out, Artie could tell by his eyes he knew. Gary nodded and smiled. Artie wanted to tell him about the match. Need he talk? It seemed Gary could read his mind anyway. There was so much to see on Gary's face, too. It changed so often. Seeing all the people in Gary was eerie.

Artie turned his eyes away, embarrassed. Am I melting, too. Near the university, they stopped to read a poster nailed to a tree. The tree was majestic. Large patches of gray were sliced everywhere by black lines that moved on the bark like snakes.

Phil spoke. "Let's head—ha, ha—get that Gary? Let's head up to the Student Union. There's an old friend I want to look up."

In the S.U., as they came in the front door, Artie could see a large abstract mural on the far wall. He stopped in the middle of the foyer. He'd seen it move! Lines waved in and out, oozing, bubbling, changing color, flashing on and off.

When he finally looked around, Phil and Ray had disappeared.

Gary shuffled his feet, glancing around. "Let's move."

Artie walked with him toward the fishbowl, a large, glassed-in area with tables and chairs. Standing in the open doorway he could see a crowd of people. Too much.

"Gary?"

"Yeah."

"I'm going over to that couch by the painting."

Gary nodded.

"Are you going to leave me?" Artie was afraid something might come up he couldn't handle.

"No, I'll be around."

On the black leather sofa under the painting, Artie sat watching the people come and go. He couldn't control his mind. It began to feel like a steam heater, hissing and clanking. When he closed his eyes, it began to boil and he opened them, afraid. The foyer seemed so much larger than usual. Like being in an airport. People coming and going. The flow was cyclic, at first heavy, then light, then heavy again. When someone looked him in the face, Artie felt he was seeing in and through them. A quick glance stretched into minutes. There was time to observe so much.

He stood up. Got to get away. Find Gary.

But, instead, Howard came from the fishbowl into the foyer.

Artie tried to turn around but he was frozen. Howard had spotted him.

"Did you come for the dance?" Howard reached for a pipe in his right pocket. "I might go."

"Well," he turned away, "see you later then."

Man, I've got to get out of here. Can't take this. Gotta mellow out. If I have to make a complete sentence I'll fail. Too easy to get tied up in words. His mind seemed to be making small trips every few seconds. He didn't want to get so far out no one could guide him back in.

When he found Gary, Phil and Ray were with him. Artie wanted to go back to the apartment, but the others wanted to go up to the dance.

"You know who's playing, right?" Phil said. "Paul Revere and the Raiders."

They climbed the long cement stairs at the back of the auditorium and sneaked in when someone came out on the balcony for air. Inside, Artie was in a fairyland. The second the music hit him he was moving, dancing frantically. The music wrapped him up and carried him along. Realizing suddenly that there were people around him, he found an unoccupied spot along the wall and sat down. The people seemed in another world. At times he felt they were all turned on and he could do and say what he wanted—but his rational mind kept warning him it couldn't be so.

Several projectors flashed pictures on the far wall. One sequence was a continuous movie of a car winding steadily upwards and upwards around a curve. Artie avoided it.

What if I got caught in it? I might never get away. Trapped.

"Let's split, Artie. Light show'll keep you here all night." Gary had materialized suddenly, coming out of the music like a genie. And looking twice as big.

In the apartment, he left the guys in the living room and found an empty bedroom. He needed to be alone.

You're up, man, up high. Going higher. Tenth floor. Top floor. Going higher.

You'll never come down. We've got you now.

Minute 157. Three lives lived.

In his mind he was once again on the roof of Friendly Hall with Phil Lockfall. But you're down there now, kid, not up here. And you're higher. You're too high to touch down. You've blown it, man.

It's getting better all the time ...

Stop the music. Blasting out of the living room. Too much. Each note was like a bullet plowing through his chest.

He blew his mind out in a car ... Watch it, man, that light's been green five hours in two seconds ... He didn't notice that the light had changed ... A road a mile long and longer ... And I just had to laugh ... Man, the Beatles knew, didn't they? They'd been here, too.

Watch the ash ... who'll eat the roach?

Sinking, reaching the elements, merge, wet grass, relax, see the stars ...

First trip ... moment 17 ...that steam radiator's your brain ... vacuum cleaner higher. One terminal ... faces faces faces, eyes look through him.

Are we still on the street?

And there he was on the street again and running. The apartment was too much. He had to get away. He hoped they wouldn't follow. He was super-high and knew it. He was living a hundred trips.

There was the time Bruce Jenkins talked him and Gary into shooting it. Howard knew about the drugs by then, but he was gone for the weekend. Artie had met Bruce again at Gary's place one evening when Bruce was visiting from Corvallis. After his year in Italy, he'd been turned down by all the medical schools and was now pushing dope. He had some pure acid straight from California. Owsley.

"It's the best. No speed in this. You guys get bad trips cause the stuff's loaded with speed. You gotta let me shoot this up you. Gives you a high in five minutes. Real clean. No side effects. It'll last you an extra five to ten hours."

Look at his veins ... break the tab in a spoon ... water ... heat ... five minutes and you're high. No air bubbles ... draw it in slowly ... shoot it clean ... The belt, loosen the belt from his arm ...

Remember your own room later? The three of you. Bruce Jenkins—who you never liked, dressed as always in fancy duds. Gary Norling—red hair to his shoulders. Artie Crenshaw. Three gods. Father, Son, and Holy Ghost. Didn't it seem you had created the universe? But for it to end, one of you had to die. Then you'd have experienced everything.

Would it be you?

"There's too much power in this room," Gary said. He was guiding Artie.

Lost, so deep this time. The fan ... lights ... the record player ... plug me in ... I made electricity ... Of the three of us, one should die. Would we return to the moment before the eternal now?

Stage five ... We're on the corner. Did you fall? Yes. I was gone.

Was our name on the list, Howard?

Ground control ... Reality number three. Would you like to be high always? Feel that song. Yeah, you're right.

Paranoia's good and bad, isn't it? It all means the same.

You're still climbing, man. Ease off.

Lying on the sofa beneath the long front window overlooking a weeping willow tree, Artie began to relax. The cushions with their criss-crossed threads were slowly cutting into his body. He could feel his head sliced into miniature cubes. Overhead, the dingy living room light began to fracture up like a prism, the colors raining down.

Man, I'm deep. This is the deepest!

So this was where it led him, into this park in San Francisco, into the dark of darkness, into this maze of paths and shrubs, this confusion. Sounds, words, music, colors, thoughts, lights—his stunned senses were in a turmoil, his mind overwhelmed. He felt his eyes open to new visions and passing before him, in the sky, fir trees with wings and their sound was like the wind on a lonesome autumn day, alone, in a wheat field, watching a solitary sparrow flitting from place to place chirping, and quiet wind swaying the stalks and the smell of earth newly plowed and black near the touching of the sky.

# — 9 —
## Crossroads

From inside the bus, the city of Portland was a whirlpool of light, a clamor of cars, taxis and trucks.

Leaving the bus, Artie stumbled and nearly fell into the driver's seat.

"Careful, honey," a gray-haired lady wearing a clear, plastic raincap cautioned him. And that was his introduction to the storm of voices around him. As he stepped from the shadows and the rumbling exhaust of the loading platform into the Post House, the glare dazzled him. Overhead, the large illuminated clock read a few minutes after four. It was still too early to leave. The walk to his older brother's place would take an hour to an hour and a half. He might be able to stretch it into two but, even then, it would only be six when he arrived. Too early for Richy.

He walked down a short flight of steps and entered the cafeteria. Buying a cup of coffee, he found an isolated table, unzipped his coat, set his small brown suitcase by his feet and sat down, opening a book.

Unable to concentrate, he folded a napkin, contemplated writing a letter to someone on it. Isolated bits of conversation from the other travelers wove their way into his mind.

Artie sensed a presence behind him. A bum in an overcoat a foot too long was staring at him.

"Say, fellow, can you spare a dime for a couple of hungry boys trying to get a can of beans?"

"I'm sorry, no." Artie raised both hands. "Student." He lowered his eyes, blocking out the voices around him and thought about his father and the letter from home in his pocket.

I guess dad's finally lost out. Sad in a way but hard to feel much pity. Trying to preserve the past was hopeless. The housing projects around the farm were increasing in size. His father had finally been surrounded. For a while, he'd tried to resist the realtors, who kept telling him he was in between two growing towns. But he'd refused and tried to keep the farm running and the woods from being cut down.

It was a zoning change that defeated him. Artie's mother had written that they were finally moving. Dad was disillusioned. Going to move on. The neighbors, she said, tried to convince him to stay. He could have a place to retire, a nice home in a residential area. Dad said he couldn't stand seeing a supermarket built where the barn had stood, so he was packing up and leaving.

But Artie had enough problems of his own to worry about. The drugs and then the girls. Fate kept stepping in and kicking him in the balls. Maybe that was what I deserved. Trying to beat Phil. The guy bragged about screwing a new girl every other week.

So the girls. His own feeble attempts.

His first date? Jan Henderson, a stocky girl in his Classic Myths class. He borrowed Howard's Pontiac convertible, kissed Jan at a stop light after a show and pizza, and later felt her over through her sweater before dropping her off at the dorm. But that fell apart after several dates because of a short trip Howard and Artie made.

Exhausted with school, depressed with their boring life, they decided one evening to leave the university and head for Mexico. They planned to stay a few weeks and return in time for finals. Trading cars with Phil—he owned a Fiat bus that would get better gas mileage and had sleeping space in the back—they left that very night, dropping by the dorm first to let Jan know.

A few miles south of Eugene, the generator blew out and they barely made it to Roseburg. They spent most of the night in a gas station, while an attendant charged the battery and tried unsuccessfully to round up a rebuilt generator. After sleeping a few hours in the car on the freeway that morning, they decided to return to Eugene. Howard had had second thoughts, although Artie wanted to go on.

When Jan found out they were back in town, she wouldn't speak to Artie. She figured, he learned later, that the whole thing was a farce to make her feel bad at his leaving. When the problem was finally straightened out, he'd lost interest in her.

Shirley Linden. Sat two seats away in his Shakespeare class. She invited him to her apartment above a small store on the corner of High Street and Thirteenth and fed him home-made cinnamon rolls and milk. A freckle-faced, motherly type with red hair. Her roommate was an old girl friend of Ray Spencer, and Artie heard he'd taken his girl to bed. Maybe Shirley wanted the same thing.

But then he asked if he could smoke and that ended that relationship. He found out later she was a Mormon. Wouldn't even drink coffee.

The third girl he met two weeks later. Winter term, an Italian class got canceled, too few students, so he was adding Spanish.

The first day he showed up, a girl in jeans was standing in the hall.

"Is this Mrs. Kaufman's Spanish class?"

It was, and they struck up a brief conversation. When the previous class let out and they walked into the classroom, she sat next to a girl in the second row. He considered sitting one seat away but, hesitating, found himself beside her. A decisive step.

Spanish was his first class in the day and, the following week, coming to school early, he found she had a free hour between classes. They fell into the habit of sitting on a bench in the hall, he reading the university newspaper and she studying. Most often, it was first-year Italian she was reviewing and he found an opportunity to help her.

To Howard and his other friends, Artie spoke of her in a hopeless tone. "She's the aristocratic type. Looks rich, sorority type. Pretty. Kind of skinny with long blond hair. Pamela. Said she was named after a character in one of Samuel Richardson's novels. I had to say I hadn't read it. Ask me something about Manzoni. *I promessi sposi*. Not some English dude. Anyway, she goes by Pam."

To himself, he said she was out of his reach, just not his type. He didn't have the class to impress her. She probably liked being taken out to clubs, dances, proms, whatever, things he hated. A nervous kid. She spent half the time talking about her problems. Holy criminy, she even took tranquilizers!

But finally one day, after getting Howard to lend him his car, he asked her out to a show. She was reading when he asked her, and he noticed her sit up in surprise.

"Yes," she said, seeming surprised herself the second she did, and adding, "But I'll have to ask my mom first. I'll let you know tomorrow."

Odd that a girl that old should have to ask permission. Talk about strict parents.

He took her to a show that Saturday. For the first hour he sat thinking he should at least hold hands with her or put his arm around her. Midway through the first feature—a war comedy set in Italy—he told himself he would count to ten and if he hadn't put his arm around her before he reached the end, he would kill himself. It was a trick he used often when his nerve was down and it always worked because he really believed he would kill himself if he didn't do what he vowed.

Feeling his arm going around her, Pam jumped forward in her seat. Artie flushed. Using the pretext of taking her coat off, he laid it behind her on the seat and removed his hand. He didn't touch her the rest of the movie. After the show, he asked her if she would like some pizza. No, she wasn't hungry. Good God, really hitting it off with her.

"Is there anything you'd like to eat?"

"Maybe an ice cream cone."

She's cheap enough, at least, he thought and, after the cone, took her home. The next Monday she was there in the hall as usual and just as friendly as ever. He couldn't figure her out.

Later in the term, he asked her out again, this time to a spaghetti dinner at his own place. He and Howard were going to prepare spaghetti alla carbonara. Pam brought a girl friend with her for Howard and they passed an enjoyable but unremarkable evening. Artie showed Pam his paintings, his art books and some of his souvenirs from Italy and that was it. When he took her home, she invited him in. Her parents were out so he stayed till two o'clock, talking until she began to yawn.

When he got home, Howard was still up smoking, pacing the room in his robe, trying to write a short story in between long steady treks from his bedroom, across the living room to the kitchen, to the far corner of the kitchen and back again.

"Man," Artie said, "you ought to see the house that girl lives in. Parents must be as rich as hell. Two fireplaces, living room, party room, two bathrooms, color TV ..."

"Bummer. Pretty though, like you said. By the way, her girl friend was a dud. I spent the whole evening talking history and politics. She doesn't know anything. Goes to a beauty school. Guess you can't expect much."

Artie laughed at Howard's idea of a good date. Unless they were philosophy majors they just couldn't make it.

Howard had been in an almost steady depression the whole term. He explained its causes briefly to Artie but didn't elaborate much. Artie managed to learn it was because of his old girl friend, Toni Walters. When Howard returned from Europe, he found they couldn't communicate.

"The thing that held our relationship together, that really made it unique," he said, "was that we were always honest with each other. Completely open. She dated a guy while I was in Italy and didn't tell me everything. I guess she even slept with him. That's what I get for respecting a virgin and leaving her alone. Someone else gets to her instead."

Howard turned away, about to go into his bedroom, but then came back.

"She's the only girl I've ever known who was a goddess. I need a goddess—someone both beautiful and intelligent. Other than her I've only found one or the other type. Never the two qualities in one."

A few nights later, Howard called him in to talk.

"I was reading Faulkner tonight," he said. "Remember when Popeye sticks the corn cob up the girl? When I read that I was ...I don't know how to describe it, I was overwhelmed by a sense of the macabre."

Spare me Howard. I've got more pleasant things to think about.

Toward the end of the term, things suddenly fell apart and Artie felt as down as Howard about girls. One day in Spanish class, Pam told him she was going back to Oregon State in Corvallis, where she'd started school.

"I just can't stand living at home," she said. "I don't meet anyone. I don't have any social life, no friends—except you," she added with a laugh, seeing his hurt look. "The people at Oregon State are different. Everyone's stuck up here at the U of O. The second they hear I live at home, I'm snubbed. If you don't belong to a sorority you just don't fit in. That's the first thing any girl asks you."

Artie felt a coldness seize his heart. Why did it seem as if he always lost the good things? He'd built so much up in his heart. He was beginning to fall in love with her.

Their parting after finals was disheartening.

"I have to go this way," he said, where the sidewalk split in two directions.

"Good luck on your painting," she called.

"Thanks. Same to you. Uh, with your Spanish."

And with that she was gone.

In the Post House, Artie took another sip of his coffee, now cold, and looked around. The place was nearly deserted and he felt a need for a change of atmosphere.

He left and, with no destination in mind, wandered from street to street, lost in thought. Soon he found himself near the freeway entrance and the long access to the Ross Island Bridge. At night, it loomed skeletal and cold. He imagined what it would be like when the sun rose high enough to splatter it with fire. It would be a beautiful morning, the orange sun on the cold black steel, the pastel shade of the grass, the river, the sky. If only his own life were as promising. It seemed he was getting nowhere.

Audrey Madison was the cause of much of it. He recalled the beginning of that. Howard had left him alone in the house one night (Artie was smoking pot) and had gone with Ray Spencer to Spencer's sister's apartment. Later that evening, the phone woke Artie from his reverie. He hated to answer, but after a few moments he found the phone on the floor by the kitchen.

"Yeah?"

"Artie, this is Howard." He was shouting. "Listen, I've got a couple of girls here who'd like to climb the butte. Want to come along?"

"Hell, Howard, you know what I'm like. I'm still high."

"The fresh air'll do you good. I have a girl for you. You'll have fun."

Artie talked and argued for several minutes and at last allowed Howard to bring the girls over. His hair was long and tousled now, and when he opened the door he could see the girls drop back. Before he could say anything though, the uglier one shoved her way in and jumped up to him. "So this is your roommate, Howard? Hi Artie. I'm Lynn Cole, your date."

Great. Thanks, Howard.

"And this is Joyce," Howard said, his arm around the husky one.

Once they were in the car, Howard said, "Hey, I know, let's go to the coast instead."

"Yeah," everyone said in unison, even Artie. "That'll be more fun."

As they left the city and the night sky darkened, Artie put his arm around Lynn. Moments later, not caring, he kissed her.

God, cold mouthed. Didn't respond worth a shit.

"Howard, you mind if I drive?"

Howard, only too happy to sit in back, consented, and Artie took the wheel. "Careful," Lynn said, as he picked up speed and began to maneuver around the endless curves on Route F, the old coast route. She sat beside him watchful, while in back Artie could hear Howard making out.

As they neared the coast, the moon appeared from behind black clouds. It was cold on the beach, the wind strong. Artie put his arm around Lynn's waist and they began to walk toward a lighthouse in the distance. Howard and Joyce followed behind.

Just then, without warning, it began to pour. They started running, Artie outdistancing the others. He dived into the car, soaked. And that was the end of that date.

The next day Howard found three cups left in the car, and in the evening he and Artie drove over to return them.

At the girls' place, Lynn and Joyce had told their other two roommates, both engaged to be married, about Artie—how odd he was, a flake, no a hippie, guy told an endless series of lies and stories.

When they arrived, three girls were there—Joyce, Lynn, and one of the engaged girls, Audrey. She was wearing a loose shift and sitting in a plush black swivel chair, in the corner by the record player and sofa.

Slouching on the sofa, Artie was silent while Howard and the girls talked. Suddenly he jumped up and reached into his pocket. "Care for a Lifesaver, anyone?"

"What kind?" Audrey asked.

"Pep-O-Mint or Wint-O-Green."

"Oh, I love peppermint." He gave her one, looking closely at her for the first time. She was rather pretty, though chubby, but not as bad as Joyce. She had nice lips and a good build. Seemed rather coy for being engaged, sitting with her side to him, feeling him looking but taking pains to look straight ahead. Proud of her profile. Her fiancé was a Marine back east; she hadn't seen him for three or four months.

In the following weeks Howard and Artie fell into the habit of stopping by the girls' apartment to chat. Slowly, Artie and Audrey began to build a relationship. Both quiet, left out of the conversation, they took to trading glances, smiles, and finally whispered jokes behind the others' backs. Whenever Artie saw her, he couldn't help smiling. He began to look forward to visits.

One evening after dinner at the girls' place, Artie was sitting next to Lynn on the sofa when she asked him playfully to write her a letter. Warm with white wine and a good fresh fish dinner, he wrote her a short, humorous letter. When she received it, she giggled uproariously, handed the letter to Audrey, and kissed Artie on the cheek.

"Oh," Audrey exclaimed, "write me a letter too!"

Artie grabbed a piece of paper and began with "Dear Audrey." He stopped and sat for several minutes. What could he say? It was difficult to write to her when he could feel his heart jump with the desire to write more than he should.

Much later that night, alone at home, he began to write her as he had promised. He tried to mask his feelings but it took effort. He couldn't understand how he'd let himself get so carried away. He'd know all along she was engaged.

Only now it was too late. He was falling in love with her. At least now, he thought, it's in the open.

He found that Audrey tacitly accepted the fact. And, what surprised him more, everyone around him—Howard, Lynn, Joyce, even Arlene the other engaged girl who was hardly ever there, Phil, Gary—all accepted the fact without ever alluding to it openly. Joyce was the only one he once heard speak and she'd said he was stupid. It made no difference to him.

In the weeks that followed, he and Audrey had several chances to be alone. They talked openly of Artie's love. He even went so far as to joke with her about her shirt with a picture of Peanuts on the front. His ears were over her breasts and they joked about Peanuts and his big ears. Audrey told him the measurements of all the girls in the apartment.

He began to a portrait of her from memory, and once spent the night lying on the living room floor with her and Lynn, talking about love, sex, and his experiences in Europe. Audrey cooked breakfast for him in the morning.

The all-night sessions became more common and more and more intimate. Audrey let him hold hands or put his arm around her under the blanket so Lynn couldn't see and they touched toes.

He was surprised at the rapidity with which things changed. In his more rational moments, he occasionally wondered about his feelings. Did he really mean his protestations of love, his claims that he wanted to marry her—or was it the realization that she was impossible to attain that drove him on? He wasn't sure.

Audrey, he could tell, felt more for him all the time. Pouring him a Coke one day, she set the glass on the kitchen counter. He put his lips down to take a sip, and as they touched the glass, he jumped back in surprise. "It sparkled on my nose!"

She laughed, a clear tinkling sound of simple enjoyment.

"Why're you laughing?"

"I just like you."

He pressed her again with "why's" until she finally told him she liked the way he reacted to things with a childlike sensitivity. "Everything you do is fresh and vibrant, awake to life." She paused. "You just make normal things new. I like it."

At that, they both stood by the sink, silently watching the February sun turn amber in the dusk.

The kiss felt inevitable.

It was a moment he wished he could stretch into hours.

Working his way along an embankment, Artie left the Ross Island Bridge behind and walked up above the brightly lit Macadam Avenue. To his left, down below near the river, he could see a steady stream of cars, funneling down an imaginary long black tunnel into the night of the city.

But in the end it all failed. After all their countless talks, after their exchanges of love, Audrey left anyway.

---

"How can I really decide?" she asked him. "I'm engaged, I can't date you, so I don't know how we'd be together in a crowd. I haven't seen Brink for so long either. I won't really know how I feel until then."

"But it'll be too late then!"

"No, it won't."

"You'll be entangled by it. It'll be too late to break away, too drastic."

"Artie, if I ever didn't feel sure of myself, I would break the engagement an hour before the ceremony."

If things had only moved faster, if he'd only pressured her more.

The day she left to return to her home in Eastern Oregon, he left with her. The night before, in bed together, he told her he couldn't say good-bye in Eugene. He had to follow her.

Outside Portland, they stopped at a restaurant near Cascade Locks. Like a young couple on a honeymoon, Artie thought. But finally, in Hermiston, he decided to go back. They had an hour until the bus to Eugene came. It was a desolate spot, an empty parking lot, deserted on Sunday. In the car, separation close at hand, they both began to cry.

But it made no difference.

He was in Eugene the night she got married. In the days that followed he wanted to write to her, wanted to tell her how much he loved her, how he missed her. He would sit at his desk writing a letter in his mind, in despair the whole time, realizing he could never send it.

But then, a few weeks before spring term ended, he received a call from Pam in Corvallis. He'd thought she was out of his life for good. But maybe not.

After the call (he could tell she was drunk), he began to write to her and invited her down one evening to dinner and another night to a concert, on a double date with Howard.

Afterward, the two returned to Artie's place and talked while they played records. He discovered why she jumped the first time he put his arm around her at the show.

"I had a Mexican novio then," she said, "a steady, but we've had trouble since then. I'm not sure where we stand. Guero asked me to marry him, but things change fast. Every time I go back to Mexico, it takes a while to start over again. We're like strangers. I'm going back there next fall to find out if I love him. I'll be studying at the University of the Americas for a year. Just outside Mexico City."

Artie had his back to her, changing a record. "How'd you meet him?"

"I went down as an exchange student in high school and stayed with his family. We were like a brother and sister, so I was surprised the week before I left when he asked me to be his novia."

"Have you seen him much?"

"I've been back twice during two summers. The last time I saved all my money and flew down for a week."

Damn. Why date her if she loved another guy?

In the weeks that followed, he wrote to her in Corvallis, saying he was starting to like her more and maybe they should drop things and not see each other in case things developed too far. It was no use being hurt if she was going down to Mexico to marry Guero, anyway. He'd been hurt like that before, he said—but didn't tell her about Audrey. Or Colleen, now a distant memory.

Pam wrote back saying why ruin a present relationship for the chance of a future one? Besides she wasn't sure if Guero was really the one or not. Encouraged by at least some positive response, he kept writing to her.

But, despite everything, here he was in Portland, going to visit his older brother. Richy was getting married in June and he wanted Artie to be his best man.

He pulled his coat tighter as the early morning chill crept in. Walking from Macadam Avenue toward Barbur Boulevard, he wondered if he would every see Pam again. He knew how things went if all you could do was write. That's how he lost Colleen.

Uncertain, hesitant, but most of all tired, he walked up into the hills of Southwest Portland. A light mist was now falling. He Wanted to forget the confusion of the last school year. So many girls, so many attempts to establish a solid relationship, so much exhaustion. And where would it all end? With Pam or not?

# — 10 —
# Aurora

In a shack which he'd appropriated as a studio, high above the corner of Aguascalientes and Medellin, Artie sat under a bare light bulb before a small easel. Around him, the walls were covered with unframed canvases tacked to the rough boards. Though it was only five in the morning and still dark, he could hear the rumble of traffic, drifting down to him from Insurgentes, five blocks away.

By his side, on the floor, lay a letter from Phil Lockfall. It was the first he'd received from his friend since being in Mexico, six months now. Tired of painting, he picked up the letter and reread it, thinking how much there was to tell Phil in return.

He's probably wondering why I'm here with Pam.

Artie stirred, wondering if he should go downstairs to bed or start a letter. Might as well stay up. Nothing better to do.

His studio was a small eight-foot-square washroom on top of a two-story, flat-roofed building. Artie rented a room on the second floor from a young widow and shared her house with two other older spinsters. He slept in a corner of the living room, curtained off for privacy.

Phil's letter had reminded him of what life was like in the States. Anti-war protests. Draft cards being burnt. People marching.

The last time Artie had spoken to Phil was in August, just before Phil had left Eugene. It was good to hear from him again.

*Dear me!* Phil began.

*It sure has been a long time since I've written or heard from you (Artie), so ... Dear Artie, Yeah, it's me, Phil. I'm still in the army, still in Georgia. Probably will head for Asia, or possibly Europe, (here there was a picture of two crossed fingers) soon. I have three more weeks in this school.*

*The biggest news of the moment is Big Ray Spencer got the shaft, in the shape of the draft. By now he should be in his third week of Basic Combat Training. I shit green balls when I received a card from him saying "Greetings from Fort Lewis." I was afraid at Christmas time they would get him. He has a pretty good attitude for it anyway since he's divorced now. He was really different the last time I saw him. He still tries to come on like King Stud, but he has loosened up some; he's closer to letting himself experience the total non-hang-up life. If anything, the Army will make him more ready for it. If there's one thing the Army does, it's to make a person value his freedom.*

*Which brings me to Gary Norling. He's on parole for stealing some car parts and is talking of going back to school to study business—that's all we need, right? More corporation crooks! But it'll do him good. Get him away from his other creepy friends.*

*I sure wish I could talk to you, Artie. We have so much to discuss, so much that is new. The girls around here really love soldiers, so I'm getting a lot of tail. When we do get together we'll have to get off somewhere for a week just to get caught up.*

*My amorous escapades, hah!*

*Back to the guys here. I get pissed off a lot, and sometimes I think of killing someone, but most of the time we get along. Too much in common. We all get fed up at times, but it is not as bad as it could be. I'm glad I'm older and able to understand (somewhat) what I'm up against.*

*Should have split for Canada when I had the chance, right?*

*Please write when able. Your friend always, Phil.*

Artie hadn't yet begun his response to Phil's letter. Almost too much to write about. The last month of summer had passed in a daze, and his life in Mexico was a mess. But he didn't want to write about Pam, sharing something intimate.

That summer in Eugene, Pam had worked for the phone company as a long-distance operator and Artie often came to meet the bus that brought her to town. He also met her at breaks and, during lunch, she would walk the short way from her job to the new place he'd rented on Patterson Street. The house was old and five guys lived in it altogether, bringing the rent down to where Artie could get along on his savings, especially if he ate only once a day. He wasn't working that summer since, after he graduated fall term, he'd been offered a job at the university teaching a beginning art class.

He and Pam would eat lunch together and then go upstairs to Artie's room, the largest one in the house. He'd appropriated it so he would have space for his canvases and easel. His bed was squished under the roof at one end where a gable cut inward. For about half the room, the roof slanted like a tent and he had to duck to keep from hitting his head.

Pam liked the atmosphere. From the bed they could see to the left an old arm chair with a pillow case pinned to the ragged cushion. Next to it in the corner stood his dresser, then a glass-doored hutch with records inside, and finally a long table stretching down one wall to the door. The rest of the room was filled with his art supplies, and his paintings covered the walls.

Pam took the bus home in the evenings when she got off work, and Artie, who was always up all night painting or walking the streets, woke up from his nap to accompany her to the bus stop by the city jail.

At night, waiting for her to appear, he parked himself in the shadows of the large doorway of the phone company, looming above him like Constantine's Arch, only not quite so big, though, if he pretended, half closing his eyes, it did seem to stretch out in the shadows. He liked the entrance to the phone company because for him it was the most majestic site in town. It was here that he met Pam.

But did he really understand her?

He couldn't figure out why she was loving at one moment, then distant the next.

Once, lying on his bed together, she told him she hated herself.

"I get to feeling I can't love anyone. It scares me. I want to love you ... but I can't when I'm feeling like this."

"Don't you feel anything for me?"

"Oh, Artie," she said, putting her head by his. He could feel her wet cheeks. "I hate to do this to you. You must think I'm terrible. Do you hate me?"

"No, I don't hate you. I love you. It just hurts me that you feel like that."

"I do care for you, Artie."

Much later that same night, after Artie had taken Pam home, Howard Montrel stopped by on his way from his home town near Portland to Los Angeles to see a girl he'd met toward the end of the school year. They talked about Howard's new girl.

"I like her," Howard said, "but I don't respect her. My problem is I can't do both with any one girl."

"Howard, you dream of too much. You've got to forget your idea of a goddess. You want someone perfect and that's impossible. You don't know what you're looking for, and you'll never find it."

Howard shrugged. "Maybe not. Then I'll go through life a bachelor."

"With Pam I feel I've found everything I've always dreamed about and yet, she's not perfect. I've never expected perfection. But she's the most complete girl I've ever known."

In his room on the roof, Artie smiled wryly. So much had happened since then. Both good and bad.

He liked to think of the afternoons they'd spent in his room in Eugene when Pam was working a split shift. They started most afternoons looking at slides of Italy through a little viewer, but both knew that was a pretext and laughed about it. They found themselves on the bed after a few slides. For the first month in the summer, they just talked and kissed, but gradually Artie relaxed her to where they would undress and lie next to each other. Pam, like him, was a virgin and it was another month before they were really making love. At the start, he told her he was just putting pressure on her and it was safe. She was making love before she knew it. When she asked him about it one day, he confessed they were and showed surprise she hadn't realized it.

"Well," she replied, "How was I supposed to know? You always said it wasn't complete."

Artie remembered one afternoon with special pleasure. They had drunk some wine together out of chilled goblets, and standing naked in his room, they could feel the heat radiating between them. He sat on the edge of the bed, holding her hips, looking at her body, the enticing color of her flesh. Pulling her closer to him he began to kiss her belly. He could feel her hands on the back of his neck. As he moved down she started to moaning. She was hot and wet and he laid her back on the bed spreading her legs to enjoy it. When he finished with his mouth, she wanted his body again. Bigger than ever with excitement, his body slipped easily into hers.

"Let me give you pleasure, Artie. Lie on your back."

They rolled over without him coming out, and she started on a story where she was a bitch, a whore, and he was fucking her. He liked it when they acted parts and she worked it slowly out of him. They passed many afternoons without thinking about the future.

When they began to talk about it, Pam told Artie she was still going to Mexico in the fall. "I've still got to see if I love Guero."

"But how can you say that if you love me?"

"I do but I guess I've got to make sure it's completely dead between me and Guero."

They argued over the matter, but Pam never wavered. She was going to Mexico to study.

"If our relationship is solid, when I get back we can start up again."

"But so much can happen in the meantime," Artie said, suspecting she wanted one last fling before settling down. They'd talked about marriage and here she wanted to leave.

Finally, near the end of summer, Artie decided he would follow her. He worked for a month, ten to twelve hours a day, painting houses for two architects in the city. Pam was shocked when he told her one night that he planned to join her in Mexico.

"But what about your teaching?" she asked. "And finishing school?"

"Jeez, don't you want me to go with you?"

"Well, sure. I think it'd be nice—but you may regret it."

Pam's father told Artie the same thing. "She's got to have a chance to make up her mind," he said. "You're throwing a lot away."

Artie tried to explain, but it was difficult. Pam's parents didn't know how deep their relationship really was. So, with only $350 saved, Artie had arrived in the city ten days after Pam. At the central station he passed an hour looking for a map of the city. Pam had given him a phone number of one of the friends she'd made as an exchange student. But in his impatience to see her, he decided to go directly to the university.

He spent the next two hours walking and changing buses until he was finally on a Toluca bus that dropped him off at the school.

It was hot under the Mexican sun. Around him, like the brick walls of a large open oven, the white-washed surfaces of four different classrooms shimmered in the heat. Pam was still in class and it would be another thirty-five minutes before she came out. Artie moved down the iron bench until he was half-in and half-out of the shade of the overhanging roof.

He wondered if Pam would be surprised. She didn't know yet that he was in the city. He could have written her telling her exactly when he would arrive but he'd been purposely vague. He preferred the unexpected encounter.

Beautiful Pam, lovely Pam, would she be wearing her pink dress that made her look so much like dawn? Was it really only ten days since he'd last seen her? It seemed that many weeks.

Then he looked up and in the glare of white on white, there she was!

In the busy days that followed, Artie escorted Pam to and from the house where she was staying and the University of the Americas. Although trying to change her residence, Pam was still living with the family of her novio, Guero Dinario, and hadn't told them about Artie yet. Whenever she and Artie drew near the condominium—Camino a Belén—Pam would tell him not to touch her. She didn't want anyone to see her and tell the Dinarios. Artie was irritated at her precautions.

After all, aren't we going together now? Why does she have to get so damn irritated at me and so damn scared?

Arrangements were made that day for Pam to move in with a different family—the Estradas—and Artie helped her transfer. He was introduced to the parents, the father, a banker, to the older son, Aureliano, an accountant, to Roberto, studying to be a tourist guide, and to Mauricio, the youngest son, a handsome kid, eighteen years old, studying politics. The youngest child, Rebecca, was spoiled by the entire family.

From the start, once they were settled, Artie with his spinsters and Pam with her large family, Artie was irritated by Pam. They were both free people, she told him, and she planned to date other guys. He could date other women if he wished, although she didn't mind seeing him, of course. But, since they weren't engaged—(even though they'd talked about marriage—hell, planned it together)—she was going to date to make sure how she felt toward him, to see if he was really the one.

Riding the bus to see Pam one night, Artie watched the faces of the people around him. Two seats down from him across the aisle sat a young fellow with a radio to his ear. The Beatles were playing and Artie watched the Mexicans relax to the soothing sounds of "Here,

There and Everywhere." The song put Artie in a pensive mood. He wished he hadn't told Pam over the phone about the Mexican girls and his landlady.

The previous Sunday, his landlady, Señora Lucia de Sonoro, had invited him to dinner with her relatives, especially so he could meet her two nieces.

"Tengo dos muy guapitas sobrinas," she'd said. "You will be a Don Juan, un conquistador." She smiled at Artie.

He returned the smile, protesting. "No, no, not a Don Juan."

One of the nieces he learned was already a novia, but the younger one, the seventeen-year-old, was his to conquer if he wished.

"I didn't tell them you had a novia," the señora told him on the bus for Santa Maria. "It's better not to say anything or they won't invite you out." Here she laughed. "Because your novia could get mad."

At least, Artie thought, we decided to present Pam to her as my novia. To her that means we're getting married.

When he'd told Pam about the two girls earlier on the phone, it had come out sounding as if he were trying to make her jealous. He told it as a joke and laughed a lot, but it was a dry, sterile laugh and they both knew it.

Rising, he pulled the cord and got off at a dark corner. The streets were wet. Two lovers stood under the awning of the Banco Comercial, enclosed in each others' arms. He quickened his steps.

Turning the corner, he found the number and rang the bell. He stepped back to see if anyone would look out the window. No one appeared. He rang again, twice now, impatient. Finally, after what seemed forever, Mauricio, the younger son, opened the door, shook hands with him, and led him to the study.

Pam was sitting on the floor dressed in white shorts and a white blouse. It irritated him that she should be so casual with two other boys in the room. He was introduced to the other fellow, Antonio something or other. It was too long to remember.

"Hi," Pam greeted him, then looked back at her books, acting, he thought, as if he were nobody. He sat down and took off his coat.

Every time he tried to open a conversation with Pam, she cut him off, remarking finally, "Will you be quiet so I can get this read?" As always, the sharpness of her attitude set him to wondering how, if she cared for him, she could act so brutal.

Mauricio called to her from a desk in the far corner. She rose and stood by his side, explaining something about analytical geometry. Artie knew he'd be tormented with thoughts of what might happen when he was gone. He saw them studying together, asking each other questions, standing side by side. Mauricio was handsome and being in the same house all the time, well, who could tell?

Later that night, their studying done, Artie had coffee with the family and left. He hated the nightly trips home. It was always pitch black—the Mexican sky never seemed to have stars—and he was in a state of exhaustion from a grueling day of bus riding.

Stepping from the Coyoacan bus at the corner of Sears and Insurgentes, Artie unexpectedly ran into Manuel Torrente, a friend of Guero, Pam's former novio.

"Are you coming from work?"

"No, I have been with my woman. But I want to ask you something. Can you come with me for an hour now?"

Artie hesitated. "I don't know. I'm pretty tired. What for?"

"My sister's birthday is today and they are celebrating. We can go to the party for a bit."

Since it was a birthday, Artie figured he'd better accept. They took a taxi to the apartment.

On the way, Manuel said, "You like Pam, don't you?"

Artie didn't know what to say. He nodded.

"Are you novios? In her letter to me, she said you were her boy friend, but down here she introduced you as a friend."

"But down here having a novia is more serious, isn't it, than just having a boy or girl friend? It usually means you're engaged and going to be married, doesn't it?"

"Not really. You can break it off at any time. Either the boy or the girl can."

Artie saw this line was hopeless. "Well, then, I don't know whether we are or not." He sensed Manuel was trying to hurt him by his questioning. "To some people she introduces me as a novio and to others as just a friend. I introduced her to my landlady as a novia."

After that, they were silent in the cab. When they reached the apartment, they climbed a few floors and found the door in a corner by the stairs. It was dark inside. Manuel rang the bell.

"Could they be in bed?" Artie whispered. "Maybe they went some-where else to celebrate."

"Perhaps." They rang again.

"Let's go upstairs," Manuel said.

On the roof, they stepped into a shack, the home of some peasants, where Manuel asked about his sister.

"Ah," someone said, "they are asleep."

Manuel looked at his watch. "So early?"

"Eh sí, sí."

"Didn't they have a birthday party?"

"Oh, Señor Torrente, didn't you know? The birthday was last Saturday."

Manuel reddened and, after a brief conversation with the family, as if to atone for taking Artie out of his way, treated him to some tacos at a small café near his sister's apartment. Artie had told him how little he was eating.

The next day, Artie was surprised to learn that Pam had already been asked on a date by Antonio, Mauricio Estrada's guitar playing friend.

"We're just going to his parents' wedding anniversary celebration," Pam said to appease Artie. "All the Estradas are going, too. So, it's not really a date."

A fight ensued. Alone at home, Artie thought about what she'd said. It hurt. "Are you going to be a ball and chain to me all the time we're down here or what?" she'd asked. "Look, my parents are spending a lot of money to have me down here, Artie, and I won't disappoint them. They want me to have a good time, to see new things. I can't do anything with you. You don't have enough money. What am I supposed to tell them when I go back?"

In his room, Artie fumed. He was eating his insides out, torturing himself with thoughts of what was going on. He hated the Mexicans. All they wanted was to get an American girl. And Pam's attitude didn't help. Antonio knew she and Artie liked each other—and yet he asked her out. And she'd accepted! That's just a go-ahead to him to get all he can. The bastard'll try, too.

For once he was partially right, but he didn't find that out until later. The evening after the anniversary party, back in the city, Pam turned to him and told him she had something to confess.

He felt like a fist had closed around his heart. "What?"

"Antonio kissed me last night."

When she saw how it hit him, she reached for his arm. "I didn't want to. I'm sorry, Artie."

"You kissed him!"

"He kissed me. I couldn't do anything about it. I don't want to hurt you. It was nothing to me. I wasn't even going to tell you, but that wouldn't have felt right."

He couldn't look at her.

"I promise, Artie, it'll never happen again. I couldn't do anything about it. I wasn't expecting it. I didn't lead him on."

"How did it happen?"

"We were out on this veranda—"

"Alone?"

"No, Mauricio was there."

"He kissed you in front of Mauricio!"

She nodded. Inside, Artie felt a dullness deadening his heart. The rest of the conversation—it developed into a fight—was lost on him.

In the Weeks that followed, Artie began to torture himself more and more, sometimes with facts, sometimes with fancies. In rational moments, he would laugh at himself, but he could never break his self-torture once it started.

One afternoon, coming home from the university, Pam asked him if he would mind coming back in the evening about six-thirty or seven o'clock to study with her.

"I think I'll rest a little this afternoon," she said. "I didn't sleep well last night, it's so cold here. Will you come by this evening?"

"Sure," Artie said. "Sounds good to me." Riding the bus home again, he passed a half-hour walking through Woolworth's (it seemed it was getting to be his only recreation) and drew for another couple of hours in his room.

He left the house shortly before six and was outside Pam's home forty-five minutes later. She lived above a clothing' store in a building that was once a bank. The ceiling was high in all the rooms and, unheated and out of the sun, the house was perpetually freezing.

When Pam's Mexican "mother," a portly woman trying to preserve her youth with vast amounts of make-up, opened the door Artie found Pam had gone out. Damn!

"What time will she return?" he asked in Spanish.

"About 8:30 or 9:00, I think," the señora told him.

Unwilling to believe Pam would have left without telephoning him, Artie went back downstairs, crossed the street, and sat before the Biblioteca Nacional waiting for her. A few minutes later, the señora came down, accompanied by her daughter and the grandmother, waved to Artie (he'd told them he was going home) and set off up the street.

Artie waited until dark, sitting on the concrete base of a fence. Across the street, the clothing store was having a clearance sale and Artie had trouble watching for Pam in the crowd. A line of cars and buses piled up at the intersection. A trolley cut off his view. Jumping to his feet, he ran down behind it to watch the doorway. But Pam still didn't come.

Fuming, Artie took a bus home. If Pam didn't care enough about him to call before she broke a date, he wasn't going to spend his money on buses to come and see her.

At home, he sat down at a small table and wrote her a three-page letter, the harshest he'd ever written.

Slamming down his pen, he folded the letter, sealed it in an envelope, stuffed it in his pocket, and set off to deliver it.

When he reached Pam's place again and rang the bell, he saw her and Mauricio both jump and then start for the door. They'd been talking in the living room. Pam saw him and smiled, but his face remained grim. She backed away, let Mauricio open the door.

Artie strode by him, oblivious to everything except his desire to confront Pam.

"What's the matter, Artie?"

They were walking to the study, alone, as Mauricio, having sensed something was wrong, prudently returned to his mother's room to watch TV.

"I've had it. I'm fed up with you!"

In the study, Pam sat down.

"What in the hell do you think you're doing?" Artie said, barely able to keep from shouting. "We had a study date for tonight at 6:30 or 7 and I waited for you for an hour and a half and you didn't show.

But what really got me is that you didn't even have the consideration to call me!

"Well, what do you have to say?" He grabbed her shoulder and shoved her back into the seat.

"You've said it all now!" she cut back, tight-lipped.

Artie stood above her, both silent. He hadn't expected belligerence. "Don't you have anything to say?"

"You didn't even give me a chance to explain. You came in here mad, wanting to blow up, and it wouldn't have done any good to tell you how worried I was. I knew you'd be irritated—but I thought you'd give me a chance to explain at least. But you didn't care. You wanted to get mad."

Artie, flustered by this counter-attack when he'd expected an apology, hesitated, but he was too angry to stop.

"What do you mean I didn't give you a chance to explain? Why didn't you call?"

"We left—"

"Who's we?" Artie said, wishing as he did that he'd remained quiet. He didn't want to appear interested in the people she went out with.

"Just Mauricio and a friend. I was sitting here about 4:30 this afternoon, bored, and they offered to take me for a walk to the Alameda Gardens. So I went. I expected to be right back."

"I don't care who you went out with. I couldn't give a damn. What makes me mad is you didn't let me know."

"Well, I didn't realize what time it was."

"You mean you didn't think of me once in four hours?"

"Sure I did. I was worried and called you the second I got back."

"You didn't either."

"Yes I did! Your landlady said you'd already left. Maybe my landlady did this on purpose," Pam added. "She told me she didn't think I should devote myself to one person."

"And I suppose you agree?"

Pam was quiet for a moment, her eyes avoiding his. "I didn't say that."

Artie took a deep breath. "I'm sorry for blowing up," he said. "And I'm glad you told me how you felt." Tears gathered in his eyes. "I hate it when we feel like this."

They were holding each other, at peace now.

Pam asked him if he wanted to watch TV.

"Not really. I don't want them to see me."

"It's dark in the room," Pam countered. "And anyway I don't think we should be in here alone."

They went in to watch TV.

In his small studio, high above everything, Artie pursed his lips. Really it hadn't all been that bad. There were good things to recall. He thought of the little restaurant on the corner of Uruguay and Bolivar where they could get a huge plate of spaghetti for a few pesos and where they ate upstairs by a window, watching the endless passing of traffic. And then there were the times they spent together in bed at Artie's place. Whenever the señora left to visit friends, they watched from the window until she was out of sight and then made love.

Two days after Phil's letter had arrived, Artie received one from Howard. It came from the Marine Corps officer training camp at Quantico, Virginia. *Dear Artie,* Howard wrote.

> *Deep in the heart of the Marine Corps, where new officers and new ideas all get maltreated, I was glad to get your letter. What a pleasure to hear from a civilian.*

Howard's beginning, the second time Artie read the letter, set him to thinking of a night and day a month earlier when his own military status had been determined. In Mexico, he'd received a letter in November telling him to report to Portland for a physical. He'd let his draft board know his address, ten days after arriving in Mexico. It was the law. He wrote about five letters before he finally had the test area changed to San Antonio, Texas. Even then it was a hardship. Pam had decided to stay in Mexico until May instead of leaving after Christmas as Artie hoped. He was borrowing money to stay in Mexico, and the trip to Texas depleted his failing finances still more.

In San Antonio, he'd been in a state of severe tension. He had letters from several physicians and the University Health Service explaining how badly he had asthma, but he was afraid they would pass him anyway. If they did, it would mean the end of everything with Pam. Artie knew he couldn't hold on to her in the service, and so much could happen in the meantime.

He'd put himself in jeopardy when he dropped out of school at Oregon.

In the morning, at the Examining Station on South Main Street in San Antonio, he arranged to have his physical test results transferred to Portland and sat in line with a horde of other guys to have his chest x-rayed, blood taken, and to write his intelligence test. He told the doctors about the boils he had continually as a kid, about his bloody noses, sinusitis, asthma, bronchitis, headaches, about the polyps in his nasal passages, and then gave them the letters from his doctors.

He was fed a box lunch while they processed some tests and then was ushered out.

After the exam he wrote to Pam. "I felt like jumping and shouting and screaming and running through the streets. I can hardly contain myself. I am now PERMANENTLY DISQUALIFIED FOR SERVICE IN THE GLORIOUS ARMIES OF THE U.S.A. God, was I scared for a bit though. It looked like they had marked me qualified. I was ready to pass out. Already starting to think about appeals when he told me the above."

Returning to Howard's letter, Artie thought, "What a pleasure, Howard, to be a civilian!"

*Here at Quantico,* Howard wrote, *they are feverishly pouring us full of huge amounts of unpalatable memorized information. At the same time they expose us more and more to the boom-boom side of war, to get us used to all that murderous and nerve-racking bullshit. Quite scientific and effective, this program they have.*

*If it doesn't sound boring and pointless, then I haven't described it well enough. Fortunately they have exposed us to it little by little. Still I am tempted to buy and send to my company C. O. the Seeds' album with the song "You're pushin' too hard." But he wouldn't understand.*

*You know, I have only one goal or value left. That is to get out of the military as soon as possible and just go. I get tired of one place, especially this place. And I get tired of being told what a fine thing we are doing stopping international communism in Vietnam. Think, Artie, of the difference between classes here and the peace march in San Francisco when we were stoned out of our minds all night. Sometimes I don't think I'm the same person.*

*Although I hate this military life with a passion, I also have the highest academic average in our company. I've been able to soak their bullshit up like a sponge and squeeze it back for the tests. In the military, they try to turn a person into a hard-working, material-oriented person. It's not impossible to resist it, but it's hard, and you have to get away and let yourself go and remind yourself that what they say is not for you. It's especially hard when you do well, because then your own pride works against you. But the paradox—you have to do well to get your choice of military occupation.*

*By the way, Phil lately sent a letter to my home in which he said he had bought some "good stuff" from Gary Norling. My father, unaware that the letter wasn't for him, opened it. So now on my bedstand I have a maudlin letter from my mother, curious as to what the "good stuff" is and expressing the fervent desire, nay, prayer, that I am not stupid enough to fool around with "those drugs" since our bodies are "the temple of God." Oh joyous, delicious complications.*

With that and a final plea for more letters, Howard had signed off.

In his studio, staring at one of his paintings, brought back to the present, Artie heard his stomach rumble. His only meal of the day, at noon, consisted of soup, rice, beans, meat, and tortillas, washed down with a Pepsi. The cost? About four and a half pesos, a quarter. Cheap, but it brought to mind his finances. In another month, by the end of March for sure, he would have to leave.

Feeling imprisoned by memories and penned up by the narrow walls holding them, he decided to take a walk down to Insurgentes. Striding down Aguascalientes as far as Manzanillo, he turned to the right towards Tapachula and Chiapas. At the corner of Manzanillo and Tapachula, he shivered at the sight of two large blocks of pale green ice lying on the sidewalk in front of a restaurant. It was too cold for any steam to rise from them. Near Chiapas, he was surprised to see a street cleaner sweeping, his broom a bundle of branches. He saw them in the day but hadn't imagined they worked at night. In the narrow, unlit street he quickened his step.

When he reached Insurgentes, a bus pulled out, leaving a little kid selling Chiclets on the corner. Are they up already for the new day? Or have they been going all night? It was hard to tell. Feeling the darkness about him—even in the glare of the lights on Insurgentes, the day seemed far away. Will it really be light in an hour?

Walking toward Sears, he passed two young Mexicans, standing by a light pole in front of a closed music store. They wore beads, Indian belts, and pointed shoes.

"Hey, American boy! You smoke grass?"

"Sometimes. How'd you know?"

"Oh, you can tell," the taller one said in heavily broken English.

"The hair, eh?"

The tall one nodded. "And the sandals."

Artie looked down. The sandals he wore, dark socks underneath, weren't unusual—well, maybe the socks were—but they were comfortable. Must appear like a hippy to the Mexicans. It was funny really. The poorer people wore sandals all the time.

The shorter, curly-haired kid touched his arm. "Would you like smoke now?"

Artie thought a moment. It had been over six months since he'd quit. "I guess so." He raised his shoulders. "I don't have too much time though."

"Come. We go look for friend."

Wary for a moment, he fingered the switchblade in his pocket, but they seemed all right. The tall one introduced himself and his curly-haired partner. "My name is Frank, Francisco, his Enrique. Henry you say."

"Mine's Artie."

"Ar-tee?" Francisco had difficulty pronouncing the name.

"Thing you drink? Like coffee?" Artie laughed. "No, no." He spelled his name on his hand, Art-ie.

"Ah, Arti!" The two Mexicans said the word awkwardly, almost as if tasting the sound like a strange candy.

They walked down Insurgentes toward Baja California, stopping at an apartment building lodged between a small goods shop and a women's clothing store. On the fifth floor, after climbing a seemingly endless stretch of stairs, Frank knocked on a door.

Number 9, fifth floor. Artie tried to imprint it in his mind—in case he'd need it later.

They waited several minutes but when no one answered, Frank got to his knees and peered under the door.

"Quizá está durmiendo," Enrique whispered.

"No, I think he is gone, left," Frank said in English.

Artie stood silent. He'd decided to confess ignorance of Spanish. The two fellows spoke to each other in what seemed to be a dialect. Artie made out they were going somewhere else but that was about it.

They left and started down side streets away from Insurgentes.

He tried to keep track of the names but found it difficult. From Nuevo Leon they headed down Astronomos, passing several long-haired Mexicans sitting on the steps of an apartment building. They eyed Artie as Frank and Enrique nodded to them.

A few doors farther on, they stopped, walked down a short hall on the main floor, and knocked at one of the back doors. Astronomos 55, number 4. Artie wondered if he could remember it.

Inside, his eyes picked out three Mexican guys and a girl. She sat silent on a mattress reading a Mexican Time, her face hidden. To Artie, she looked American. The walls were plastered with posters and drawings. A small electric heater warmed the room.

They locked the door behind him.

Artie was introduced again. The names were difficult and he remembered only one—Botas. Boots. The fellow pointed to his long black boots. "A nickname, you say."

Artie sat in a big chair, laying his coat, with his knife in one pocket, beside him. The Mexicans were smoking. Artie smelled the grass. Botas, a short rugged fellow with several days' growth of beard and an orange and red scarf around his neck, handed Artie a joint. He inhaled, feeling immediately the coolness in his brain.

Sitting there smoking, a moment of guilt assailed him. He'd promised Pam never to do it again. How'd I get mixed up in this? he wondered. He felt awkward—no one had asked him how he'd met Frank and Enrique—who he was—or anything about him.

"Do you know Paul?" one of the fellows finally asked.

"No. Who's he?"

They were surprised he didn't know Paul.

The girl on the mattress laid down her Time. "He's a kid out at the University of the Americas. He and some of his friends live in the arroyos below it. These guys turn on with them all the time."

So! he thought, she is American. "Where do you come from?" he asked.

"Canada. Toronto. My name's Kathy. I'm leaving in three days to go home. I'm broke but my parents mailed me a ticket."

She didn't look very poor to Artie. She wore an expensive-looking leather jacket, some iron-gray burnished bracelets, big leather belt, and jeans. She squatted on cowboy boots. When the joint was passed, she smoked too, but Artie thought she didn't seem to do it very naturally. He wondered how she came to be there. Maybe she slept with one of the guys. He could see her belly beneath a loose shirt. She was a slim girl but not good-looking. Maybe she helped them run drugs out of Mexico.

The cigarette had been passed to Artie several times and he felt the high easing over his body. He wanted to lie back and listen to the music. They were playing a new album of the Beatles. It was the first time he'd heard it.

I am the eggmam ... Yes, I am, he thought, as if he were talking to Pam, and you've broken me up. Splat!

I'm crying, I'm crying.

He saw himself in the song, cracking. Yellow matter custard dripping from a dead dog's eye.

Feeling the eyes of the Mexicans on him, he sat up. Kathy was in the middle of the room, dancing, and the others were sitting around the room, watching.

Shit, Artie thought. Get her high and make her dance. You can take turns screwing her afterwards. All the hatred he felt for Mexicans because of Pam took hold of him. He despised the girl, too. Couldn't she tell they were using her? It seemed this was always the fate of plain-looking girls. He wanted to leave.

He could see she was stripping. She still wore her bra, but they were asking her to take it off. Long jeans, boots, and a bra. He seemed to be viewing them through a glass partition. He could feel the adrenaline, the desire for sex, but it made him uneasy.

How to leave? Don't want to stand up and just walk out. Maybe they'll think I'm going for the police. Maybe grab me and find the knife.

The girl had the bra off now, bouncing, swirling, swinging her breasts. Two of the Mexicans were dancing with her, their heads swaying.

Should I run for it or just tell them I've got to leave? Maybe they'll get mad. He'd interrupt their act. She might stop stripping. She'd kicked off the boots now. Do they all screw her? A bed huddled along the back wall by the record player. Who will she sleep with? Who would get her first?

The crack at the top of her butt appeared, her pants with the big belt hanging low. One of the Mexicans loosened the belt. Artie felt sick, imagining Pam there dancing, the Mexicans around her eager, waiting.

He closed his eyes and sank back in the chair. Fire from the electric heater. Orange, like the sun. He turned his face away, then opened his eyes. The girl was sweating now. Slipping out of her pants. They fell to her feet. She wore no underpants. He saw her buttocks, black hair in the crack. Her waist was thin, but she had a broad butt. As much as he felt sick, he wanted her to turn, but she danced facing the Mexicans. He was surprised they didn't strip, too.

When would the music end? He no longer remembered the song. He felt slightly nauseated. The smoke was too thick, the air too hot. Each breath, it seemed, went to his lungs by way of his brain. That the grass had made him this high, especially after so long without it, surprised him. Maybe it was hash, he thought, or had opium in it. He felt the song would never end, the girl would never stop dancing. There would always be two Mexicans standing in front of her. He would always be planted in that chair, locked there by the force of their will, staring at her butt. He closed his eyes, feeling his brain grow until it burst and diffused through the room on the thick, stale smoke, on the red heat of the orange coils.

Suddenly, after a jumble of activity, he felt coolness and found himself in the street in darkness. He had a dim recollection of standing up, of mumbling some excuse, and of slipping from the room.

In front of the apartment, he forced himself to concentrate. The street seemed different. Someone had moved things around, adding a building here, destroying one there, stacking things higher, cutting things down. Even the pavement felt different—darker and rougher.

When he finally discovered the way and made it to Insurgentes and familiar ground, he settled down. He only needed to walk five blocks to his place.

For a moment, looking down the street, he thought he saw Pam. Yes, there she came, waving, a block away, wearing her pink dress. He broke into a grin, feeling his heart rise as the first rays of the sun burst over the horizon, splattering the store windows with fire. He shut his eyes. Yes, there she was all right, a vision of beauty, waiting for him.

At his door, finding his key, he looked again at the sky. The sun wasn't quite visible from the steps, but he sensed its warmth. About to go in, he turned for one last glimpse, greeting a light morning breeze. The breeze ruffled his shirt, waved back, wafting over his tired mind, refreshing him. For a moment, still on the threshold, he paused, took a deep breath, exhaled, and then went in.

# The Echoes of Our Two Hearts

*We view it now as if we were strangers—or rather, aliens. Not from Mars—merely from another, far distant continent. Undeclared aliens from the present, we slide down the steep slope into the past, arriving finally where the detritus of time forbids further passage.*

*We stop and listen and wonder if we have learned. Surely, if we were to do it over—live those days again with the knowledge of the present—everything would somehow be different ... somehow easier ...*

*But if we couldn't distance ourselves then, what makes us think we could do so now?*

*Back then, we had no time for thought of what we might be in the future, what we might want. No way of visualizing the problem—or the problem's answer—before it occurred. Our brain cells could simply not expand beyond the narrow confines of the reality that passed before our eyes.*

*And this was that reality.*

# Part One • Scudding
## (1971)

# chapter 1

Artie and Pam Crenshaw stopped for the night at a squat, concrete-block motel along the old highway near the outskirts of Klamath Falls. For a few moments, as a frumpish maid in rubber galoshes drew the drapes for them, the sun, festering on the horizon, transformed the drab room, smelling of camphor and naphthalene, into a crepuscular sea of yellow and gray. Once the maid was gone and the sun down, however, the room resumed its dreary state, revealing ceilings discolored by winter leaks, cigarette burns near the bathroom sink, carpet stains throughout, and a tattered quilt spread over the double bed. Still, at ten dollars a night, the room would do.

While they unpacked, both silent, the late afternoon flies gave way to gnats and then, soon after, to moths, which now swooped near the saffron-colored light bulb outside the lavender door.

From a narrow writing table near the window, his back to it, Artie stared at his wife as she lay nearly hidden in the smouldering darkness.

Pam finally spoke: "Artie, could you at least turn on the light?" It was an accusation, not a question. "I'm having trouble breathing."

How'n hell does light help breathing? Shaking his head, he strode to the door and flipped the light switch. As if cramps aren't enough. She'll blame me for losing her asthma pills too.

Oh, hell. He needed to get away.

"Why don't I go out and see if I can't find you some pills? Something to help your cramps." Anything for an escape.

She looked at him and then shut her eyes. "You said you'd write the postcards."

"How am I supposed to be able to concentrate with you moaning behind me every two seconds?"

Fuck! "Go on and get out of here." Pam stifled another moan, feeling the swelling of tears. She turned away from him, toward the wall. "Go!"

Artie threw his pen on the table and shoved the upholstered chair away. "Do you think I like seeing you suffer?"

She didn't reply.

If he didn't get out of the room now ... He'd already told her in one angry fight that he was ready to leave. And he didn't mean for fifteen minutes. Shit! This was supposed to be a vacation.

"Look. I won't be gone long. Just try to breathe deep, okay? I'll find you something. That corner pharmacy we saw by the Safeway store? They might still be open. That's close enough to walk."

"I'm suffocating. Why do we always stay in such lousy places?" It was a waste of time to ask. She knew why. Wasn't it always money?

"Be back as quick as I can." He patted her shoulder, was going to give her a kiss, but she didn't turn around. "See you soon."

Artie Crenshaw, twenty-five years old, one year older than his wife, had what his wife called hippopotamus eyes—sometimes gray, sometimes green, and sometimes yellow, as if mud speckled. Standing beneath a scrawny oak tree at the corner of a one-block park dominated by an old Southern Pacific steam engine, he stared at the darkened shape of the drugstore. Damn! Should've known it'd be closed this late on Sunday. Grocery store, too.

Where to now? He had to keep looking or Pam would bitch all night.

He trudged down the nearest street, his anger incarnated into a rigid let's-get-ready-to-draw-and-fire posture.

At the moment, a fall night in 1971, he was wearing cowboy boots, though he'd long ago rebelled against all his father stood for. The boots, rough and mean, represented his pseudo Hell's-Angels outfit. They were biker's boots in his mind, the flat-toed kind with a brass ring at the sides holding straps that passed over the top of the foot and behind the heel. He wore them especially when he went out at night—not so he could hightail it and run when assaulted (he was convinced it would happen someday) but so he could kick and fight and stomp whoever had it in for him.

As was his habit, he wore corduroy Levi's, the current pair worn thin like a field overrun by a herd of cattle. He sported a green cotton T-shirt, frayed at the neckline, and a heavy leather coat with thick cotton lapels, his prized possession. If he ever succeeded as a writer, which was his ambition now that he'd given up painting (damn, just no talent, a wasted six years), he wanted to make sure he was going to be ready with a bit of style.

His writing would be a lot harder to describe than his looks. It's easy to say Artie had wavy brown hair, a broad forehead, prominent nose, lips on the thick side, a rugged chin—in short, a rough handsomeness about his features, but his writing changed from one day to the next. He'd read Norman Mailer's *Why are we in Vietnam?* and start out the day's work like this:

> *I don't aim to spread the hot shit on you but we'll lay it on cool like a big pile of foamy shaving cream slapped on your face. We'll skim over the top of this story plucking out bits and tits here and there.*
>
> *It's all about me egotistical bastard, smart-assed prig. We shall delve down into the lower realms, you and me. And don't worry, I won't piss in your tea.*

His reading Norman Mailer was not beneficial to his style.

When he wasn't writing, when he wasn't blundering his way out of a mess or performing some overwhelming act of clumsiness, he would be preparing little bits of speeches, most unoriginal, to spice up press conferences. Speeches like: "Well, I was born in the rubber shortage at the end of World War II, hee, hee, hee!"

Wandering off up the store-lined street, drifting into fantasies of fame and fortune, soon to forget his promise of a swift return, Artie raised his arms and embraced the night, as if his were the foggy paws of Jupiter around Io.

# *chapter 2*

> *Nobody loves me*
> *Everybody hates me*
> *I'm going to go eat worms*
> *Long thin slimy ones*
> *Short fat gushy ones*
> *Itzy bitzy fuzzy wuzzy worms.*

P am sang the song to console herself. During low moments, especially at period times, she found herself singing it often. It was almost as much with her as her finger typing. No - bo - dy - space l - ov - es - space m - e

… Odd. She typed the letters out in her mind, separating them in groups of two, and at the end of each sentence she checked to see if the words came out odd or even. Sh - or - t space - fa - t - space - gu - sh - y space - on - es. Even.

It wasn't easy to stop typing in her mind. Especially when typing was all Artie gave her to do. Him and his "exercise your mental powers." She didn't even like telling him about her weird habit in the first place, but sometimes it would become so unbearable and distressing she felt she would go crazy if she didn't ask for help.

Think of something else, he'd say. Force yourself to stop. You won't unless you do it by an act of will.

Always bragging about his many "acts of will." He could eat a huge Chinese meal and half of hers or get along on one apple a day. "Mind power," he'd say. Sometimes he wouldn't eat all day until ten or eleven at night just to impress her. He expected the same stubborn determination from her.

Sometimes, more often this last year, she hated him.

I should have stayed in Mexico and married Mauricio. At least the Estradas were wealthy.

Hitched to Artie for three years now and life only getting worse. Any thought of companionship long gone. She shook her head. Now it was sex and only that.

Son of a bitch! I told him to check the bathroom and he leaves the pills there. Now the damn motel's three hundred miles behind us and he's mad at me. Well, fuck that asshole.

In between stabs of pain—her cramps were worsening—she tried to think of happier times. Why do I have to go back so far to find them?

The sand dunes near Coos Bay—spotted with pine, stippled with scotch broom—appeared before her eyes. The dunes were always a mystery to her. At the age of six or seven many things had seemed strange and scary. She remembered the time she and a friend had ventured away from the beach into sugary dunes which eventually became thick with pine and scrawny fir trees. Somewhere in the vast silence of this sandy forest they'd come across a long, straight, expanse of asphalt. It was a road, absolutely deserted, seeming to stretch from here to eternity at one end and to die in the ocean at the other. And then suddenly a man appeared and frightened them in the silence by unzipping his pants and pulling out his penis. It was an impression that went deep into her and which she knew she'd never forget. She felt an arrow in her chest even now sometimes at the sight of her husband's penis as he came bounding from the shower or appeared before her unexpectedly nude.

As much as she hated him sometimes, she wouldn't mind making love now. A good tonic during bad cramps.

He was acting like a tool, so he might as well be one.

For a second, the thought brought a smile to her lips, and then the pain hit again..

She touched her temples with her middle fingers, feeling for the swelling of veins, stretching and massaging the tautness of the skin. Oh, God, don't let it be a migraine.

Her forehead, to which her fingers next moved in a circular flow, was a smooth auburn color of California health. The opposite of what she felt.

The vacation days in the sun had been nice, even though its rays brought out the freckles on her nose. Still, her face acquired its more youthful pixiness, bright rose cheeks, paler under the eyes which were hazel, with a fine gray rim around them. Artie was always telling her how much he liked her eyes, all her features, but then she heard him at a party once telling another guy she was a thin-lipped bitch. That night, in the middle of a fight, was the first time she'd said "fuck you" to him.

"Say that to me again and it's over," he said. "You can file for divorce."

When two hours had passed and Artie still hadn't returned, Pam threw a pillow at the room's TV.

Stupid imbecile! He'd get lost in a men's john and probably drown in the toilet bowl. I'm not going to lie here and wait all night.

She got up and dressed in warmer clothes, putting on her blue and pink plaid wool pants and a pink sweater. When she felt low, looking pretty helped so she went into the bathroom and began to fix her face. She'd just had her hair clipped short and already she could tell the haircut was lousy. That's what I get for going to Sophomores at a Beauty College just because they're cheaper than Seniors. Maybe I should use some lighteners. This brownish-blonde look is getting me down.

The mirror in the bathroom, opposite an ancient, four-legged, dragon-clawed bathtub, covered the length of one wall—almost six feet long—and had a small shelf running below it. Meticulously she laid out her eye liner, blush-on, mascara, and eyelash curler, and then washed her face, thinking again of yesterday.

\* \* \*

Yesterday had been a stupid day. They'd driven by freeway from Sacramento to Klamath Falls and Artie's attitude had peeved her from the start. Somewhere in between Weed and Klamath Falls they'd entered a thick, cottony fog and Pam had ordered him to slow down.

"I can see alright. You just watch the scenery."

Fog-shrouded trees poked isolated, black branches into the sky. Occasionally a hay barn or a chip-burning silo loomed high yet indistinct. As Artie roared along in the fog, a bird flew up from the gravel at the side of the road and took off across the highway. Instead of going straight, the bird swerved to avoid the car and hit the top edge of the windshield with a resounding whack.

Pam screamed and covered her face.

Artie's voice cut at her, quick and sharp.

"Jesus Christ, Pam! What the fuck?"

"Murderer!"

"Dumb bird you mean. Stupid thing would've lived if he'd flown straight. Anyway," he added, as he steered the Fiat around a gentle curve, "it was an instant death."

"Yeah, like you being hit and run over by a cement truck or a semi. You'd like that."

"You don't remember the pain. Ever been knocked out?"

She was silent.

"You don't feel any pain till you wake up."

"Well, I hope it didn't leave any blood on the car. Poor bird."

And what was Artie's response?

"Shit," he said. "It's as hard to get along with you as it is to pick fly manure from pepper."

He probably thought that was original. Something he'd read in a book somewhere. Thought he was smart. She'd liked him better when he was a painter, although with his failure at that, he'd turned into a grouch.

Finishing her make-up, she went back into the main room and shuffled through her purse until she found a quarter. There was a small, coin-operated TV on the wall at the foot of the bed. She didn't know what the Sunday evening programs were and didn't even bother flicking through the channels, leaving the TV on the channel last set. I'd be a real smoker if I smoked, she thought, biting at a fingernail and resigning herself to a centuries-old movie.

# chapter 3

Towards what appeared to be the center of town, Artie found a side street with a semblance of life. A few neon signs buzzed with static, sputtering the names of various bars and night attractions.

As he approached the first bar, he heard someone shout from across the street. "Hey, Artie! Man, what a surprise! What're you doing here, kid?"

"Well, I'll be dammed! So you survived Vietnam." He hadn't seen Phil since the guy had gone off to basic training.

"Yeah, got me a Purple Heart, too. Guy jumped into a fox hole on top me and broke my scapula. How's that for heroic? Hey, did you know Howard didn't make it?"

"Oh shit. I hadn't heard. I knew he joined the Marines. Always said if he had to go to war he wanted to fight with the best."

"Yeah, and then he winds up getting killed somewhere in Quang Nam province. Remember Ray Spencer? He tried for conscientious objector status. Didn't get it and left for Canada. I haven't heard from him since."

"Yeah, I think we all lost touch with each other."

Phil, he could see, the ladies man, was starting to lose his curly, black hair. His forehead shone in the light from the bar. Barely five foot five and thin as a pine needle. Wearing a black leather jacket with silver studs.

"Well, Artie," Phil grabbed him in a hug, "we lucked out finding each other." Artie, after hesitating a moment, returned the hug.

Guy must just be happy to make it back alive. He knew a couple of guys from his high school in Gresham who hadn't made it.

Phil took a step back. "So, they never got you?"

"They tried. I had  to come up to San Antonio for my physical when I was living in Mexico. I was an idiot to leave school—and to let my draft board know where I was every time I moved. But I failed the physical. 1Y, not 4F."

"How'd you do in the lottery?"

"Not good, they'd have called me up. But it didn't matter at that point."

"Yeah, I should have gone to Canada with Ray. Saw too much. Hey, man, let's grab a beer and get caught up."

"Oh shit! I told my wife—"

"Your wife! You got an old lady?"

"Three years now. Anyway I was saying—"

"That's great man! Happy for you."

"Well …" He was about to say things weren't going so good but thought better of it. "I told her I'd be right back. Got to find a store that's still open."

"Nothing's going to be open this time a night. Not on Sunday." Phil grabbed his arm. "Ten, fifteen minutes. That won't kill her, right?"

"I guess not." Shit, Pam's going to be pissed.

As soon as they were seated at the bar and had a draft beer in front of them, Phil said, "Listen, man, you knew Gary Norling and I went in on the buddy plan, right?"

"Hadn't heard that. I thought he was going to claim he was gay."

"Changed his mind. We took a lot of acid together. I convinced him we should go in together. Easier with a buddy."

They clinked glasses and drank. Artie drained about half of his, anxious now to get moving.

"But he surprised me!" Phil looked at him as if waiting for a question.

"How's that?"

Phil swirled his beer in the moisture on the counter. "Whole thing started in this shit-hole hamlet. Maybe five, six huts in the whole ville. Anyway, we had this guy on his knees, thought he was VC. He was blabbering away when Gary up and shot him. Then he tried to get a ring off the guy's finger."

"Shot him in cold blood?"

Phil grinned. "Ain't nobody's blood cold when you're looking for Charlies. Shit! Stuff like that happened all the time. Gook probably stole it from a dead American. No way a fuckin' peasant's going to have a gold ring. It's why Gary shot him when he saw it.

"Anyway, one of our boonierats, a black dude we called Lawrence of Nigeria, pulls out his K-bar and says, 'Fuck, he's dead. Let's cut the bastard's finger off.' This little dink—must have been the guy's son—runs up and starts screaming. Gets on Gary's nerves, so he slams his rifle butt in the boy's mouth. Knocks him flat on his ass. We had this FNG with us—Fucking New Guy, a Marine lieutenant."

Phil snorted. "They were the worst. We'd been in Nam a year and he flies in, one week in-country, thinks he knows everything. He starts coming back toward us and Gary says, 'Quick, drop your knife.' The brother drops it and Gary shoots the kid through the head."

"Jeez, no way. That's as bad as the Nazis."

"Got away with it too. Black dude says the kid had grabbed his knife and was trying to stab him. They're not going to string up a grunt cause he killed a slope."

Artie frowned. Tell the guy I object to his racism? He'd finished his beer and wanted to leave. Not worth the effort.

"I've got to go to the can, Phil. Then I need to get back."

"Let's have one more." Without waiting for Artie, he gestured to the bartender, pointed to the empty glasses. "You haven't said anything about yourself. When you get back, you can tell me about your wife."

Artie hesitated. Okay, maybe he owed him a word or two. For old times sake. They had been best friends. For a while at least.

"One more and that's it."

When Artie disappeared around a corner, looking for the men's room, Phil reached into his coat pocket and pulled out two blue plastic capsules filled with white powder. After looking around, he opened one, dumped it in Artie's beer, made sure it dissolved, then swallowed the other.

"Little pure acid. That'll give ol' Artie the heebie-jeebies. Bring back lost memories."

When they came up from the bar, from the noise, the smoke, the voices, the glitter, the leering bottles of liquor and the lights, it was foggy. Artie was lost, dazed. Phil led the way. They crossed a footbridge over a creek. Fog rose off the water and hung around the street lamps like clusters of grapes. The moon slipped out between clouds, then disappeared again.

He wanted to tell Phil he was having a flashback but couldn't get the words out. Did I tell him about Pam? That I've got to get back?

They stopped before a stranger and Gary asked for a light. The stranger, out of matches, cupped his hands around his own cigarette, inhaled, brushed the ash off, and the two moved closer—Artie, transfixed, watched this strange ritual, an anthropologist before live specimens—the red and white tips of cigarettes meeting, smoking, the fire of life passing from one soul to the next.

When Phil's cigarette caught flame, he stepped back from the stranger, nodded thanks, and stumbled on around him. It was then, walking down the street, that Artie felt the sky shudder. Like a movie reel that flickers, the buildings around him began to quake. It was a movie world, a shutter going click-click-click, click-click. With that quick warning, the world fell apart and like broken glass the sky hit the pavement and shattered.

# chapter 4

Pam rose and shut off the TV when the movie ended, in bed over two hours, unable to sleep.

Just like Artie to go out and not come back.

Bastard.

Was he that fed up? He'd threatened to leave the other day during an argument. But she'd taken the threat as just a weapon meant to hurt her.

Nothing more. But it seemed divorce came up in every argument these days. Go out and look for him?

She didn't like being alone for long, especially in a strange town.

In her high school days she'd even taken girls with her down to the toilet for company. She'd been sure she was slowly going crazy. It seemed a barrier existed between her and everyone else and when she talked she felt as if her face were a mask. Someone else was talking through her. Someone false. Once, after getting off a bus, she thought she saw herself still on it, sitting in a seat by the rear door. She clenched her fingers, almost as if pulling strings taut, strings controlling a marionette. The figure in the bus, mannequin-like, turned jerkily—with jointed limbs—and she was afraid for a moment that she was outside herself, detached, controlling her moves not by natural reflex but by logical thought processes. Processes which were breaking down.

Artie had often asked her what brought her out of it, but she didn't know and couldn't tell him. Her trouble just ended.

Only once since then had she had serious trouble, and it was meeting Artie again, she told him, that had distracted her then. One day as she was taking notes in a beginning Italian class—like Artie she was majoring in Romance Languages—she happened to see a wisp of gray smoke drifting from her fingertips. A moment of fear rattled in her throat, passing through her like ice, and she clutched at the smoke as though to reabsorb it. From then on she was convinced her essence was slowly seeping from her. Her astral body was leaving her, not in one mighty break but in elusive little flights.

When she'd come to back to the University of Oregon from a term at Oregon State, she'd met Artie outside the arts building. He wasn't painting. He'd found a job through the university placement board and the part-time work was helping him through a tight stretch. Plus, he told her, he was going to spend a year abroad. He was making money any way he could.

Her first thought was, well, this won't be a long relationship.

But whatever it was, it helped. Didn't take long to get close. Just no sex. She kept wondering when Artie was going to kiss her, forget about making love, how about a kiss? but he never made the move.

One night at Oregon State, a guy had touched her. A football player—and she hated jocks! But she was hard up for dates. She'd even volunteered through the Student Activities Board to be a go-go dancer at the Friday night dances in the Student Union. They wore miniskirts and danced on stage in colored spotlights. After a brief performance—(she loved to dance; she'd watched American Bandstand all through high school, mimicking the best moves, and she knew she was good), the women would go down to the dance floor and pick a partner. It was an easy way to get chosen—to choose that is!—no waiting like a wallflower. No stigma in asking. In fact, the spotlight dancers were almost always surrounded by frat brothers trying to cut in. And the fraternity boys were always the most handsome, though most were jerks when you got down to wanting to meet them and talk seriously.

Jack Martin, a linebacker on the team, had danced with her and offered to drive her back to the dorm. She was excited to see he had a Jaguar, dark blue with rich, tan leather seats. He took her out on the old highway and gave her a scare or two, hitting one hundred and ten at one stretch, wetting her pants in pleasantly scary terror.

When he dropped her off at the dorm, it was nearly two o'clock, and he walked her to the door and into the lobby. The waiting room was empty and he asked to come up to her room—men were prohibited from the floors—so she refused. She didn't know him well enough. Plus she disliked men who only wanted sex, who didn't really know you or care.

While they were kissing goodnight at the stairs, he'd slipped his right hand up under her skirt and jammed it down her panties before she could do anything. His finger had her wet and breathless before the kiss broke and then she shoved him away and said good-bye as if nothing had happened. She'd gone to bed frustrated, not even touching herself. She'd never masturbated herself to an orgasm. Didn't masturbate at all. In fact, even now, after almost three years of marriage, she wasn't sure she'd ever really experienced an orgasm. An old friend, Mitsy Fabner, had told her she'd know if she truly had orgasmed.

Thinking now of the sensation, she remembered a similar feeling in grade school. After school, alone in the playground near her home, she would slide up and down a pole by the monkey bars, feeling the tingling in her crotch, a tingling which she increased by whispering, "fuck me, fuck me,." Somehow at age nine that had been daring and sinful. And the spotlight dancing had been equally titillating.

Artie, unfortunately, didn't like to dance. Or, if he did, he didn't show it. She was always after him to go out on Saturday night, but he seemed to think sitting in a club was a waste of time. He'd rather go out to a dumb movie or stay home and watch TV. Pam hated television, especially sports. Most of their arguments, it seemed, were occasioned by Artie watching football when she wanted to do something else.

After countless screaming fights, after numerous bitter arguments and stinging castigations, they'd finally come to an uneasy compromise. Artie would watch only one game on Sunday and Monday Night Football. No Saturday college games. No Sunday doubleheader.

That was one thing she'd enjoyed about the stay in San Francisco. No TV. They were coming back from a summer in Cuernavaca, where Pam had studied Spanish-American novels and Artie spent his time writing.

The stay in San Francisco was their "second" honeymoon, taken two years late but what the hell. They'd returned to the Villa Roma, a round hotel where they had a room overlooking the bay. Pam was enamored of the waterfront, despite the mass of other tourists.

While Artie slept in late—he was usually in bed over ten hours, although he claimed it took him two hours to fall asleep—Pam would get up at seven and take a morning walk down to the wharves. She walked in behind the restaurants, where the fishing boats docked, and found her favorite, a clumsy hulk which was always in the same berth, a dilapidated, junk-strewn scow moored near a davit. She never saw anyone on board, but the boat was full of dogs. She discovered a new one almost every day of the vacation. There was the black bitch with swollen teats, near delivery; the brown and white collie; the Skye terrier, a feisty fellow; the black mongrel with two rear legs white from the hock to the paw; the now gray clumber spaniel, and even an old, lumpy beagle who slept in a coil of rope and scratched his belly on a low box full of nuts and bolts of all sizes and shapes. Who fed them? There was barely room for them to move on deck. They sat on the stern gallery, or roamed along the gunnels, jumping over scattered tackle blocks, piles of clew jiggers, and buckets of belaying cleats, then disappeared down three narrow steps through a galley door jammed halfway open.

Pam loved the peace of the docks, once the tourist and commercial fishing fleets were out. The slap of the water on hull, the twangy whine of rigging clanking in the breeze, the fishy salt-water smell, all lulled her into a dreamy daze, a state of ease in which she envisioned herself in earlier times, other ages, far-off places, exotic locales.

She often thought she would've liked to have lived in pioneer days, when choices were few and decisions simpler—when work was a necessity that brought rest at the end of the day, fruit or grain or vegetable at the end of the harvest, the wood stove or crackling fireplace in winter. The modern world of cars, polyester fibers and plastic, of steel surfaces, sirens and glaring acrylics was an orchestra warming up out of tune and destined, conductor-less, never to find harmony. Give me instead, she thought, burnished oak, a cotton blouse, and a dappled Appaloosa! But Artie never understood that.

If she had one value in life, she thought, it would be health. Unscathed, untainted, country-fresh. What Artie took for granted. If there was anything which destroyed that vision for her, it was menstrual cramps. Exercise, she thought. Hard work and a natural flow. It's time I started an exercise program. That's what she would do once they got back to Eugene.

Maybe I can persuade Artie to start jogging with me.

Once we get back …

# chapter 5

Artie sat across a small wooden table from Phil. His mind was insane. The chaos of the club overwhelmed him, and Phil's incessant grin ate into his body, bite by bite. How had they got here? Someone had plugged him in to too many stations. TVs blaring. Someone selling used cars. He wasn't ready for this.

He lit a bummed cigarette, smoked, felt his chest swell. His head was leaking oil like a rusty old car.

He could taste the phlegm in his throat, slightly tainted, tarnished by a medicated Parke-Davis throat lozenge. Someone was talking about parts, fittings, accessory equipment. Will that damn commercial never end?

The coupe drooped, the drum sticks clipped and clopped, trochaic belly flop. Rhythm schism syncopated strobe light. His curb weight (God, get me out of here), self centering drums on rear something or other (his mind rolled along like a radio dial tuned in to AM and FM) *mañana van a prender mañana par avion 2422 metros sobre el nivel del mar van a tomar Coca-Cola ben fria.* He was lost, back in time, between stations, the past and the present merged.

Doped up, deep down, lost, in Mexico again. God, I hope not. A bad trip. His brain felt like a steam radiator, clanking and hissing.

And, always, the fear that he was caught in this loop and would never come back.

He was huddled on the train when it left the station, his body gently rocking, in tune with the rhythm of the wheels.

# *chapter 6*

A woman answered the phone when she dialed 911.

"I'd like to report a missing person," Pam said.

"One moment please." The line went dead and Pam got off her knees and sat on the edge of the bed holding the phone in her lap.

A police officer came on the line and asked for an identification, the last time she'd seen her husband, where he was going and a few other seemingly irrelevant details, and then told her not to worry, he'd probably be back soon, but they'd look for him in the meantime.

Yeah, right. Patronizing asshole. But what can you do? She'd reported it, that's what mattered.

She saw Artie up an alley, robbed and stabbed.

The hospitals!

She flipped through the yellow pages—there were two it appeared in town, one a clinic, the other called Emmanuel Hospital.

Neither had admitted any injured males that night.

She considered calling home to her folks but it was close to morning now and she hated waking them. Besides, she thought, if he's run off, I don't want them to know yet. It'd be just like him to take off and make his way home to Eugene without her. She went to the suitcase to see if the checkbook was there and felt relieved to find it as well as close to a hundred in cash. I can get home at least. She thought about the apartment. It would be weird to go back without him.

Maybe I should wait here till he's found. Maybe he's been hit on the head and is wandering around amnesiac. Unless I'm here he'll never know this is the place. Oh hell!

She lay back on the bed. If I could only relax and think straight.

It would be weird if he were dead. She couldn't resist considering the possibility. Even lovers hate each other sometimes. Maybe married people more than lovers. In a way, to love another was to surrender control, to place one's emotional well-being in the hands of another person. A voluntary death, right?

What would she do if he was dead? Three fourths of the apartment was filled with his things. It's funny. I must be different than most women. I made the place around his things. So much junk. So damn many books and art supplies that he never used these days. He'd given up on painting, said he was going to be a writer instead. I was lucky I got him to throw away half his school notes. All the way from high school. What in the world was he going to do with chemistry notes? He hoards paper like his dad hoards junk.

She thought of her in-laws with mixed emotions. Artie's dad, retired from farming and construction—and from the ministry, Artie was happy to say— had moved the family, or what was left of it—Artie and his older brother Richy were gone—to Westville, a modest two-story house near the grange, close to the outskirts of town where the roads begin to rise, the timber thickens, and fresh creeks flow.

Anytime you stopped by, it always seemed his dad was cooking potatoes at a wood stove. He'd greet her at the door with a kiss and then immediately rush back to his skillet. It seemed he must have never fried up less than ten pounds at a time. They lived off fried potatoes.

I feel sorry for Artie's mom. She's always talking about the new home she wants. She wants a white rug in the living room and no boots allowed. There's to be a shed for the boys to leave their manurey boots in and a big sink to wash up at.

She'll never get it. That's one thing I'll never let Artie do. Promise me something all my life and never give it to me.

Beneath the curtains, which came just to the bottom of the window, the darkness began to drain away. It was too early to open the curtains. Pam found some notepaper, left Artie a note in case he returned, got her coat, a wool tweed with a fake fur collar, and left the room. The Fiat was still out front, the windows lightly frosted. She warmed up the engine. The motor coughed at first and then struggled to a throaty roar, the tail pipe dripping moisture.

Wiping down the windows, she stared at the impersonal lavender door of the motel room and then drove out of the lot and on to the main drag. Coasting along, looking for a coffee shop, she finally found a Sambo's open, parked, and went in.

"What'll it be, sweetie?" the waitress asked.

Look you shit, Pam felt like saying, don't sweetie me.

"I'd like this fifty cent pancake breakfast," she said, looking up and smiling.

# chapter 7

Coming back from the water dispenser, looking for someplace to put his cup, Artie saw a young woman smiling at him from a window seat near the end compartment. He paused, thinking of saying "hi," and she said it for him.

"Hi! Where're you going?"

Artie wavered, thinking, a slow grin crinkling his face. He felt as if his mind was out of gear. "I bet you think I'm acting stupid," he said.

"Are you?"

He laughed. "May I sit by you? This is going to take some explaining."

"Sure. It's going to be a long ride. I never can sleep on a train anyway. Where're you from?"

Wow! She was a talker! It was a two-second sputter. The words still smothered him like waves of feathery foam. He'd forgotten already what she said. He was looking at her face instead. Her cheeks showed the ravaging marks of youth; plagues of pimples had left a field beaten down by hail, pock-marked, a close-set lunar surface. She wore no lipstick.

"You asked me something, didn't you?

"Weirdo. Where'd you get on? I didn't see you in San Fran."

"You've been on this train since then?"

"Yes, since then. Now look here, whatever your cotton-pickin' name is—"

"Artie."

"What? Fartie?"

Was she joking—or deaf?

"Artie's my name. A-r-t-i-e."

"You mean, Arthur."

"No, Artie." He didn't want to talk about his parents and family names.

She sat there staring at him, laughing. Okay, so she was joking. He noticed she had abalone shell barrettes holding long chestnut hair out of her eyes.

"You have pretty eyes."

"Hah!" She turned her head and looked out the window.

On the opaque window Artie imagined he saw a frenzied dog groveling in slobber, and for a moment he shuddered. Damn. Flashback still flickering. What 'n hell had happened to Phil. Was he on the train or had they got separated somehow? And then he remembered that it wasn't a flashback. Phil had confessed to putting acid in his beer. Maybe that's why he was alone. A dirty trick from an old friend. Jeez, what about Pam? He was royally fucked.

"I bet you don't even know what color my eyes are," she said, keeping her head averted. "I bet you didn't even notice."

"They're brown."

She turned to look at him. "Look again, joker."

"You're not too sweet, are you?"

"I'll tell you what," she said, grasping his arm. "You go down, get another drink of water, and when you come back let's start over, okay? I'll tell you who I am, where I'm going, and you can do the same for me."

"Okay. You wait. I'll be back." Getting up, he bumped into a porter.

"Watch it, will you!" The roughness of the voice startled Artie. God damn it, these porters are supposed to be friendly. Already the guy was down the aisle, his greasy back luring at Artie.

"Hey you," Artie called. The guy turned, his eyes red as if he'd been drinking, flaming wheels of fire.

"You want something?"

Artie hesitated, then shook his head. He was in no shape to cause trouble.

He'd seen this guy before. The archetype of all bullies. A trouble maker. The type that wasn't happy unless he was in a fight or kicking you when you were down.

"Did you see that guy?" Artie asked the girl.

"Yes, stupid. Go get your drink. That was the conductor."

At the drinking machine, Artie watched the water fall and lost himself.

Pam, jeez, what was he going to tell Pam? No way to get to a phone until this train stopped—and he didn't even know for sure where it was headed.

Or if he even wanted to talk to his wife.

# chapter 8

P am loved the pancakes. Thick, wavy streams of raspberry syrup, rolling outward and down, swirling in the melted butter. She cut neatly into the pancake, squared a mouthful, and then savored it slowly, eyeing a fish-eyed reflection of herself in a Volkswagen hubcap, the car parked sideways just outside the window.

Before leaving the restaurant, she bought a novel and began reading back in the motel. After a series of yawns, which left her eyes watering, she closed the book, unable to concentrate. She didn't like sitting there alone, waiting.

Gathering all the dirty clothes she could find, she packed them in a suitcase, left another note for Artie, and took off again with the car.

After circling several blocks, she came across a launderette, parked the car, and entered the deserted room. A row of Bendix commercial washers extended down one side of the room, with dryers at the far end.

With the load finally running, she sat down and for a while stared vacantly at the soap light on the square box with the little circular pothole which snatched up quarters. WATCH YOUR SUDS LEVEL!! TOO MANY SUDS SPOIL THE WASH!! The signs had been painted in large red block letters behind the machines. Did they really need two exclamation points. And capital letters?

The door swung open and a hippy girl entered with a bag of clothes over her shoulder. Barefoot, though it was still early spring, early morning, and cold, she wore only an ankle-length cotton dress and couldn't have been over fifteen.

Pam nodded and picked up a magazine.

"Hey," the girl said, "you know how to run these screwed up machines?"

Pam grimaced, fearing the next thing the girl would ask for would be money. She got to her feet and forced herself to be pleasant. "You fill the washer, add your soap here, and then just stick a quarter in and the rest takes care of itself."

"I can dig it," the girl said, nodding. "You use these things often?"

"No, my husband and I are just traveling through and I thought I'd do a wash."

"Oh groovy!"

The hippy's enthusiasm was unwarranted, and Pam ignored the veiled request to be sociable. Sitting down again, she watched the girl stuff the washer, her hair, mud brown and straw straight, eclipsing her raw cheeks. When the girl finished, she turned to Pam. "Hey, I hate to bug you, but do you have any extra soap?"

Pam swore to herself, glad she didn't have a box with her. Her cheeks twitched once. "No, I had to buy one for a dime out of that machine."

"Oh," the hippy said slowly, staring at the machine. "Well, let me see." She untied a handkerchief and flicked through a few coins. "You say you got to have a quarter, or will it take change?"

"Well, the washers take only quarters, but the soap dispenser gives change. Do you need a quarter?" Her tone was perhaps too direct, as if to suggest, "Bug off!"

The girl paused, looking at her money. "No, I guess I got it."

Pam picked up a magazine and buried her head. When the girl turned her back, she watched her fumble with the machine. Was she retarded? Finished finally, the girl sat down a chair away and looked at Pam.

"That's a pretty bracelet you're wearing."

"Thank you." Pam resolved to be patient. "My parents bought it for me."

"What's that written on it?"

"This engraving? Nothing, I guess. They're just Mexican designs."

"Oh, really? Can I see it?"

Pam hesitated.

"I just want to see what they are," the girl explained. "I bought this bracelet from a junk dealer in Portland and he told me some crazy story about this bracelet having a pair and if I ever found it, the two together would tell where this lost kingdom is. Isn't that interesting?"

Pam faked a smile. "Really?"

"Yeah, no kidding! It's in South America somewhere. He told me he got the thing from this old woman he helped across a creek during a storm in Mexico one night." The girl's words rushed from her mouth. "She said she'd been looking for it all her life and never found the other half. I'm looking for it now." She smiled. "You know, kind of on and off when I see one."

Handing her the bracelet, Pam noticed for the first time a tiny, red rose tattooed on the side of the girl's cheek. The girl took the bracelet with both hands, as if it were a precious object, and examined it closely, running her finger along the designs. "No," she said finally, handing it back, as Pam got up to put the clothes in a dryer, "I guess this isn't it."

While Pam worked, the girl continued talking, an incessant chatterbox. "You should've met this guy that sold me the bracelet. He was full of the wildest stories." She grabbed a pipe running to the ceiling and swung around in a half circle, holding on by her left hand.

Not going to ask the question the hippie was waiting for.

Ignore her.

Pam inserted a dime in the dryer, reading the directions for temperature control.

"He said his great-great-grandfather had the distinction of being hung by a bunch of vigilantes on a telegraph pole on the very day the Castello Circus, Menagerie and Abyssinian Caravan came to town—which was Laramie, by the way, on June 6, 1869. It was so funny how he had it all down. I memorized it!"

"Hilarious," Pam said, focusing her gaze on the open magazine and shaking the pages.

Just what I needed to know.


# chapter 9


Coming back up the aisle with the cup full of water, Artie stopped at the seat. No one was there. Was I mistaken? Maybe she was a fantasy. He heard a smothered laugh across the aisle and turned to ask if they'd seen the young woman.

"Fooled you, didn't I" she chirped.

Artie stood there. Not sure what to say.

"Come sit down, dummy. Don't look so stupid."

She patted the seat beside her.

"Now," she turned to face him, "My name is Ady Gleason and I'm going all the way up to Bellingham. By train just to Eugene, where I have some friends to visit, and then by bus from Eugene. I have some relatives in Ferndale, outside of Bellingham. I haven't seen them in a long time. Then I'm off to Canada. Just to live. Now, let's hear about you."

"So we're going north?"

"What'd you think, dummy? Don't tell me you don't know where you're going."

"Nope. No destination. Just along for the ride. To tell the truth, I don't recall how I got on this train, but I know one thing for sure and that is I've got one hell of a mad wife waiting for me somewhere and I also lost track of a friend I was with. How's that?"

"You've been drinking, haven't you?"

"I was but one of my old friends kicked up a tornado in my mind with a little dope. Hey, maybe he's on the train too."

"Well, if he takes drugs, I don't care to meet him," Ady said. "I don't like drugs."

"You sound just like my wife ... "

"What is this about your wife?"

"I guess I left her behind in Klamath Falls. She's going to kick my butt. I got to get off and call her."

"You're kidding. Let's see your left hand."

Artie spread out the fingers of his left hand. "There it is. Right on the old finger."

"You didn't just leave her, did you?"

"Yes. That's what I said."

"Were you fighting?"

"For a year! I'd just as soon forget her for now, because when I get back things are going to be bad enough."

"You do have a ticket for somewhere, don't you?" Ady said. "You'd better check and see where you paid to go."

"Paid? Hell!" Artie grabbed his wallet. Whew! Still with him. Inside he found a five dollar bill. He checked his coat pocket and felt the reassuring rectangle of some travelers checks. "Well, I haven't spent a cent all night," he said. "That means I got some free beers, a little dope, which I'd resolved to give up, and a train ride."

Artie leaned back into the cushioned seat. Damn. What in hell is Pam going to think? That's a confrontation I'd just as soon avoid.

Ady had her knees up, leaning back into the window, facing him.

"I was just thinking," Artie said. "My wife and I live in Eugene and we can't be too far from there. I'll get off at the next stop, try to call her, and then just hitchhike home."

"Listen," Ady said. "My ticket's only paid to Eugene, like I said. I have some friends there to visit before I head north to my aunt's place. If you don't mind, why don't we both get off. If you don't think it's too far, that is. It'll be fun to hitchhike. I get bored stiff riding all the time with no one to talk to."

"I'm not sure hitchhiking is ever fun. By the time we get off, it'll be light out at least. Otherwise we'd never get a ride."

"Maybe you could show me your place in Eugene."

Artie caught her eye and didn't look away.

"You could stay there if you need a place for the night," he offered, "except maybe, yeah, my wife might be back today. I don't think she'll stay in Klamath Falls, since we're so close to home. I'd hate to have her see me with you."

"Why? You're just talking to me."

Artie leaned forward, elbows on his knees, head in his hands. "What a mess! I'm almost afraid to go back!"

"Coward!" She poked his thigh with her foot.

"Hey, the train's slowing down, right?"

Ady nodded. "We have to be coming into a station. I have a suitcase down at the end there. Can you help me?"

Artie got the suitcase while Ady used the bathroom, and when the train came to a stop, he opened the door and jumped down, turning around to help Ady off.

Standing on gravel, large white chips, rather than the asphalt he'd expected, Artie looked down the track for the station and saw nothing. "I think we got off on the wrong side," he said, turning to Ady.

"Well, let's just wait till it leaves and we'll cross over."

Ady sat on the suitcase, beginning to shiver. The fir trees along the track were dripping water, frost melting in the early morning sun. Artie squinted. "It's going to be a good day, isn't it? Bright."

Ady nodded. "I wish they'd move."

"I hear another train," Artie said. "Maybe they have to let it pass."

In a minute, on the far side, a freight train roared past, shaking the gravel as it rumbled over the tracks. When it passed, the passenger train thunked into motion, couplings clanking as each car took up the slack. When the caboose passed, Artie stared after it up the tracks. "Shit!"

"We're nowhere!"

"We're on a siding, is where we are. Come on. Give me the suitcase. We'll have to walk."

"We could wait for another train."

"It might not stop. Best to walk until we can find a station—or a road."

Ady stared at him. "Way to go," she said.

Okay, I don't need another Pam.

He grabbed her suitcase and set off down the tracks.

It was noon and Artie's spirits had risen by the time they came across signs of life. He recognized the terrain. "We must have gotten off at Oakridge," he told Ady. "We can't be more than twenty miles from Eugene. Let's climb on down to the highway."

He helped Ady down a muddy bank and they began walking along the highway. An old man in a white pickup finally stopped and carried them on into Eugene. He talked the whole time about an antique auction where he'd bought some junk.

Getting off near the university on Franklin Boulevard, Artie offered to treat Ady to lunch. "Let's get a quick bite at the Millrace here and then we can find your friends."

"Have you decided what you're going to do?" Ady asked a few minutes later, munching a hamburger. "About your wife."

Artie grinned—"I don't think I'll go back yet"—then grew pensive. "It's funny being in the same city. I could leave her a note I guess, saying not to worry about me—that I've taken off to think for a while."

"You don't want to see her?"

"Not right away. I think we both realize the marriage is over."

"Shit, that bad?"

"This gives me some time." He shrugged. "But come to think of it, maybe it'd be better to go there now. I don't think she'll be home yet. She would've stayed in Klamath Falls all night for sure, since we'd paid for the motel, and maybe all day today. I'll pack up some of my clothes and get some money. You don't mind me coming with you for a ways, do you? Maybe I'll go as far as the border and then come back."

"Really? Are you serious?" She stared at him in disbelief. "Well, don't expect anything out of it." She blushed. "I mean, permanent."

"No, I just thought I'd keep you company. Until you get to your friends' place now, and then ...." He paused. "What were you planning on doing in Canada?"

"Finding a job. I dropped out of school this last term. Cal State Hayward. Tired of it."

"What were you studying?"

"Biology."

"Biology!"

"What's so strange about that?"

"Nothing. I just hated it in high school is all. So, what would you do? Go on to study medicine?"

"I could. I'm more interested in being a veterinarian though. I grew up on a farm near Ferndale. We had Guernseys."

"Hey, I know what that's like."

While they polished off their lunch, down to the last dark brown French fry scraps, Ady told Artie about her friends. They'd attended the same high school before taking different paths to college.

Having paid the bill, they set off to find her friends' apartment on Patterson Street. It was a fifteen minute walk, traversed in silence, the opalescent spring sun overhead and budding trees along the sidewalks having lulled them both into a relaxed and somnolent torpor.

"This must be it," Ady said finally, pointing. "1275."

"It's funny. I've seen this old place a hundred times. Walked right by it on my way to campus."

The front door was open so the two knocked and walked in. To the left a stairway led to the second floor and to the right stood a long, narrow room with a fireplace at the back. Looking over Ady's head from the vestibule, Artie saw a refrigerator down the corridor in what he figured to be the kitchen. A young woman, resting on a blanket-draped sofa in the living room, saw Ady and shrieked. Ady ran in and the two hugged each other and laughed while Artie stood in the vestibule.

When Ady introduced him to the girl, her name was Nancy, he said "Maybe I should go and come back later. You guys can talk."

Ady hesitated, but Nancy grabbed his arm and told him to relax. "Is this your boyfriend, Ady?" she asked, looking Artie up and down.

Ady blushed. "Not quite. We just met last night, but we're traveling together."

"Oh, how romantic!" Nancy said, embarrassing everyone.

The three sat and talked for an hour. Ady clued her friend in on what had been happening to her at Cal State. When Nancy asked Artie what he was doing, he suddenly remembered the note he was going to leave for Pam and the clothes he needed to pick up.

"Listen, Ady. I forgot I wanted to get that stuff packed. Why don't you tell Nancy what's happening, and I'll take care of my clothes."

In the street, he felt a sense of panic and hurried on foot to the apartment. He doubted that Pam was there but if she'd left early that morning it was possible. She was a slow driver at any rate.

Was he being an idiot? Thinking about taking off, even if it was for just a few days? Might as well admit the marriage was over.

Outside the apartment on Ferry Street—they lived on the sixth floor of a apartment complex—he listened, heard nothing, and entered. In his desk, he found twenty dollars in cash he and Pam kept on hand for emergencies, took it, and packed his clothes in a flight bag. The packet of travelers checks had over a thousand dollars in it but he knew he couldn't take it all.

Artie walked downtown to the bank on Willamette Street and cashed enough for $500. Back home, he left Pam the rest of the travelers checks and a note saying he needed time to think, and then left. By then, it was four o'clock in the afternoon and beginning to cool. A dense layer of gray clouds was moving in and before he reached Ady's friends, a light patter of rain had wetted his hair and jacket.

"Hi Artie!" Nancy shouted, as Artie bounded up the walk. She and Ady giggled. "Come on in," Nancy said, taking him by the arm.

In the living room, Artie nodded to another girl as Nancy presented her. Allison, a chubby teenager in green jeans and a sweatshirt. She smiled and waved a cigarette at him. "Wow," she said, "you won't believe what I've been hearing about you!"

"I probably would," Artie said, sitting down on a mattress across from the sofa. "Unless Ady's got a bigger imagination than I think."

After ten minutes of desultory conversation, Artie, feeling the pangs of hunger, offered to take them all out for dinner and the women scurried to get raincoats and an umbrella. "Why don't we just walk up to the Mandarin?" Artie said. "It's only a block."

During dinner, Artie talked to Ady and, by the time they were through, the two had decided to take route F over to Florence and then go north along the coast until they reached Astoria. From there, they would head in to Portland and hitch on up to Seattle by freeway.

In the apartment on Patterson, they played records until late, when it was awkwardly settled that Artie and Ady would sleep in the living room on two mattresses the women used for couches.

When the house had settled into silence, except for the dying embers of a fire, Artie whispered to Ady, "You asleep yet, Ady?"

"No, I was wondering if you were."

"Why don't I come over and we'll talk."

"Okay."

Artie got up in the dark, having removed his trousers under the blankets, and slipped across the room in his white underpants.

Ady giggled. "You look funny."

Artie slipped under the covers. "Can't help that."

"It reminds me of the night I stayed with a girlfriend in Vancouver. Summertime. We caught her brothers outside in their underpants. We were all sleeping in tents, and they came out to pee."

Artie put his arm over her and felt naked flesh. "You're not wearing anything?"

"What? You think I wear pants to bed?"

He reached down, kissing her cheek, and, when he touched her body, felt her mouth search his.

# chapter 10

In the motel room Pam packed the toilet articles and loaded the suitcases in the car. She'd waited the day, fretting, calling the police twice to ask if anyone had been found that night and then was too embarrassed to try again. She was sure now that Artie had run off. She didn't like to drive at night but, after filling up at a Chevron station, she aimed the car like an angry arrow and headed out of town towards Ashland to get back on the Interstate for Eugene.

On the trip home, to break the monotony of driving alone, she rehearsed her outbreaks, imagining what she would shout when she met Artie. In the back of her mind, she knew she would be relieved to see him, but before this was straightened out there would be some wild words between them. Wild words and stormy tears. They'd fought before, both stubborn, neither one wanting to give in, but somehow unable to sleep until they'd laboriously rehashed the fight over and over and reached a settlement, sealed quite often with tears.

Pam remembered the worst fight they'd ever had. Artie had tried to grab her hands when she was already angry and this had infuriated her. She'd seen her father beat her mother too many times. No one was going to touch her. She let out a blood-curdling yell and ran to the kitchen. When Artie appeared at the doorway, shouting at her to shut up and calm down before the neighbors called the police, she reached into the sink, full of water and dirty dishes, and began throwing them at him. She'd shattered three or four when he rushed in at her. Terrified, she raised a plate in the air, swung and smashed through the bare light bulb in the kitchen. The hot fragments of glass shattered down on both. Pam, lightly shocked by the contact of wet plate and filament, fell to the floor screaming. By the time Artie had calmed her, hugging her and saying he was sorry, they were both cut from the glass.

That was their worst. Pam relived a thousand more it seemed, worse yet in her imagination, on the trip home. On the way she also drove off the road a thousand times in her mind, winding up shredded in a bloody wreck. He would feel sorry for her then. When she pulled into the apartment on Ferry Street after midnight, however, she was still alive. Alive and tired.

Opening the door into darkness, she listened for Artie and then stepped in and switched on the light. Reading the note, high above the city, in the cold light of the kitchen, she called Artie a bastard and then broke down and cried.

## *chapter 11*

H ey you kids! Time to get up," Nancy shouted, and Artie rolled away, finding Ady snuggled beside him. They were both awake now, a frightened look on Ady's face.

"Do you think she came in and saw us, Artie?"

"I don't know. I doubt it. It's not that drastic, is it?"

"You'd better hurry and get dressed, anyway. They might tell my folks. Nancy's pretty religious."

"Why'd she even let us sleep in here together then?"

"What could she say? We both hung around."

Ady had been planning on staying for another day but the awkwardness of the situation induced her to change her mind. After breakfast, she announced they were leaving right away, since the coastal route took more time, and she needed to cash in her ticket before they left.

On the way towards 6th Street where they would hitchhike, Artie had them slip near the apartment building to check for the car.

"It's there," he said, "the red Fiat. Come on, let's get going." He turned back towards Patterson and they skirted the apartment building. On 6th Street they caught a ride taking them out to the big Y, where Artie had a flash of inspiration.

"There's an overpass right behind us here," he told Ady, "with tracks under it and I know the freight trains go over to Coos Bay or somewhere on the coast. Why don't we hop a train?"

Though at first she thought he was joking, Ady jumped at the idea. "That'd be fun. But isn't it dangerous?"

Artie shrugged. "If we're not careful."

"What about the cash you're carrying?"

Artie looked around. "Let's go into the store here and see if we can't get something for protection."

Fifteen minutes later, they danced out of the store and ran across the parking lot, whooping like idiots. "A bow and arrows, would you believe it?" Artie laughed. "What a weapon, huh? Let them try to get us now and we'll scalp 'em!"

By the time they caught a train it was shortly after eleven. Ady had been afraid to jump the first train, although Artie had gotten on and off. "Next time," he said, "you go first. I'll pick a good car." When the second train, longer and slower, passed, they managed to scramble into a box car.

They sat down at one end, watching the land roll by, staring at the old factories and mills and occasionally the cars passing along the highways skirting the tracks. The day was already warm and lazy, a beautiful early spring day, the willow trees along the tracks waving as the train passed. When they drew near Fern Ridge Reservoir, Artie got to his feet and watched trees, water, and swampy fields flicker past.

"Great, isn't it?" he shouted to Ady.

"I don't like those people in cars seeing us,"

"They can't do anything."

"They might report us."

I doubt it,but I'll close the door on that side."

"Not on both, okay?" Ady leaned away from the wall, her hands supporting her from behind. "I don't want to get stuck in here."

Artie pulled the one door shut. "There. It's darker in here, but at least the sun's away from the highway side. I think I'll practice with my bow."

He moved down near Ady and emptied his quiver into the far wall which was lined with cardboard tacked to the wall by slats.

"Want to try it? It's fun!"

Ady took the bow and shot for the wall. The arrow skittered along the floor like a pebble over water. "I'm not strong enough to use it right."

"Sure you are. Just hold the head of the arrow up with your left hand. And don't shoot the arrows out the door."

They were going around a curve now, the cars rocking and banging, and Ady sat down.

"You don't get car sick, do you?" Artie felt fine, his head clear. No trace of his acid trip.

"I did all right on the passenger train, didn't I?"

"What a view, huh?"

Artie sat beside her and touched her leg.

"Artie,'" she said.

"What?"

"I hardly know you."

Artie laughed. "That didn't stop us last night."

"What if somebody sees us?"

"In the fields?"

"Yes, farmers, or cars at some crossing. Besides, if we ever stop at a crossing, a brakeman might walk by and see us."

Artie rose and walked to the far end, pulling a two by four loose from the wood frame at that end. "I'll wedge this in so the door can't close all the way, okay?"

Ady hesitated. "Just be careful, please Artie. I'm afraid of being locked in here."

"I will be." She was afraid of everything. "The other door didn't lock when

I shut it anyway. And no one's going to come along and padlock them while we're moving."

With the left door nearly closed now, a thin shaft of light illuminated the bare freight car. Artie sat down by Ady and she kissed him.

"Kind of dusty in here, isn't it?"

"A bit. Kiss me again."

Artie leaned over, kissed her, and began to unbutton her blouse. He rose to his knees before her. "You're built nice," he said, opening her blouse and unsnapping the bra. "My wife is small."

"Artie, let's not talk about your wife, okay?"

"Sorry. It's just a change for me."

"Good, come here and enjoy it." Spreading his coat and shirt on the floor first, Artie undressed Ady until she lay nude, languorous in the dim mottled light, and then stood up to take off his pants while she watched. Artie stripped to his underpants. He stood for a moment enjoying the sight, the swelling breasts and smooth belly, her hips beckoning, her pubic hair like the waving grass outside in the sun.

Ady enticed him with a lift of her body and with her tongue licking her lips. "There's more than just looking."

Before each was through riding the other, they'd passed through many fields, by ponds and creeks, over bridges, through hills, across soft valleys. Artie had never seen such sensuous country. And, finally, he'd slept with more than one woman. He'd always wondered if he'd die having made love only to Pam.


# chapter 12


P am knew she would have to call her folks and of course they would expect to talk to Artie. She pondered not saying anything but finally decided to drive out, explain everything in person, and get it over with. Before leaving, she stopped off at the neighbor lady's place and knocked.

"Hello, Mrs. Clairwood," she said to the gray-haired lady dressed in black.

"Oh, come on in, Mrs. Crenshaw."

"I can't stay today. I just stopped by to pick up Oedipus. How is he?"

"Oh, he's as frisky as he was when you left him!" she cackled. "Fatter maybe.

I fed him some cans of some of this new cat food and he went wild." Mrs. Clairwood clacked her dentures and sucked her lips in and out as if to see if they were still working.

"Oh, you shouldn't have," Pam said, looking around for the cat. "You'll spoil him. Was the five dollars enough to cover everything, or shall I leave a bit more?"

The old lady, who had a tendency to keep her for hours when she could, raised her hands and shrieked in mock horror. "Oh, it was plenty, honey."

While Mrs. Clairwood went to get the cat, Pam stepped from the hallway into the apartment. The living room had an air of rouged antiquity, like the old woman's cracked cheeks. Mrs. Clairwood spent half her day dusting off the myriad memories contained in each knobby and gnarled knick-knack. Pam heard her cheerful voice from the kitchen, which emitted a glow of light down a dim, picture-lined corridor.

"What was that?"

"Come look at him. Isn't he cute?"

Pam walked into the light of the kitchen and saw Oedipus on the window sill, batting at a house fly. "He does that all the time," she said. "He just goes wild, like a bear after honey.'"

"I'll say. Gosh almighty, he's sure a doll!"

The fly, a big, blue bottle monster, zipped up to the ceiling, bumping it with a rasping staccato, a B-52 of the entomological world, and the kitten stood up on its hind legs, swiping at it. Leaning back, he lost his balance and fell twisting on to the kitchen table, knocking a bowl of sugar flying and tipping over a glass of milk the old lady had set out.

"Oh, no." Pam forgot the cat, which had dashed under the bed at the up-raised voices. "I'm so sorry." Her cheeks flushed. She righted the empty glass, somehow blaming Mrs. Clairwood and not the cat for all this. It was as if the woman wanted to detain her and this was the only way she knew how.

"That's alright, honey. You go on now, you said you had a lot to do."

"No, let me help you clean up."

"No, I'll get it'," she insisted, clutching Pam by the wrist and pushing gently. "You said you had chores. Here's a biscuit for Oedipus."

Pam hesitated. "It's just that my folks are expecting me and ..."

"Where's your husband? Writing away I imagine."

Pam stopped at the door with Oedipus in her arms. She had coaxed him out with the biscuit. "Artie's downtown right now. Thanks again for keeping

Oedipus."

She slipped out the door, ran down the hall, threw the cat into the apartment and took the stairs, afraid to stand in the hall and wait for the elevator.

In the car on the way out to her folks' place, she grimaced. "As if I don't have troubles enough."

A half-hour later, she parked the car in front of her folks' home, a low, ranch style house with a blossoming wild cherry tree in the front lawn, and went on in.

"Mom," she called. "Anybody home?" No one answered, but she heard the lawn mower in the back yard. "Probably Dad," she thought, "I wonder where Mom is."

She went through the living room and out into the patio. "Hi, Dad," she called. He saw her and came over to kiss her. "Where's Artie?"

"Where's Mom?"

"She's down at the grocery store getting some steaks for tonight. I wish you kids had let us know you were back. I could have told her to get more. The Caldersons are coming over tonight."

"Oh really. Well ..." Pam looked away, her eyes moist, unable to explain about Artie. Her folks, she knew, thought highly of him and it was going to be a big shock.

"I guess I'll just wait inside for Mom," she said. "Can I get you anything to drink?"

"No, I have a beer out on the picnic table. Help yourself to the frig."

Pam went inside and sat in the coolness—the shades were drawn to keep the sun out—waiting and thinking.

The front door slammed and Pam rose to help her mother with the sacks. "Hi Mom! What'cha got?"

"Hi, Pam. Saw the car outside. Where's Artie? Did you get him a beer?"

Pam walked into the kitchen by her Mom and when her mother sat the sack down announced, "He's left me, Mom." Mrs. Walters looked up, eyes wide. Pam stared at her until a tear began to form in each eye and then her Mom put her arms around her and the daughter cried in the warm embrace of her mother's arm.

After a moment, her mother said, "You can do better. I don't think Artie ever knew what he really wanted."

"I guess it wasn't me." She turned away and looked out the window at her dad. "He always told me I was his soulmate ... Now I hate that word."

# *chapter 13*

I t was late afternoon by the time Artie and Ady, having jumped the train in Reedsport, had hitchhiked north as far as Siltcoos Lake. Overhead the sky was changing rapidly, now dark with the threat of moiling clouds.

"Hey, Ady." Artie sat down on her suitcase, tired of standing at the side of the road while cars whizzed past. "Let's cut through those dunes to the lakeshore and try to find a place to stay for tonight."

"I think we should find a town, Artie. We need food."

"We can get along on what we bought in Reedsport." He tried to sound jovial. "It'll be cold but sandwiches are better than nothing."

In Reedsport, they'd bought a box of Ritz crackers, a small sack of red delicious apples, a loaf of bread, and a small jar of peanut butter. A guy at the deli had given them a plastic knife.

The two struggled hand in hand over sand dunes spotted with scotch broom and came upon the shadowed, puce-colored lake near a dock where several small boats were tied to bollards.

"Let's sneak out and eat in a rowboat." He searched Ady's face for a glimmer of shared enthusiasm.

"What if they catch us?"

"It's deserted. No one's out in this kind of weather."

A gimlet streak of pale yellow filtered through the slate-gray clouds, while a cool breeze ruffled the scrawny pine around the lake. Artie found a rowboat with a tarpaulin tied over it and loosened an edge so he and Ady could slip in. Once inside, he used a short seat board from one end to prop up the tarpaulin. Ady spread the food on the middle seat. Giggling, bumping each other, they stretched out on the bottom and opened the sack of apples.

"I was going to eat a sandwich," Artie said, "but I think it'd be too dry. We should've bought some jam."

Ady unscrewed the peanut butter and dug a finger into it. "Mm. Try some straight. It's not bad."

By the time the two had satisfied themselves, a light mist had begun to fall.

---

Artie peered out from under the tarpaulin and watched the mist build up until sheets of rain were blowing and undulating across the water. He could hear the trees creaking as they swayed in the wind. The water danced, flecked with tiny white caps. A peal of thunder rolled out of the flagstone clouds, and Ady shivered.

"I saw some cabins on the far side of the lake. I was thinking we could sleep in one if they're deserted."

Over Ady's protestations, Artie untied the bow and, with the awning still protecting them, shoved the boat out from the dock with an oar. They were surrounded by motor boats without their motors and a few rental rowboats padlocked together. Scraping the sides of the boats, and adding to the screeching of wood and clanking of chains in the wind, the little boat finally floated free. Artie lifted the awning at both sides and began to row away from the dock. The wind whipped the edges of the tarpaulin.

"Ady," Artie called. "Can you tie the front of the tarp down better? I'm getting sheets of water every time it flaps up."

"You're splashing water back here with the oars, too. We'll be soaked."

"Just try … look … wait! You'll knock the board over." Artie held her back.

He left the oars hanging in the oarlocks and crawled to the front of the boat. "Get out of the way. I'll tie it down."

Ady shivered. "This is terrible. I'm freezing."

Artie crawled back to the middle and knocked the seat down. He lay for a few seconds in frustration and then rose to his knees. "Ady, I'm going to tie the tarp down tight on this side and we'll keep it facing the breeze. We'll just rest a bit until this passes."

With the tarp down tight, the two huddled together, squinting out of the side facing away from the dock and the unseen ocean beyond the dunes. Hugging each other, they began to warm.

Moments later, Artie said, "I think the wind's pushing us closer to the shore where those cabins are."

Ady looked out over the side. "It's getting dark fast. All I can see now are trees."

"At least we know the places are deserted if no lights are on."

Artie let the tarp drop and the two rested in silence. Ady lay on her side with her back to Artie and the pressure of her curved buttocks against his body began to arouse him. He kissed her neck.

Overhead the wind tap danced across the tarpaulin and over the water, swishing. Ady turned her head back over her shoulder, her lips seeking Artie's.

"Oh, I like these kisses," she murmured. "They make me dizzy." She shifted her hips. "I just wish this wasn't so uncomfortable."

"Raise up a bit and I'll slip my coat under you."

With the coat arranged, Artie pulled up Ady's sweater and slid down to kiss her back. "Raise your hips again, Ady," he asked. She did, silently, and he slipped her pants down, biting and caressing her buttocks.

She reached down to stroke his hair as he slipped between her legs, his lips finding her wetness.

Later, he kissed up her back, tugging her sweater higher, until he reached her neck and then her ear. Holding her buttocks, he slipped into her from behind and they lay there moving slowly, rocking softly with the force of the wind.

"I like this, Artie," she whispered. "I've never been so aroused in my life."

"It's nice being warm and hearing the rain."

While he held her, caressing her breasts under her sweater, she began to thrust back against him, drawing him deeper and deeper into her. Kissing each other, pressing together with force, they forgot the bobbing boat, the lake, the sand, and the combers crashing to shore beyond the dunes.

# chapter 14

I don't know what Artie's doing, but if he's with some woman so help me I'll cut off his penis."

Close to midnight and she'd just left her folks' house after a stormy session of tears, soul searching, and anger.

She'd spent most of her hours since Artie's disappearance dissecting recent events, probing into the past, deconstructing and reconstructing it, searching for the clue, the spur, that could have caused him to leave.

But wasn't it clear? They'd both wanted an escape. It's just ... when it's forced on you ... what do you do then?

She thought about how close they used to be. A perfect marriage. The same likes and dislikes. Both were jealous. They'd cut off their friends. Pam didn't like Phil and Artie didn't Pam's best friend from high school, Mitsy Fabner. She smoked too much, was a bleached blonde and wore short skirts. Pam didn't like Mitsy being around Artie too much anyway, so she was glad he didn't like her.

But, in time, their closeness had turned bad. Artie had started complaining about their insularity, the lack of stimulating conversation, of new ideas, of different people.

In the apartment, unable to sleep, hesitating a hundred times, she picked up the phone book and looked for Mitsy Fabner. Couldn't find her name. She hadn't seen Mitsy in a few years, but expected her to be in Eugene. She dialed Mitsy's folks before she realized how late it was.

"Mr. Fabner," she said when a gruff voice answered. "Yes, who is this?"

Pam thought fast. "Nancy DeLong," she stammered, using the name of a classmate who she knew had gone to Germany with her husband. "I'm in town for a few days and I wanted to get in touch with Mitsy. I'm sorry I called so late. Has she moved away?"

"No, she's still in town. Hasn't she written to you? She's been married about six months now. I've got her number here somewhere, but maybe it'd be easier if you just looked it up. It'll be under Jim McAllister."

Pam thanked him profusely and hurried off the line. She paused again, realizing it was near one o'clock, but then dialed the number, planning to hang up if she heard a man.

"Mitsy, is that you?" she asked, when a sleepy voice answered.

The voice picked up immediately. "Yes, what is it? Nothing's happened to Jim has it?"

"Mitsy, this is Pam."

"Pam, wow, it's been a long time. You know I'm married, don't you?"

"That's what your dad said. I made the stupid mistake of calling him a few minutes ago."

"He won't mind." Mitsy's voice grew stronger. "Jim's not at home now, and I was a bit scared by the phone call. He's a policeman. I'm always afraid they'll call saying something's happened to him."

"Oh, sorry if I ..."

"Forget it. It's good to hear you. What's up?"

Pam hesitated. "Nothing much ... well, I guess that's not true. I was feeling lonely and I thought maybe we could talk some." She picked at a button on her blouse, waiting for Mitsy's response.

"Sure! Why don't I telephone and leave a message for Jim, and I'll come pick you up. We can get a bottle and relive the good old days, and I'll drop you back at your place before Jim gets off in the morning."

After the usual polite hedging, Pam agreed and gave Mitsy directions to her place. A half hour later Mitsy pulled up in a Cougar and took Pam for a ride.

"Why don't we stop at a bar and get something," Mitsy said, after Pam broke the news of Artie's splitting. "I bought some bourbon with me but we might as well get a little music and share some company before the bars close at two."

Pam hesitated, knowing Artie wouldn't approve, but then, on an impulse, to spite him, angry that she should still feel his authority, agreed. "It's funny," she said. "I've never been in a bar in my life and I'm twenty-four now."

"Didn't you guys ever go out drinking?"

"We don't drink much—a little wine or beer at home, but that's about it. Our budget's been kind of tight."

Mitsy drove up 13th Street toward the University and parked near a hamburger restaurant. "I'll take you to Maxie's," she said, opening her purse and applying some lipstick. "It's always fun."

In the narrow bar, feeling uncomfortable, Pam ordered a cuba libre and scanned the crowd, averting her eyes whenever she caught anyone else's. One woman, with sharp, angular features and a hard metallic voice, sat at the bar talking with two men. A couple of others, looking like students with dates, were in a booth and the rest of the place was full of guys.

She looked back at Mitsy. "How does Jim feel about you coming here alone?"

"I'm not alone, I'm with you!" It was good to hear Mitsy laugh. "But he doesn't mind. I come here every now and then with Jane Vanton, remember her? Jane's got two little boys by the way."

"Wow, she had them fast, didn't she?"

"Yeah, she's divorced from the guy already too. You know, she married Greg, the guy she dated all through high school."

"I always wondered if they'd make it to the altar."

"Greg settled down quite a bit, actually. It was Jane who caused the divorce."

"She was always messed up, I thought, by what happened to her folks." Pam was happy to talk about someone else's problems.

Mitsy nodded. "Never should have married in the first place really. She was always saying she didn't think she could make it."

"Too bad she had kids."

Thank God I don't. One less thing to worry about.

Mitsy hesitated. "She only had them to try and tie herself down. What really bothered her was she didn't like sex with him."

"Really? Why not?"

They'd seemed a perfect pair.

Mitsy frowned. "On their wedding night—you know, all those years they kept from it—anyway, she says he about raped her after trying to get her drunk. So, it was a pretty lousy experience to start out on."

Pam sipped her drink, eyes downcast. "Artie and I started out before we were married. It was a month before I even knew we were doing it. It was pretty easy on me. I think it'd be terrible to have to make it in one night."

Mitsy leaned closer and lowered her voice. "My first lover had a pecker as big as a pencil so I was lucky!" She grinned, a flush brightening her cheeks. "Don't tell anyone but I was up to carrots and zucchini by then."

Pam laughed along with Mitsy and for the first time all evening forgot her own problems. Giggling in embarrassment, she shared her own youthful experimentation. "I tried a banana once," she said, "only I made the mistake of peeling it first!" They both broke into uncontrollable laughter, attracting the attention of a group at the far end of the bar. Pam put her finger to her lips, trying to shush Mitsy but unable to stop herself.

"Nothing like mashed potatoes," Mitsy said, gasping for breath. "That sounds like my luck with men before Jim. Pencil pricks or sponge dicks. Ain't that a killer?"

Pam had to admit that it was.

# chapter 15

Following a rigorous day of ten-mile rides along twisting, sheer-cliffed, coastal roads, Artie and Ady clambered exhaustedly from a cramped Ford pickup somewhere south of Pleasant Valley. With the sun hanging above the ocean, like a basketball in mid bounce, they walked north along Highway 101 the three miles to South Prairie. Ady was tired and wanted to stop, but there were no motels in sight. Tillamook, they were told, was only eight miles further north.

"Let's start walking, Ady," Artie said, urging her on. "We'll get a ride along the way and if we don't it's better to walk the distance rather than sleep in some field."

Ady's didn't respond but set out ahead of Artie, angry he could tell. He was responsible for their plight. Should've stopped in Lincoln City, but he'd wanted to go on. Three o'clock had seemed too early to stop.

When they were a few miles north of South Prairie, the sun flattened out on the ocean, then disappeared from view. Ady stopped and faced Artie, arms akimbo. "My feet are killing me."

Artie looked down. Both their shoes were covered with a light gray powder. Road dust. He'd carried her suitcase the whole way. so why bitch?

"They're burning," she said. "I quit." She looked at him as if expecting him to come up with a solution.

"Let's look for a barn or shed," he said, trying to ignore her crankiness.

"I'm not sleeping in cow shit!"

"There's hay in a barn, you dolt. Just shut up and let's look for shelter."

They trudged on as the shadows steadily increased. Finally, off to the right, in a clump of fir trees, Artie saw the lights of a house and a stronger glare from an outdoor lamp on a telephone pole. Leery of dogs, he had them cut off the road, traverse a soggy meadow, and come up behind the farmhouse.

The barn, a battered and unused silo nearby, was set back from the house near an orchard. They walked beneath a row of apple trees, scaring themselves when they stumbled upon a sow and her litter. The piglets squealed as if being murdered, and the two stopped, terrified at the noise. The sow, a monster, grunted and moved off.

Damn. She had to have weighed three hundred pounds or more.

At the barn, his heart still thumping, Artie slid open one of the double doors and peered inside. The interior was pitch black. Stepping inside, into the musty, sweet smell of dried alfalfa and fescue, he pulled Ady after him and slid the door back in place.

Ady held his arm and started to complain about the darkness. "Shh," Artie whispered. He was listening for animals.

As their eyes adjusted to the dark, they could see a row of stanchions and beyond them a hay loft.

"Let's see if we can find the ladder," Artie said, feeling his way down a freshly washed concrete floor. "They must have milk cows."

Ady followed him silently, her hand on his back. At the far end, they turned and moved across the width of the barn until Artie found a wooden ladder nailed to the wall. Overhead, barely visible, a square hole was cut in the ceiling.

"Do you want to go first?" he asked.

She shoved him. "You go first."

He started up the ladder, feeling for each rung. He could smell the crisp odor of last summer's hay. Ady was beside him then.

"It stinks up here."

"What? You won't find anything sweeter than this. Unless you want to sleep out in the orchard."

The hay was stacked in bales. "There're kids in this family," Artie said. "The hay's been arranged in forts. See that dark hole? That's a tunnel leading back in."

Ady grabbed his arm when he moved toward it. "Don't go in there. It might collapse."

Artie shook his head. "No way. Come on." He walked across the front of the loft.

"Just remember I'm not screwing here in the hay," she said.

Shit, who asked for a screw?

No use in arguing though. Ady lay down on some loose hay, and before he could get settled, he could hear her snore.

When he awoke, it was nearly four. Still too dark to see clearly, but cows had gathered in the yard below, mooing and shifting about.

Ady sat up, rubbed her eyes, and sneezed. She poked Artie. "I'm thirsty."

What am I supposed to do about it? She could go drink out of a trough if she was so thirsty.

He rolled over, his head striking an object. He reached out. "It's a basketball!" He stood and tapped out a knee high dribble on the straw-strewn floor. "A basketball!"

Ady moved over and sat on a hay bale.

He knew she was sulking. Tough shit. He'd had enough of crabby females.

When the sky lightened outside—a few rays crept in through the loft door above and the trap door below—Artie found the hoop.

"There're two," Ady pointed out, as Artie dribbled away from her and dunked the ball in a low-hung hoop at the far end. He whooped softly and passed the ball to Ady. Ady threw it two-handed toward the basket behind her. The ball hit the rim and bounced dangerously toward the trap door while the rim clanged with a dull, vibrating sound.

"Careful," he warned, scooping up the ball. "Don't lose it down the hole. Let's play!"

For a few minutes they played against each other until Ady tired of Artie's weaving around her and slam dunking the ball. She quit when he stole the ball and dribbled the length of the barn to dunk it again.

"Bastard!"

Artie wiped the sweat from his brow and sat on a bale at his end of the hay-loft. Just as he was about to suggest they leave, he heard the barn doors being shoved open, rolling with soft squeaks along the overhead tracks. Artie stood and motioned for Ady to keep still. She was looking at him in alarm. He put his finger to his lips and motioned for her to come toward him.

She shook her head, crabby, still resentful.

Artie waved angrily, gesturing for her to come on. After she'd tiptoed over, frowning at him the whole way, he pulled her head roughly toward his and told her they were going to have to crawl back through one of the tunnels and hide in the hay.

Ady tried to pull away, but Artie held her firmly by the head, drawing her ear towards his mouth. "The kids'll be getting ready for school and the guy doing the chores'll grab the nearest bales. Just follow me!" he ordered.

He left her there, got on his hands and knees and crawled back into the pile. Inside, he found not only a hollow, but one open to the roof.

When Ady joined him, he whispered, "Plenty of air."

The wait extended late into the morning. The milking, even with machines, took over two hours. For another two hours, they could hear the fellow clean-ing milking equipment and doing other chores in the barn. The whole time Ady refused to look at Artie.

No one came up to the loft. When Artie and Ady finally dared climb down, Artie saw why. They were feeding the cows from some alfalfa bales stacked on the ground floor. Just as he was about to go out a small side door, a milk truck drove up, and they had to hide for another half hour while the milk was pumped out of the storage tank and into the truck.

Back on the road, Ady still sullen, they caught their first ride at eleven. A farmer in a pickup took them the few miles into Tillamook, talking all the while about his herd of ten Herfords and how he was having a rough time getting rid of warts on them. One poor little girl, he kept insisting, had them hanging in clusters all over her neck. Poor little girl! Terrible things! Terrible things! And the Herfords weren't polled so he always had to watch out for their horns.

Artie looked skyward, begging for mercy. It was all he could do to resist telling the fellow he should've bought Angus instead. Then he wouldn't have to worry about horns. Besides, nothing could match a deep green field dotted with shiny black Angus. Much as he hated farm work, in the evening, under a sky of gray storm clouds, that was the party dress of the universe.

# chapter 16

Pam woke after ten, her head stuffy. She felt as if she'd come down with a bad cold. Her head rang, her ears buzzed, her eyes swam. She took three aspirin and lay back down till noon. Her mind lingered fitfully in a state of waking dream. When she awoke, she felt an ache nagging at her, a worry.

What's happened to Artie? The question gnawed at her while she heated a can of soup. What does one do when one's husband disappears?

I could go browse in a bookstore. A smile crossed her face. A fine response to a lost husband! What else?

Well, there was always what Mitsy had said last night.

"You need to get fucked, girl."
"Mitsy!"
"He fucked you over. It's your turn to fuck him up."
"I don't think like that."
"Give it some time. You will!"

Three years! Three years with one man and then … And then what? Did things start out bad from day one? They'd picked a wedding date just one month after their time in Mexico City. Maybe that was too soon. Neither had finished school by then.

The marriage ceremony itself was what she'd always hoped for, although her parents were embarrassed when Artie's folks refused to drink any alcohol. His dad had resisted even the seductive attempts of Carol, Pam's mother's resident socialite.

The marriage night itself wasn't the greatest, though.

Artie wanted to make love and I was too tired. We'd been doing it all week! But he thought protocol (or is it ritual?) called for it. Maybe that was the first false step.

But there were bigger things. School was hard on Artie, now that they were married. He felt responsible for their livelihood, and to make it worse, the time in Mexico City—he never stopped telling her he'd only gone there to follow her— had left him in debt. He was working nights for Georgia-Pacific. In a veneer plant outside Eugene, striping panels, dragging himself through the graveyard shift in a daze. Sprawled on a couch in the Honor's Center, he slept through most of his classes. Pam would wake him every hour for the next class, and he would mutter in exhaustion that he needed another hour. Then, in the afternoon, he couldn't sleep. By the time work came, he was a wreck, frustrated at not having been able to sleep, tired just when he needed to be fresh, angry when he wanted to be calm.

Finally he'd dropped out of school for the winter term and came back in the spring of '69 , finishing with two C's, two B's, and one undeserved A. The A was "earned" in his minor, a Fine Arts class, and the ceramics instructor who gave it to him said if Artie's writing was as far-out as his pots, he'd make a great hit in New York. Artie didn't know if the teacher was mocking him or not. And if she wasn't, was it a compliment? I should have chosen ceramics not writing for my concentration he'd joked to Pam and remembered the joke every time a freelance article, short story, or poem was turned down.

Near the end of that spring term Pam had started talking about going back to school in Mexico. A summer course.

"But what about your phone job?" Pam had worked summers for Pacific Northwest Bell, a long distance operator, ever since her senior year in high school.

"I can work somewhere else when we get back if I have to," she said. "How am I going to get a job teaching if I don't practice my languages?"

"You're not even majoring in Spanish anymore."

"I know what my major is," she shouted.

"You switched to Italian! And that was my influence."

"So what? I'll need to teach both in high school. Or maybe I'll go to grad school, ever think about that?"

They'd traded more accusations, stopping only when Pam stormed into the bathroom and slammed the door.

And then it was Artie's turn to throw a fit, slamming the bedroom door.

Once they'd hurt each other's feelings a compromise came. They'd wait a year, save up until the summer of 1970, and then they'd have the money to go back to Mexico, but not to Mexico City. Artie didn't like her friends there.

---

She picked a school in Cuernavaca instead.

So in the fall of '69, Pam went back to the university and Artie, having received his degree in the spring and taught a summer course of remedial English for the university that summer, had no job in the fall. He'd decided against graduate school.

He made the rounds of the mills. No one was hiring with winter layoffs approaching. He'd already tried the Register-Guard three times—as a reporter, a proofreader, and a copy editor—and had been rejected each time. He went back, asked to be a clerk, and was turned down again. Finally, in frustration, he went to work for two architects who bought old homes, upgraded them (Artie's job), then sold them for profit. He was paid $2.75 an hour for nine months work and quit the day Pam graduated that spring.

They still planned on going to Mexico for Pam to study but realized they'd need more money. So both agreed that a gap year would do them good. They would postpone the trip to Cuernavaca until the summer of 1971.

Pam, knowing he was frustrated by his attempts to find more meaningful work, let him write for most of June and July before her fears of a financial crunch drove her to nag him about a job. Artie resisted, but with every rejected short story manuscript or feature article, he grew more sullen. Finally, unable to justify his writing, he telephoned his former employers and went back to work refurbishing old houses.

The job was bearable, partly because the manual labor distracted him from the problems in their marriage. And, since Pam staffed a split shift at the phone company, from nine to one and five to nine, Artie put in a twelve to fourteen hour day, starting as early as eight and finishing at dusk.

If they'd been crabbing at each other the evening before, Artie sometimes worked on at night. When it got too dark to work outside, he would move indoors, stripping wallpaper, cleaning fireplaces, many which had been painted and needed a brisk brushing with chemical solvents to reveal the brick, sanding wood floors, removing and spray painting the steam pipes of old radiators, replacing cracked or broken windows, whatever needed to be done. By the end of the August he was tanned and brawny.

Pam, in a more enclosed job, spent her afternoons building a tan at Fern Ridge Reservoir. She would drop a lunch by for Artie wherever he was working, chat for a few minutes, join him in a cold drink of juice or beer, and then drive out to the lake in the MGA convertible.

Now that was another problem! After spending nearly a thousand dollars over the last two years on the '59 MGA, a flashy red softtop they'd bought together before their marriage, they'd made the decision to sell it at the end of the summer. Though a beauty, the car was a continual headache. Their first mistake was buying it, Artie always said, knowing it was Pam's idea. If she couldn't have a Jag or a Corvette, her high school fantasies, they could at least buy a sports car and a convertible! That's what she'd said and he'd gone along with her. Anything to keep the peace.

On their first trip to Portland, the car had overheated. Three garages along the road replaced minor and not so minor parts—a thermostat, hoses, a water pump—and one rodded out the radiator, all to no avail. They finally towed the car back to Eugene, where they learned the MGA had a cracked block, a cracked block which had been illegally welded. After that expensive repair job, a series of car accidents beset them, all caused, Artie claimed, by the other drivers.

That school year, '69-'70, Pam's last as an undergrad, their financial anxieties had reduced them to a two hundred dollar a month budget. The strain told on both. Pam still wanted to spend the summer in Cuernavaca and Artie resented that, even though she'd promised him he could spend the time writing. No outside work, not that he could find any in Mexico.

As the months went by, they fought more often, sometimes over something so minor Pam wondered later how it had even started. Worse yet, they seemed to have forgotten how to stop once a fight started.

Thinking about it now, as she picked her way through a used bookstore feeling alone and angry, she realized the only reason she'd continued to refer to a high school job when she talked to Artie was to lessen his financial burden. Graduate school, if she had only herself to consider, would be her choice.

The realization came as a blessing. Easier to make decisions without Artie! Easier just to think of herself. Something positive thing to take out of this mess.

A "second" honeymoon, that was Artie's term. More like a last gasp. No matter what happened now, she knew she was through with him.

She would have to make more friends, she thought, stepping into the empty apartment and setting down the bag of books she'd bought that afternoon.

Before she could get her coat off, the phone rang. She picked it up, expecting to hear her mother.

"Hi Pam," she heard Artie say. "I want to come home."

\* \* \*

Return Artie did. The fight that developed lasted a month, at times smoldering beneath the surface, at times blazing, and ended only when Pam asked him to move out. The separation, when it came, was by mutual agreement. Artie's breakaway had awakened both to new possibilities, brought each to an awareness of the value of freedom. Freedom of choice for Pam, freedom from responsibility for Artie. And so, with some turmoil, Pam welcomed the change. Artie knew she'd applied last winter to graduate school at Berkeley and been accepted, something that never pleased him.

The semester hadn't started yet at Cal, but a job was waiting. She had a month to get ready for the move. Tuition paid and a position as a graduate teaching assistant. Pay? Twelve thousand a year. And cheap housing in the University Village in Albany. She could forget Artie and start fresh. A relief!

She'd gained a prestigious job and lost a husband. Mitsy, her best friend, would have thought her fortunate.

# Part Two • Flux and Reflux
## (1971)

# chapter 17

Days, it often seems, pass slowly. Changes slip by unnoticed, like the movement of the hour hand on a wristwatch. Years, instead, flash by flickering, fast like the cards in a shuffled deck. Five years pass and one looks back in surprise at all the changes. At the growth.

It took Pam two years to like California, a third year to think of herself as a Californian (although deep inside she still felt she was an Oregonian and, when asked where she was from, always replied, "I was born in Eugene, Oregon, but I've been living here in Berkeley for three years"). Two years later, when it was time to leave for New York for her first teaching job, she looked back on her life in the Bay Area with deep and painful nostalgia. She'd made friends, had shared good and bad times with them, had learned much about herself. She loved the climate, the freedom to be whatever one wanted to be, the city's acceptance of the abnormal.

Three years of marriage to Artie, half a decade on her own in Berkeley. Yes, she had changed. It had seemed such a long, hard grind. From the age of twenty-one, a new bride, to twenty-nine, a new Ph.D. Looking back in more negative moments, she felt old. Her twenties were gone and what did she have to show for it? A degree and a string of experiences. Was any of it worth the effort? She'd almost never asked that question during the process. At the conclusion it was too late. Time, no one needed to tell her, did not willingly retrace its steps.

Pam thought that after Artie left she would go to pieces. How could she pass those endless evening hours by herself? Where would she acquire the brute strength to open a fresh jar of pickles? How could a woman who didn't know where the spare was kept in a car change a flat tire?

She surprised herself. The answers to all her questions came, if not always easily, with not undue effort. First, in the evening, she read books, studied, watched TV, or chatted on the phone with old friends. The lonely moments, the tears, the recriminations, the bitterness, were all shared. Second, she realized she didn't eat as much as Artie. Half the food items in the refrigerator were for him. She tossed them, pickle bottle and all. Besides, to open a stuck lid you cracked its lip with a knife a few times or tapped the lid on the counter, or held it under hot water until it expanded, or asked your next door neighbor for a hand, or did without.

Third, changing a tire meant finding the jack and spare tire in the trunk under the floor panel (so that's where it was hidden!) and setting aside a few patient moments of practice. At worst you called a towing service.

Surmounted difficulties quickly became confidence builders. She met challenges and found she could exist on her own. She wanted and needed friends for support but she was also happier with herself. Some nights she cried, but as do all nights that too passed. Sometimes she missed Artie's company, his sense of humor, making love. But there were other compensations. For the first time in her life, masturbating, she realized what an orgasm was! Three years of making love and she'd never truly experienced one before. She didn't blame Artie. They'd tried every thing. Simply put, neither one had know how much direct stimulation it took. Even when love-making sessions with Artie had lasted an hour, they rarely focused steadily enough on her. But now she knew! One more step on the road to self-knowledge.

Too bad that it took me till I was twenty-five.

She was also able to devote more attention to her school work. For Pam, after a period of alternating elation and turmoil, her re-emergence into the world was a rebirth. She turned to studies as a relief, a diversion, better yet, a vocation. At the University of Oregon, she'd written her honor's thesis on women poets of the Renaissance. Feminism, at the time, was not the issue with her—it was then called, rather, relevancy. One of her retiring Italian teachers, Professor Kantubus, the same guy Artie had studied with in Pavia, suggested the topic in a tone of condescension—"Why don't you write on one of those minor women poets of the Renaissance?"—implying, as well, that only a woman would be interested in or could empathize with another woman.

Pam recognized the superior attitude in a man who, forced to give in to the current demands for "relevance," attempted to show somewhat sardonically what that demand led to—that is, to "inferior" women poets not worth "serious" study. But she took his suggestion as a challenge and wrote a two hundred and eighteen page thesis, not on one woman poet, but on all the women poets of the sixteenth century, from literary courtesans like Veronica Franco, Tullia d'Aragona, and Gaspara Stampa with their psychological penetration into human sentiments and their sexual freedom and joyous acceptance of sensual love to the opposite religious and political conservatism and severely formal elegance of nobles like Vittoria Colonna and Veronica Gambara.

Delightful to find that Gaspara Stampa fell in love with the noble Collaltino di Collalto, not on Easter as did Petrarch with Laura, but on Christmas! The courtesan poets were like the movie stars of today. Only they preferred literature to lovers. Even if some, like Veronica Franco praised the worth of their voluptuous activities above their literary achievements ("I'm much better in bed than writing poems"). They were the Aspasias of the day. Cities vied for their presence. It was a sign of honor, of touristic boasting, for whatever city possessed their talents. Delightful Veronica, when criticized by Maffio Venier for her way of life, responded by castigating homosexual love. These poetesses were a refreshing breath of natural vivacity and human veracity. Their sincerity was a joy.

Earlier in her last year as an undergrad, long before her separation from Artie, Pam had written two papers in a course taught by a visiting professor from the University of Michigan. In a private conference he'd pronounced both papers "forse pubblicabile." "Perhaps publishable" had been stimulus enough for her. She submitted both articles to journals. To her surprise, both were accepted, one rushed into print by Italian Literary Studies that very spring, in order to appear in an issue devoted to the Renaissance, the other appearing in Cinquecento Review in the summer, after she'd received her degree.

That September, before her move to California was a time of intense mental activity. She had just enough money left in savings to make it until her checks started coming from teaching. She'd thought of writing to Artie for a loan of a thousand dollars but had resisted the impulse. Artie had taken to writing to her occasionally in care of her parents but she wasn't eager to open up a direct correspondence.

Now that they were apart, now that she'd made it through the emotional suffering (her lawyer was taking care of the divorce papers), she didn't feel like re-entangling herself. Her emotions had given way to her mind and she was finding that her intellectual achievements not only gave her pleasure but provided an immense source of self-esteem. With Artie, she'd quit living. She'd lived his life. She'd typed his stories and poems and had taken satisfaction in his achievements. When he left, after the first few weeks, she came to realize she was no longer a person. She'd been an appendage—an arm—lopped off suddenly, discarded, good for nothing without a mind behind it to move it. So she'd turned within. It was her mind she wanted to nurture, not her feelings. Let Artie do that. From his letters it seemed he was drowning in a sea of emotions. Fine. That was his way of coping. For her it was going to be different.

Pam wasn't sure what had impressed them most at Cal—either her article on penile imagery in Politian—entitled "Poliziano as Pederastic Poet: Homo or Uomo?" and published in *Italian Literary Studies*—or her note on Bembo's theory of sexual love in the *Asolani*—entitled "Bembo's Bee: Pricker of Rose Buds or Honey Sucker?" The first article, published in *Cinquecento Review*, was chosen to be included in an upcoming critical study of Renaissance mores, edited by the famous critic Cesario Gilletti-Franconia. Both were real coups for someone so young and surprisingly no one had objected to her tongue-in-cheek titles.

Pam arrived in Berkeley, suitcase in hand, six days before classes were to start. She'd lost the apartment in the University Village. Turned out they were for married couples only. Divorced, she was out of luck. Once she found a place to stay, her dad had promised to bring down a trailer load of clothes and furniture.

Fortunately, she remembered the name of a young woman she'd met once at a conference in Eugene, Vera Lovati, and found her in the Berkeley phone book. Vera was living on the north side of campus, on Euclid, and offered to take Pam in until she could find an apartment.

Vera, though Italian by birth, was a Canadian citizen. She was working on a Ph.D. in Linguistics with a minor in Italian. A short woman, older than most of the students, stocky but well-proportioned, she liked to wear second-hand clothes, a patchwork of various colors, rumpled and out of style. The first thing she did was to take Pam shopping in a Goodwill store on San Pablo Avenue in Oakland.

Then she advised Pam to use more makeup. Vera herself had black, shining eyes, lined in kohl, most often smudged. Despite her makeup, she was an ardent feminist, the first Pam had ever known. "I love to turn on the boys," she said, "and then turn them down."

Vera offered to help find an apartment. Most of the numbers they called from the ads in the papers proved fruitless. The apartments were either rented or too expensive. Finally, late the next afternoon, after perusing the listings in the Student Housing Center, she found a room in a large, three-story Victorian house on Dana Street, south of campus. Vera said the area wasn't the greatest, but Pam was anxious to get settled. The apartment was listed as a studio, but the kitchen was really a room apart, shared by others, and the house had an enclosed sun porch open to all.

After Vera left, Pam went to unpack her suitcase.

Berkeley—here I come!

The Berkeley aesthetic was brought home to her at the end of her first week on campus. That Friday, by chance hearing rock music at noon, she made her way following the sounds from below Dwinelle Hall, across the bridge over Strawberry Creek, by the cafeteria, to Lower Sproul Plaza up a short flight of stairs.

"Shrimp Pan and the Jelly Busters" was the name on the bass drum. The lead singer was a blonde wearing a striped turquoise and pink jerkin, purple leotards, an Indian bead belt running through the crotch, and gold lamé boots. But what first drew Pam's eyes was a woman in the crowd, dancing topless. Not that she was big bosomed. In fact, she was rather normal. A boyfriend held a sign proclaiming women's right to go topless and the young woman was encouraging others to do likewise. No one, however, seemed quite as brave.

After enjoying the music for an hour, luxuriating in the (for her) unusually warm fall sun, Pam set off down Telegraph Avenue to find someplace to eat. So far, until she got her kitchen stocked, she'd been eating out. She'd tried three places already, Larry Blake's, Joe's Soup Kitchen, and Mario's Mexican restaurant. Today she was pondering whether to eat at an Indian restaurant— the Darvish—or at the Belgian Pancake House next door.

"Spare change?" Telegraph Avenue was a circus at noon. The street was lined on both sides with vendors, ready to reap the shekels of the newly arrived students before the spare change artists got to them. "Filthy lucre?" a bearded, barefoot, dirt-encrusted ogre asked her. "No thanks," she replied, as if he were offering it to her rather than asking for it, and stepped around him, embarrassed. She'd learned fast not to carry a purse.

At night, as she soon came to find out, Telegraph Avenue became a ghost town, a concrete desert of garbage strewn gutters, of flying placards, pamphlets, posters, and discarded Daily Cal's, of empty beer cans, whisky bottles, drug-crazed zombies, heroin pushers, and other souls footloose and fancy-free.

The first night she happened to walk down the street alone, heading to her apartment on Dana, a white-robed hippie followed her, shaking both hands as if he were beating off a pair of peckers, shouting, "Repent and be saved. Save your soul with rock and roll. Roll on, oh mighty Hebron!"

As she clenched her jaw and strode on, trying to ignore the fellow, a tall, red-haired kid leaning against a chopped Harley-Davidson laughed. "He's one of those 'Monks for Mohammed.' Better watch out or he'll convert you."

Pam's first teaching assignment was a section of Italian 1, meeting at 1:30. It was a small class of twelve students. Two hours before class started she lost count of her trips to the bathroom. She kept telling herself to relax. What was the worst that could happen? So what if she flubbed up, made a mistake, stuttered like an idiot? She'd live to see another day.

She practiced as many anti-fear techniques as she could think of. It didn't help much. She told herself the students were dumb, she was smart. Cast your audience into an inferior role. Feel superior. Look down on them as imbeciles. None of it helped. She had visions of brilliant Berkeley students cutting her to pieces, mocking her, laughing. Perhaps there would be class disruptions, students who would want to make political statements. Perhaps the whole class would walk out to join an afternoon rally in Sproul Plaza.

In her morning classes, she found it hard to concentrate on her professors' lectures. Then, during the pilot class that all TAs had to attend, butterflies fluttered in her belly. The pilot class was taught by Natalia Carucci, an Italo-American with a perfect accent. She'd grown up bilingual, looked Italian with her brown eyes, brown skin, dark hair; even the mannerisms, the inflections in the voice were pure Italian. Pam was envious, jealous of those who possessed a natural edge, of those who didn't have to work at the simplest things.

She looked down the row to her right. She and the other six new TAs were stretched in a taut line at the back of the room, conspicuous by their whispers, giggles, know-it-all attitude. Pam was taking page after page of notes, but most of the others seemed bored. Jeff and Sally Henderson, a married couple, separated in their seats by Margarita Piccone and Wally Ferguson, were passing notes back and forth. Pam even saw Vanni Lorenzini, an Italian native, give Gina DiPietro a kiss. Vanni was a handsome guy she thought, a real Latin lover type, but at the same time a bit effeminate. If she'd seen him by himself or with a group of guys, she would have considered him gay. He wore his shirt open, two or three gold necklaces glinting on a bronze chest, and the shirts were always silky and iridescent. His slacks fit his body like the peel on a shiny Bing cherry, hugging two round buttocks and outlining his bulge in the front. Pam had heard Margarita and Vera Lovati joking about how with Vanni you could always tell which side his balls were hanging. Vanni's father, from what Pam had heard, had been a friend of Palmiro Togliatti, the Italian Communist Party leader, and had fled Italy when the fascists came to power in the early twenties. He settled in Southern Idaho near Shoshone Falls and made his living running a rope-drawn ferry across the Snake river. Vanni had been born there, but was raised speaking Italian in the home.

Gina, apparently, was his girlfriend. In the TAs' office, their desks were facing each other, the rims touching like illicit lovers grazing each other's thighs in public. But other than that and the kiss she'd just seen, Pam would never have guessed they were lovers. Vanni flirted with all the women, and Gina never seemed to pay attention to him. She was just as often sitting on the edge of Jeff Henderson's desk, chatting vivaciously in Italian with him, while Jeff's wife, Sally, across the room at a desk in the corner, glanced up every minute or two and glared. Gina was a pretty women, with flashing eyes, bright cheeks, bouncy hair—sorority type to a T. Dressed to perfection.

It was funny, Pam thought. The married couple had their desks as far apart as you could get them while the two who tried to feign indifference to each other most of the time were right on top of each other.

To Pam, experienced in marital discord, Jeff and Sally's marriage seemed doomed. She couldn't see how two people could be so different and still get along. Sally, first of all, was a big woman, about a foot taller than Jeff, who was small, and in his own way, despite his mustache, effeminate also. He and Vanni would make a good pair, she thought. Maybe the four of them—Jeff, Sally, Vanni and Gina—got it on together. They could all swap partners, men and women.

Sally was stacked, blonde, given to sexual innuendos and loud laughter. Jeff was quiet, withdrawn, serious, asexual, and professorial in manner. He carried a briefcase, wore a sportcoat and tie. She hardly ever carried any books, and if she did they'd be jumbled in a wild pile, papers sticking out, pencils marking reading spots. Her clothes could best be described as weekend backyard barbecue. In a way, Pam admired her free spirit. She herself wouldn't mind sometimes wearing a sweatshirt and cutoffs to school.

The other two in the back row were also opposites, but, since they weren't a pair, it didn't seem to matter. Margarita Piccone was a three p's—prim, proper, and pouty. She was glacier material, cold and formal, a stickler for rules. If the rigidity of her features would ever soften into a laugh, Pam thought, she'd be a real beauty. She had nice features, a small, slim—even elegant—body, and didn't seem to notice either. She was the prototype of the cold woman professor. A virgin cloistered in coldness.

Wally, on the contrary, was red-haired, freckled, jovial, and over-weight. Not terribly so, though. The friendly chubby type, quick to make a joke. Wally, Vera told her, was best known for running through a drive-in movie lot during a showing of Franco Zefirelli's Romeo and Juliet and screaming, "She's not dead, she's not dead" as if he expected Romeo to hear him.

When the pilot class ended, Sally Henderson walked out of the room with Pam. She stage-whispered a comment which Pam, blushing, hoped Natalia, standing at the front of the classroom talking to students, couldn't hear. "It would help if these people who think being Italian is enough to make a good teacher, would take a proper methods course. Jeff and I couldn't believe some of the things she does, and here she's supposed to be a model for the rest of us."

Sally and Jeff had come to Berkeley with M.A.'s from Brown. Both had taught for two years already but, as new TAs at Berkeley, were required to sit in on the pilot class for four weeks. Pam and the other M.A. candidates had to attend for six weeks. The class was a burden on her schedule but Pam felt the need of it. Each day after writing Natalia's procedure in her notebook, she'd rush to the office and redo her own class plans before her 1:30 section. It helped.

"You know," Sally was saying, "That's one thing you'll find out soon here at Berkeley. We Americans have to stick together. The Italians are a clique and they'll put you down as inferior because of your accent."

Pam stared at her for a second but didn't respond. She'd just as soon not hear about intradepartmental student squabbles. But Sally rushed on.

"Jeff and I think the universities in this country should prohibit foreigners from getting jobs. There're hardly enough anyway and they should go to Americans. We can teach the language better half the time anyway. You know Bruno? He's the guy finishing his dissertation on Sannazaro. He never prepares a class plan. He thinks it's enough to speak the language. He walks in and bullshits for an hour. His students like him because he never makes them do anything but they don't learn anything either."

Pam had to leave for another building and the one-sided conversation stopped at that point. But it was to be a familiar complaint of the Hendersons. Without them, Pam thought, everybody would probably get along. They belonged in the eighth circle of hell, ninth ditch, right along with the other disseminators of schism. One thing they have in common.

When Pam, after a quick sip of water at the drinking fountain, walked into her class the first day, she felt the focused attention of twenty-four expectant eyes. The eyes were like computers, judging and cataloguing a host of impressions in the briefest of seconds. "Buon giorno," she said, and then smiled at the silence that greeted her. Yes, it was true. First quarter students did know less than she did. It wouldn't be so hard after all. "Ripetere," she said, gesturing so as to include all the class. "Buon giorno, professoressa. Buon giorno, signorina."

Halfway through the semester, Jeff and Sally invited her and Wally Ferguson for dinner. Were they match making? Wally was fun but definitely not Pam's type. She had her eyes on a graduate student in the history department, Mike Clemmons. He'd stopped once to ask her for help with a history text in Italian, and she'd been the only one still at her desk.

Her interest was perked when Gina DiPietro mentioned Mike's ex-wife Laura. She was finishing her dissertation under Professor Donata Sturmgard in Romance Philology. Pam had seen Laura once or twice, an imposingly mature Italian woman, made up perhaps to excess, but flashy. Mike himself overwhelmed her initially. He was older, she couldn't tell how much, but surely in his mid-thirties, handsome, in a rugged Irish way, with the build of an athlete. In fact, she learned in reading the Daily Cal one day, he'd won the city's squash tournament in the B class. When she mentioned she'd seen the notice and congratulated him, he grinned as if abashed, gave a self-deprecatory shrug, and invited her to see a match. So far, she hadn't had a chance.

At Jeff and Sally's, they barbecued some shish kabob on the balcony porch—against regulations Jeff said—and then sat around the living room talking about the department. Wally, though in his first year like Pam, already seemed to know more than she. She listened in near silence, broken only by an occasional question, as the other three exchanged gossip.

Before the evening was over, having seen Jeff put down Sally every time she spoke, Pam decided she would have to tell Sally about the women's group that met on Wednesday evenings to discuss feminist literature. She had just started attending the sessions and they were an eye-opener. Sally, though older, needed to know what was going on, what was being done to her.

Why let yourself be stomped on?

Jeff was a bastard and fuck his lofty judgmental professorial attitude. That's what Sally should say.

A few weeks after dinner at the Hendersons, Wally asked her out.

She blushed. Not really interested. But how to let him down?

She finally told him she had a paper to work on. He never asked her again.

Mike, she couldn't get to ask her out. So finally, taking a clue from Gina, she asked if he'd like to go to the opera with her. "I had a girlfriend who was going with me, but she had a conflict and couldn't make it. I've got an extra ticket if you'd like to go."

To her chagrin, he said no.

"Sorry, I'm going to a Raiders' game at the Coliseum. "Don't think I could stay awake at the opera after that." He grinned. "Besides, with as much beer as we drink, I'll be wasted by then."

Maybe I ought to just ask him to take me to bed. Would that get him away from his football game?

Mike, she learned one day, was part-owner of a shoe store his father had started in Palo Alto. Apparently Mike made quite a lot of money, even while attending school, because he told her one day he'd blown nearly two thousand dollars gambling at Golden Gate Fields. During the racing season, he was at the track daily, an addict who let his grades suffer.

Pam knew he'd given his ex-wife a home in the hills as part of the divorce settlement. Apparently a wedding gift from his parents. So, obviously rich. A party boy. Negatives for her—along with his machismo.

Still, she enjoyed his visits to the TAs' office.

Calm down, girl, she told herself, then heard Mitsy's voice. Fuck him, but don't get involved

The Wednesday night following the party at the Hendersons, Sally told Jeff she was going to the library to study with Pam and the two went to Professor Alice Holmes' house where about twenty women from the university had gathered to discuss Jane Austen's *Emma*.

The leader of the group, Professor Nancy Vogel, handed out a syllabus of readings for the next two months. While she recognized all the names, Pam had read only one of the works, Charlotte Bronte's *Jane Eyre*. Ibsen's *A Doll's House* was on the list, along with Willa Cather's *O Pioneers!*, Virginia Woolf's *To the Lighthouse*, Doris Lessing's *The Summer Before the Dark*, and an anthology of women's poems.

Professor Vogel—she asked everyone to call her Nancy—talked about stereotypes. Pam found the presentation stimulating. She saw in her mother the martyr figure as well as the dominating wife. It was as if the proverbial thunderbolt had opened her eyes to the reality of her parents' relationship. She'd always thought her father controlled her mother and, while he did in certain ways, she also realized that her mother controlled him in other more subtle fashions. It was her mother who provoked the fights that made her father look so mean and act so boorish. She got him started and then sat back to play the martyr's role. She actually wanted him to blow up.

And the other types? Were any of them her?

The submissive wife, a woman who hides her anger out of fear of being left alone, often a slave to her husband's image of her as a sex object. The mother as angel, the woman on a pedestal, often two vastly different types, one "motherly" and protective, the other a hellion, a witch, a force of love as evil, beauty as treachery. The sex object, the spinster, the woman alone, a creature to be pitied? Or admired? And finally, the liberated woman, strong, resourceful, sure of herself, striving for and gaining self-esteem through her own actions, not those of a man.

Following Nancy's short presentation, Alice Holmes lead the discussion of *Emma*, beginning with a brief analysis of women's place in the society of the time, her choices in the social structure of the early eighteen hundreds.

Though unable to contribute to the discussion, Pam was enraptured by the forceful women in the group. She could see that Sally was impressed, too.

Near the end of the session, a woman, whose name she missed, announced the topic for the following two weeks. "When you read *Jane Eyre*," she said, "I want you to concentrate on the work as a particularly feminine version of the quest novel. A novel in which the heroine grows up and sets out into the world in search of some greater value, What is Jane looking for? Why is it so difficult to attain? Does she find what she's looking for?"

And with those words the meeting broke up. She and Sally found themselves talking to Becky Laller, a graduate student in the English department. "Any quick clues," Sally asked, laughing, "to help us with the answer to those questions? I'm not sure I'll get the time to read *Jane Eyre*, let alone come next week."

Instead of answering, Becky asked a question of her own. "What are we all seeking? Women as well as men for that matter?"

Both Sally and Pam waited, having thought the question was going to be answered by Becky, but she said no more.

At home that week, unable to read the novel, what with teaching and course work, Pam began to ask herself what she was seeking in life. The best answer she could come up with was self-esteem, a sense of personal worth. She'd lived off Artie for a while and that had destroyed her as a person, turning her into the typical crabby bitch, much as she hated the word. It was one word she'd forced Artie never to use with her. He hated being called a bastard as much as she hated being called a bitch, so they'd bargained the two terms out of their fights. But he was a bastard and I was a bitch. Getting rid of the words wasn't enough. *Nomina sunt consequentia rerum.* It was a law they'd tried to ignore but the labels applied whether they used them or not.

She talked to Sally later that week between classes in the TAs' office. Margarita, prim and proper as always, conservatively dressed (my God, this type exists in Berkeley?), hair pinned back in a bun, eyeliner meticulously applied, eyebrows perfectly shaped, Margarita also listened, although from her place, two desks away, she feigned indifference, correcting quizzes, scowling occasionally, smiling at other points, as if engrossed in the answers of her students.

"Sally," Pam said, "as women, we've had our sphere of emotions circumscribed by society, by men. We've been excluded too often from the spheres of ideas, of reason, of power." And, though it was probably a touchy subject to bring up in public, she mentioned Jeff's habit of putting her down. "Sally, he's no better than you. You shouldn't let him run over you like that. I'd set him straight if he tried to do that to me."

Sally, clearly miffed, threw her pen on the desk, "Pam, you don't know what you're talking about. Wait till you're married and then you'll see."

"I've been married," Pam said. You could've heard an angel fall off the head of a pin. Margarita even looked up for a moment, caught Pam's eye, and dropped her head, blushing.

"I never knew that! You never mentioned it."

An accusation, as if Pam had held back a significant fact, such as her social security number on a tax form. She wished instantly that she'd kept quiet. Now the whole department would find out. "

Are you divorced?" Sally again.

"Well, I'm not a widow."

With that, the bell rang and the topic was dropped, but Pam knew, having let the tale out of the pouch, rumor would fly like the winds of Aeolus. Better to tell all than to have gossip create its own mythology.

When Jeff broached the subject that very afternoon, she knew Sally had told him.

Might as well tell as much as I can. The non-Italian clique would know the story in more or less its original form at least. The Italians, she hoped, couldn't care less.

When she'd finished, he asked, "So, what's your ex doing?"

"I don't care what he's doing and I'd just as soon not know. He's in Chicago and that's enough for me." Out of sight, out of mind. There must be a good Latin rendition of that, she thought. Wait, I know that in Italian. Lontano dagli occhi, lontano dal cuore.

# chapter 18

*Welcome to three sevenths of a chicken*
*two thirds of a cat*
*one half of a goat*

Artie arrived in Chicago on a Tuesday. Bam! Wham! Rolled off the freeway in his rented U-Haul, singing, bouncing on the seat. Hit Lake Shore Drive, rolling past beaches (the Lake, like an ocean!), harbors, sailboats, Lincoln Park. A taxi pulled alongside, horn tap dancing, arm waving. Artie just grinned and shrugged. Hit the road, Jack! He had an amphetamine track, down the mainline into a pink heaven at the end. Frustrated taxi pulled away, driver shaking his head. Three minutes later, it's a voice from blue and white clouds. Chicago cops, loudspeaker lips, screaming to get the fuck off the road. Artie hit the brakes (holy crap!), swerved to the right, clipped the toenails off a car or two, and pulled over just beyond an entrance ramp.

Screaming voice, burnt toast, spilled coffee, shit he'd broken the law! ChiCAgo polICe! Can't you read? You imbecile. Signs every hundred yards. No trucks. No commercial vehicles. Shit, said Artie, sure I saw them, ain't blind, but, hey man, I'm not commercial! I'm private! That's for other business trucks, isn't it? Mothafuck, says the cop, turning to his fat-faced partner, we got us a moron today.

\* \* \*

Welcome to Chicago. City of inferiority complexes, Biggest this, biggest that, tallest skyscraper—don't forget the modifier!—that has electrical wiring, toilet bowls on every third floor, marble elevator shaft, pink windows. All five stories. Widest this, longest that. Tallest, ugly black box building in the world. (Thank God for the white marble elegance of Big Stan! Even that's the biggest something.) The John Hancock. Largest cornuto sign (over one thousand feet high!), spreading its beneficent and protective aegis over the city of losers. Now let's see, that's also the world's tallest, all-electric office, commercial, and residential building. Wow! That is special!

He felt bad for the city near Christmas (despite the pretty white lights everywhere) when contractors finished the North Tower of the World Trade Center in New York. Let's see ... only 1,368 feet. Oh, wait, that's the tallest building in the world.

City of money-grubbing corporate asslickers, neatly suited striving professionals, junior juvenile executives, worshipping god dollar, practicing T-M on the El, on their way to the world's most bourgeois shopping mall. Pseudo-hipsters, pseudo-artists, pseudo-this, pseudo-that. Frigging cold, frigging hot, two days of spring, two days of fall, nine months of winter. And the fucking idiots boast about it! Midwestern mentality—save us, O Lord, from that. Mayors Payley and Blandprick, playing pseudo-politics. Welcome to Chicago! City of business suits, high heels, brokers, condo camps, Church of Banks ... Words fail me ... Give me, God, a virulent pen, harsh words, guttural sounds ...

Why had he come? The answer to that wasn't hard to find. Soon after his divorce, unemployed (although his former boss at Georgia Pacific said he'd take him back), Artie had read an article in the travel section of the Eugene Register-Guard on the marvels of the midwestern city on Lake Michigan (I thought it was in grain fields and stockyards), and, at that point, he was ready for a change, a new environment, a fresh start. Especially since Pam was now in California.

Any job had to be better, less hectic, less mentally taxing, than his work in the mill. So bore and dulling, as he put it. Surely, there would be many jobs in a city the size of Chicago. He wanted a lazy man's job for once, a job that would leave him time and energy to write. Perhaps one of the newspapers would hire him, or an advertising agency. One of those glamor jobs. At worst he had enough money saved up to last most of the fall.

On his arrival, unfamiliar with the city, he drove from the freeway north on Lake Shore Drive until the police forced him off into the city streets. He had no destination in mind, could find no parking spots, and simply bounced out Broadway dodging potholes until he found a motel where he could pull off the road. He was, he realized later that day when he took his first walk, nearly at the city limits, just beyond Loyola University on Sheridan Road. Stumbling upon the university by chance, he was delighted by the campus, so small and snug, a green jewel set against the blue of the lake. And it was there, his first day, in the basement of Mertz Hall, that he found the notice that led him to his first apartment.

The building, in Rogers Park, was a three-flat with a garden apartment in the basement available for immediate occupancy, Artie signed a lease that evening and moved in, happy at his good luck, the following morning.

The apartment was the most modern he'd ever lived in, with walnut cabinets, new appliances, and a dishwasher and disposal. His living room window looked out on a flower bed and a small grassy patio, complete with a wooden picnic table. Beyond that a cyclone fence divided his landlord's property from Pottawottomie Park. Beyond the fence, across a strip of grass and a sidewalk, were two tennis courts and to the left of these a squat fieldhouse for the park. The fieldhouse had a small gym, a few racketball courts and a row of classrooms.

At the East end of the three-flat, behind the garage, there was a large playing field with a baseball diamond in each corner. The park was lit at night, and that fall, on the weekends, it roiled with slow-pitch sixteen-inch softball.

Later in the fall, the center of the field turned into a gridiron. In the winter, which came too soon, a circle in one corner was usually plowed out, filled with water, and used for an ice skating pond. During the big blizzards, the city plowed the entire field and used it for a parking lot for towed cars. By early spring, when only a few cars were there—the derelicts which wouldn't start—vandals attacked at night, breaking windows, ripping apart upholstery, and in general creating havoc. But what else, he once wondered, is there to do in the winter in the BIG CITY? No one minds. Right?

Artie's landlord, Paul Cerini, lived on the third floor of the building with his wife Debbie and two kids. Paul worked for the city, in the accounting department and Debbie wrote children's books. She'd already published three, and one day, about a month after Artie had moved in, she showed him a story she was working on. He traded a few of his own and enjoyed chatting when he could spare the time from job hunting.

Above his apartment and below the Cerinis, three young women had moved in shortly after Artie. The landlord told him they were good "Christian girls," but Artie found them obnoxious. Good if you didn't mind clogs and high heels tromping on wood floors over your head all night. They all seemed to work different shifts, and one liked to play the piano at four a.m. Every weekend, they threw a party and sang a few hymns before turning on the stereo to rock music. Artie liked rock himself but not coming from someone else's apartment, so finally in late July he broke his lease and moved.

His second apartment was within sight of his first. If one walked from the Cerini's place along past the tennis courts and the fieldhouse, one came to Rogers Avenue right where Wolcott dead-ended into it. Artie rented the upstairs apartment (never again anyone overhead!) in a white two-flat which fronted the intersection and sat catty-corner to it. The only trouble with the place, other than having old appliances and poor water pressure, was the street noise. There was a stop sign at the intersection on both Wolcott and Rogers. When buses or trucks rolled by, accelerating, the whole house shook. Artie expected it to drop into a storm ditch or sewer any day. Everywhere else the roads always seemed to be caving in. You'd think this was Mexico City!

Despite his move, he remained friends with the Cerinis. Especially Debbie. Debbie was the opposite of Paul and for this Artie liked her. Not that Paul was unlikeable. Paul was a tall man, Artie's own height, and carried himself with confident ease and self-assurance. From the way the man talked about himself, he was the sole guardian of the city's finances. He also had pretensions to nobility, going back to some Tuscan or Ligurian countess. It was hard to ruffle him.

Debbie on the contrary was easily ruffled. Easily given to outbursts of emotion, which Artie liked all the more precisely because her husband was embarrassed by them. Debbie was politically more liberal than Paul, and younger, more creative. Paul liked the arts but only as a connoisseur of what he called the "fine things" in life—opera, museums, historical events—the fourth of July celebrations at the Chicago Historical Society where they read the Declaration of Independence, for example, and similar highbrow events. Debbie herself was an artist. Of sorts. Successful actually from Artie's point of view, considering she'd published three children's books and illustrated them herself.

\* \* \*

Paul and Debbie introduced him to Anne Elston that spring at a barbecue held in the Cerini's backyard. Anne, Artie thought, was Paul's type, more than Debbie's. She seemed someone to match wits with, to duel verbally, to relate to with repartee. Too cultured for me. But when she called a week later, inviting him to go to a play with her on Sunday night, he accepted.

Anne was a small woman, thin as a sheet of ice, with short black hair framing a face dominated by a leptorrhine nose. She dressed in business suits most of the time, and spoke in a voice pitched too high for Artie's comfort. She had a habit of talking nervously and, while that made it easy on a first date (when Artie never knew what to say), after a while it got to be tiring. If he wanted to point something out to her, he usually had to interrupt.

She was too introspective for Artie. She liked to talk of life and the arts. Artie preferred action. Ideas, when discussed on a date, and with complete seriousness, bored him. On the way home from the Loop, riding on the El, Anne drove him crazy analyzing the play. When she invited him up to continue their chat—(chat! he thought, monologue you mean)—he almost said no, but changed his mind, hoping she might invite him to stay all night. He knew when the idea flashed through his mind that his hope was probably futile. Anne had given no indication of being even vaguely sexual. She seemed to want only a friend, a companion, not a lover. She avoided his touch, removing her arm from the armrest if Artie's touched hers, never bumping him as they stood in the El or walked along the street, maintaining a distance both physically and emotionally. Maybe that's why ideas bore me, Artie thought, as they climbed the stairs to her condo. They're too abstract, too unfeeling, too emotionless. He needed to reattach himself to someone and Anne was not the woman.

When he entered her apartment, he saw a pier table with a series of different colored stuffed unicorns, all reflected in a tall, thin mirror. Seeing his disheveled reflection, he ran his hand through the front locks of his hair to restore some degree of civility, patting the hair down and pulling it across his forehead. She asked for his jacket, said, "Make yourself at home," and disappeared down a long corridor leading back into the darkness. He heard a light switch on at the end and a few minutes else later a toilet flush. While she did whatever else women do in the bathroom—freshen lipstick, powder her face, comb her hair—he looked around the room.

An old, oak coffee table sat in the middle of the room on an attractive, light blue and beige Persian rug. He saw a stack of books on Zen Buddhism, a few on meditation in a separate pile.

Had she placed them there, strewn carelessly, on purpose? A Buddha squatted on a corner stand next to a thin ceramic vase with sticks of incense.

She was back in the room then, apologizing for the mess—"What mess?" he said—and then she excused herself again. "I'll be back in a minute. I'm going to get into something a little more comfortable. Why don't you take-off your shoes? If you like, there's juice or mineral water or some beer in the frig. Help yourself."

He could tell she was nervous. She talked too fast, was trying to act casual. "Sure," he said. "Go ahead. I'll look at your books. You have a good collection of books on religion, it looks like."

"That's only part of them," she said, walking down the corridor again. "I have a couple of boxes in the bedroom I haven't been able to unpack yet."

But the early promise of greater ease and a change of subject proved fruit-less. When Anne returned in elegant, gray slacks and a long-sleeved green blouse, she took up where she'd left off. Artie lounged on her sofa while she sat forward on a big chair across the coffee table and jabbered incessantly. Finally, reading his boredom as exhaustion, she commented on his tiredness and said they'd better call it a night.

"Yeah," Artie agreed. "We both have to get to work early tomorrow." He shook his head the rest of the way home, promising himself he'd never ask her for a date. Dating her was like eating olives straight from the tree: One bite was enough to sour one on ever doing it again.

Artie's job, to which he'd alluded, was not quite what he'd envisioned on his cross-country journey. In fact, he'd been unable to find a steady position doing anything—and it seemed he'd tried that fall and winter the whole range of jobs listed in the classifieds, from administrative assistant, bookkeeper, and clerk to Xerox operator, yearbook editor, and zoological guide. After three months of scattered work and living off of dwindling savings, he'd reached a bank balance of three hundred dollars and was beginning to panic. As a last resort, he went to Kelly Services in Evanston and told them he was available for clerical or secretarial work.

He did fine on all their tests, spelling and typing, and was all set for some assignments in the neighborhood, when they called and asked him if he'd mind helping out their Loop office by going downtown to accept a three-day assignment for the Northern Trust Bank Company. He'd told Kelly he could only work three days a week since he was also writing, but he hadn't emphasized enough his desire, his determination, to avoid riding the El downtown.

Still, since it was his first assignment, he thought he'd better humor them and accepted on the condition that he only work three days. They sent him down on a Sunday for four hours of special training on a Wang word processor.

Monday morning, things went bad from the start. When he arrived ten minutes early, at 8:20, on the seventh floor at Personnel, they said, "Oh, Mr. Petig handles the Wang pool. He's on the eleventh floor." When he arrived at the eleventh, the office manager put him to work immediately. He started going over his manual and familiarizing himself with the equipment.

At noon, when he called Kelly to see if they'd done anything to find a replacement for him after his three days, the assistant started screaming, wondering where he was. The bank personnel office had been telephoning them all morning, saying Artie hadn't arrived yet.

"I've been working here since 8:30."

"Go back to personnel and report in to a Mr. Van Thorsen."

At personnel, they accused him of by-passing them. He had to explain that a secretary told him to go straight on up to eleven. It took them another half hour to get his lunch pass ready, and then he was sent back to the pool.

First thing, Petig ran over, this young M.B.A. grad, smug in his three-piece suit, executive hue, and accused Artie of not following the right reporting procedure. Artie felt he was being talked down to, as if he were a high school student, and he sat there burning, ready to walk off the job, but needing the money.

He did get through the three days and he warned Kelly Services that Wednesday was his last day. They asked if Mr. Petig wanted him to come back. "He hasn't said anything," Artie said, "but they need the work here." "Well," Kelly told him, "don't worry. We'll take care of it."

Instead, Petig blew up and came screaming to Artie, trying to badger him into staying. Artie told him it was impossible. He had other obligations. "No, I couldn't make an exception," he kept repeating. Pissed off, Petig glared at him, left to call Kelly, and returned five minutes later, throwing Artie's time card on his lap. When Artie picked it up, he saw Petig had written, "No charge to Northern Trust" in big, black, pencil strokes. He made Artie feel like a shit and Kelly, Artie was sure, wasn't too pleased at having to train him on Wang and then to pay him themselves for three days work.

When the assignment was over, he called Kelly and resigned. He'd starve,

THE HORNETS' NEST OF OUR DESIRES

he decided, before he'd take that kind of shit. All year he'd been pondering the proper job. He'd lost his illusions. He no longer thought in specifics. No newspaper was going to hire him, no advertising agency, no editorial office. Instead, he thought of qualities that mattered to him.

People, first of all. He wanted work that was meaningful and people-oriented. The money was secondary. The job would have to enrich him as an individual, would thus indirectly help even his writing, The work, if possible, would integrate him into the community, would provide a service of value to others, would allow him to develop as an individual, not as a cog in an immense, impersonal machine.

But, despite his ideals, at the moment, he had a part-time job as a janitor for a rest home.

In September, on a Wednesday, just over three weeks after the barbecue, the Cerinis invited Artie and Anne to go sailing. Each summer, along with seven of his colleagues, Paul rented one eighth of a twenty-six foot sailboat, moored in Chicago Harbor in front of Grant Park, and it was his final week to sail. He went out with a different group of friends nightly. "If you sail with me," Paul boasted, "you learn to run the ship. First off, you can connect the halyards to the jib and main sail."

When Artie glared at him, Paul grinned and explained, "The halyards are lines that raise the sail. The jib is the front sail; the main is the big one coming back over the boat. The other lines are called 'sheets.'" Paul sat at the tiller, attired in the proper sailing gear, while Artie scampered about in his ragged cutoffs, trying to attach the lines as directed.

Once they'd motored beyond the breakwater, they set sail toward one of the water-intake plants far out in the lake. The sun was dropping behind the city skyline and the night was mild, with a slight wind from the north, soft but strong enough to move the boat over the slow swells. Anne, despite the calm waves, wasn't feeling well. "That sandwich was too rich," she kept saying to Artie. She'd asked Artie to bring her a turkey sandwich from Captain Nemo's, a sandwich shop near his apartment in Rogers Park, but they hadn't had any turkey that night, so Artie had bought her a tuna sandwich instead. While eating it, Anne had exclaimed, at least three times, "Gee, I didn't expect to see an orange sauce on it! There's so much stuff in this!"

She complained most of the trip and Artie, whenever Anne looked away, rolled his eyes at Debbie. Debbie tried to repress a grin, failed, and had to manufacture a reason for it when Paul asked her what she was laughing at.

Halfway through the evening, Anne began to worry about the time. She'd told Artie on the dock that she didn't think she should've accepted the offer to go sailing. "I don't like to do things on work nights," she said. "I have enough trouble with insomnia. I have a routine I like to go through at night. I won't have time to read now."

Artie had felt like asking, "Well, why'd you come then if you're going to bitch all night?" but just nodded. "It's a special occasion," he said finally.

Paul, after four or five hints from Anne about how dark it was, finally turned the prow toward the city about nine o'clock. The trip in took over an hour, since the wind had almost died. Paul finally dropped the sails and started the motor. He'd promised to have Anne back home by ten. She usually liked to be in bed, she said, by nine or nine-thirty. Anne interlaced their work with peeved comments along the lines of, "Gee, I didn't realize it took so long to tie up everything."

On the dock, waiting for Paul to make the last trip in with the dinghy, Artie and Anne watched the colored lights playing on Buckingham Fountain. It was the first time Artie had seen it at night. He tried to talk to Anne but she made sure brusque answers showed how peeved she was.

In the Cerini's station wagon, Anne leaned forward and told Debbie, "I'll probably not go in to work tomorrow."

Artie looked over at her, amazed. "I thought you said you didn't fall asleep till around 11:30. It's only 10:45."

Paul looked in his mirror and added, "We'll have you home by eleven. You just lost your reading time."

Anne scowled and sat back. "I need that or I don't relax. It's hard to do something and just go home, jump in bed, and fall asleep."

Artie was going to joke about sex being a good cure, and would have if Paul hadn't been present. After they'd dropped off Anne at her place, Debbie, as if she'd read Artie's mind, told the two fellows about a conversation she'd had with Anne. "She likes living alone, she told me, except for what she called her 'sexual tension.'"

"What's that?" Paul asked, cocking his head.

"Come on," Debbie said, laughing. "You know what that is."

"I don't think so," Paul said. "I never had to worry about that. But Artie probably does."

Artie was going to joke, "Not with Debbie around," but thought better of it. Neither of the Cerinis would appreciate that.

Debbie continued her story, her arm stretched along the back of the front seat so she could see both guys. "I finally said to her, 'Well, Anne, there's always masturbation.'"

Artie and Paul laughed.

"What'd she say?" Artie said. "Did you ask her if she did it?"

"I don't remember exactly how she put it, but I guess she does sometimes. She was blushing like crazy but trying to act cool."

"That sounds like Anne alright," Artie said. "Especially the cool part."

Neither Paul nor Debbie responded. In his imagination, Artie created the outing again, in his horniness depicting everything as a sexual metaphor. Getting out into the lake and coming in. Putting up sails, taking them down. All the effort for so little action, at least as far as Anne was concerned. Mast up, penile erection. Turning on the motor to get in to the dock. Was that the vibrator bringing her over the edge? For some reason, it was hard to imagine making love to Anne.

He sighed. He was getting too horny. Time to do something about it.

The following Friday night, Artie went to a bar and grill near Loyola University to hear a disk jockey play reggae records. He didn't know much about reggae, but a black kid he'd met in the Employment Office recommended he attend.

When Artie stepped into the bar, the music was so loud he looked for a corner where he could hide from the direct blast. The place was jammed with dancing couples, not all of them, he noticed in the dim light, heterosexual. The air was full of smoke—cigarette and grass. The crowd ranged from long-haired hippies to punky teenagers dressed to clash. In between the extremes, there were even a few in leisure suits and glossy fashion rags.

Beyond the dance floor, Artie saw a bar and to the right a group of tables and tubular chairs. The record being played reminded Artie of sixties music—Eric Burdon and the Animals, or Eric Clapton. Most of the people at the bar, he thought, had probably never even heard of the Animals.

"You skank so, you skank so." Artie was rocking to the lively beat when a blonde with one-inch hair, porcupine style, said, "You mind if I sit down? My feet are killing me." She didn't wait for his answer, just plopped down and turned her back to him.

A Bob Marley tune got a crowd on their feet.

The girl turned back around. "You wanna dance?"

"I thought you were tired."

"What?"

Damn. She couldn't hear a thing and neither could he.

He leaned forward and raised his voice. "I'm taking off. Too loud."

"I'll go with you," she said.

He was about to ask "why?" when he realized how stupid that would sound.

Outside, he asked her if she wanted a coffee.

She looked around, as if searching for a better option. For someone else not so dull as him. Finally she said, "Why not?"

"We can walk to the Heartland Cafe. If you're hungry they have some good vegetarian dishes." He paused when she didn't respond. "Or there's a Baskin-Robbins not far from the cafe."

Her name was Dourine and she was only eighteen. Artie, at twenty-five going on twenty-six, suddenly felt old. Seven years difference. She belonged to a different generation, for sure had different tastes.

"You have a beautiful name," he said. "Unusual."

"A diseased name! My fate."

He didn't understand.

"No one's heard of it but it's a disease passed by horses in copulation."

Smart for her age. Who said "copulation" anymore?

But then she added, "The mule cock's desire for the she-hinny's ass. Sterile spermatozoa, fertile protozoa. That's my name."

Damn. "I don't know diddly about mules." He'd never heard of the disease, and he grew up on a farm. But then pigs and Angus were different. Dad would never have bought horses or mules. Good-for-nothing creatures, he called them. Forget that the kids might have some fun. No, it was work, work, work.

A bummer.

Dourine chattered away, while he sipped a chamomile tea. She'd ordered something flavored, a fruity Italian drink made with Torani Amaretto and milk.

When she said her apartment was nearby, he walked there with her, wondering, What am I getting into this time? This girl wasn't his type. Still, he hadn't made love to a woman since the break with Ady, and Pam had refused the entire last month they were together. Was this girl on the make? He could hope, right?

Turned out her apartment was south of Devon on Glenwood, in a large U-shaped complex. She led him to the back and up two flights of stairs to the top floor.

When Artie stepped into her room, he was stunned. The walls and ceiling were covered with iridescent paintings, vibrant as flaming tattoos, studded with jewels, whether glass or gems he couldn't tell. Each wall was divided into three panels and painted from floor to ceiling. Overhead, in the middle of the room, a golden light, with a plastic cover of projecting spikes, radiated around the room, dimming to darkness and white specks of stars at the far edges of the ceiling. The walls, he realized almost immediately, despite the lurid expressionism of the art work, contained abstract depictions of the signs of the Zodiac.

Taurus, his own sign, was staring him straight in the face, a flame-snorting, monstrous black bull, head twisted, horns fearsomely silver. Around the bull danced sinuous maidens, spreading rose petals beneath stomping hooves. In the bull's eyes, Artie thought he saw lust gleam and wondered if it was only his own randiness. Dourine had disappeared into the bathroom and Artie, ignoring the Ram to the left of the Bull, did a slow swivel to the right, taking in the Twins, Nordic giants with blond curls descending to their shoulders, russet armor gleaming on their chests, two massive shields centered around effulgent carbuncles.

Beautiful! Put anything he'd ever tried to shame. And she was an eighteen-year-old kid! Holy criminy.

On the right wall, against turquoise blue, a giant crab moved spidery legs while miniature, dancing dolphins sported in the froth. The center panel opened in a burst of tawny gold, the lion, in a sea of wild grass. Awesome. Next to the lion, he recognized Virgo, a maiden, rosy as dawn, dressed in violet.

He couldn't believe what he was seeing. He turned around. Behind him, the door held a blood-red scorpion in a desert of orange flame, pincers open, spiked tail arched to sting. To the left of the door as one went out, in a balance of white and black, he saw the Scales. To the right of the door, an archer, half man, half beast, with taut-stringed bow, arrow pointed straight at the viewer.

Artie was dizzy with color. The luminescent tones, the bold, passionate brush strokes. Behind him, as he turned to look at the other wall, he heard the sound of Dourine entering the room.

---

"I'll put on a record," she said.

"Did you do all this?"

"All mine." Acting like it was nothing.

What had he missed? An agile goat, cloven hoof, leering at a nude nymph—had to be a naiad. The nymph poured water from a jug, smiling at the viewer, not watching the water, which splashed down the wall and on to the floor. A wet spot was painted on the wood, spreading slowly outward. And finally, flanked on the far side, beyond the corner, by the ram, a sea of fin-flicking fish, varied as a medieval bestiary, dominated by the sharp, saber-tooth jaw of a razor-thin predator, its jaws looking strangely like a slightly open pair of thinning shears.

When he turned, Dourine was at his elbow. She was so hot he could feel the heat radiating from her. She wore only a sheer nightie.

"Take your clothes off," she said, letting the garment fall to the floor.

He liked the way she seemed to beg and order at the same time. Hard to believe she was this free.

I mean, how often is this going to happen? Once in a lifetime?

He was ready to believe it was a wet-dream, but no way could he imagine the way her place was painted. Too much!

He did have the presence of mind to ask her again how old she was.

"Old enough to fuck" was all she said. But she'd already told him she was eighteen.

Okay, the gods had smiled on him for once!

When both were nude, he lead her to the couch. He knelt before her and spread her legs. When he began licking up her thighs, pressing out on her legs with his arms even though they were already spread, she wet her fingers and began to rub her small breasts. The sight of a woman giving herself pleasure turned him on and he pulled her bottom toward the edge of the couch. She had her head back, lolling from side to side, her eyes facing the ceiling but shut. When he licked up the outside of her pussy, separating the folds and rubbing over her clitoris, she jumped and dropped her hands to his head. He pressed his nose against her clitoris and buried his tongue in her as deep as he could, thrusting in and out, and then sideways, and back to her clitoris, thinking now only of giving her pleasure.

Her body went into a quick shudder, as if she were bouncing on a hot car seat, and she cried, "Fuck me now."

Artie drew back, his cock rock hard and grasped her buttocks. She was so wet he slid in all the way with one thrust and Dourine gasped, as if in pain, but then thrust back. He pounded her bottom into the sofa cushion, trying to keep from ejaculating. When she finally quieted down, moaning softly, he slowed his pace and pulled her buttocks to him in slow, easy strokes.

Smiling, she opened her eyes and looked directly into his. He smiled back, feeling the sweat drip from his forehead on to her belly. "Was it okay?" he asked and she nodded, wiping his brow with her hands.

But, shit, not something he should have asked.

"Lay back on the floor," she ordered, "and I'll ride you a while."

She kissed him then, poised over him on her knees, working her pussy up and down his cock. He thrust up into her and she told him to relax.

"Your body feels so good, it's hard to just lie here," he said.

She leaned over and pulled his head under one arm. "Suck my tit while I fuck you."

Right, nothing like making it harder not to come.

He twisted his head and tried to keep his mouth on her nipple but his lips kept slipping off. She was getting excited again, he could tell, breathing heavier, and closing her eyes.

He took some saliva on his fingertips and put them on her anus, rubbing around her butt. When he stuck his finger up her ass, she groaned with pleasure. He began to thrust again, pulling forward on her anus with each thrust. And then, excited by her passion, by the shudder when she came, he shot his load into her, coming for so long he thought he'd never stop, and, when he did, he collapsed, luxuriating in the pleasure.

Damn. Should have asked if she took birth control.

Too late now. About time I had a good fuck.

Now if Anne tried a little of this she might find she didn't care if she had insomnia!

He wasn't quite sure why that came to mind. Anne was the least fuckable person he could imagine.

# *chapter 19*

The class Pam enjoyed most winter quarter was a seminar taught by a woman professor, Ida Svendson. Svendson, a native of Utrecht with a strong Dutch accent, shared an appointment between the Departments of Classics and Italian. She was married to a professor in the philosophy department named David Reynolds, but she taught and published under her maiden name. That fact was enough for Pam to assume Svendson was a committed feminist. Her husband, as Pam learned at a department function, a too-long TGIF party, was an absolute bore. He cornered her at one point in the evening, and talked for a half hour—drinking Scotch and spitting cheese and crackers in his enthusiasm—of Duns Scotus and the conflict between the Franciscans and the Dominicans over the ideas of Avicebron, the purported author of the *Fons Vitae*.

Her eyes glazed over after the first five minutes and she spent the rest of the time nodding, a rigid smile frozen on her face, saying, "Oh," and "Um," and "Interesting." When she finally made her escape, all she could remember was that Reynolds was teaching a seminar on the conflict between philosophy and theology. It was enough to chill her against ever finding herself within ten feet of him again.

His wife, on the contrary, was down to earth, clear-spoken, interesting, willing to listen as well as to explain. The seminar she taught dealt with the uses of classical mythology in the Italian Renaissance and concentrated on four genres—epic poetry (including chivalric romance), pastoral drama, narrative dialogues, and mythological poems.

What Pam enjoyed most, besides Svendson's approach and the material itself, was the chance to reread the classics she'd skimmed in undergraduate honor's classes. Once again, she wandered and battled her way through Homer and Virgil; for the first time she dallied over Theocritus, Bion and Moschus; she descended into Lucian's *Dialogues of the Dead* and lost herself in Ovid's

*Metamorphoses.* For her research paper, which she published a year later in the *Journal of Renaissance Studies*, she concentrated on mythic patterns in Ariosto's *Orlando Furioso*, tracing his use of mythology in elements as brief as the title, based on Seneca's *Hercules Furens*, to the more extended plot structures, based on classical myths and archetypes.

In the class itself, Pam, for the first time in her life, felt truly confident of her abilities to read and analyze literature. It seemed every time Professor Svendson asked a question, Pam knew not only the answer but why the question was asked. It was as if she could read the teacher's mind. She invariably left Svendson's seminar with ideas swarming in her mind, energized, intense, exhilarated, brimming with self-assurance. Her years of reading the classical myths for pure pleasure, the hours spent delightedly perusing handbooks like those of Robert Graves and H. J. Rose, were paying off. She was becoming a disciple, finding a mentor. From her first year of grad school at Berkeley, she knew who she wanted as her dissertation director, who she would model herself after.

Her only moment of disillusion, and it was severe, came one afternoon when she was talking privately to Professor Svendson during her Thursday office hours. Ida, as she'd asked Pam to call her socially (something Pam could never do with comfort), was responding to Pam's questions concerning discrimination based on sex. Brushing back her black hair, streaked with gray at the front, the professor smiled. "When you are good," she said in her strong accent, "there is no discrimination. No one ever stopped me from doing what I wanted. I don't believe it happens. It's the excuse of weak minds."

Pam didn't like the superior tone, the adamant and brisk stand so uncharacteristic of Ida's demeanor. She'd always come across as confident in her classroom encounters but never as overbearing. In private, she seemed to be showing a different face. Having made it to the top of her profession, she needed to assert (with smug satisfaction, Pam thought) that she'd met no obstacles on the way, that no man had ever even thought of putting her down or holding her back.

Knowing from what fellow women graduate students had told her that such was not always the case, that there were abuses and acts of discrimination, having experienced it in subtle ways herself, Pam was aggravated that Svendson refused to recognize the existence of a problem for others. She wanted to tell her of Panizzi at Oregon and his condescending attitude but decided not to pursue the matter. It was clear from what Professor Svendson said that she wouldn't accept Pam's interpretation of the matter. If you were good, it didn't matter what sex you were.

From then on, though she admired Svendson's professionalism and tried to emulate her mastery of the material and her methods, Pam saw things with clear eyes. She noticed, for example, that she was the only woman disciple accepted by Ida. Her other proteges were all men. It disappointed Pam and she understood when Vera and Gina, or Sally, talked of Svendson's coldness.

Here was a woman who could've encouraged the members of her own sex and she refused to see the need. In the end it came down to this: Pam loved the course itself; she admired Professor Svendson's control of the subject matter and respected her brilliance as a critic and scholar; but she didn't like her as a person. She resolved that when she made it to the top, she wouldn't forget to help other women who might need a word of encouragement.

One February day, after an afternoon seminar, she was in the TAs' office correcting papers when Mike Clemmons glanced in.

"Hi," he said, stepping inside and letting the door close behind him. "Would you like the light on?" He flipped the three light switches in unison.

Pam lifted her head, drumming the white eraser of her red marking pen on the stack of papers. "Not really," she said. She had a headache and preferred a dim room.

She turned back to the paper, her red pen correcting an error. "I prefer the dark," she said, glancing up again. Mike had not moved from the door.

He shrugged, turned the lights out, and opened the door to leave.

Pam took a deep breath. "Mike?" she called. He looked back. "I didn't mean to drive you out."

"That's okay I should've asked first. I just stopped by to see if Vanni was here. We're going to a hockey game tonight."

"Oh." She'd hoped he was stopping by to see her. She thought of asking, Who's playing? but the words wouldn't come.

Mike stepped toward her desk and sat on top of Gina's, his leg swinging toward her and lightly thumping the side panel of the metal desk. He was wearing a wool sweater, light brown with a darker stripe across his chest. It emphasized his ruggedness. No socks.

"Do you lift weights?" she asked, breaking what to her was a stiff and awkward silence.

He grinned and she wished she hadn't asked. Why let him know he was attractive? He was self-assured enough as it was.

"I work out in the gym a few nights a week. Helps my squash game?

"Are you any good?"

Jeez, who's controlling my thoughts? Could I be more inane?

"I won the B division city championship."

She didn't know if that was an especially noteworthy feat. Besides, who played squash anyway? She imagined boys in a ring jumping delightedly on yellow squashes to see who could get theirs the flattest.

"But I'm good at every thing. He laughed. "Nothing like being pretentious, huh?"

A little false humility?

"That's what I was going to say. Only I had other words in mind."

There was another moment of silence. She dropped her head to the sheet in front of her and felt his eyes roaming over her body. "How good are you at correcting exams?" she asked.

He glanced at his watch. "Terrible. I'd like to help but I've got to be running. That is, unless you'd like to come down to Café Giovanni's and grab a bite to eat. I've got to meet Vanni by 5:30."

She pondered the invitation. A fifteen to twenty minute rushed meal. A high and dry feeling. "Not tonight. I've really got to get these papers corrected."

"Don't stay too late. I wouldn't feel safe in here alone."

She glanced at his blunt jaw. "I'll be packing up soon."

"You're sure you don't want to grab a sandwich together?"

She looked out the window. The sky was darkening to a clear, deep blue. "It'd be dark by the time we finished," she said, "And I don't like walking home alone from Shattuck Avenue at night." She hurried on, not wanting him to feel obliged to offer his company. "If I leave from here, I'm closer."

"Are you on the north or southside?"

She could tell it didn't really matter. He didn't have time to walk her anywhere. "Southside," she told him. "So that's out of your way."

"See you later then. I've got to run."

At the door, he turned and caught her eye. "Another time, okay?" And with that he was gone.

Nick Resin, a graduate student one year ahead of her, called her at home that evening, as she was nearing the end of the papers to be corrected. He invited her out, spur of the moment, for pizza. Nick was a tall, slim teaching assistant, with friendly eyes, given to moments of gaiety, with an aquiline nose, and thin but sensual lips. His desk was near hers in the TAs' office, and he liked to interrupt serious discussions of literature with either jokes or off-the-wall imagery, comparing plots of novels, for example, to soccer games, pomegranates, or carburetor repair work.

"Can we meet at La Val's about eight-fifteen?"

Sure. Only a few blocks on the other side of campus. Near Vera's place.

Pam turned on a small desk lamp and left the apartment around eight. Nick was waiting for her in front of the Northside Art Theater.

"I see they're showing "The Conformist." He pointed to a poster with a picture of Dominique Sandra. "Have you seen it?"

She nodded. "I wouldn't mind seeing it again, though. Let's check the show times." They walked up the passageway between the pizza parlor and the theater. At the box office, Pam saw the timetable. "We've missed the eight o'clock showing ... I can't be out till midnight tonight."

"Onward to La Val's then."

While they ate—a vegetarian pizza on whole wheat crust—Pam found herself looking at Nick and thinking of Mike Clemmons. She listened with an air of distraction while Nick talked of Professor Bempelli and his class on Italian Romanticism. "You tired?" Nick asked, noticing perhaps the fixity of her gaze.

She focused in on his eyes, blushing. "Sorry," she said. "I was drifting there a bit. I guess I am tired."

"Well, I'll walk you home and we can call it a night." Nick finished the last of his beer. "Do you want to take this extra piece or shall we just leave it?"

Pam looked at the platter. She barely remembered having eaten. "How many have I had?"

"Three."

So he'd counted. "Why don't you eat it?" she said. "I'm full." She pushed it playfully toward him.

"No, it's yours," he said, grinning as he shoved it back across the table. Giggling like idiots, they played a game of bouncing the platter from one to the other.

"Let's just leave it," Pam said finally. The two beers she'd drunk had taken their toll. She wasn't used to alcohol.

If Nick asked me tonight, I'd probably go to bed with him, she thought. And if Mike had asked? The answer surprised her. She would say "no." And yet it was her desire for Mike, she realized, that made Nick an attractive compromise.

When Nick left her at her door, she realized why she would've slept with him (if he'd asked!). He liked her as a person not as a sex object. Mike, more attractive, would probably have looked on her as just another conquest among many.

Am I being foolish about sex? she wondered. Vera Lovati would've told her emphatically "yes." Her heart told her "no."

Two weeks later, in early April, Mike Clemmons asked her out on a date. During the course of the evening, he let slip that he'd waited so long to ask her out because he'd been involved with another woman.

"A barmaid. I met her after a football game. We celebrated in Jack London Square and she moved in with me a week later. I didn't want to tell anyone about her." He paused. They were seated in the North Beach Restaurant in San Francisco. Mike speared a calamari, lifted it, and put it down uneaten. "So, I guess I'm on the rebound again."

She noticed he'd said again. "How long were you married?"

"Would you believe eight years?"

"I was married three years myself," she said, thinking he'd probably heard the news anyway.

"Never would've guessed it."

She stared at him. What was marriage supposed to do? Mark you for life? Artie would've liked that. A brand in the middle of her forehead, saying, "Property of Artie Crenshaw."

"Why?"

He shrugged. "You just don't seem the bitter type. Have you met Laura?"

Pam shook her head.

"My ex-wife. A bitch. You'd like her, of course. You're a woman. " He said the word with a moment of unveiled disgust.

Pam bristled. "Don't sneer at me."'

"Let's just say my wife was fucked and leave it at that."

"In more ways than one, I assume. I can see why she got screwed up, if you want the truth."

"Why'd you go out with me?"

She put down a bite of saltimbocca. "Why'd you ask me out?"

"Why not?"

"That's not good enough."

"Well, I wouldn't kick you out of bed for having cold feet."

"What about a cold heart?"

"As long as the pussy's hot, I don't care."

Mike speared another calamari, lifted the fork while she watched, slipped the squid into his mouth and chewed it with what she could only call sybaritic lust.

"You're gross."

"That's one of my few abiding traits. "Grossly carnal."

But despite his grossness (because of it?), she went to bed with him that night. The evening, which had started poorly, ended well. Even Pam had to admit that Mike, for all his egotistic hedonism, was an experienced lover. After they'd made love so many times she lost count and when Mike finally flopped back exhausted on his gigantic mattress, Pam forced herself to get out of bed.

She could see the surprise in Mike's eyes. "Aren't you staying all night? We can make love in the morning and have breakfast together."

Pam shook her head, slipping into her underwear. "Not tonight," she said, and was thankful when he didn't ask why. "I had a great time," she said, thinking that despite his bravado he might wonder if he'd been adequate. "It's not that. It's just something I promised myself." But Mike, she could tell by his snores, was already asleep.

Walking home alone, hurrying because of the dark streets, Pam pondered her feelings. It should have meant more, right? The second guy she'd ever made love to. Only, it wasn't making love, was it? Just sex. Nice, but not the only thing she wanted. Could he even give her that, and if he did, would it be something she'd want from *him*? Not the ideal partner.

But no reason to get angry just because she'd succumbed to physical attraction.

I did what I wanted. I slept with him because I wanted to, and that's that. Why make such a big deal of it? Maybe that's a sign of repression, ingrained in me by Artie. Now, I make my own decisions.

But then the next minute she changed course and called herself a fool for sleeping with him. When we were fucking, if he'd have asked me to move in with him, I'd've probably have said yes. Why am I so dumb?

While Pam had only fleetingly faced the question of independence in her three years of marriage, after the split she'd been forced to reassess her attitude. She'd not been instantly strong. Her first thought had been, how do I face the world alone? Nothing in life had prepared her for that.

After high school, she'd gone straight to the university, first in Corvallis, where she roomed with a family her folks had known since the 1940s, before Pam was born, and then in Eugene where she lived at home. Neither situation provided an opportunity for independence. In both, her meals were prepared for her, she had constant companionship, and all bills were paid by her parents. It was an artificial and at times idyllic existence.

From the university and living at home, she'd moved straight in with Artie. Her responsibilities, of course, multiplied. She had to cook, she had to think of Artie's needs, sexual, emotional, and physical, she had to pay bills, she had, like him, to work. But mentally, the responsibility for their livelihood remained with Artie because this was what they both had been raised to think. Rather, it was so natural they didn't have to think, it seemed ingrained in their DNA along with the other elements of the genetic code.

After Artie's departure, then, she felt alone, in ways that provided both pleasure and pain.

Should've lived alone after high school. Before marriage. Should've developed, without Artie's influence, her own likes and dislikes, her own goals, her own personality. Now, at least, she had the chance to do so, and this was pleasure, despite the fact that the initial purity of experience had been lost. Her independence was not by choice, not planned for. The pain, in turn, came from loneliness, but even loneliness had its advantages. Loneliness changed in time to self-sufficiency and self-sufficiency to self-esteem. She'd learned she could get along by herself. She learned she was a person, she had an identity. She also learned that she preferred being alone—at least for a while.

Free at last. Why jump so soon back into the nest? Why gum up one's wings with pitch? Why strike the bait only to find the hook within? Better to stand on one's own. To enjoy men but not to be entangled in their needs, not to let them force her into a traditional mold. That was best,right?

And so she continued to do two things. She worked to establish a network of women friends, and she kept an emotional distance from men. She'd developed what her women friends would've called a healthy mistrust. If she *consorted* with a man, it was not, as the Latin root of the word suggested, to share his fate. No, it was simply to share pleasure. She didn't deny herself their companionship, as she didn't deny herself physical release. That she might be using them did not cross her mind (or if it did the thought was soon rationalized and accepted) since the balance stood level. They used her as much as she used them. They received as much back as they gave. They knew from the start—or from the moment when they showed more serious intentions—that she planned to finish her Ph.D. before becoming emotionally involved with anyone. "No commitments" was a clear signal given to all. Friendship, yes Sex, yes. A long-term relationship? A big no.

Late in the semester, two of her fellow grad students, Vanni and Gina, invited her to their apartment in the basement of a house on Hopkins Street near Grove. They'd been living together, Pam learned, for two years, hiding the fact from both sets of parents. Gina prepared a green salad and mashed potatoes to which she added raw onions, while Vanni grilled shish kebab in the back yard.

After dinner, they sat on the floor in the cramped living room, drank Orange Pekoe tea from delicate porcelain cups, and savored Pepperidge Farms chocolate chip cookies. The talk turned to sex. Vanni and Gina surprised her with their openness. Vanni's father had died of a heart attack in his early forties and as a result he himself was afraid of the exertion brought about by intercourse. "When we make love," he said, "I usually don't come—and Gina usually doesn't come without a lot of manual stimulation."

She looked at Vanni. "Wow. That'd be hard—not to orgasm. *Ever!*"

Vanni laughed. "I come once every other week or so. Sometimes we don't even make love for a month."

Pam's tea cup clattered down to the saucer. She opened her mouth, but everything that came to her mind sounded impolite. Along the lines of, gee, that's weird, or, wow, my ex-husband would call that abnormal, or …

But before she could say anything, Gina pipped in with a chirrupy laugh, "Once we went three months without sex."

Was it some type of game? A challenge to see how long they could wait?

"We just don't feel like it," Gina confessed, as if sensing what passed through Pam's mind.

"I suppose that makes it more exciting when you do make love."

"Some people think Vanni's gay," Gina said, abruptly shifting the conversation.

Pam blushed. She'd had the same thought a time or two.

"They interpret his European mannerisms as feminine," she said. "Do you think he's feminine?"

Pam cleared her throat. "Well, Vanni, you do have a gentle air about you. Some people might mistake that." He laughed. "And your clothes are more flashy than most of the other grad students. That might give some people the wrong impression."

Vanni nodded, neither affirming or denying. So, Pam wondered, was he gay? He'd just laughed at their comments, as if enjoying them. Was it his "effeminate" manner that made him feel like a "safe" friend. She hoped not. She hoped she could have guy friends who didn't always want to get into her pants.

That Saturday evening spent with Vanni and Gina had resulted in a discussion of Pam's relationship with Artie. After she'd described their romance and the early years of marriage, they asked her how things stood at the present.

"We're not actually legally divorced yet," she said, "but that's tenuous at best. The final decree should be handed down any day. He's in Chicago now and writes to me occasionally. Out of a guilt complex probably."

"Maybe he just wants you guys to be friends," Vanni said,

"I don't think so. I don't know myself. To be honest, I usually avoid analyzing how I feel. I guess I'm afraid if I dig too deep it'll hurt."

That was something she'd never admitted before, not even to herself.

"You must feel something for him," Gina said.

Pam shrugged. "We were married three years. Didn't even get to the seven-year itch."

"You were too young."

Maybe, but that wouldn't explain everything, would it.

"I think he is changing," she said, "which is good. I thought, being by himself, that he'd turn into a stud trying to screw every female he met. He did run off with a girl before we split up." She paused. "But now, judging from his letters at least—and who knows what he hides—he seems more sensitive."

"Not a pussy hound."

"Vanni! No, I got the impression he must have a feminist girlfriend. Maybe someone's indoctrinating him."

"Did you guys screw around during your marriage? Maybe your husband just needed a little more variety."

"We've even talked of that ourselves," Gina said.

"Of what?"

Vanni spoke. "Of letting me date other women. I'd like to, but I don't think Gina's too happy with it."

"I don't like to think of you screwing other women if we only fuck once a month!"

But Vanni wouldn't drop it. "Maybe your husband wouldn't have run off if you'd've let him have a little freedom."

"I'm sorry," Pam said. "You're not married, so I won't judge what you feel you should do, but there's no way I could accept my husband making love to other women. I'm too jealous."

"You're jealous too, Vanni," Gina said. "Maybe I wouldn't mind if it were reciprocal."

"I've never said you couldn't date."

"You wouldn't like it."

"So? Neither of us likes it. That's why I don't do it. But I think I'd be willing to swap partners occasionally, if you were willing."

Pam interrupted at that point to lighten the exchange. She looked at Vanni first and then at Gina. "Don't look at me!" she joked. "I don't have a partner so we can't swap!"

The affair with Mike was just that, an affair. By the time the summer of 1972 ended, it was over. Her summer, in her mind, was wasted. First because she'd had to get a job she disliked, working as a switchboard operator for Alta Bates Hospital, and second because her relationship with Mike ultimately had been so unsatisfying.

The more she came to know him the less content she was. She was attracted to him, she had fun with him. He was gregarious and lively. Her free time was spent in a whirlwind of activities. Mike was always wanting to do something. But it wasn't always with her. She had to compete with his friends.

That didn't bother her as much as he seemed to think it did. Near the end they argued about it often but, deep down, Pam realized it was a secondary issue. After all, she wanted to maintain her independence. She hadn't stressed that enough to Mike. She realized she'd come across as a grasping person. If Mike had shown her more affection when he was with her, she wouldn't have bugged him so much.

She also came to realize that the glint in Mike's eyes, which she'd always attributed to his vivacity, was actually one of nervousness. His cool control was a facade. He was relaxed only around his men friends, rarely around her.

Realizing this, she also began to analyze his sexual attraction. She'd always considered him sensual. Sensitive no. Sensual yes. But, really, he was neither. At best he was sexual. There was a clear distinction in her mind between sexual and sensual. Sensual meant caring for the other person, meant communication, meant openness, meant showing one's emotions. Sensitivity led to sensuality. Sexuality by itself led to nothing but sex. Mike, she noticed, found it impossible to express his feelings. She wondered if he had them. "Do you love me?" she'd asked more than once, and he'd said, "Sure, why do you ask?" or "You know I do." But never the same words back.

So, in the end, the relationship faded away. There was no big bang. No last bitter fight. Pam merely decided to let Mike call her (rather than vice-versa) and after a time or two (those times out of obligation, it seemed), Mike ceased to telephone.

She was free again, damn it, and she decided to stay that way a while. She thought she'd learned that once from being with Artie.

# *chapter 20*

In the winter of 1973, with snow two feet deep, with winds whipping off Lake Michigan and dropping the temperature below zero, Artie found a steady job. The pay was as low as the temperature, minimum wage, but the challenge was as sharp and biting as the wind chill factor. The Food for People Cooperative Grocery Store on Greenleaf—only five blocks from his apartment—hired him as one of five staff members to run the store.

Artie had no retail experience but he had drive. Somehow his work ethic had impressed the other four co-managers enough for them to hire him. Most of his competition for the job, he learned later, had been weirdos who were looking for a "laid-back" job where they could smoke grass and take things easy.

Not that the current staff was that normal. Ed Harrison, a member of the Board of Directors, caught Artie in the coachhouse after the first Board meeting he attended—he was there only to be introduced—and asked him, "You into drugs?"

To allay suspicion (these days it was the truth, anyway) he said, "absolutely not," only to learn that Ed thought it essential that at least half the staff be into weed.

Talk about being flabbergasted! What did smoking grass have to do with running a co-op grocery store?

To increase his knowledge of the store's product line, Artie signed up for a nutrition course offered by a private cooking school in Roger's Park. The first half of the course was taught by a Chinese acupuncturist, Lu Wong, and the second half by a macrobiotic dietitian, Azib Odonau.

Struggling with foreign accents, Artie learned how to cook with miso, tofu, wakame, nori, kombu, shitake mushrooms, and agar agar—this from Wong (his first name, he was told, names were backward in Chinese)—and how to eat according to the seasons and with natural foods grown in one's local environment from Azib. By the end of the course, following a four-day, apple-juice fast, concluding with olive oil to bring about a liver flush, Artie felt spring clean and healthy.

They say you are what you eat. Here's a picture of Artie's refrigerator in 1971 and that of 1973, words he'd jotted down to show how much he'd changed.

*Artie and Pam's Frig (1971)*

*Top shelf: jar of pickles, package of bologna, head of iceberg lettuce, jars of Mayonnaise and mustard, loaf of Wonder Bread, cans of Root Beer and Fresca, gallon of milk.*

*Middle shelf: left-over meatloaf, left-over canned corn, left-over Spaghetti O's, package of bacon, eggs, bottles of Thousand Island, French, and Italian dressing, container of cheese dip, package of cheddar cheese, jello.*

*Bottom shelf: package of ground beef, package of chicken thighs, package of hot dogs, scattered tomatoes.*

*On the door: endless bottles of processed foods, margarine, imitation this, imitation that.*

*Freezer: Imitation orange drink, ice cream, frozen pizza, frozen meat.*

*Artie's Frig (1973)*

*Top shelf: pitcher of tomato juice, two bottles of Peters Val mineral water, gallon of spring water (hand pumped by Artie out on Irving Park Road in the Forest Preserves of Chicago), a quart jar of home-grown alfalfa sprouts, container of wheat germ, plastic container of Japanese Honba shiro miso, a cantaloupe, Parmesan cheese, olive oil, glass of salad dressing made from tofu.*

*Middle shelf: brown rice left-overs, bulgur soaking for tomorrow's breakfast, cup of pesto, container of tofu, package of feta cheese, sharp*

*cheddar, a vegetable salad, cucumber soup, fresh mushrooms, stalk of*
*celery, two ears of corn on the cob, fresh parsley.*

*Bottom shelf: bunch of green onions (which his teacher always*
*elegantly called scallions), half head of red cabbage, cauliflower, two*
*lettuce heads (Boston and Red Leaf), container of left-over stir-fried*
*ginger vegetables, apples, Red Flame grapes, pears, oranges.*

*On the door: two pounds of unsalted, uncut butter, eggs, ginger root,*
*four cans of Olympia beer (no potato yeast for those allergic to that, but*
*a vegetable yeast like Red Star), umeboshi plums, safflower oil, corn oil,*
*soy oil, mustard, fresh ground peanut butter, apple butter (no sugar,*
*no preservatives), yogurt.*

*Freezer: ice cubes, home-made whole wheat bread, frozen peas.*

The trouble was he couldn't tell if he actually felt better or not.

On the job, when someone asked the difference between tamari and
Worchestershire sauce or between arrowroot and cornstarch or between
sunflower and safflower oils (or between cold and hot pressed), Artie would
launch into a spiel. The benefits of whole foods, organic produce, sugarless
products, preservative- and additive-free delicacies. The uses of millet, bran,
bulgur, rolled oats, rolled wheat, wheat germ, organic raisins, sunflower seeds,
molasses, honey. The differences between bleached and unbleached flour and
whole wheat. He knew the vitamins in brussels sprouts and eggplant, the
nutrients in brewer's yeast, the medicinal value of comfrey root or fenugreek
tea. When to use basil and when oregano, the taste benefits of fresh coarsely
ground spices, what foods supply vitamin A, or Niacin, or Pantothenic Acid, or
magnesium, what lecithin is made from (soybeans) and its three forms (liquid,
powder, and granules), and the fact that cultured milks like Kefir and yogurt
help stabilize the intestinal flora, an aid to digestion.

When he wrote to Pam of his accomplishments, she wrote back that he
deserved to be in Berkeley. "You'd fit right in here," she wrote, and added,
"Why don't you come cook for me? You owe me three years!"

After studying nutrition and macrobiotic diets, Artie moved into iridology
and foot reflexology. He would've liked to have studied Esoteric Psychology,
ah, yes, as dictated to Alice Bailey by the Master D. K. and its theory of the
seven rays. (Sometimes he had to laugh at himself.) Or, if not that, perhaps

Rolfing or even the Alexander Technique or something more physical like the Feldenkrais exercises—oh to understand the pelvic clock!—but he didn't want to appear too unfocused so he limited himself to things like finding the heart chakra below the big toe, the illeo-cecal valve near the base of the foot on the left, the gall bladder point in the center of the sole and then up to the left an inch. Or he ascended from the foot, source of all movement, cornerstone of the body's building, to the eyes. And there on the eye, he found the tombstone-shaped areas of the kidney, the vagina, the thyroid, and liver, the rectangular grids for the spleen, the scapula, the trachea, the outer circle for the lymphatic and circulatory systems, the inner circles (foremost among all, largest in size, and standing next to the black hole of infinite space), that of the stomach.

The eye was not the window on the soul. The eye was the window on the body, the organ to be looked in at, as well as the organ looking out upon. It was all a lot of fun. Even the nonsense.

And finally, not the least of his endeavors, he tried to learn how to run a store: stocking shelves, manicuring produce, doing the biweekly buy at the Water Street market, ordering products from wholesalers, supervising workers, operating the cash register, revamping the physical features of the store, preparing advertising copy, and reckoning accounts, which meant endless amounts of paperwork. And that seemed like only a small part of what there was to do.

His co-managers, Bill Spimling, Bev Watson, Walt Gefford, and Herschel (the "Hearse") Levine, possessed varying talents and operating personalities. Bill was the hard-nosed tyrant, who came on like everyone's boss. Bev was the customer-relations expert, sloppy, occasionally lackadaisical, but sharp when it came to store operations. Walt (a history buff) was usually drunk, smoked Camel cigarettes, wanted to stock more meat, and talked your ear off, whether he was enumerating baseball records (all memorized), the struggles of the Wobblies, or the attempts of the labor unions to thwart the Taft-Hartley Labor Act. And the Hearse was a gloomy, long-haired, semi-freak who came to work stoned and was given to bursts of unrestrained gaiety. He would be sulking in the back by the spice scales one minute and dancing helter-skelter in the aisles the next. Oh, and he was gay. Once, he came up behind Artie, when Artie was talking to a customer, and laid his chin on Artie's shoulder.

"At least you're not a homophobe," he said later. Artie hadn't shied away.

Blending their various working styles and personalities was never easy. Artie would come in to work the evening shift sometimes, after Bev had opened, and spend the first half hour cleaning up the mess she'd left. The cash register and check-out counter would be covered with scattered papers, price lists, catalogues, open bags of potato chips, half-full cans of pop or bottles of juice. In the back she would have left a pan on the hot plate (unplugged fortunately) with rice droppings caked inside. And he'd find her plate and fork on the meat cooler by the spice scale. In the sink would be a pile of dirty cups, cheese knives, peanut butter scoops, and silverware.

Working after Walt, however, was sometimes worse. Smoking was prohibited in the store so Walt spent half his time out on the front steps consuming his Camels. If he could find a worker skilled enough to run the complicated cash register, he'd sneak off to the bar next door and quaff a few brews, as he put it. You could usually hear his voice through the walls. Walt liked to preach and his topic was usually politics. He'd majored in poli sci, with a minor in history, earning his M.A. at Columbia, where both his parents taught. When he was drunk he'd carry on a one-way conversation with whomever he could corner, talking one day of the decline of the I.W.W. and the rise of the Communist Party and another day of the Progressive Party which, as he would tell you, in 1924 nominated former Wisconsin governor Robert M. La Follette for President. Poor Fighting Bob. The only electoral votes he won were thirteen in Wisconsin, but he polled five million popular votes.

If there were women in the bar, Walt would throw in a line or two about La Follette's ardently feminist wife Belle Case. "Shit," he'd exclaim, "you think you're the first feminists that ever existed. The feminist movement in the U.S. was active ten years before Belle Case was even born. Ever hear of the Declaration of Independence for Women? People like Elizabeth Cady Stanton and Lucretia Mott issued that at a woman's rights convention in Seneca Falls, New York, back in 1848." And he'd add a clincher to put them down a bit more. "Shit, the only reason you've heard of Susan B. Anthony is because they're gonna put her face on a dollar coin."

When he was drunk, Walt also liked to rave about the Anti-Saloon League and the Prohibition Party. Frances Elizabeth Willard, who helped organize the Woman's Christian Temperance Union in 1874, was frequently the butt of his aggressive arrows, as was the eighteenth amendment to the Constitution and the Volstead Act. Most of the time his audience was young enough not to have heard of any of the political and social events of which he spoke, and Walt, having sufficiently mystified them, was able to hold the floor alone for ten to fifteen minutes. He was an expert on the history of the labor movement in America and unfortunately he liked to talk more than he liked to work. His favorite interjection, if someone else tried to explain something, was, "Does that have anything to do with oral sex?" The phrase was one of his least objectionable. Walt was the original foul-mouth.

So, when Artie followed Walt, he found the store half empty. Walt never had time to stock the shelves. There would be bricks of cheese in the cooler waiting to be cut and wrapped, lentils to be bagged, produce to be priced, signs to be changed.

Bill was a different case altogether. He'd alienated most of his co-workers and was barely civil to Artie. Artie fell into the habit of jokingly mocking him by genuflecting and making the sign of the cross whenever he saw him. Bill took it in good humor, half believing it was due obeisance. He let slip to Artie one day that he had a circle of vassals among the co-op members. "They even blew up a photo of me and had it printed on T-shirts," he said.

Artie had heard the same story, only from Walt's point of view. Walt said they'd done it to make fun of Bill's god complex—Bill considered himself an avatar of the chief-executive principle—but Bill chose to ignore the derisive aspects of the deed.

Artie had walked into the store a few times to find Bill and Herschel literally screaming at each other. Bill would be angry because Hearse had forgot to deposit the previous night's earnings in the bank." "Every time you fuck up, we bounce checks. I outta take the nine buck fee out of your salary—or your hide."

Artie had been assigned the duties of bookkeeper by the Board of Directors, partly because he'd been a clerk, mostly because no one else wanted the job. Bev had been responsible for the books but had ceased to do them two months earlier, following a break up with her boyfriend. She'd told no one for the entire two months. Bills had piled up, records were a shambles.

Artie had looked forward to the duties at first, even signing up for an evening accounting course at Loyola University to help him handle the complicated budgetary matters. But, after a while, he realized why no one else liked the job. Sure, it meant you could get out of the store for a while, but it also meant you felt the entire burden of the store's failing finances. Taxes were due, loans over-due. Suppliers couldn't be paid. The store's dealers were requiring cash or certified checks (after all, the co-op's regular checks regularly bounced). The float was around three to four thousand, their cash flow, if it was a stream, would barely cover the pebbles. Just to catch up on what Bev was supposed to have done was going to take months it seemed. The other staff members didn't appreciate the immensity of the task. They were always asking, no, expecting, Artie to put more hours into store operations. The books, for all they cared, could wait.

Weren't they of secondary importance to running the store?

Artie could see why Bev had given up in frustration.

One night after Artie had been on the job a little over a month, Bill, who'd worked the closing shift, stopped him just as he was walking out the front door. It was 10:30, pitch black, and a bitter February wind blew frozen snow crystals through the air. Artie had spent all day trying to get the books caught up. He was exhausted and eager to get home.

"I don't think you're putting in enough time on the books," Bill said. "It's taking too long to get them into shape."

What the fuck? "The co-op's been running for two months with no one touching the books."

"Yeah, and we've been bouncing checks. This last year we paid over $450 on bounced checks."

"That's not because of the book work. Beverley could've been doing them all along and it wouldn't have made much difference. The trouble is, Herschel forgets to go to the bank. Every day that he's there after two p.m. we bounce all the checks that go out that day." He could see Bill didn't like his own complaints thrown back at him.

"I still think until we get this mess straightened out you're going to have to put in fifty or more hours a week."

He turned away from Bill. The wind struck him in the forehead like a cold axe. He felt like saying, fuck off, Bill, you're not even a member of the Board. Go take care of your own work.

Before he could respond, however, Bill grabbed his arm. "I think you should come in tomorrow." He knew Artie had the weekend off. It was his first two days back to back since he'd started.

"I think I should stay away. You come in if you want to. It's my day off."

He turned to go.

Bill, standing in the doorway to the store, caught the outer screen door before it could slam shut. He shouted after him, "You're not dedicated enough to the co-op. We need someone with collective principles."

Artie turned, already fifteen feet down the street, in front of the bar. The door was open and he could see Walt inside playing darts, a beer bottle in his left hand.

"Fuck your collective principles," he said. "I do my work and I do it well. Bev fucked up for two months because of personal problems and we should've fired her. Don't try to blame me for what's happened in the past. I've only been here a little over a month, and now I've got every jackass in the co-op sitting on my shoulders. You're not even on the fucking Board. And another thing, quit telling me to devote all my time to the paper work. If you want that done, you bring it up before the Board or the staff. The rest are always screaming at me to work in the store. We're a collective you know. We discuss things. I'm not going in to the other three staff members and tell them I've got to devote all my time to the books. What'n the hell are we hiring an outside accountant for? Why don't you butt off for a while and let us take care of it?" But Bill was already back in the store, the door slamming behind him.

Walt, having overheard the commotion, was on the doorsteps of the bar. "What'n the fuck was that about?" he asked, slurring the words. He was drunk already.

Artie stared back at the store, his hands on his hips. "Bill has a burr up his butt. He's harping about the books again."

Walt pulled his wispy goatee, swaying slightly on the steps. "Now Bill is a strange, fucked-up guy. You've got to understand Bill. Let me tell you about him." And he began to wander on about Bill starting the store and why he thought like he did.

Shit, Artie thought, now I've got to listen to a drunkard. Walt was such a bullshitter, but at the moment he didn't want to alienate him.

"Come on, Walt," he said finally, interrupting his slow-paced spiel. "Speed up the reel, I want to get home sometime before midnight."

"Just wait a moment, listen to the prophet," Walt said, mocking himself. "'Scuse me while I get another beer and I'll tell you in two minutes how you handle Bill." He gestured at Artie to wait and turned to go back in the bar.

After Walt staggered up the two steps and disappeared, Artie set off up the street, kicking the telephone pole on the corner as he stepped around it into the gutter. The parking meter received a second kick and then Artie settled down for the walk home.

Damn, it was cold! How in hell did people live here? What did the gods have to do? Freeze the damn lake solid before people'd leave? Shit! This was the arctic. This was uninhabitable.

* * *

Walt and Artie clashed at the next weekly staff meeting. Artie, worried about loans coming due, suggested raising the "bump" an extra five percent for non-working members—the percentage mark-up they'd have to pay. Non-working members currently paid ten percent above shelf prices and non-members twenty percent.

"Five percent! Are you crazy?"

Artie flushed.

"We should be dropping the bump five percent. That's how we'll get more business."

Bev, apparently in agreement with Walt, pursued the matter. "If we raise the bump, we'll wipe ourselves out. Our competition would eat us alive."

Artie rocked forward, hitting his pen on the desk in the attic office. "We're going to be wiped out anyway if things continue as they are. We're not doing a good job. We're losing a thousand dollars a month. Cutting the bump will cost us at least another five hundred a month. It won't increase our business. We don't do any advertising anyway! We need to generate more income."

The jab concerning advertising was another sore point. Artie had been pressing to set up an advertising budget of at least a hundred a month, but the other co-managers were reluctant to increase expenses.

Bill, surprisingly, took his side. "Artie's right. We need more money and fast. Walt, if we lower the bump, sales won't increase fast enough to make up the difference. If we raise it five percent for everyone, I think the increased income will more than make up for the customers we lose."

"Bullshit."

Artie sighed, tipping his head back and counting holes in the ceiling. Going to be another productive meeting. The joys of consensus. Unless everybody agreed—Bill, Walt, Bev, Herschel, Artie—nothing could be done. Five people in accord, when it occurred, was a Pythagorean miracle.

That night, alone at home, he wrote a brief letter to Pam. His motto had always been "Never regret the past," but now he felt like apologizing. "I've been wishing I wasn't so stupid, that I'd been less selfish, more understanding, not so immature." And he went on for a few more lines of regret.

But the letter, rather than being a release, oppressed him.

In the morning, awakening to the burdens and responsibilities of his job, he could barely get out of bed. By the time he finished breakfast, his mind was made up. Next month, at the Wednesday board meeting, he would walk in and say he was through. Forget a letter of resignation. Do it in person. A moment of satisfaction.

"So tell me about your ex-wife," Liz said.

Liz Butler was one of the co-op's more faithful customers.

Artie shifted on his stool. The two were in CC's bar next to the co-op, drinking beer. Outside a hard rain thrummed against the windows. Artie thought of a simile, didn't know if it was original. Pellets of rain eating into the snow like acid on styrofoam. These days he wasn't getting any writing done.

The bar was a glow of blue and gold in the dark, almost deserted now.

He took a sip of beer, then brushed his lengthening hair behind an ear. "Why?" he said finally, blurting the word like a slap across the face.

It was an effective way to end a conversation. At least he thought so, but after a few minutes, she said, "Why don't you like talking about her?"

"You like talking about your ex?" He knew she was divorced. She had a nine-year-old boy named Brian.

"But you haven't asked me about mine."

"Right." The way he said it was meant as a message. I don't ask you, you don't ask me.

"Does it bother you? I'm interested, and it'll be good for you." She paused. "Besides, I want to know you better."

"If I talk about my wife, you won't like me any better."

"Your *ex*, remember. Try me."

Artie leaned into the bar, sorting through thoughts. "I've always had a motto. Never regret the past. Never feel bad for something you've done if, when you did it, you did it with intention. You would've always done it that way."

"I'm listening. Still haven't heard a word about the ex."

"Shit!" He shook his head. "She wanted a blotter, and I couldn't be one."

"What's that mean?"

"She had a lot of frustration to vent. She wanted me to share her problems. Just to listen really. But I couldn't listen without getting angry myself, without trying to tell her how to live her life. So, instead of absorbing and diffusing her emotions, I intensified them and tossed them back at her. She'd complain about something bad that had happened on her job or at school, and I'd get frustrated. Why didn't you do this or why didn't you do that? And then she'd get angry at *me*. Instead of us both getting angry at someone else, we'd scream at each other."

Liz touched him on the arm. The touch felt good even through his flannel shirt. "Do you regret breaking up?"

"Why do you ask that?

"I think you do."

"Oh, women's intuition at work? Then you know more about it than I do."

"Come on." She poked him in the ribs. "You know I throw the tarot. Let me psychoanalyze you."

And partly to get even for forcing him on unpleasant terrain, he said, "Is that what you did to your husband?"

Later, at home alone, he wondered why he'd said that. She was just trying to get to know him and he'd shut her down. A woman he liked! She was good looking, smart, put in her member hours without complaint, always bumped him when they were working side by side. In fact, she seemed the most joyful person he'd ever met.

That was no way to win her affection, was it?

Shit! The co-op had sourced his personal life.

Liz called him the following Saturday—(neither one apologized for the two-week break)—and asked if he'd like to go for a bike ride along the lake in Evanston. "We can dress warm," she said, "and watch the waves. Wear gloves. The bike paths are clear but there's a lot of neat ice formations along the shore." When Artie paused, thinking of the cold lake winds, she added, "Brian's staying over night with some friends, so it'd just be the two of us."

Artie was pacing in his kitchen, swirling the long telephone cord like a jump rope. "Sure, that'll be fun. Friggin' cold but fun."

"Great! I've missed you! Let's meet at Loyola. Three o'clock. We can bike from there up to Northwestern and back. Have some pizza at My Pie. I like their deep dish spinach and cheese."

When he got off the phone, Artie danced from the kitchen down the hall to the living room. Wow! Just the two of them. Alright!

When Liz hadn't shown up by four, the sky already darkening, snowflakes drifting in off the lake, he walked across the street from Loyola's campus to the pizza parlor and asked if he could use their phone. No answer at her place.

Unwilling to wait longer, he decided to bike along the route Liz would've taken. No sooner was he out along Sheridan Road than he noticed two police cars, parked near the gas station on Albion. He hesitated, realizing they could cite him for biking without a light, but pulled up next to the driver's window of the first car.

A young, mustachioed police officer rolled down the window. "Yeah?"

None too polite. Maybe he didn't like the cold creeping into his warm cockpit.

Artie blew his nostrils clear. The air was icy. "I was supposed to meet a woman who was bicycling here along the lake," he said. "She hasn't shown up and I'm worried about her."

The officer looked away from him toward his partner. Artie bent down and saw it was a woman. She looked white as Ivory Snow in the pale light of the overhead lamp.

"Why do people bike in this weather," he heard her grumble. "What was her name?" the woman asked.

"Liz Butler."

Both officers stared at him.

"What's the matter?" Artie's stomach sank. Before they could respond he guessed. "An accident."

The mustachioed officer nodded. "A car tried to turn in front of a bus and forced the driver to swerve. The bus hit her. I'm sorry but the woman was killed. Instantly we think. She was trapped between the bus and the parked cars. Don't tell anyone we told you."

A wave of nausea doubled Artie over the handlebars, tears freezing in the corners of his eyes. Why her? And what about her son? Nine years old.

He straightened and shook his head. Why do we create such metal monsters? Cars which then kill us? Were all the benefits even worth one life? He tasted sour bile at the back of his mouth.

Liz was hit on the one stretch with no bike path. It was only a few blocks long. The bike path died along the lake and cyclists were forced to ride along Sheridan Road. Most rode on the sidewalk, but the sidewalk had "No Biking" signs painted on them at every intersection. Liz had obeyed the signs. Why? And why didn't he agree to meet her in Evanston at her place? That wasn't that far away. A fifteen minute ride …

The police officer was talking, but Artie was too numb to reply. He brushed at the tears in his eyes, gloves icy, kicked the pedal around backwards, found it at the top, and bicycled away, choosing not the safe sidewalk but the open street.

* * *

When Artie arrived home, he wished he'd told the police about Brian. Throwing his coat, hat, muffler and gloves on a rocking chair, he tried calling the Rogers Park police station but no one seemed willing to give him any information. After several phone calls to different sections, the best he could get out of them was that the next of kin had been (or would be?) notified. They were sufficiently ambiguous on the latter point ("We're taking care of it") as to leave him unsure.

He tried calling Liz's number to see if Brian would pick up. No answer. Where did her parents live? Would they step in and take care of things? He had no way of knowing. He looked in the phone book, hoping she was using her maiden name. There were fourteen Butlers in the Rogers Park directory alone, eighty-four in the Near North Suburbs, five columns in the Chicago book!

He busied himself in the kitchen. He cooked a dinner and didn't eat it. He cleaned up the dishes and refrigerated the left-overs. He even vacuumed the living room. Finally he called Liz's place again. Still no answer.

He called long distance information for California. There was no listing for a Pam Crenshaw. Five minutes later he dialed back. Yes, there was a Pam Walters in Berkeley. So, in the phone book, she was using her family name, not Crenshaw.

Overcoming his hesitance (it was so much easier to write letters, less personal, less a sense of her physical presence), he dialed her number. She picked up after two rings.

"Hi, Pam," he said. "This is Artie."

There was a long silence at the other end.

"Hello," she said finally. "This is a surprise."

He bit his lip, unable to speak because of the compression in his chest. I'm acting like a woman, he told himself, trying to gain control. The silence was extending itself.

"So," Pam said. "Did you call to talk or just to breathe in my ear?"

"I just wanted to see if you were okay. I was worried about you."

"Me? I'm fine. Why now?"

"I'm sorry, Pam," he said. "I can't talk now." And with that he hung up, leaving her on the other end in California, perplexed, shaking her head, wondering then why in hell had he bothered to call?

# *chapter 21*

P am's second and third years in Berkeley existed in her memory only as a haze of nebulous and repetitious events, days spent teaching, study- ing, preparing for her M.A. exams in the spring of her second year, and working toward her Ph.D. after that, probably another three or four years.

She taught her usual Italian I class each semester. She audited an intensive Latin course along with her usual two Italian literature classes. She read vo- luminously, beginning with the Sicilian School poets of the Duecento and ending with contemporary novelists. Her master's exam covered all of Italian literature, her Ph.D. only her specialty, a hundred and fifty-year period.

She dated occasionally, attended films and guest lectures, took long walks through the Berkeley hills. She even began corresponding with Artie. But that was only as the second academic year ended.

Her weekends were spent in the library. She was rewarded for her hard work when a paper she'd revised that fall was accepted for presentation at the 47th Annual Conference of the Medieval and Renaissance Society of the Pacific Coast, held that December in Los Angeles.

Unlike most conventions where one read his or her paper and then answered questions, the MRSPC distributed the papers a month early and arranged for a respondent to critique it, after which the author of the paper had his or her turn to clarify matters. The critique was shared ahead of time.

When she arrived in L.A. Pam was happy she wouldn't have to read the paper. She'd come down with a bad cold and sore throat two days before the convention. She'd been resting her voice, trying to resist the normal syndrome in which she lost her voice entirely and was laid up in bed with a fever and headaches.

When her respondent, Professor David Palude, had finished his critique—he was a youthful colleague teaching at the University of Washington, a fellow she'd met in Berkeley one summer when he was conducting research as a NEH fellow—she rose, clutching her file folder and the sheet of paper on which in her daze she'd jotted as many points of conflict with his critique as she could get down. David had *not* sent her his critique ahead of time.

When she began to speak, her voice was a rough rasp on the saw-edge of laryngitis.

"Thank you, Professor Palude," she said, nodding to him where he sat in the front row, his hands between his legs clasping his briefcase, his shoulders hunched forward in expectation.

Asshole. She was sure he wanted to sabotage her.

"In my tiredness this morning, I will probably not be able to recall all the points raised by my colleague," she said, "but I've jotted down as many as I could. Please forgive my voice," she added. "I'm struggling with a bad cold and I've been up since four driving to get here." Though she felt like she was giving excuse after excuse, she added, "I would be better prepared if I'd been able to see Professor Palude's remarks in advance of today's session."

She was the third speaker and noted that the other two respondents had given copies of their critiques to the authors of the papers. David had spoken to her on the phone one day—it was her call—and had obliquely mentioned one of his points. It was in fact the first one he'd made and she was prepared, at least, to respond to it.

"David has pointed out that my statement regarding the optimism of the Humanists in the Quattrocento is not entirely accurate. While no one would contest his contention that a pessimistic strain ran through many of the writers of the fifteenth century, witness Salutati's letter on his son's death, in general terms I think that there can be no doubt that the civic humanists looked forward with confidence to the building of a rational and well-ordered state."

She paused, ready to go on—her response to this point had been clear in her mind for a week—when, looking down at her notes and then back at the audience, her mind went blank.

She looked down again, feeling the silence, hearing a chair creak, and then a sniffle from someone else with a cold, sitting in the back.

"I'm sorry. I forgot what I was going to say." She grimaced. "My mind is fluttering with various medicinal drugs"—she made sure she said "medicinal" so her older colleagues wouldn't think she was stoned—"in a vain attempt to clear my head and soften my throat."

She could see a few looks that said, I feel sorry for your debacle but I'm glad it's not happening to me.

"I remember now," she said. "I was going to say there's a distinct change in tone in the writings of the Humanists following the disastrous invasions of Charles VIII and Louis XII. By the time Francis I and Charles I of Spain, soon to be Charles V, Holy Roman Emperor, are fighting in Italy, and especially following the Sack of Rome in 1527 and the Siege of Florence from 1529 to 1530, the situation was so grave that tragedians like Rucellai had lost faith in the ideal states of an earlier generation. The concept of a Divine Providence, of man's blindness ..." She stumbled, searching her tired mind for the correct locution. "The awareness that nature is orderly, that the cosmos is regulated according to divine principles, that man is the source of disorder and confusion ..."

She paused again, absolutely panicked, unable to remember what she'd just said and how she was going to finish it. She felt heat rising into her cheeks, burning. "I'm sorry," she said finally, tears building up and blurring her eyes. "I'm in no shape to speak today." She reached into her suit pocket for a handkerchief and on the pretext of blowing her nose, turned away and dabbed at her eyes.

With her back to the audience, feeling her chagrin thick in the air about her, an absurd thought flashed across her mind and she had to laugh at herself, regaining in that moment her self-confidence and an awareness of the insignificance of the event. Life would go on. Just that morning, eating two grapefruit halves—one left over from yesterday and one half from a new grapefruit, she'd come to the conclusion, counting, that all grapefruit have thirteen sections. (A year later she found, to her dismay, another type with twelve.) As she sliced each segment from the connecting membranes, she'd counted 1A, 1B, 2A, 2B, a stroke on each side of the membrane, until she reached thirteen. Thinking it was a bad luck sign, she'd cut into the other grapefruit, hoping it might be different. But no, it was the same and she concluded that all grapefruit followed this pattern, forced by ineluctable fate into a convention, into a common homogeneity. This was now the thought that flashed into her drug-hazed brain.

Controlling her impulse to share this observation, wondering distractedly, however, how many people in the world had ever counted, how many shared this esoteric knowledge, she gathered her papers into a file folder, said, "Thank you," and stepped from the podium.

Perhaps to save her, or at least in an attempt to start a discussion without her, a professor from Colorado, whose name she hadn't caught earlier, asked

Palude a question on the source of the Rosmunda episode. In her own seat in the audience, she tried to remember, testing herself as if she were still at the podium. She knew the answer was somewhere in her reading notes, but nothing came to mind. Probably couldn't have answered that even if weren't befuddled.

Palude, of course, with his precise Eastern accent and shifty eyes, was happy to talk of Paulus Diaconus and his eighth century *History of the Lombards*.

Show-off, Pam thought, as the conversation puttered along fitfully. You know Paul the Deacon, but do you know that all grapefruit have thirteen sections? She grinned, hiding it behind her handkerchief. Who was to say, after all, which item was more important?

In the spring of '73, perhaps sensing Pam needed a respite from her intense study (her exam was only six weeks away! panic!), Gina Di Pietro invited her to a political gathering one evening in her basement apartment. Giacomo Mitraglia, a professor from the University of Padua, was going to talk on *Autonomia Operaia*, Workers Autonomy, and the radical left in Italy.

In inviting Pam, Gina had explained her connections with the leftist movements in Italy. She spent her summers in Italy organizing workers, women, the unemployed and marginal members of society. Pam, surprised by the intensity of Gina's enthusiasm, accepted the invitation. It was the first time Gina had mentioned her political activities. She hadn't seemed the type. Underneath her languid beauty, apparently, lay a militant in the mold of the Symbionese Liberation Army.

Gina's apartment was jammed with Italians when Pam arrived. Some of them were students in the department, but most she'd never seen before. In the discussion that followed Mitraglia's impassioned plea for aid in support of the upcoming summer offensive, Pam learned that the audience ranged from Italian immigrant laborers to professionals with leftist leanings.

Mitraglia was a galvanizing speaker. "This is the summer," he proclaimed, "for the militarization of our campaigns. Groups like *Lotta Continua*, Continuous Struggle, and *Potere Operaio*, Worker's Power, will carry the confrontation to the heart of the state. We will extend the struggle from the factories to the cities, we will ground our movement on the daily life of the workers, we will fight for better housing, better health care, better schools, greater economic power. The conflict is social and must be spread to all of society."

And later, while Pam listened entranced, he talked about the U.S.

"In the United States the radical movement of the late sixties has effectively disappeared. It has lost its political perspective, it has dissipated at all levels of society. In Italy, instead, the impact of 1968 has proceeded with uninterrupted vigor. The desire to transform society, from the bottom to the top, has gained in momentum. Frustrations are increasing daily, class warfare is the inevitable and the only solution."

Listening to Mitraglia, Pam felt that what she was experiencing must have been what Berkeley students experienced daily in the late sixties. It was a period she'd just missed. When she'd arrived, the campus still had a revolutionary reputation, but the reputation hid a different reality. Her students weren't interested in improving worker conditions. They wanted a tool that would guarantee them instant wealth. Mass layoffs, inflation, chronic unemployment, poverty, hunger—none of it mattered as long as they were at the top of the heap.

Excited by Mitraglia's rhetoric, Pam wished she had more time to be involved. Gina, apparently, was once again going to Italy in the summer to help organize protest marches. The Italian feminists, said Mitraglia, were ready to press their demands on a national level. They would take to the streets in mass, not just to force specific claims, but perhaps more importantly simply to affirm themselves as a presence on the political level.

"It will be the masses united against state terror," he said. "And our aim is not that of the *Brigate Rosse*. We don't agree that insurrection should aim to appropriate state power. We want to destroy state power. For us, confrontation is a means of providing for the needs of the proletariat. The needs of the proletariat can only be met by breaking the domination of the capitalist machine.

"Democracy is a dictatorship of the bourgeoisie while proletarian dictatorship is the highest form of freedom. State power, unable to resolve the underlying problems confronting Italian society, is becoming state terrorism. Violence when it is employed by the State in the so-called defense of democracy is, in their words, legitimate, but, I ask, when true democracy does not exist, does not state violence amount to terrorism?

"If the systematic fiscal evasion of the capitalists is democracy, then we have democracy in Italy. If the systematic mutilation of the work force in our factories is democracy, then in Italy we have democracy. If social inequality and exploitation perpetuated in harmony with the laws of the state are qualities of democracy, then Italy is democratic."

The room burst into applause at this point and Pam, glancing around, saw rapt faces. Was Mitraglia advocating armed violence? He'd spoken of the militarization and the Vietnamization of the conflict. Or were these merely inflammatory statements supporting a less bellicose means of protest, ranging from mass demonstrations to general strikes? It was one thing to speak of battling with sword in hand (might not the "sword" be the pen?) and another to train members in the use of semiautomatic pistols and automatic weapons.

Having slipped from Gina's apartment following the question and answer session, just as refreshments were being served, Pam walked home pondering Mitraglia's points. It would be nice to be politically committed, but she didn't think she was the type. For her, violence of any sort, by the state or the individual, was anathema. She'd seen her father beat her mother enough times to hate the thought of physical confrontation.

It didn't take Artie long to learn that violence terrified her. He'd tried to grab her arms in their first big fight. Her response? A horrifying, help-I'm-being-murdered scream, the cry of a person literally frightened out of her wits.

Walking down a sloped and deserted stretch of Oxford Street, by an empty field of mouse-trail-skeined weeds and scattered rubbish, she suddenly experienced an emotional insight into Artie's behavior.

She thought she understood now why he'd run off. If he'd stayed, his frustrations would've erupted in violence. Instead of committing violence on her, he'd committed it on the marriage. His infidelity, if this made sense, was less a crime against her as an individual than it was a crime against their marriage.

She laughed at the thought, deciding, no, it didn't make sense. His running off hurt her as much as it hurt the marriage. What was the marriage but parts of both of them? She'd seen the Random House dictionary definition and thought they had it backwards: Marriage, the social institution under which a man and woman establish their decision to live as husband and wife by legal commitments, religious ceremonies, etc. It wasn't until meaning four, the first of the abstract definitions, that one read: any close or intimate association or union.

A union was a oneness, a state of being indivisible except by rupture. Artie's leaving was an act of violence not only against their marriage but against her. A part of her was torn away. Had the wounds healed yet? What about her own anger? Was she dealing with that?

That night, for the first time, she sat down and wrote a serious letter to Artie in response to one of his. It was a first step.

# *chapter 22*

When Artie was finally free of the Food for People Cooperative, he took a two-month break from work. He felt he'd neglected his writing long enough. It was time to read, to absorb, to reflect, to rest, and then to write. He returned to a book he was calling Nocturnal Emissions.

Ever since he'd left Pam, the work had gnashed its teeth in limbo. Artie added a few fragments, but couldn't seem to develop the discipline needed. It was easier to write poems, to compile lists of melodramatic novel titles, to begin novels every other day or so, even to doodle.

In May, Trab Kulman, a former staff member of the co-op, opened a café in a building on the corner of Ravenswood and Greenleaf, two store fronts down from the co-op. Trab had inherited over twenty thousand dollars and had decided to go into business for himself. He'd recently moved to Park Forest, a suburb south of Chicago, but felt the northside location held greater promise. Once the business was established, he planned to let other people run it and go back to school in order to get a degree in agri-business.

When Artie saw the café being set up and learned that Trab was the owner, he applied for a job. Trab was a likeable fellow, burly, given to wearing overalls and flannel shirts, always in a good humor. He'd left the co-op before Artie started there, but Artie knew by hearsay that Trab had been a hard worker.

Trab put him to work immediately helping to remodel the store, and when they opened a month later Artie was named general manager. The title was more glorious than the position. Artie worked one shift himself and supervised two other workers. He came to work in the early afternoon (the café was open all day), relieved Carla Martin, a young married woman whose husband taught math at Northwestern, and stayed until closing time around midnight. He and Denise Delucca, a young woman who made her living as a free-lance artist, designing ads for small stores, making signs, drawing up posters, covered the weekend shift.

Artie enjoyed the work. The responsibilities seemed less demanding than they had for the co-op, the pace slower since the café had just opened. He didn't have to consult anyone before making minor decisions, and the clientele came in not to take care of a chore (like shopping), but to relax and enjoy themselves.

Initially, the café had a limited menu. They offered the usual coffees, espressos, cappuccinos, hot chocolates, and teas, as well as pastries, cheesecake, and cheese and bread plates. When business picked up, Artie added eggs, muffins and jams for breakfast, a soup of the day for lunch, and crepes for dinner. The dessert menu was expanded to include Italian sodas, ice creams, pies, mousses, and other treats.

Many of his customers, especially in the slow, late evening summer hours, seemed to enjoy talking to him, single people especially. He developed a small group of regulars, people who came in at various times during the week, not so much for refreshment, but to unburden themselves it seemed.

One guy he enjoyed teasing was an Indian named Dashi, born in a village outside Delhi, in the U.S. now for over twenty years. Every time Artie came to take his order, the fellow would intone "Aham brahmasmi." Artie thought it was an Indian greeting. Finally, after getting the pronunciation straight, he greeted Dashi with them himself and stared wide-eyed as Dashi pounded the table in laughter. When he calmed down enough to speak, he said, "Aham brahmasmi" means "I am spirit. I am not this body.

"You should not say so," he added, "unless you understand that you, the Brahmana, the dog, and the dog-eater are all equal. When you understand that you can say it truthfully. But you are not a true devotee, are you?"

"Of whom?" Artie asked, setting Dashi's coffee before him.

"Of Krishna, the avatar of Vishnu."

Artie emitted a "Hm," shrugged, then said, "Oh, the Hare guy," and was about to return to the counter when Dashi showed him a book—*The Bhagavad-Gita As It Is by his Divine Grace A. C. Bhaktivedanta Swami Prabhupada.* The pictures inside the flyleaf reminded Artie of those inside some of the family Bibles he'd seen as a kid. Only here, the colors were so much brighter. He laughed when he saw the pictures of the Swami and his teacher.

"Why do you laugh?" Dashi asked, offended.

"They're both wearing watches!" he said. He couldn't understand how a spiritual master could wear a watch.

"Only the soul is eternal," Dashi said, closing the book. "The body is in time."

"Well, time for me to get back to work," Artie said and left Dashi to his coffee.

"You're breathing too fast," Dashi said one afternoon.

"Breath is life. It's the only thing that never changes from birth to death. The only thing we never give up, never stop doing."

Artie bent over to wipe the table clean. "There's a lot of things the body never stops doing."

"They all depend on the breath. And modern man never breathes correctly."

Artie put his hands on the top of the empty wooden chair opposite Dashi, the wash rag hanging over the edge like the drooping tongue of an overheated dog. "How so? oh swami."

"You never notice your breath. You breathe in shallow breaths, with your chest."

"So, that's where the lungs are."

"Have you ever noticed a child breathe?"

"Probably. So what?"

"The kid breathes with the stomach. The chest never moves. You must breathe from the belly. From the center. You are fragmented because you no longer breathe from the middle of your being. You are not centered."

"Well, maybe you're right about being fragmented, but I doubt it has anything to do with breathing."

"When I said you, I meant all modern man," Dashi said, tapping his spoon lightly on a napkin. "But you feel your fragmentation, do you?"

"I'm split every which way." Artie said. "What? Breathe deep and find out who I am? I wish it were that simple."

The next time Dashi came in Artie wandered over and told him he'd been breathing so good that he'd written a poem. "First one in over a year. Want to hear it?"

"If I must."

Artie glanced around the café. He didn't want to share it with a crowd. "It's called 'Coming home to Ithaca.'"

> *Sitting on an El train*
> *going lickety-split*
> *staring at my wristwatch*
> *as it slowly*
> *as it slowly*
> *as it slowly*
> *crystal face back-blacked by night*
> *ticks.*

*Watching Venus float to shore*
*flesh dressed by three nude nymphs*
*watching Vulcan as he stoops*
*—ah he wishes!—*
*to kiss her lips*
*wondering*
*wondering.*

*But she, shock-lit by spark-over and clackety clack,*
*is only a picture*
*a name with no address*
*the scene his self-forged family portrait*
*in-doored where Mars can knock*
*laughing, mocking,*
*smudging the shiny steel*
*as she*
*to admit her lover*
*opens the artist's dream.*

Dashi snorted. "You call that a poem?"

It was Artie's turn to be offended.

"Dashi, have you ever noticed how all the Children-At-Play signs in Chicago show the kids decapitated? Either that or they're high. You must've been the model for that."

Dashi took it in good humor. "Just playing with you, Artie. It was a good poem. And I see you added a wristwatch. The influence of the Swami."

Not long after, on a Saturday, one of the workers Trab Kulman hired, Mark Wilson, came in wearing a pair of baggy blue cutoffs and a ragged light blue T-shirt with a fading picture of two radio dials placed strategically over the nipples. Below the picture, equally faded, one could read the words, "Don't mess with the knobs. I'm already adjusted."

"Isn't that shirt meant for a woman?" Artie asked, as Mark sipped a beer and leaned on the counter overlooking the kitchen. Mark had stopped by to return a short story Artie had let him read and had invited Artie over for a drink after work that night. Turned out Mark was a writer, too. He'd published a handful of short stories.

"This is my sister's," he said, pulling at the shirt. "We got up in the dark this morning and put on each other's clothes."

"Huh?" Artie looked up from the head of lettuce he was shredding.

Another of Mark's jokes?

"Incestual alliance," the guy said. "We spent half the night nude together and dressed in the dark. Happens all the time."

That's what I get for asking stupid questions.

That night, Mark opened a bottle of cabernet sauvignon and poured each of them a glass.

"So, when are you and your old lady going to get it on again?"

"She's not my old lady." He let the silence lengthen, then shrugged. "I wouldn't mind visiting her in California. It'd have to be in the summer when she's not teaching. It's too late this year. Maybe next summer."

He'd surprised himself. But, no, not in the cards. Pam had changed. Another person now. Someone he didn't know any longer. No reason to get sentimental. And he'd changed, too, right?

Outside he could hear someone coming up the back steps.

"That'll be Cheryl," Mark said.

"Your sister?"

Mark nodded.

Cheryl pushed the door open with her foot, a box balanced precariously between her body and the doorjamb. It didn't look like she was even going to greet her brother, but then she saw Artie.

"Oh, hello," she said. "Didn't know we had company."

Cheryl, as Mark had already told him, was a student, early twenties, working days as a secretary for a food processing corporation in the Loop. At the moment she was attending Loyola's downtown campus at night, working on a B.A. degree in psychology.

When she joined them, after introductions, she sat cross-legged on a faded cotton mat and flashed a grin at Artie which lit up her eyes like sapphires in the sun. She had perfect teeth, he noticed, glistening behind moist pink lips. Her eyebrows, though unplucked, were delicately arched and tawny. He wasn't sure he liked her hair, to put it best a brown between clover honey and apple cider. She'd fastened her hair with two gold barrettes.

Cheryl asked about Artie's writing. "Mark let me read your short story. I liked it."

He didn't know if he approved Mark having shared his story. Anyway, not a subject he cared to talk about. Instead, he asked what she did at her day job.

She giggled. "As little as possible."

"She don't do nothing," Mark shouted. He'd already drunk three-fourths of the wine while Artie was only halfway through his first glass.

Cheryl gave her brother a dirty look. "That's what he thinks," she said. " I work eight hours a day, five days a week, and I'm taking two night classes at the moment."

She went on to talk about her classes while Mark sighed in boredom and began drinking straight from the bottle. He was glassy-eyed by the time she finished describing a course on theories of personality.

Artie had listened closely, his eyes focused on her face. Her eyes were as blue as Paul Newman's. Hard not to stare.

She smiled and gestured toward her brother. Mark lay slumped back against the foam cushion. "He's asleep," she whispered. "Let's go outside."

"Okay, I have to be going soon, anyway."

In the back yard, Cheryl opened the fence gate. "I'll walk you back to Custer," she said. "Seems like a nice night."

"A little cool for summer." He hated to think of winter. It would come soon enough. Artie had a long-sleeved flannel shirt over his T-shirt. Cheryl, in shirtsleeves, crossed her arms, holding her elbows.

"Want to wear my flannel shirt?"

She shook her head. "I'll be okay." A minute later, however, she said, "Yes, I'll take the shirt." She laughed when she saw how long the sleeves were. "Here," she said, "hold your arm next to mine." Artie's was a foot longer.

"How tall are you?"

"A little over six feet two."

When they reached Custer, they stopped under a street light. Traffic was thin. Artie could see a few distant beams stopped at a red light a block away. The maples and oak trees along the walk were in full leaf and the streetlights filtered through the branches. Facing each other, Cheryl said, "Well, I guess I'm going to have to part with your shirt."

"You can wear it back if you want and I can get it another time." The excuse was ready-made, but a little too obvious, he thought.

She touched him on the arm. "No, I couldn't make you walk that far in your T-shirt. I only have a few blocks."

"I could jog."

"No. That's okay."

He paused, while she removed the shirt and handed it to him. He was unsure what to say. Both began talking at once, and then stopped.

"I hope you were going to say the same thing I was," she said.

"What's that?"

"I was wondering if you wanted to get together tomorrow evening."

That was a surprise. But why not?

"Sure," he said. "I could pick you up and we could eat together. There's a new restaurant near Loyola's lakeshore campus I've been wanting to try."

"Why don't I just meet you at the Loyola El stop. I'll be coming back from the downtown campus."

"Great. What time's good for you?"

"The sooner the better," she said playfully and he blushed, hoping it wasn't obvious in the dark. "I can get there by eight," she went on. "Is that okay?"

It was.

After dinner the next night, he took Cheryl to the Volume II bookstore near Loyola, to check out the café upstairs, part of the same store. He ordered a latte and Cheryl asked for the same. They decided to split a piece of cheesecake despite having eaten too much Italian food. Cheryl's eyes were like blue neon, glistening in fog. She'd asked if she could read more of his short stories.

He'd enjoyed her company so much during dinner that he felt he was levitating. Treading on thin air, half out of his mind.

"Do they ever flash red?" he asked.

"Huh?"

"Oh, sorry. Just talking to myself."

Crazy. Yes, he knew, she already had guessed too. That's how she made him feel.

"Crazy," he said.

She looked around. "I suppose you could say that."

He followed her eyes—to see what she'd seen. Tables, chairs, bookshelves lining the walls, tables with more books, wood floors, wood counter, silver coffee machines, a refrigerator case, windows, Mertz Hall visible beyond the student cafeteria.

"I like your eyes."

"Thanks. Yours too."

He didn't know what to say to that. For the moment their conversation died.

To break the silence, Cheryl told him about a two-week workshop her company was offering. One hour every morning during her work day. They'd asked her to attend. "It's a course in business ethics."

"Ethics ... well, your corporation is ..." He searched for a word, saw her waiting for what he'd say. "So ..." He looked again into her eyes, hoping she'd hold his gaze. "So ..."

"So?" she said.

"So ... neon crazy."

"Blue neon?"

He grinned. Damn, she'd caught on. "Buzzing blue," he said. "In fog. Like your eyes."

"Buzzing blue neon crazy eyes?"

"Yes," he said. "That's what I've been trying to say all evening."

"Artie, let's go to your place and fuck."

Wow, compliments do pay off. What was it with women these days? Too much!

Was that what Pam was like now?

They were standing, he noticed, under a maidenhair tree and a flash of associations overwhelmed him for an instant or two. Fleshy fruit and edible nuts. It sounded somehow sexual, as did its name. The leaves themselves, Chinese fans, were like winged V's. For virgin or Victory? Scientific name equally expressive. Ginkgo biloba, gin for silver, kyō for apricot, and biloba for the dual lobes—which brought to mind, in their associative train, aplets and cotlets, somehow suggestive of sweet dainties wrapped in candy paper, and labia, moist and folded. The labia brought him back, *immensus circulus*, to her lips and he bent to kiss her, wondering what had gone through her mind in those few seconds between first eye and then lip contact.

When they kissed she flicked her lashes and theirs brushed, the sensation strange yet intensely erotic.

This must be it, he thought. Love's struck again. Going down for the third time. Would it be the last?

That night, after they'd made love and he'd taken her back home, he wrote a short sketch for her, an imaginary fantasy about two lovers. He wanted to tell what kissing her made him feel.

\* \* \*

*It seemed everywhere they kissed that day was connected with a tree and each tree had its own ambience, its own string of associations. Under the hackberry tree,* Celtis occidentalis, *he thought of the small, edible, cherry-like fruit, the slim leaves; under the* Littleleaf Linden, *with its dropping, yellow-white flowerlets and cordate leaves, he thought not of cords or cordeliers but of hearts, of the core, the heart of the fruit, and perhaps for a moment, of Cora. Cora as symbol of virginity, eating the seed of no return, Cora as maiden, with blonde tassels of green corn. Under the spindly and spidery honey locust, delicately filigreed, he thought of sweetness and thorns, of pulpy pods, and dangerous pleasures. The honeyed scent, the seed-eater, the maidenhair—in all, the arboreal ambience was polysemous and erotic.*

God, not much better than when I was imitating Norman Mailer. No way I'm showing that to her. He was still feeling dafty. A fool for love.

The following Tuesday, Artie received a brief letter from Mark. It read as follows:

*To Artie Crenshaw, peasant.*

*Greetings in the name of Mark Tray, esq., M.D., S.V., T.p.l., L.S.M.F.T., Protector of the Paulist Fathers, Director of the Royal Gymnasium at Wiesbaden, High Priest in the University of Gottingen, Comptroller of Augustine's College, Canterbury, Fellow of Hertford College, President Pontifical Institute of Allegheny, Canon of St. Ninian's Cathedral Perth and Honorary Canon of the Cathedral of the Holy Spirit, Cumbrae, Monk of the Benedictine Congregation of St. Maur, Westminster, Rector of the Academy of Poitiers, Abbot of the Ecclesiastical Seminary of Mantz, Secretary of the P.T.A., and King of England.*

*Are you fucking my sister? Confess before it's too late! You know what happens to people who don't confess? They go to hell. Hell is a deep, dark, fiery, hot place down below heaven somewhere. It is guarded by fornicators and onanists. Everybody that goes to hell burns forever! Can't you just see God laughing at them all? What else can you expect of him? He can't feel sorry. After all, he is a just God and while he would hate to hurt anyone who didn't really deserve it, he must punish those who do. People who are too happy on this earth or try to be deserve punish-*

*ment, of course, and God should think nothing of condemning them.*
*But enough of this echolalia (how do you like that for "meaningless*
*chatter"?). Beware of lewd and indecent behavior unless I an included.*
*Yours sincerely, M. T.*

"Shit!" Artie said, having read the letter twice, "He's preaching to me and I ain't even Catholic!"

# chapter 23

With her M.A. proudly ensconced on her parents wall in Eugene, Pam plunged onward. In the Fall quarter of her third year at Berkeley, she made a discovery which, although it dealt with her minor in Spanish, was to gain her professors' esteem and install her in their good graces for the next two years. Even without her discovery, Pam had captivated the Italian department by continuing to publish articles at a pace unmatched even by the new Assistant Professor hired by the department out of Harvard,

Pam had been working in the Bancroft Library, Berkeley's rare book room, reading Leone Ebreo's sixteenth-century *Dialogue on Love* in the Aldine edition of 1525. By chance she came across the chronological file of the library's manuscript collection and decided to glance at a few of the Italian holdings from the sixteenth-century.

Several earlier works intrigued her, but they were written in a crabbed and hasty Gothic cursive, too difficult to read. The Cinquecento scripts, however, most in fine humanistic bookhand, were a joy to peruse. Her discovery, however, was not a humanistic treatise, not an epistolary or a collection of poems, not an early sixteenth-century comedy, not a fragment of a mythological manual, not a school teacher's notebooks—all of which were there to be read and edited—but a skillful forgery which purported to be a seventeenth-century English translation of a passage deleted by Cervantes in the final version of the *Quijote*. She proved, through a linguistic analysis, that the text was in reality an early nineteenth-century work written by an Italian in English. The process was a brilliant piece of sleuthing and Pam felt she'd proven herself in the mold of the literary critic as detective.

After her heady success in the Fall, the second quarter of 1974 took an ugly turn when a particularly troublesome student named Adrian Cacciati enrolled in a section of Italian I she was teaching. Adrian showed his true character one day the first week when one of the women in the class pointed to a smudge on the floor and said, "Is that what it looks like?" Adrian, just arriving, paused in front of the class, announced dramatically, "Let's see," bent, ran a finger through it and lifted his finger to his mouth.

"No," he said, sucking it. "It's not dog shit. Dog shit's a bit more acrid."

He broke up the class, of course, and Pam found it hard to control the pace for the rest of the period. Once Adrian discovered that his antics peeved her, he took a perverse pleasure in causing trouble, particularly whenever he could do so innocuously.

One day he brought a beautiful golden retriever to class and Pam, while she loved the dog, had to tell him it was not allowed in the building.

"Oh shit," Adrian said, staring at her with brazen impudence, "You're not going to get uptight about that, are you? None of my other profs said anything."

"It's not the rule I care about," Pam said. "It's the interruption. You've already taken the first five minutes of class and you can't expect a pup like that to behave."

"Okay, so I'll put him in a box. I can't leave him outside. I haven't got a collar for him yet."

"And just where will you get this box?" Pam asked, and wished immediately she hadn't. It would be like Adrian to have one outside the door. In effect she'd capitulated to him by asking the question.

Sure enough, he'd seen one by the elevator on the first floor near the history department. He left for the box and she'd just started an oral drill when he barged back into the room, triumphantly carrying the dog in an empty book box. She felt she'd lost the class's attention, and the day, like so many others, was ruined.

She pondered asking Adrian to drop her class but, when she thought of the one legitimate way to go about it, he had an excuse. Her suggestion was that he move from Italian I to a section of Italian II. He'd grown up hearing Italian at home and obviously knew more than the other kids. His lackadaisical approach, possibly because of his verbal abilities, was setting a bad example. He'd developed his little clique who laughed at everything he said and alienated the other half of the class who were serious about learning the language.

When she made her suggestion, he protested that he didn't really know the grammar and he didn't want to lack the fundamentals when he went on to take advanced courses. "I took a placement exam, anyway," he said, "and the department told me to start with Italian I. Originally, I wanted to start with II but they wouldn't let me."

It was a duel the entire quarter, and she hadn't realized how unpleasant the class had become until the semester ended. She felt a tremendous weight lift from her chest. She knew she wouldn't be teaching Italian II in the spring, so some other teacher would be bequeathed the bugbear.

When spring quarter started and she learned Sally had Adrian she kept silent for two weeks, waiting to hear her complain. When Sally said nothing, Pam stopped her in the hall outside the office one day and casually mentioned that she'd seen Sally had Adrian Cacciati in class. "He's a real terror, isn't he?" she said. "I could've killed him a hundred times last quarter."

"Oh, not at all," Sally said, tossing her hair over her shoulders. "He's sweet. You just have to know how to handle him. I haven't had any problems. Really, he's a doll once you get to know him." Ignoring Pam's dour look, she asked, "Did you ever meet his family? He's got the neatest father and mother. I'm inviting them over when I have the class party at the end of the term. You'll have to come and meet them."

Pam walked away burning and vowed never to go to the Henderson's place again, but when Jeff called her up at the end of the term and invited her over for a spaghettata, she found herself accepting. She resolved to go early and leave just as quickly. When she arrived Jeff was in the kitchen, making a salad, and Sally was sitting on the floor in the living room, laughing and drinking a glass of red wine, surrounded by three of her male students.

Pam joined Jeff in the kitchen and when she asked him if she could help, he said no but put his arm around her waist and asked her how she was. She felt uncomfortable, she could feel the firmness of his hip, the heat radiating from his body, but she said "fine" and then moved away toward the counter. He smiled at her and she felt her face flush. She remembered what he'd once said in the TAs' office.

She and Sally had been talking about Vera Lovati who'd returned to Canada for a semester to help with a family crisis. "Don't you think Vera is sexy?" Sally asked her.

"Don't ask me," Pam said. "I wouldn't know." Really she thought Vera plain but didn't say so. Sally turned to Jeff and asked him the same question.

Jeff nodded. "Sure. I've always thought Vera was sexy. Remember the time she danced at Professor Daniele's party? We were sitting on the floor and you could see Vera wasn't wearing underpants every time she spun around. We had a group of guys who really got turned on."

"Did she know she was doing it?" Pam asked, embarrassed by Jeff's open lust.

Jeff shrugged and turned to Sally.

"I don't doubt it," Sally said. "She asked me one time if she could sleep with Jeff."

Jeff grinned.

"What'd you say?"

Sally shrugged. "I said that was up to her and Jeff."

Ever since then, Pam had felt uncomfortable when Jeff touched her, and the Hendersons were great ones for embracing every time they saw you.

She left the party, just as she thought she would, a half hour after she arrived. She was fleeing not only Jeff, who continued to touch her whenever he could, but also her own feelings—of embarrassment, discomfort, shame, and, yes, maybe, lust.

That night she masturbated herself to sleep, picturing herself, Jeff, and Sally in a threesome. Fantasies, thank God, were secret!

When she thought back on the events of that year, Pam realized she should've seen the pattern developing. Jeff had talked to her for hours on end in the TAs' office, and she'd accepted the attention, thinking he was impressed by her academic efforts. Jeff continued to denigrate Sally every opportunity he could, but Sally seemed impervious. Or did she? In retrospect, Pam saw that Sally's anger came out in less obvious ways.

Sally took pleasure in talking about sex and in admiring other men in front of Jeff. Pam had assumed it was for her that Sally raved about so-and-so, but, after Jeff's advance, she realized it was done as a dig at Jeff. Sally had even laughed at Jeff's inabilities as a lover. He put her down intellectually and she put him down sexually.

"Jeff was too tired after studying all evening to get it up last night so I had to use the banister," she joked. Or, in private with Pam, she'd confess that Jeff couldn't keep a hard-on for more than fifteen minutes. "I don't think we're going to make it," she admitted once. "Just not sexually compatible."

Did Jeff tell Sally he wanted to make love to Pam? she wondered. They joked and talked about an open marriage often enough. Maybe that was why Sally had seemed cold and distant sometimes. Perhaps it was jealousy. Did she even think they'd already gone to bed?

They hadn't.

Pam was again nonplused by her feelings. Why could she be turned on by someone like Mike or Jeff but not by someone like Nick, her only male friend?

Asking herself the question, she wondered if it was because Nick was so available. Mike, although divorced, had seemed the independent type who wouldn't ask for a deep commitment. Jeff was married and thus couldn't ask for much beyond a casual affair. With Nick, she sensed that sex would lead to entanglements. He would be the indefatigable pursuer. He would be possessive. He would be Artie all over again. And for marriage she wasn't ready.

From the pranks of Adrian Cacciati in the Fall, Pam skipped to the puppy love of Frank Peterson in the Spring. That was a distraction whose effects were felt into the summer.

On July 12, 1964, the number one hit song was the Beach Boys' "I get around." Ten years later to the day, Pam was driving the Hendersons' borrowed Saab towards Modesto, with the window open in the heat, listening to the same song on a tape deck. Jeff and Sally had a box full of '60s songs on cassettes. Rolling over the slow hills from Walnut Creek down to San Leandro on 680, she had selected, reaching into the box, choosing by feel, first the Lovin' Spoonfuls' album *Do You Believe in Magic* and then a miscellaneous tape with Joey Dee's '62 hit, "Peppermint Twist," and in succession, the Crickets' "Maybe Baby," The Cryan Shames' "Sugar and Spice," Desmond Decker and the Aces' "Israelites," Tommy Jones and the Shondels' "Mirage" and the Chiffons' "Sweet Talkin' Guy."

From San Leandro, full of nostalgia, she took 580 over the Altamont Pass toward Tracy, bopping to the early '60s hits of Brenda Lee (ah "Sweet Nothings") and Dion (oh "Runaround Sue"). From Tracy on, the car vibrated to the rhythms of the Monkees' *Headquarters* album, sides one and two, and two Animals' albums—*Animalism* and *The Best of the Animals*.

As the music rocked her along, the tires humming in the heat, the air sultry, she grew pensive, at times driving by feel. The hypnotic reel of telephone poles, the hawks hovering in the upper air currents, the monotonous stretch of fruit orchards detached her from her immediate surroundings, sending her back to her high school years, years now heavy with nostalgia.

A Herman's Hermits' song from 1964, "Something tells me I'm into something good," came up on a miscellaneous tape, followed by Percy Sledge's

"When a Man loves a Woman," and tears blurred her eyes like heat waves rising in the distance on hot pavement. She shook her head, feeling the tears rolling down her cheeks, not wiping them, letting them dry in salty tracks as the hot air rushed by.

In Modesto waited one of her students, Frank Peterson. In Spring semester, obviously infatuated with her, he'd given her two art works, one a lithograph entitled "The Screaming Woman" which, turned sideways, reminded her of a Giorgio DeChirico. In the sky floated multi-colored blocks hanging over a landscape of decaying sculptural remains.

She'd helped Frank struggle through his first semester of Italian by meeting with him twice a week during office hours. She knew he monopolized her time, and she would've resented it—there's nothing a TA likes better than free office hours—except for Mark's obvious emotional need. The sessions were less for Italian than for human contact. Frank, as she soon learned when the conversations turned personal, had no friends. He was contemplating dropping out of the university, having lasted one year only because of his art classes.

Pam found herself opening her own life as if Frank were an impersonal therapist. In class she treated him with studied impartiality, making sure no one glimpsed the special attention he was receiving outside of class, but in her office his openness, lack of guile, and intense sympathy made her feel that when she spoke of her past troubles he understood as only a co-conspirator could.

But, despite her help, Frank had received a D. She'd agonized over his grade for a week. He was just a few points below a C and she contemplated how easy it would be just to give him the higher grade. The TAs were each responsible for their own sections including final grades. So, as far as that went, she could give him an A and no one would know he hadn't deserved it. But, perhaps in reaction to her feelings of sympathy, she forced herself to be rigidly scrupulous. Frank had earned a D. He received one.

She didn't see him again after finals and wondered how he took the grade. Finally in late June she received a letter from his home in Modesto. He spoke little of the grade, merely saying he knew he deserved it, and going on to say that he'd decided not to continue at the university. He made it clear that the decision had nothing to do with her class. "Your course was the only good thing that happened to me all year," he said. "Without it, I wouldn't have made it through the term. I enjoyed my painting classes but no one made me feel like a person except you."

The purpose of the letter was to invite her to visit him at his folks' place some weekend. Though hesitant, not wanting to get further involved, never having felt a romantic or sexual attachment, unsure of Frank's intentions, she wrote a letter of acceptance and set the date for the second week in July. Now, pulling in to Modesto, fresh doubt assailed her. Was this a wise thing to do? She pulled to the side of the road, saw a Dairy Queen, a block off the main drag, and drove down.

Eating a thick strawberry shake with a long, red plastic spoon, she rehashed the possibilities for the weekend. In her current emotional state none seemed particularly inviting. Frank was a former student, probably five years younger, an immature romantic, carried away by a youthful infatuation. She didn't want to deal with that outside the confined boundaries of the academic situation.

Calling herself a fool for coming this far, for ever agreeing to the visit, she drove until she found a phone booth. In the booth, sweating in the heat, she deposited a dime and dialed Frank's number.

Frank answered on the eighth ring. "Sorry," he said. "I was out cutting the back lawn. My folks are out shopping."

She got right to the point. "I called to apologize. I won't be able to make it this weekend." She paused, sensing his disappointment. He was silent. What next? She knew that was inadequate, yet in her panic she hadn't thought of an appropriate excuse.

"What about next week?"

"Frank, to be honest, I don't think I can make it this summer." She rushed on. "If you're ever in Berkeley, give me a ring and we can have lunch together."

She stopped, hoping he wouldn't ask why, wouldn't continue to suggest alternatives, wouldn't cry. As if this were the melodramatic end to a romance. But he didn't.

"Well," he said, "sorry you won't get to see Modesto. Perhaps some other time."

She smiled. He thought she was calling from Berkeley. "If I ever get out there, I'll give you a ring. I want to thank you again for the paintings. I appreciated the gift."

"It was a good class."

"Yes. It was ... Well, I'll be running."

"Yeah. And ..." He paused. Her heart jumped. Please no maudlin declaration of love. "Good luck."

"Thanks," she said, more for what he hadn't said than for what he did.

On the long drive home, Pam no longer saw the scenery, no longer played the tapes. The music accompanying her now was the melancholic hum of the tires, the buffeting of the wind through the open window, the memories of simpler times.

Her grandparents, now dead, were with her often, brought back by a subtle smell or a faint sound. On days her grandmother baking cookies, her kitchen smelled of cloves and nutmeg, of cracked walnuts and honey. If she was making soup, it would be thyme; if meatloaf, sage; if baked chicken, rosemary; if pasta, basil; if pizza, oregano. Her grandmother had loved spices. Her cupboard was always full of teas—not just chamomile, but goldenseal, mullein, hibiscus, and skullcaps.

To counter her malaise, Pam began a daily exercise routine, jogging around the campus and occasionally up Strawberry Creek Canyon as far as Lawrence Hall of Science and back. Vera Lovati, who might have jogged with her, had returned to Canada for good, so Pam went out by herself. Jogging fulfilled both physical and mental needs. While Artie had always been athletic, Pam, though on the thin side, had developed fat thighs and buttocks. Her running didn't seem to lessen the bulk around her hips, but the weight turned from fat to muscle. Her lungs, always weak, became stronger. She felt good about herself.

Every now and then that summer, Pam would wake up in the night sweating waves of humiliation. Humiliation, at times, from way back. From years ago in high school. And then more recent events. She remembered her Master's exams and how she'd referred three or four times to Montale's poem as "Non chiedèrmi la parola." Finally, after her fourth time, Professor Daniele, unable to take it any longer, had corrected her. "It's 'Non chièdermi la parola," he said, and of course he was right. It was one of those stupid errors. She always said "chièdere" so why not "chièdermi"? Adding the direct object pronoun wouldn't change the pronunciation of the verb. She'd emphasized the wrong syllable.

Waking up with the scene in her mind, she could still feel the tightness in her jaws, the tension in her head and neck. Even her palms were sweaty. Despite her publications and other achievements (perhaps, as a perfectionist, because of them), the seeds of humiliation once sown came back as full sheaves. And what a bountiful harvest.

Things, it seemed, were coming to an end. But to what end? Was it what she'd always shot for? Or had someone changed the target on her? Were things not what they seemed after all? Things. Why was life just a succession of things? What was the driving force behind her activities? What tied them together?

Her life seemed a succession of events, like a train with countless box cars. Only someone had released the brakes, had cut the pressure, had set each car adrift, rolling alone, isolated from the rest, all on the track, but going where?

# chapter 24

One day Dashi lingered over his tea longer than usual so Artie figured he had another lesson to impart and when a free moment came sat down opposite him unbidden. When Artie didn't say a word, a smile flickered over Dashi's features.

"How's your third eye been doing lately?"

Artie sat back in his chair, the hard wooden ribs doweling his back. "My third eye? It hasn't seen much action lately. No dark caverns to explore." He laughed, assuming Dashi would catch the metaphor. "No nookie," he elaborated in a whisper.

"Beg pardon?"

"You asked about my pecker, right?"

Dashi looked truly startled. "You call that your third eye?"

"What are you talking about then?" A light flush hazed Artie's cheeks. He'd thought Dashi, for once, had descended to the common but apparently he'd been mistaken.

It took Dashi a minute to speak and when he did it was as a teacher chastening his pupil's failure to read the lesson at home. "Your third eye," he retorted, "is the eye in the middle of your forehead. The eye of Shiva. For you scientific Westerners the pineal gland."

Artie tried to make a joke of it. "I wouldn't know a pineal from a pituitary. So, what's it do?"

"Yours does nothing."

Just like Dashi to be aloof and superior.

"And yours, pray tell?"

"With training the third eye sees thoughts. You become a witness. An outsider." Dashi spoke with a pause between each phrase. "You empower the imagination. The imagination becomes real. It has a life of its own. What you imagine will be. Imagination and actualization become one and the same.

Dreams become reality. You will observe your own life as a psychodrama. You will be a witness to yourself playing a part in life. There is much more one could say." Having said so, he fell silent, waiting perhaps to see if Artie was ready for more.

Artie, as always, was a willing if sometimes mocking pupil. "Okay, enlightened master, elucidate."

"No questions?"

"You want questions?"

"Only if you have them."

"So, where's this third eye again?"

"In the middle of the forehead, between the eyebrows. If you close your eyes and look to the middle, your eyes will stop when they find the third eye. It is like a magnet. It feeds on attention. It is starved for attention.

Artie shut his eyes and moved them toward a point in the middle. "Okay," he said. "They've locked on a spot. Is that it?"

"When it is difficult to move, then you have found it."

Artie opened his eyes. "So, what do you do when you find it?"

"Many things are possible."

"Like?"

"If you are focused in the third eye, you are able to feel the essence of breathing, of air itself. The life force in air. Now, you think you feel the breath when you breath in and out, but you feel only the vehicle, not the essence. If you are correctly focused, you feel the prana, the energy."

"I was at a health seminar recently where a naprapath talked about some people who claim they can live off the energy just in the air."

Dashi nodded. "Some can live in a state of Samadhi—merged in cosmic consciousness—and draw energy, draw prana, from any substance. They can live even without air."

Artie snorted. "Yeah, but for how long?"

"For a long time. Many years even."

"So, is that it for the third eye?"

"Not at all, but I tell you only one more thing and then you go back to work."

"Sounds fair," Artie said. "Shoot away."

Dashi looked Artie in the eyes. "Death," he said.

Artie didn't flinch. "So what?"

"You can control death. If, when focused on the third eye you can fall asleep and maintain awareness, you will understand and experience death and no longer fear it."

Artie nodded. "Out of body travel," he said. "Astral projection. It almost happened to me as a kid." When Dashi didn't respond, he decided to tell the story. "I was lying in bed one night, trying to go to sleep, counting sheep and so forth. At a certain point, I started saying my name over and over again until it lost meaning and suddenly I felt like my body was falling asleep and I was floating out of it. I was so frightened at the thought that I jerked myself awake. I've never been able to let go since."

"Perhaps you were closer then than you are now. It came naturally. Effortless. Now perhaps you try too hard."

"I don't know that I'm really trying even now. But you got any last minute words on death?"

"I said you can control death but I meant more than just understanding it and accepting its inevitability. You can choose not only when to die but who you will be in the new life. A master of life and death."

"So who you coming back as?" Artie said, laughing and rising. "My grand-kid?"

Dashi's face gave no sign that he thought the idea worth joking about. "Who would you come back as?" he asked.

Artie paused, thinking. "I think I'd like to be a ..." He lifted his eyes, trying to visualize a life. Dashi stared at him, waiting. Artie's mind ran through a host of careers, personality types, both sexes even. "Shit," he finally said. "I don't rightly admire anybody, except unpretentious people. So, who can I be? I know. I'll come back as me! How's that? I'll live my own life over again. Maybe I can do it better the second time."

But if he came back a second time as himself could he avoid any of the *endearing* episodes of childhood? Those oh so *pleasant* days?

When he told Cheryl about his dad, she marked him as anal-retentive. "He was toilet-training you in his own original way," she said. "Instilling his values in you."

"Only I rebelled, thank God." He paused. "I should tell you I don't believe in him."

"Your dad?"

"No, God. You know, *In Elohim We Trust. Allah bless America. One nation under Zeus. Or is it under Marduk?*"

Cheryl laughed. "What your dad was doing was trying to regulate pleasurable activities. You saw him as the authority figure—like the God you don't believe in."

"He was an authority. On everything. He always talked about gumption, you know, doing things on one's own, but then he'd restrict us kids so much we were afraid to cross the street without asking permission."

"You mentioned that you'd rebelled against your father by feeling free with money, but I see a lot of controlled behavior in you too."

"Oh God," Artie moaned. "Control! Here we go with my favorite word!"

"Well, you are a neatnic, right?"

"Not really."

"You're so organized. All your lists. You budget all your time, if not your money."

"Actually I even budget my money." He grinned. "I just make sure I budget plenty for pleasure." He reached over and put his arm behind her neck. "And talking about pleasure, Miss Psychiatrist, how about telling me, if I may imitate the favorite expression of my former co-op colleague Walt, why I like oral sex so much. Is that some fixation?"

"Now that's a good question," she said, laughing. "How about we go fixate some and see if we can't answer it."

That summer his headaches turned to migraines. Was it the bright Chicago sun on the water of Lake Michigan? Was it stress? Was the café too much? Had the migraines begun before Cheryl left?

Cheryl told him her plans for the first time one hot evening in August after they'd exhausted themselves making love in Artie's apartment. Limp, polka-dotted with beads of sweat, he listened numbly while she told him of being accepted into Columbia University. She would begin a graduate program in the fall, working for a degree in developmental psychology.

He tried to accept the necessity of her leaving. He even discussed the benefits of studying in New York. And yet, it was hard not to show that it hurt. "You can come visit me as often as you want," she said, "and I'll be coming back during vacations to see my folks. We'll get together and still enjoy each other."

Later, alone, he asked himself why all the women he liked wound up going for their Ph.D.s? The question, flitting into his mind haphazardly, gave him a jolt upon reflection. He'd automatically included Pam in the list of women he "loved." But why not? He'd loved her once. He still loved her really. You can love a person and not like some of the things the person does. He was well aware that he was as much to blame as Pam. Maybe even more to blame? He often felt that way but tried to tell himself it was just another guilt trip. His running off was just a small part of a whole. Oh hell, he usually concluded, I was a bastard.

That night Artie sat down to write a letter to Pam. In it, he reminded her of a night they'd spent together in Taxco in the spring of '68. A windy night, late, streets deserted, no hotel in sight. They'd gone into a train station—not a soul there—forced their way into a locked waiting room.

Neither could find the light switch. They felt their way to a long leather-covered couch. There, Pam on top of Artie, they proceeded to make love in rhythm with the wind rattling the casement window at the far end of the room.

In the middle of their passion, they heard the double doors swing open and a thin shaft of light streaked in behind the body of a little girl standing in the doorway, staring into the darkness, light-blinded. They watched her slap the walls but fail, like Artie and Pam earlier, to find the light switch. Looking behind her the girl scurried into the room and squatted in the shaft of light.

Neither one said a word. Artie was still hard, Pam wet. He thought of a joke he'd heard once. Love will keep us together, forever. Gee, I don't know if I can keep an erection that long.

They watched while the girl began to pee on the floor. When she finished, she ran back to the doors, pulled them shut, and disappeared from sight, leaving a puddle of urine trickling along the cracked marble of the floor.

Afraid a parent might show up, they stopped short of climax and left the station, huddling the rest of the night near the shafts of a water tower.

In the letter, Artie hinted that he still dreamed of that night and still desired to finish what they'd left unfinished, despite all the times of making love afterwards. Being away from Pam was an interruption that never should've happened. And though he was responsible for the break, he'd been, in effect, a child himself. A child who stained a marble floor by peeing on it, who did so perhaps even maliciously, but who was answering to a real need at the time.

It was a stupid parallel, he realized—what am I saying? That now I can control my bladder?—but perhaps at worst she would laugh when reading his letter, easing some of her bitterness, remembering a moment only they had shared.

That night he made a decision. Things could not go on as they were. He would go visit her. Not right away. His job was not that elastic and, at any rate, the way would have to be prepared. It wouldn't do to go to Berkeley and be rejected before he could say anything. He would have to write again, and more seriously now.

Determination. Will. That's what it would take. Strength of purpose. Be like the sparrow who tried to drink up the ocean to retrieve her eggs. Dashi had mentioned that once. Desire. One has to desire something so much that one dares the impossible. Only then, in Dashi's words, would Garuda, the avian transporter of Visnu, come to one's aid.

# chapter 25

Pam had been troubled all day. She welcomed her classes as moments of respite, moments when her mind was too focused to think, when her emotions were too restrained to allow for extraneous impulses. In between classes the situation was different. In the student cafeteria, she ate a hot lunch without tasting it. She'd left Artie's letter at home and all through her meal, while her mind ran over it, she wished she had it before her. It was so jumbled with thoughts and emotions that her own were now equally confused. Perhaps with the letter in front of her again she could straighten them out.

But at home her hopes were deluded. She read the letter twice more and still wasn't sure of her feelings. How did she feel? It was a question she hadn't asked herself in a long time.

A week later Pam telephoned and invited Artie to come visit.

In October he transported a drive-away car from Chicago to San Francisco and stayed in Berkeley for five days. Pam was teaching four days a week but their evenings were free and they spent all day Tuesday together.

Before Artie's arrival, Pam had agonized over where he would stay. Neither had discussed the matter. She knew she could get in touch with one of the guys in the department and find Artie a room where he could sleep for free, or, if he didn't mind paying, there were hotels. The Carleton wasn't far away. And of course there was room in her place. But wouldn't that be awkward?

When he arrived—actually he was sitting on her front doorstep waiting for her when she returned from classes—with his big grin, she was genuinely happy to see him. The first glimpse even took her breath away for a second, although as she told herself perhaps it was only the shock of seeing him unexpectedly.

They talked a mile a minute the rest of the day and when night came—Pam had fixed a meal while Artie helped set the table and did the dishes—it seemed only natural to let him stay all night. There was nothing terribly awkward about it. She simply said, "You can sleep on the couch," and Artie said "fine."

Following the first night in, it seemed they walked all week. They walked out to Albany to see an old French movie at the Rialto. They walked from Pam's apartment down to Shattuck and all the way north as far as Solano. One evening they made a complete circuit—from Shattuck to Solano, down to San Pablo Avenue, and back to University Street where they headed up to campus—in all over five miles. Most of the time they talked; sometimes they walked in silence, Pam's arm through his. Once they'd even argued—and both were happy afterwards!

"We still know how to do that," Artie said. "Only ..."

"Only we know when to stop," Pam concluded.

"Maybe that's it. We know ..."

"We know what?"

"That's a good question."

"What's a good question?" She was ricocheting her questions off his and when he said, "Who knows?" they both laughed. It was fun to get carried away, to feel free to be absurd and zany. Even to talk nonsense. Artie was so lost in thought, and abstracted at times, that he talked backwards, mixed words, transposed vowels and consonants.

"You should've been a Latin poet," she joked after one particularly garbled comment.

"I feel a little archaic all right," Artie admitted. "Or is it senile?"

It was also good, though it bothered both, to talk about relationships. Artie told her about his entanglements and she told him about hers.

"Being in harmony with oneself is what really matters," Pam said at one point. "That's the quintessential condition of a good relationship."

"Are you in harmony?"

Pam sat on the sofa facing Artie, her legs thrown over his. The only light in the room was a lamp behind Artie. It framed his hair, which had grown longer and wilder. She liked it.

"Outwardly, I probably seem to be," she said. "I've tried to develop stable relationships. I've developed a lot of women friends, which I like. Inwardly I don't know. I used to think it wasn't as important, that it didn't matter. I thought the inner state would automatically come to mirror the outer, in time."

"I'm not sure I ever feel in harmony," Artie said, his hand resting unconsciously on her knee. "I'm trying I guess. I'm learning more about myself all the time."

"You seem different to me."

"Do I? How?"

"You're more thoughtful."

He shrugged. "Maybe."

"You try to understand. You listen. You don't act so uptight."

"That's probably because you don't either."

She nodded. "I'm a lot happier with myself. For a long time I blamed you for everything that went bad in my life. I finally came to realize I was responsible for myself. That helped ease a lot of bitterness."

"I was pretty shitty," Artie conceded, a crooked grin creasing his face.

She didn't smile. "You had your reasons. I can be pretty bitchy sometimes."

"Can't we all?"

On Friday, the last day of his visit, Artie bought a small glass vase with two receptacles for single flowers and filled it with two pink rose buds. When Pam returned from her classes, she found the table set, with the roses in the centerpiece, and a bottle of chablis chilling in the refrigerator. Artie had prepared an elaborate lunch. For appetizers they had an antipasto plate accompanied by French bread and paté. Artie had walked over a mile to the Pig-By-The-Tail charcuterie for the ingredients. He'd also made a pot of split pea soup, thickening it with carrots, mushrooms, celery, and onions. Following the soup, he served a salad of red leaf lettuce, sprouts, garbanzo beans, and chopped parsley and for dessert a cheese and fruit plate.

"This was really sweet of you," Pam kept exclaiming. "Why didn't you ever do this before?"

"You wanted to cook. I was working nights a lot, too, remember? Plus I think in those days it was just assumed the wife cooked."

"Those days aren't that long ago."

"It seems like it," Artie said.

Pam thought he had tears in his eyes, but he left the table before she could tell for sure.

When Artie left that night by plane, they hadn't made love.

Following Artie's week-long visit in October, late autumn was singularly bare. The trees and shrubs, the clematis and bougainvillea continued to thrive as always. It was hard climatically to tell the seasons were changing, but the passing of fall semester and final's week were there to help say it was December.

During the weeks following Artie's visit, Pam found herself often in a questioning mood. She was full of queries and cross-examinations, although it all boiled down in the end to one question. How do I feel about Artie? She asked herself at least once a day it seemed. Most often the questions came after she'd finished her class plans and was reading in the evening. She would sit on the veranda on the second floor and watch the sun set out over the hills of San Francisco beyond the Golden Gate. The sunsets were magnificent.

So, she wondered again as night fell, how do I really feel? It was a question harder than any on her preliminary exams for the Ph.D. With study those questions were, if not easy, at least answerable. Sometimes she thought of Artie and the past would disappear. Try as she might she would find it impossible to evoke the first years of their marriage in Eugene. Was it a fatal amnesia? A hiding from the truth?

She thought of Artie at such times as a new person in her life. Someone she'd just met that fall. A pen pal who prepared his coming with a series of spring and summer letters. The visit had shown her a different Artie. And I suppose, she realized, he sees a different me. We've both changed. She played with an inflated rubber ball left on the veranda by the neighbor boy. Absentmindedly, she kicked it to the railing, watched it bounce back, and tapped it away again. Bouncing back and forth. Her mind performed the same routine.

Wouldn't it be just as hard, if not harder, to try and make it as a couple now? In the old days she'd been content to sacrifice herself, her goals, her ambition to his. But no longer. And he, at least, realized it, too. Realized it and, it seemed, accepted it as good and necessary. Perhaps it freed him in a subtle way as well. But someone would have to make some changes if they were ever to get back together again. More than likely it would have to be Artie. He wasn't bound to Chicago by his job. His writing could be done anywhere (couldn't it?) and his jobs in support of his writing did not add up to a career.

She rose in the twilight—the sun had gone down, the sky was bluing behind her, the hills darker than burnt amber—and walked to the railing overlooking the back lawn, the parking lot and a huge hedge. The streetlight in the alley beyond cast a ghostly pall over the cars in the lot. Disembodied cocoons they seemed, empty and dead.

She was surprised to feel tears in her eyes. She hadn't been thinking sad thoughts, had felt no melancholic forewarning. Was it better, then, to ... ?

The question stopped as soon as it started. She wasn't sure what she was going to ask. Was she going to ask if it would be better to forget Artie once and for all? To let the past recede, decay, like an empty cocoon? Or might one imagine a seed implanted in that shell? A worm but one destined to become a butterfly. A line of Dante's came to her mind. "... Noi siam vermi / nati a formar l'angelica farfalla." We are worms, born to form the angelic butterfly. Were moths born from cocoons, she wondered, like butterflies? Perhaps their love would breed a moth, a creature who, once born, would seek light and, finding it in fire, consume itself.

"Our love." Turning to go in, she examined the expression she'd used as if it were a word she'd never used before. Do I have any right to use it now? she wondered. It was another one of those questions asked only to raise others. Benumbed by the failure to answer she shut her mind to her feelings and decided if she was going to get any work done that year she would have to forget Artie.

But Artie, out of the blue, telephoned in March with an invitation. She'd just started a load of wash in the basement when she heard the phone ringing upstairs. She answered it breathless, afraid whoever was calling would hang up the second she lifted the phone. She didn't feel like running up two flights of stairs just to hear a click of disconnection.

"Is that you, Pam?" The line had a long-distance hum. She nodded, gasping for breath. "It's me, Artie. Just a second. Let me ..." Another gasp. "Catch my breath."

When she recovered, he sprung a question on her which left her, though breath intact, speechless for a moment. "How would I like to spend a week in Jamaica? Why do you ask?" She felt stupid, playing dumb at the same time her heart was thumping. Obviously he wanted her to go with him.

Artie rushed on, not waiting for a proper response, telling her if she'd pay for her way to and from Chicago he'd pay for the round trip to Jamaica and cover the expenses for the entire week.

"We wouldn't have to wait until summer. We could go during your spring break.

She hesitated and he sensed that it was because of the money. "I only volunteer to pay because I know the trip to Chicago and back is bad enough and your TA salary can't cover much more. Some day when you're richer"—here there was a dry chuckle—"you can return the favor."

"I thought you were barely able to make it," she protested, realizing as she did that the statement was a tacit acceptance of the offer.

"My mother got a settlement on an old insurance claim and sent each of us kids two thousand dollars. I need a vacation and I don't think I can get through another cold spring here without one."

"Is it still cold?" she asked.

"Is it cold! Winter doesn't end here in February. Wait till you step off the plane."

"But I haven't said whether or not I can go."

"Well, can you?"

"I suppose." Really, no use playing a childish game of hard to get. "It does sound like fun. At least coming to Chicago first, I'll get a taste of cold so I can appreciate the sun. But have you made plans?"

"I talked to a travel agent in Evanston. There's a package deal we could get—not really a tour—but we'd have to stay in Negril the whole time. The airfare's tied up with the accommodations."

"I don't know anything about Negril, but any place is fine with me. Have you picked the days?"

"You're free toward the end of March, right?"

"Uh huh. I've got a friend who could cover for me for a few days. Our break isn't long enough."

And so it was set. She found that the vacation, something to look forward to, was an effective smotherer of questions and doubts. Instead of pondering where her true feelings lay, she fantasized an idyllic week of utter relaxation. Instead of asking, is it worth it to start the struggle over again? she visualized a white sand beach, turquoise water, tanned skin. Instead of tiring herself with endless questions, she calmed herself with daydreams and awoke from reveries excited at what lay ahead.

When school finally let out for spring break, she packed her beige suitcase and caught a flight to Chicago. Unmindful of the weather, taking only a coat for the chill, she wore a light spring dress, feeling vain since she preferred jeans, but wanting to strike Artie with her chic appearance. Besides, she thought, I need one good dress if we go out to any clubs, and in Jamaica I'll want a light one. She'd only packed three shirts, two cutoffs, and a swimsuit. For the latter, she selected an iridescent, blue two-piece which tied behind the neck and back. She'd made it herself. In Berkeley she rarely wore it. When she swan in the university pool, she wore a one-piece suit so she didn't have to worry about the top coming loose when she did her usual backstroke.

Stepping from the plane into the movable loading platform, she was shocked by the change in temperature. It was like stepping from a sun porch into a freezer. Incredible, she thought. I thought I'd felt cold in Oregon, but the high twenties would feel like summer next to this. In the car to Artie's apartment—she would have a one day visit before their Jamaica flight—she chattered and shivered, unable, despite the heater, to stop her insides from shaking. She wasn't sure how many of the barely suppressed quivers were from the cold and how many from excitement and, yes, tension.

But Artie put her at ease as soon as they left O'Hare and got off the freeway on to Touhy Avenue where he could direct his attention from the traffic to her. "You should've seen the heads turn when you walked into the waiting room."

Her smile, her cheeks, her hair—she knew he'd always loved her looks. When he leaned over at a stop light and kissed her, she didn't draw away.

Here I was worried about being intimate, wondering how and when the first kiss would occur, and it's happened just right.

"Nice to see you," she said, as they sped along a dark stretch through the forest preserves. She could see a grin light up his face.

"Nice to see you, too."

Both were pleasantly surprised by Negril. Unlike Montego Bay, which seemed full of slums—but then their bus had left the main highway, following a torturous route past hulking wrecks, to find gas—Negril was a necklace of pearls. The sand was as white as the beach in Pam's fantasies, the water just as variegated with its hues of turquoise, blue, and bath-water green. Their cabin, she was happy to see, was located along one of the nicest beach fronts. Pam knew they were sharing a room, but a room with two double beds.

Soon after they entered the room and plopped down their suitcases, one on each bed, Artie suggested they take a quick swim to freshen up from the long ride. Before she could say anything, he went on hurriedly. "I think, to make things easier, that we might as well just forget modesty while we're here."

She stared at him, standing at the foot of the bed, while he arranged his toiletries on a nightstand.

"Half the beaches are nude anyway," he said, "and we've seen each other nude"—here she gave him a look with her arms on her hips, her head bent to the side—"so I think it'll be easier if we just act natural."

She didn't say anything.

"I don't care," he said then. "Dress in the bathroom if you want. Will it upset you if I walk around nude?"

"I didn't say I wanted to dress in the bathroom."

Artie looked at her and started to speak but changed his mind.

The first night, unfamiliar with the town which stretched, it seemed, in a thin line along the beach, they walked in pitch blackness to the first lighted restaurant they could find. "Evan's Native Food" the sign said.

"The travel brochure said don't call them 'natives,'" Artie noted. "So that's what the first sign we see says!"

"You positive you want to eat here?"

"Why not? We haven't seen anything else and I don't know about going on in the dark. This is fine for tonight."

"It's in a shed," she said, but inside they went.

As soon as they were seated, Evan himself greeted them, shook hands, and then disappeared behind a curtain into what was obviously the kitchen. The waiter, introducing himself as Lamonte, sat down facing the back of a chair and enumerated the menu choices. Artie chose the fish and Pam the chicken. Goat meat was the other option.

Contrary to their expectations, the food was good and the portion hearty. Eating in an open shack—neither could think of a more appropriate term— with insects buzzing about, with the heat still lingering, with the restaurant empty at that hour, was not as terrible as it might seem. True, both ate in silence, Artie polishing off a bottle of Red Star beer, while Pam drank water, both finishing in less than a half hour. They asked a few questions of Lamonte, who'd told them jokes while they were eating, left a tip for the service and then walked along the beach back to the cabins. Both were too tired for any romantic interludes. They fell asleep as soon as their tired heads hit their respective beds.

# chapter 26

Jamaica—a broad, low sky, morning clouds fanning out like sun beams from a spot on the horizon. In the afternoon came thicker and blacker clouds, sweeping from behind the hills, from inland, out over the ocean. The water deepened in color. The waves seemed to break with a more ominous sound. Rain fell, hot and heavy. The road steamed at first and then was calmed as puddles crept over it, mirroring the sky where thin shafts of sunlight slit through the rifts in the clouds.

When the clouds passed, the air was heavy and moist, the humidity so high, they stayed either in the ocean or in their air-conditioned room. Outside the cabin, the tropical vegetation shone. The grass matted roofs of the bungalows and the outdoor restaurant dripped water at the edges, while the flagstones collected small puddles of water in the rougher areas.

Two days into the vacation, Artie was surprised to learn that the room next to theirs was occupied by two women who lived in Rogers Park and had frequented Trab's café. Lois was a short stocky woman, an accountant for a law firm in the Loop, and Janice was a stockbroker. She looked younger than Lois.

Janice still had a high school freshness to her features. Her blonde hair fell to her shoulders in soft strands that blew around her face in the lightest breeze, and her cheeks had a chubby rosiness to them that recalled budding apples and bees. The image was not Artie's but Pam's. Janice, she said, was "la semplicetta Silvia" of Tasso's *Aminta*. The naive young girl tricked into kissing Aminta by the faked bee sting on the lips.

Lois, instead, came across as a self-assured executive. She had kinky black hair framing her face in an oval of ringlets. Her nose was pug, her eyebrows heavy, a thin black mustache covered her upper lip, and she was wearing braces. While Pam noticed her facial features, Artie, she assumed, noticed the body. Lois was what Pam's high school chums would've called "stacked" and had a big butt to match.

---

Pam fought an impulse to link her arm through Artie's when they stopped to chat with the two. In her earlier years, she realized, she would've latched on to him. She would've let the outsiders know he was taken. That he was hers. Hands off. Now, she forced herself a bit to the other extreme, inviting the two to join them for breakfast. She was glad when they both chimed in with the news that they'd already eaten.

"You guys should go out on the beach to get breakfast," Lois said. "It's a lot cheaper than at the restaurant here."

"What's there to eat?" Artie asked.

"There's excellent banana bread," Janice said, unselfconsciously patting her bottom to remove some sand. That, Pam thought, was something I could never do without feeling self-conscious. "And fresh-squeezed orange juice," Lois added, bouncing her—excuse the expression but it came to Pam's mind— "jugs."

When the two women left, Pam said, "Let's just eat in the restaurant."

"Why not try the beach? We can always eat here another day. It'll leave us more money for dinner."

To herself, Pam chalked up another lesson: spend your own money, make your own decisions. Spend someone else's money, live by theirs.

The second encounter with Lois and Janice occurred late that afternoon. Pam and Artie had lotioned up and were stretched on chaise longues to catch the declining sun. The two women stopped to chat and after five or so minutes of shared experiences, Janice excused herself to go shower. Lois stood at the foot of Artie's lawn chair and shifted her weight from one foot to the other as she talked. Her arms were never stilled, resting either akimbo, or at her sides, or waving before her. She wore a one-piece brown suit with lace netting covering the stomach and back. Pam could see her black pubic hair pushing outside the crotch, pinched between the suit and her fat thighs.

"Did you guys know they got great ganja cake here?" Lois said. "I bought a big piece from a woman up on the hill. I can't wait to try it." She rattled on, not giving either of them a chance to respond. "Why don't you guys stop by tonight and we can smoke some grass and share the cake?"

To their noncommittal shrugs she replied, "Great, we'll knock for you. You know, if you unlatch that connecting door in the corner and we do the same, we have a walk through. It's like a big suite." And off she flounced.

"Did you see her crotch?" Pam couldn't keep from asking.

Artie looked up from a paperback. "What'd you want her to do? Shave? Like she should've done for her mustache." He laughed.

"Funny," she said sarcastically. So obviously he'd noticed.

The women invited themselves in that night around ten o'clock. Artie and Pam were on their respective beds reading. Lois, in bikini pants and T-shirt, sat on the end of Artie's bed and Janice, in a pair of white jogging shorts and a blue blouse, took the chaise longue in the corner.

"Can I use your book?" Lois asked.

"Sure," Artie said.

She opened it and laid a bag of grass in the seam. "Where's the roller, Janice?"

"Oh sorry. Left it in the room. I'll get it."

"Here," Artie said. "I'll roll one while she's getting the roller."

Lois handed him a cigarette paper and he leaned forward, toward her, to pick up the grass, their heads almost touching. Pam, impolitely, continued to read. Out of the corner of her eye she saw Lois uncross her legs, her arms resting on her knees as she hunched over the roller. Soon, they had four joints rolled.

Lois lit one, took a lungful and offered the joint to Artie. He motioned to Pam. She hesitated, aware that she could easily be thought the left-out martyr if she refused. "After you," she said. She gave in, she told herself, not only out of pressure. She'd smoked one other time in Berkeley with Jeff and Sally and hadn't gotten high. She really didn't have anything against people smoking if they felt like it. It just didn't do anything for her. But, she was willing to admit, perhaps Jamaican ganja would have an effect.

When they finished the second joint, Janice excused herself and went to bed. Artie got out a deck of cards and he, Pam and Lois began to play Hearts. As luck and Pam's inexperience would have it, she lost a game each to Artie and Lois.

Artie, she knew, was familiar with her angry outbursts at losing games—he'd regularly trounced her at Monopoly in their early years—so she said nothing, trying to mask her sullenness by asking Lois questions about her job. When Pam got up to go to the bathroom, she left the door ajar to hear what they were saying. She could hear Lois shifting on the bed. Probably spreading her legs, she thought, and then was angry at herself for feeling jealous and being so stupid.

The next morning, Artie watched the two women again as they sunned on the beach. Janice, he noticed, had round cheeks—they reminded him of hamburger buns—and a wide mouth. Her lips were full and country-fresh. She could have been a milk maiden in Victorian England. While not fat, her body had a fullness to it, a solidness of flesh and bones, her body well-defined, her calves shapely, her thighs firm, her waist not blubbery like Lois's, her breasts full but not to excess.

Lois, shorter and stockier, could have been one of those women who become a fire fighter or police officer. Or perhaps a jail guard in a woman's prison. A corrections officer. She affected a nervous restlessness as if to call attention to her energy. She was always referring to some activity she had planned for the next day. Artie and Pam wanted to relax; Lois wanted to cram everything into one week. Which was fine as far as Artie was concerned, as long as she didn't involve them in everything.

That morning, when they were invited to go horseback riding, he declined. When they were asked to share a fare for a reef tour, Pam turned thumbs down. At lunch, when Lois mentioned renting cycles … Wait. That was something that sounded okay. Just the day before Lois and Janice had rented bikes and toured the coast line north. On cycles, Lois noted, they could head inland and cover more territory.

Artie looked at Pam and they traded a glance of acquiescence. "Okay," Artie said. "Let's do it tomorrow early so we don't lose half the day."

"Great!" Lois said. "There's a place right next to us that has enough cycles. I'll go reserve four."

Pam sat up in her chair. "I've seen some of the cycles," she said. "I think one will be enough for Artie and me. I don't need one of my own. Ask for one of those Honda 100s for us."

"Don't you want your own?" Lois asked, implying it was the liberated way to go.

"Not really," Pam said. It had nothing to do with independence. "Just reserve one for us."

"Okay," Lois said. "If that's the way you want it."

Later in the week, Lois came up with yet another bit of news. She'd found a nude beach and was raving about how great it was to swim in the natural. "Everybody's so cool," she said. "It's great. You two guys'll have to go there with us. No one's got any hang-ups. When everyone's nude, you don't feel like everyone's staring at you."

Pam and Artie glanced at each other, looked back at Lois, and said nothing. Lois was glancing around the beach.

"Do you think anybody'd mind if we went topless here? Some of the Americans are pretty uptight."

"Probably the people with kids," Pam said.

"You think so?" Lois assumed a skeptical stance.

"Most people with a ten year old boy wouldn't be too happy seeing women walking around nude." She'd raised her voice, annoyance showing.

Artie recognized an undeclared hostility between the two women, unsure himself what caused it. Unless it was Lois's overt sexuality.

He spoke to ease the tension. "They'd rather have them catch glimpses of bosoms in Playboy."

"Or Penthouse," Lois said. "I can't stand those sexist mags. Talk about using women as objects. Out here it'd be natural." Again a moment of strained silence. She pulled her swimsuit away from her bottom and wiggled her body. "One bad thing," she joked, "I got sand up my butt."

Artie nodded and looked back at his book and Pam slid her sunglasses from the top of her head down over her eyes. She was flapping her sandals against her heels and Artie recognized the suppressed resentment.

"Well, see you," Lois said after a moment. She shuffled off, sliding her thongs over the flagstones of the walkway.

Artie, looking at Pam, caught her eye and shook his head. "Just our luck," he said, hoping to appease her.

"Well, you'd probably like to go."

Artie shrugged. "No big deal. I've seen nude bodies."

"Yeah, in sexist mags."

Artie grinned, recalling that they'd occasionally read Penthouse together prior to making love. "You're just upset because you're not big bosomed," he said.

"Doesn't bother me. Go look at tits if you want. I'm satisfied the way I am."

"I didn't say I wanted to look at tits. Yours are fine enough."

"Who said you could look at mine?"

He leaned over and pretended to straighten the strap of her two-piece. "Woops," he said, pulling the string out and revealing her nipple.

"Artie!" She slapped his hand. "Not in public, do you mind?"

"Just wanted to see if they were still there," he said.

* * *

375

Later that afternoon, after a snack of club sandwiches and beer at the outdoor restaurant, they went to their room to cool off. Artie slipped out of his trunks and lay facing her on his bed. She was lying face down, her head turned toward the far wall. He stroked himself absentmindedly, staring at the inviting pillows of her buttocks. A minute later, he sat on the edge of his bed, fully aroused. She wouldn't turn to look. He rose and stood above her.

"Like a massage?"

She shrugged her shoulders. Her hair, bleaching out in the sun, covered her face. She blew a breathing hole through the locks and lay still.

"I'll give you a freebie," he said, and straddled her, his knees on the bed, his penis hanging between her thighs. He moved towards her butt until there was a comfortable pressure on her vagina and then began to massage her head and neck, pulling her hair back into a pony tail. From her neck he moved to her shoulders and arms and untied the strings behind her neck and then moved to her back.

"You need some medicine on your back," he said. She had two spots of eczema below her shoulder blade. Recalling her skin allergies and his medicating her back, he wondered briefly who applied the Lidex for her now.

"The cream's on the dresser," she said. "Put some on."

At the dresser, shuffling through the vitamin bottles, chap and lip sticks, suntan lotion, deodorant, jewelry, and loose change, he saw in the mirror that she'd turned on her side and had removed her bikini pants. "Here it is," he said, turning, his penis swaying like a boom from side to side. "Fluocinonide," he read out loud, "a 21-acetate ester of fluocinolone acetonide, in a cream base of stearyl alcohol, polyethylene glycol 6000, propylene glycol, 1, 2, 6-hexanetriol and citric acid. Wow! My friend Dashi would love this!"

"Who's he?"

"An Indian guy. Into Zoroastrianism."

Having applied the cream, he replaced the tube and returned to the massage, kneading her back muscles and then her buttocks. He pondered running his hand under her but decided to finish the massage. No use antagonizing her with haste.

When he finished her buttocks and upper thighs, he slid off beside her and lifted her feet one at a time, rubbing the calf, putting pressure on the soles of her foot and then bouncing the leg toward her buttocks.

"Still don't touch, I see," he said.

"You're full of flattery today."

He bent and kissed her bottom. "Firmer though. You must be exercising."

"Jogging," she said. "I'm up to five miles three to four times a week."

"That's good," he said, remembering her reluctance to take part in any sports.

"Helps my breathing, too."

He made a noncommittal grunt and bounced her other leg signifying the end of the massage. Before she could move, however, he stretched out over her, his penis again in her crotch. She shifted, didn't reproach him, and he moved forward kissing her neck. She turned her head and he slid his chest off her back so he could kiss her on the lips. While they were kissing, he felt her buttocks rise and his penis slipped easily into her body, her vagina moist and hot. After a few thrusts, he settled down so as not to come too quickly. It was nice to be making love again.

She pulled her head away and he lifted himself with his arms to give her room to breathe.

"You're crushing me," she said.

"Want to get up on your knees?"

She nodded. He pulled back and she came to her knees, her face down, her hair a sheath around her.

"Lie on my back," she said.

"Your knees'll get tired."

"No they won't. I'll let you know if they do."

He leaned over, resting his face on her back.

"Grab my breasts," she said.

The instructing was new. Before, she'd never taken much initiative.

With one hand he cradled both breasts and reached back for her pussy. Her pubic hairs were drenched and he felt his balls soggy with her juices. Finding her clitoris, he began to rub his finger back and forth and she moaned with pleasure. The sound excited him. He stopped moving for a moment to rub the sides of her vaginal lips, stretched tight around his penis. "Don't stop," she said. "It felt good."

He moved back to her clit, trying to slow his thrusts. But she moved back into him and the pressure was too much. Unable to stop, past the point of release, he wrapped both arms around her thighs and pulled her to him, thrusting deep with each ejaculation. When he'd recovered, he kissed her back and said, "Sorry. I know I came too soon for you."

"It still felt good," she said. "Can you suck my tits while I masturbate?"

"You never came before, did you?" he said, and she shook her head.

"It was as much my fault as yours. I didn't let you know what I needed. I didn't know what an orgasm was like."

He lay beside her then and while she thrummed her clit he lapped, sucked, tweaked and tongued first one breast and then the other.

When she came, arching her back, he slipped into her a second time.

"Now we can make love slow," he said. "We had to wear away a little of that youthful excitement."

She smiled at him and nodded, and he saw the sweat beading her lips as it beaded his own.

That night, as they were again reading—on one bed now—the women next door knocked again. When Artie slid the bolt and swung the connecting door open, he was surprised to find the frightened face of Janice.

"Can you help Lois?"

"What's wrong?"

"She's sick."

"Let's see." Artie, glancing quickly at Pam, still on the bed, shrugged and stepped into the other room. "Where is she?"

"She's in the bathroom."

Artie followed Janice who stopped at the open door and pointed in. He stared around the edge, saw Lois squatting on the floor, her head over the open toilet bowl.

Lo how the mighty have fallen. "What's the matter?"

Lois stared at him, her eyes red with weeping. "I'm scared," she said.

He recognized the look. "Did you eat mushrooms?" Ever since they'd arrived, it seemed every kid they saw had tried to sell them mushrooms.

Lois shook her head.

"She ate that piece of ganja cake," Janice said. "She's really psyching out."

"Did you throw up?" Artie asked.

She nodded.

"Good. That'll get most of it out of your system but you've probably already digested some. It must be potent stuff."

"I've never been so scared in my life," Lois said, quivering, her hand slipping on the rim of the toilet bowl as she shifted her legs. "I've never been so high. My mind is going crazy."

There was a moment of silence and then Lois whimpered, "I'm afraid I won't come down. I just want to get back to normal."

By now Pam was at Artie's elbow.

"How you doing, Lois?"

Lois's response was to break out in shivers.

Artie stepped back out of sight behind the bathroom wall. He looked at Pam. "Want to take her out on a walk?" he whispered.

"Will it help?"

"She should be moving. Wear it off."

"Okay, I'll get my sandals on."

"Lois?" He stepped back into the doorway. Janice was leaning against the door jamb, staring.

Lois looked up.

"I think it'd be better for you if we all went on a walk. You need some movement. Something to help burn it out of your system."

"Have you ever been this high?"

"Sure. On LSD. Most of the time I felt like I'd never come down. But you do. Just a matter of time."

They stayed with Lois for the next three hours. The three of them took Lois out on the beach. It was pitch black, only stars and no moon in the sky. Along the bay, the white sand was a thin strip of cotton next to an expanse of obsidian sea. As they walked, small crabs shuttled quickly to their holes, and in the trees and savannah to their right birds were calling to each other.

Occasionally they passed a couple or a group going the opposite direction and the passers-by all stared at Lois. She was walking with her head down and kept shaking her wrists and hands as if to circulate the blood. "I'm losing feeling in my hands," she said, when Artie asked if the shaking helped. "My cheeks are numb. I can't even feel my tongue." And a minute later. "Am I making sense?"

Everybody assured her she was, despite having noticed a few creative slips of the tongue. "You're doing fine," Artie said. "It just takes time."

And time it did take. Unlike grass when smoked, the chemicals were deep in her digestive system and slow to be expelled. She drifted off to sleep in her own bed around two in the morning. Pam had also gone to bed, telling Artie to stay until Lois felt better. Lois seemed to trust him since he'd been high on acid and knew from experience what she was feeling.

Sitting on Janice's bed, with Janice leaning on a pillow at the headboard, he asked her is she was glad she didn't use pot.

"Well, I smoke it," she said, "but I know now I'll never eat any ganja cake. She drank three piña coladas this evening before eating the cake."

"No wonder she got sick. She would've gotten just as high but probably wouldn't have felt so bad to her stomach." Lois shifted on the bed, rolling on her side away from them. "Do you think we ought to cover her?" Artie asked. "This air-conditioning might chill her."

Lois had taken off her top when Pam left the room. She'd vomited down the front and didn't want to sleep in it. Artie had never seen breasts so immense—too much so, he thought—but the sight had aroused him despite his earlier love making with Pam.

After they covered Lois with the rough cotton quilt, Janice straightened, saw Artie's penis standing hard in his tight cutoffs and smiled. He saw too that she'd seen and grinned back, shrugging sheepishly. She seemed unembarrassed.

They stood, both hesitant, staring at each other.

"I love Pam, even though we're separated," he said, "but of all of you, you have the nicest body." He watched the color rise in her cheeks. "Don't mean to sound sexist," he said.

She laughed. "I don't mind. I'm glad you like it."

Artie made no move to leave. Janice stepped around the end of the bed. "Can I tell you something?"

"Sure."

She moved closer to him. "I've desired you ever since we've been here. You know why I left so early the other night?"

He shook his head. She was close now. He put both hands on her sides. She felt soft and warm, sensuous to the touch as if she wore no clothes.

"I left because I had to masturbate and didn't want Lois to know."

"Would you like to make love now?" Artie said. "It's not like adultery."

He felt foolish after he'd said it. What was it like? Could one just enjoy another person for the pure physical pleasure of the act? Without harming an emotional attachment to someone else?

Making love to Janice that night, Artie didn't have to go slow. Pam had taken off the edge. Afterwards, thinking again of Pam, asleep on the other side of the wall, he felt a lecher, full of shame, guilty of lust.

He knew where Pam, had she known, would have placed him in Dante's hell. Not with Paolo and Francesca among the *Lussuriosi* but much further down. In the ninth circle among the betrayers, the traitors to family.

* * *

So the vacation, meant to unite the two, was only partly successful. To Artie it proved he was still weak, still not to be trusted. That was the hardest blow. A sexual tryst in Chicago with Pam in Berkeley, with the two of them officially divorced, was fine. But, fresh from her arms and body, next door to her sleeping figure, that, he realized, despite numerous rationalizations, was not right. That only a fool would do.

For Pam, the vacation was also only a partial success. Unaware of Artie's liaison, she still found his behavior annoying at times. He seemed more vivacious with Lois and Janice than he was with her. When she accused him of this directly, veiling her pique with joking comments, he explained that that was just his social face. It meant nothing. With her he could be relaxed and natural. With others, he had to work to be sociable. She accepted, grudgingly, his excuse, an indirect compliment, but her conclusion, when he accused her of jealousy, was this: "The next time we take a vacation together, we'll go with two guys I know, and see how you like it. We'll see who's jealous then."

# chapter 27

Back in Berkeley, relaxed and renewed by the slow pace in Jamaica, Pam plunged again into work. She planned on taking her final set of qualifying exams for the Ph.D. in June of '76. To prepare herself she wanted three free months and so cut down on all extracurricular and social activities. She continued to teach one section of Italian, as required by her assistantship, but she signed up for Individual Study for Doctoral Students to avoid taking any other classes. This left her free for intensive reading and review.

She'd decided that her specialty would be the Renaissance and Early Baroque and thus chose for her required hundred and fifty year period the years from 1475 to 1625. By beginning with Lorenzo de' Medici's circle and the re-emergence of the vernacular in the late Quattrocento, she avoided the early years of Humanism, which she saw as a preparatory movement for the Renaissance, despite the fact that various strains of Humanism, as a cultural movement, ran throughout the fifteenth and sixteenth centuries. The price she paid for avoiding the Latin treatises of the Civic, Philosophical and Rhetorical Humanists was the necessity of extending her competence into the later

Mannerist and Baroque writers of the early seventeenth century. As regards Marino, she didn't mind. She found the *Adone* to be an eminently enjoyable mythological epic and felt that the centuries of negative criticism had been unjustly severe. True the Marinisti had carried the word games and wit to excess but the master was still deserving of praise.

For her generic specialty, she chose another underdog—the theater and in particular the tragedy of the sixteenth century. From Pam's point of view, the Italians, although lacking a Shakespeare or a Lope de Vega, had almost disgracefully misrepresented the importance of their theater.

Despite her immersion in study, she continued to respond to Artie's letters and occasionally, when a backlog of unanswered missives had built up, she picked up the telephone and chatted with him for a half hour or so.

The day before her qualifying exams for the Ph.D., she called Artie at the café. She could hear the hum and bustle of business in the background and knew from Artie's fast breathing that he was busy. "I tried to get you at home last night but no one answered," Pam said. She realized that sounded accusatory, but it was too late to rephrase it.

"I unplugged my phone." Artie said. "Too many calls. They've been driving me batty." He kicked himself. "Not your calls, though," he added quickly. "I didn't think you'd call until after your exam."

"Tomorrow morning I have my final orals," she said.

"How long's that?"

"Three hours. First my minor field and then the Italian material."

"I'd wish you good luck, except I know you don't need it." He didn't tell her but ever since he'd read *The Catcher in the Rye*, he'd never been able to wish anyone "good luck." Holden hated that, right?

"I hope I can sleep tonight," she said. "I'd take a tranquilizer, but I'm afraid it'd kill off a few needed brain cells!"

Artie laughed. "Wish I was there. We could do a few other things to put you to sleep."

She responded with a "hmm," waited a few seconds, and then said, "The only other thing I was going to mention was that I might go to Italy this summer."

"I was hoping we'd be able to see each other this summer."

"I told you before we went to Jamaica that I might go to Italy. You know that. I even told you you could go if you wanted."

"I do have a job."

"That's up to you then. Anyway, I'm not sure. I just wanted to mention the possibility again. I still haven't heard about the grant yet."

Pam had applied for a one-month scholarship to attend a class for Teachers of Italian Abroad at the University for Foreigners at Perugia. If she was accepted, she planned on traveling for a month before beginning the course.

"How's work going?" she asked, to break the silence on the line.

"Same as always, I guess. It's okay. I probably should be going. I know you'll do well tomorrow. I'll be thinking of you."

"Thanks. I'll do my best. Talk to you later."

The exam, like most, began inauspiciously. Professor Ida Svendson, whose protégé she was recognized to be, asked the first question. To Pam's irritation, Svendson, after all their discussions on the Renaissance, decided to focus on the concept of Humanism. The idea was one Pam had ignored on the whole, picking her specialization dates with care so as to avoid the early Humanists.

It was impossible, of course, to point out that the question dealt with material outside her specialty and was therefore unfair. Humanism, as a concept, could be ignored by no one who studied the Renaissance. Fortunately, Pam had recently read Ferguson's survey of scholarship on the period and was able to sound more learned than she actually was. In response to a string of five questions, she was able to come up with the names and ideas of various prominent critics. Though she tried not to show it, her face was tinged with a flush of anger.

When the questioning moved on to her specialty, she shone. Five professors grilled her and none was able to stump her. Finally, when it came time for Professor Spinoso, the medievalist, to ask his questions—he was the one she feared the most—merely said, "I think Ms. Walters has shown us she knows more about the period than some of us do. I have no questions myself."

With Pam waiting nervously outside the door, the committee discussed her responses. Pam expected the discussion to last the usual ten to fifteen minutes. It was said the faculty waited that long even if they had nothing to say. They wanted no one to leave with a swelled head, no one to think it had been simple, no one to assume he or she had passed with ease.

To Pam's relief, however, two minutes later the door opened and she was called in to a chorus of smiles. All six committee members shook her hand and offered congratulations.

"So I passed?" she said, raising her eyebrows.

"Was there any doubt?" Ida Svendson put in somewhat sarcastically.

---

Pam shrugged and grinned. "One never knows."

Professor Spinoso took her by the arm. "I bet you found my questions the hardest," he joked, not having made any.

She smiled and nodded. "They were the only ones I couldn't answer." Though having made the statement as a joke, she winced immediately, realizing the faculty might take that as a sign of pride. Spinoso himself, however, merely smiled in response.

In the hall, by herself finally, she laughed and clapped her hands. She felt like skipping. Done! Finally done! At least with exams. There was still the dissertation of course. But after this exam, that seemed a minor task, a formality. She already had a topic in mind.


Sure enough, Pam got the fellowship to study in Perugia. After agonizing about the matter for two days, Artie told her he wouldn't be able to go.

She flew into Milan, then took the train south.

From Terontola, where she changed to catch the train to Perugia, Pam shared her compartment with two professors of art history at Santa Barbara, a man and a woman, and with a young American student from Belgium. When she arrived at the Stazione Ferroviaria, the young man, introducing himself as Brad Richey, asked if she minded if he tagged along.

"Not at all," she said, recognizing his need for a translator and her own for company. She would've preferred to be there with Artie but she'd understood when he said he couldn't afford the trip. She'd resolved, despite being alone, to make the most of her time in Italy.

Together she and Brad went to the Tourist Office on Corso Vannucci, named after the famous Umbrian painter, better known as Perugino, teacher of Raphael, and from there Pam took charge, making two telephone calls to the recommended pensioni. It helped, she found, to refer to herself as a professor. After all, she did teach in a university.

Both Pam and Brad found a room in the same pensione, a modern but quaint building perched on the sloping Via della Canapina just outside the ancient city walls. The padrona, at first, said she had room only for "Lei, professoressa," speaking to Pam, but after Brad stammered out a few awkward questions, she seemed to soften. In fact, she would have a room opening July 3rd, if Brad wouldn't mind sleeping in a "camera brutta" for three nights. The "ugly room," however, was quite charming and Brad moved in at the same time as Pam.

Pam's room was in the back of the building, one level below the street passing in front. From her room, however, given the steepness of the hill, she looked out over the valley toward the unseen Lago di Trasimeno. What she could see, from her balcony, was a small garden, beyond that an infrequently traveled winding road, and then trees and, in the distance, haze-covered mountains.

The room itself was delightful. She had a large armadio and chest of drawers to her right, standing next to a slender three-tiered stand which she soon utilized for her purchases of food. To her left lay a narrow metal-spring bed, and next to it, sitting catty-corner in the room, was an immense desk, with three drawers on each side, and a brand new swivel lamp clamped to the back edge. The wall opposite the door consisted of two large windowed doors which led out to her balcony and a clothes line.

From the first, accompanied by Brad, she liked the city. The twisting medieval lanes, barely wide enough at times for little Fiat 500s, the vaults, the arches, the aqueduct, the old churches and houses, the medieval and Renaissance palaces, all were a pleasure.

And the food! She loved the pasta. Her first day in Perugia, she stopped at a small trattoria near the Via dei Priori and ordered tortellini alla panna. The pasta al forno, a simple lasagna-style dish, baked in the oven, was another favorite.

She made sure she didn't miss anything Artie had recommended.

In the middle of his list of places to visit, he hadn't been able to resist one cutting note. "I was supposed to be the Italian professor. You were going to teach high school."

"No, you were going to be an artist, and when you gave up on that, a writer."

"I'm talking about before I even met you, after my year in Pavia."

"We each made our own choices."

A quick flare-up, and he moved on sites she had to see.

The second day after she was settled, Brad left for Florence for a three-day visit, and she was left on her own. A situation she preferred. Brad, she knew, she would see enough of at the Università per Stranieri, despite taking different courses. She was with faculty, he was a beginning language student.

While he was friendly and handsome, a sandy-haired fellow of medium height with rosy German cheeks, she'd rapidly tired of his intellectual bent in conversation. He preferred to discuss Milton or Boccaccio, she preferred conversations dealing with restaurants, rosticcerias, trattorias, tavola caldas, sights to see, things to do.

Brad carried his scholarly ideas on his shoulders like a back pack. Pam left hers in the classroom or study. "I'm here as much for a vacation as for language work," she told him. "I'd just as soon skip classes if there were anything else to do." Brad, it seemed, took her pronouncements as heresy.

She was happy, when Brad returned, to be seen walking along the promenade with a tall, handsome fellow from her class for Teachers of Italian Abroad. She introduced him to Brad—he was an assistant professor at Princeton named Joe Besome—and all three sat outside at a sidewalk caffè along Corso Vannucci. Brad's twin brother was enrolled in Princeton so he and Joe talked of academic matters while Pam observed them in silence. She was sipping a Sambuca, drifting in and out of the conversation, as she watched the passing crowd.

Brad, over confident and abrasive (My God, the kid's only twenty), was telling Joe about a conflict he'd had with Joyce Carol Oates in a creative writing class. The way Brad told it he'd refused to buckle in to her demands, maintained a contentious relationship the whole quarter, and received a D from her. "She was a real bitch," he exclaimed, "I did as much work as everyone else, hell, I wrote a play, but she claimed I hadn't put enough effort into the course. She put me down a few times in front of the class, which I didn't appreciate. She thought I was stuck-up and that I felt I was better than the rest of the class." He paused, and then, with a smug look of superiority, informed both of them pointedly, "Of course, I was."

From his confrontation with feisty Ms. Oates, he moved on to other academic gossip, asking Joe which universities had the best Comp Lit programs and who was teaching where. Joe was up on all the avant-garde critical currents and knew where to find the structuralists, the deconstructionists, the left-over New Criticism theoreticians, the phenomenologists, the scholars working in Reader-Response criticism, the Marxists, the Neo-Positivists, the critics favoring a psychological approach, and a range of other critical types.

Brad, she saw, even though an undergrad, had a better grasp of the current scene than she did. At Berkeley, somehow, her teachers had never stressed critical theory. The students who took French received a healthy dose of modern critical thought but not those who limited themselves to Italian. It was ironic, she thought. Here she'd just finished her final qualifying exams for the Ph.D. and some smart-aleck sophomore from a fancy school in the East made her feel inferior.

The following weekend, Joe Besome took Pam to Gubbio for an afternoon excursion. He'd borrowed a beat-up Renault from an uncle who lived in

Torgiano, just outside Perugia, and asked two others in the class to join them.

The others, a cheerful Dutch fellow named Sandro, and Lien, a young woman from Switzerland, spoke English poorly so all four communicated in Italian. Again, Pam felt inferior. Most of the people in the class, these two included, seemed to speak better Italian than she did. Sandro was not even a teacher. He was studying medicine and took the class purely for interest as part of his summer vacation. He, like Joe, had relatives living in Umbria.

Lien was a dark-haired, angular woman in her late twenties. She was a smoker, the only one in the group, and asked, on the return trip, if she could sit in front by the window so the smoke wouldn't bother the rest. Pam was irritated. The smoke and Joe's fast driving on the winding mountain roads had given her a headache.

Joe seemed as attentive to Lien as he'd been to her. He was an attractive man, sure of himself, muscular, a smooth talker. The only thing she didn't like about him was his moustache. Lien was also fascinated by Joe, Pam could tell. Lien had ignored Sandro throughout the trip. Sandro, in his early twenties, was too boyish, both in looks, with his fuzzy tan hair and bright cheeks, and in mannerisms, with his over-exuberance, to take for too long at one sitting. He drove Pam batty pointing out all the sights. Lien, she could see, wearing a skirt, sat facing Joe with her legs spread. Pam had to laugh when she learned that Lien was rooming in a convent. That would slow her down. Of course, Joe had his own apartment, so maybe not.

During the next two weeks, Joe split his time between both women. Pam found out when she invited him to the Cinema M to see *Il Gattopardo*. Joe had blushed and informed her he was planning on going, but had invited Lien. She saw them there later. Other evenings, when he wasn't with her, she saw them walking down the Corso, eating gelati and laughing. When Joe was with her, he brought her ice cream also. Saronno di Amaretto was his favorite, and she liked nocciola. She marveled at his ability to spend time with both and never mix up what she told him about herself with something shared with Lien.

She couldn't do it herself. Sandro and Brad occasionally invited her out to lunch or dinner and she was always referring to something the other had told her. She would remind Brad that they'd tried pizza at the Medio Evo, only to learn he'd never been there. Later, she would remember that it had been with Joe or Sandro.

Finally, tired of Joe's equanimity and his failure to devote more time to her, she gave up on her romantic fantasies and avoided his company. She didn't care for Brad as much but she didn't have to share him. Sandro, apparently eager for variety, had passed on to others, running through two or three women, each lasting approximately three days. One afternoon, Pam had laughed with Lien about Sandro's predilections. He needed a new flavor every other day, as Lien put it.

With Brad, she didn't have to worry about her own emotions entangling her. She'd gotten involved emotionally with Joe before she realized it. Joe had remained impervious. It was just as well, she learned later, for he was married and had two children. From Brad, on the contrary, she felt detached. He was there, another soul to help pass the slow evenings, but he wasn't an object of desire.

As she sat thinking of Artie outside her room one Saturday night, overlooking the small garden and twisting Via Checchi Arturo, the flutter and glide of frenzied bats lent movement to a scene of stillness. From dark tree-greens below and tones of gray (the stone balcony, gravel path and faded highways beyond) her eyes rose to a lilting sky, first slow waves of lower viridian growth and then, above this, the gauzy haze of dusk against distant, sloping hills, the sky almost viola at the edge and then, coming back towards her, peach-fuzz pink, shading to light blue and, at the roof line, straight above, deepening to azure and ultramarine. And between the dark waves of the trees and viola of the sky, a line of streetlights extended out over the road on long, thin, praying mantis necks. Sporadically, a string of cars gutturaled up the road or rollercoasted down.

The scene brought tears to her eyes. It was beautiful but also lonely. The sky was not her sky, which hung crimson and gold over the evening horizon beyond the Golden Gate. Here, the sunset was smoother and less violent, reminding her of the lonely colors in Antonioni's *The Passenger*. In Berkeley, the sun slammed into the ocean like a rock in a paint pot, scattering the sky with intensity, with life. From the balcony of the pensione, she saw only silence and an occasional cat.

She moved back inside after an hour and sat at her desk, a box of Oro Saiwa biscotti close at hand, beyond them a small glass of Bianco dell'Umbria. She wrote a short letter to Artie and, when she finished, it was still only eight forty-five. She faced at least three more hours of solitude before sleep. Her desk was gradually acquiring a topography. A dictionary, a travel guide, two books, an alarm clock and a pack of envelopes grew like scattered outcroppings on a desert plain. Directly to her left, taped to the wall above the woven straw headboard of her bed, was a Communist party manifesto: "Una Vittoria delle Donne, una Vittoria Civile e Democratica." It celebrated the recent passage of the law permitting abortions and affirmed the PCI's support of women's rights. Next to the manifesto, less political, was a poster of Perugino's "Miracle of the Baby of Rieti," a painting which she'd just seen that day in the National Gallery of Umbria. The wry juxtaposition of the two posters had been unintentional. The Perugino print, a view of the countryside seen through the arch behind the miracle, had been on her wall throughout her stay. In a few weeks it would come down, along with the other posters she'd picked up at the tourist office. If she'd given way to her impulse, the posters would be rolled and packed by now, and she'd be heading home. But she still had days to fill. Empty walls would not help.

Getting up, she lowered the suspension shutter, cutting herself off from the outside, which was now uniformly black except for the string of street lights. The bats had had their hour. Or were they, blind to the light, still out there flying in the dark?

As the weeks passed, Pam grew slowly more despondent. She tried to analyze her mood. Maybe her depression was the aftereffect of her intense preparation for her final written and oral exams. That was as good an explanation as any. She found it hard now to motivate herself. Her dissertation research never got off the ground. She dozed through most of the course lectures.

She wrote to Artie nearly two or three times a week, but half the month passed before he received the first letter. When he replied, she had to tell him to stop writing because his letters would never arrive before her departure. She'd decided to leave Italy early, one week after her course ended. She would make a quick tour of a few cities she'd never visited before, Urbino, Ferrara, and Padua primarily, and then take the train back to Milan for her trip home. Since she'd be on the road, Artie's letters would never reach her. She did receive two more the last week in Perugia and that was it.

On the road, taking buses and trains, her loneliness increased. She met many vacationing Italians who were friendly but after a while their conversations were repetitive. She found herself using the same phrases to talk about herself with each new acquaintance.

When she was finally on the train heading north out of Florence, she settled back with a sigh and shut her eyes immediately so as not to be drawn into talk. She was exhausted and too lonely to face another empty chat. Rather than help, the casual and sometimes prying conversational ploys of the male Italians only made her feel more isolated. She resolved that the next time she came to Italy she would do one of two things: find a serious Italian lover (were any serious?) or come with a companion of her own. She knew her situation was bad when she found herself recalling with fondness the disastrous times she'd shared with Artie in Mexico. Still, she thought, even though he's sometimes a creep, Artie made the stay more fun. Hadn't they had a great time in Jamaica? It would be good to get home, she realized, with or without Artie.

# chapter 28

Artie, that summer, was in the process of refining his first novel. His first novel was not Nocturnal Emissions. Rather it was a work he'd written almost nine years earlier. Having unwillingly and by chance obeyed Horace's admonitory dictum to shelve a work for nine years, he reaped the benefit of that advice. That is, after nine years, he didn't like what he'd written.

The novel, in its earliest version, had been over six hundred pages long. His first few rejection notices, before he finally ceased to circulate the manuscript, referred to the "maze of adventures" of his protagonist, to the work's "sprawling nature," to its "detailed account of many and various events, which fail to become anything else," to the "tedious length of the chapters," to his "labored figures of speech."

Sometime in the early seventies, in the aftermath of his divorce, he'd taken the manuscript in hand and had cut it to three hundred and eighty pages. At that stage he sent it off to a literary agent advertising editorial services in one of the writer's magazines. After an exchange of lengthy letters, Artie agreed to pay for a detailed editing of the book and in return received what he called, as most offended writers would have, a hack job. Much of the criticism was just, despite his inability to accept it, but much was catty and some plainly foolish.

Artie, feeling that the agent had farmed his book out to an English major in some college, wrote an angry letter back, excoriating the editor for several of the suggested changes and lambasting the insensitive mind of the reader. Some of the cuts, he felt, were justified, but he couldn't help but be dismayed by the reader's total lack of knowledge regarding rhythm, phraseology, and what Artie felt was his style. Having discharged his bile as best as possible, Artie put the work away, discouraged, and only recently had he pulled it out.

His latest efforts on the text had reduced it in size to just over two hundred pages. He was afraid now that the work was so thin it was no longer a novel. At least, he told himself, he'd avoided the errors made in cutting by the hired editor. Whoever had worked on his novel had paperclipped lengthy sections together with comments such as "College dates are a crashing bore" or "Why don't you write a travel book?" or "Oh my God, do we have to listen to more of this?" More than once they'd cut a character and not corrected the manu-script in later sections to reflect this. Characters sitting on trains, for example, suddenly appeared in swimming pools. To Artie, that was as bad as Sancho Panza riding off on his mule—just after it was stolen! His final version, while sparse, was, he hoped, consistent.

By the middle of the summer, he was mailing query letters and receiving negative replies. He wrote to ten literary agents, sending a sample chapter and plot summary, and not one asked to see the manuscript. Despite being discouraged again, as years earlier, he wrote to ten presses as a last resort and then watched them slowly fade away as publishing prospects. A few requested sample chapters, most told him they were too busy to accept unsolicited manuscripts, some recommended he go through an agent.

"There's one thing that aggravates me," Artie told Mark that summer, both at work at the café. "Every now and then I find a book published in the last few years with an idea or a theme or even a technique that I used myself almost ten years ago. Only my book didn't get published, so I don't get credit. If I use it now, it'd be called derivative. Ain't that the shits?"

"You'd better not complain about that," Mark said emphatically. "Everybody'll jump on you. You can't go claiming to have been first at things if you weren't published first. Every hack would claim that distinction then. You gotta be satisfied with things as they are. Just let 'em go. If you weren't first in the race, it ain't ever going to be rerun for you."

Throughout the summer, as time permitted, Artie also continued his work on Nocturnal Emissions. He'd acquired the habit of restricting himself to one sheet of paper for each fragment and he added sketches at the rate of about two a week. He hoped eventually to have 365 stories, a year's worth of reading, if one read one page a day. Occasionally, he let Mark read a few. Mark seemed to enjoy them but offered no helpful criticism. Some Artie even sent to Pam, although he knew she wouldn't get to read them until her return from Italy.

Too bad Mark's sister, Cheryl, had stayed in New York that summer to take classes at Columbia, a course on behavioral neuroscience and another on abnormal behavior. She written once and then stopped.

Too busy, he assumed.

Work at the café dragged on. Artie was growing resentful of the hours the café required. In the evenings he would've liked to have been out walking along the lake. In the day, he wished he had more time to write.

He learned from Mark that Cheryl had only returned for a few days to visit the family and had gone back to New York where, in addition to the two classes, she had a summer job in a mental health clinic. Although Mark was never too clear on the matter and Artie didn't want to press him, it appeared Cheryl had also found a boyfriend there.

The clientele at the café was also slowly changing. Old acquaintances disappeared without warning and the new customers seemed less friendly. Artie wondered if it was perhaps himself. His mood was less cheerful. His first novel continued to be rejected. Work was more of a drudge, and he missed Pam. Nothing seemed to be going right. Sometimes, with Pam's example in mind, he pondered going back to school. He would be enthused for a day or two and then the arduousness of the five to seven-year grind would wear down his drive. He wasn't sure he could stick it out. For that he admired Pam. It took a lot of endurance. All Pam had left to complete was the dissertation. If he were to go back, he'd be at least five years away from that stage! It was dismaying.

One evening, Dashi came into the café for tea and told Artie he'd decided to return to India.

"Don't you like it here?"

"It's not that," he said. "I want to help the people of my city. I will come back some day perhaps." He smiled. "To have a good cup of tea."

"I may not be here either," Artie confessed. "I'm thinking of moving to New York. I'd be closer to the publishing industry then."

"Will that help?"

"I doubt it," he blurted out, grinning like an idiot. He brushed the hair back off his forehead. "Pretty soon no one will be left around here. I haven't seen half the people who used to come in. Everyone's new."

Pulling a chair around, he straddled it and sat down, resting his chin on the back. "Life beats a person down.

Dashi lifted his black caterpillar eyebrows. "Life is within and without," he said serenely. The light overhead reflected off his glasses. His black hair glistened. "Misery need never come in contact with what is within."

"Easy for you to say."

"You're angry no one wants to publish your writing. But the ultimate goal of life is not to achieve success in the material world. That is only a temporary relief."

"What's wrong with temporary relief. Better than nothing. If we all thought like you, we'd sit back and contemplate our navel."

"You misunderstand me. I did not say one withdraws from the world, although that is always a possibility. Mere renunciation of activities, however, is not enough to lead one to enlightenment."

"This abstract talk doesn't do me any good," Artie said, hunched over the back of the chair. "I go to two extremes: Either I think I should just relax, give up trying to achieve success—like in publishing—and enjoy life. When I'm dead what difference will it make what I've done? Why sacrifice for something I'll never know? And then I think—" He paused, playing with a fork on the table. "No, I feel a compulsion to accomplish something. A drive for recognition."

"And that is happiness?" Dashi asked, cocking his head in mild reproof.

Artie snorted. "Who said life was happy? That keeps one busy, that's all. Maybe it's better to keep busy so you don't have to think. The more you ponder life, the worse off you are. That's why I hate philosophy. It's a dog that pisses at every corner. "

"Well, I must leave you, now," Dashi said, "but not on that note. Think of it this way. When you work, you should work for the satisfaction of the whole, not for self-satisfaction. You need to see everything as the same. The dirt clod, the diamond, the pebble, the gold nugget. An experience is an experience, whether good or bad. In the end, it's better to do your own job, even if poorly, than to accept another's occupation and perform it perfectly."

"I don't quite follow you there, but that's okay. You left the road and ran off in the bushes."

Dashi smiled and swallowed the last of his tea. He rose to his feet and held out his hand. "One of your western playwrights has said it best. One does not conduct a ship to port with a wind of sighs."

As Dashi turned to go, Artie whispered, "The trouble is, this ship may be sinking!"

But Dashi had caught the whisper. He looked back. "If you try your hardest with absolute devotion, you will accomplish all you wish. Best of luck, my friend." And with that he was gone.

In the fall, Artie rented a car and drove to New York. Since he was paying a per diem rate on the car, he gave himself two days to find an agent. Near Tompkins Square Park, he spotted a phone booth and pulled over. Two dimes later he was speaking to an associate of the Patricia Reynolds Agency.

"I wrote you about a month ago," he said, "sending a capsule summary of the work and ten representative pages."

"Well, I'm sorry, Mr. Crenshaw," she said pleasantly, "but you've caught us in the middle of a move. We really couldn't accept anything at the moment."

"Okay. You needn't bother to answer my letter or return my material then. Thanks for your time."

Had his snide comments been too subtle for them?

Crossing Patricia Reynolds off his list, he called Ben Deght. The old man himself answered the phone and Artie, after Artie explaining who he was, asked if he could drop off a manuscript. He'd sent a chapter ahead of time, but it didn't seem the agent remembered.

When he arrived at Deght's office, a young woman ushered him in.

"Where's the book?"

Obvious, wasn't it? He had a box in his hands.

She took it from him and laid it on a scale. $1.09," she said. "Return postage."

He reached for his wallet. A small, balding man stepped around a cubicle wall. "I'm Ben Deght."

Artie introduced himself again, fumbling to shake hands, wallet in his left hand, two dollars in his right.

"Here, this'll cover the cost of a mail pac," he said, handing the money to the assistant.

"Just a minute and I'll give you your change."

Artie looked nonplused. The old man was watching the transaction. "That's okay," Artie said. "Keep the change. The mail pac must cost something."

He followed Mr. Deght into his office. The woman kept the manuscript but appeared with it a minute or two later, sans box.

While they talked, Deght riffled through the pages, reading passages at random. Artie suffered each time the fingers found a passage and faltered. Mr. Deght would say, "Please go on," and Artie would talk to the top of

Deght's head.

Suddenly, Deght stood, shook hands, told Artie he'd read the manuscript that weekend, and said good-bye.

Two weeks later, back in Chicago, he received a mailpac—yes, the postage was a $1.09—and a brief note. The letter read as follows:

*Dear Mr. Crenshaw:*

*I have read your novel and, even though you write well, in my opinion you are not a novelist and thus I am returning your manuscript to you.*

That was it. Artie was stunned. No criticism. The bastard could at least have said what he didn't like, what he considered worth working on. Sure, he thought, I'm not a novelist, if being a novelist means having a book published, but I am a writer. Maybe not a good one, maybe not published, but still a writer.

One day, at the start of his writing session, he pondered the alphabet. Just twenty-six letters. Not even the number of squares on a chess board. And yet look at all the works of literature that had been written using just twenty-six fundamental building blocks. The atoms of the literary universe. That's what they were. Elementary particles, with the vowels swarming around like protons, neutrons, electrons and mesons, around a nucleus of consonants, the whole forming matter, words. Words like molecules or elements formed chains to create sentences. And these compounds joined to form paragraphs. And these substances joined to form chapters and chapters to form books.

A book was like a jar of jam. It might have everything in it from amyl propionate to lysinoalanine. And behind it all was energy, the mind, the *nous*. Twenty-six letters. Use them once and they were still there, ready to be used again. Indestructible. Letters—now linear, now cubic, sometimes diamond or hexagonal, occasionally rhombohedral, and tetragonal, even orthorhombic or monoclinic. Wow! They could do anything ... or nothing.

And so went his writing. At the end of his session he looked at the piece of paper. It was pure white. At the top he copied the twenty-six letters of the alphabet and then closed his writing pad. He'd done his work for the day. Mind work, right? Feeding the pump.

But every day the pump seemed to run dry, leaving just droplets behind.

---

# chapter 29

During a busy fall of research and voluminous reading, Pam made steady progress on her dissertation. She expected to finish by June.

But spring brought two events that upset her equilibrium.

The lesser event, actually rather typical, occurred three weeks into the semester. Mary Ellen, a bio major, red-haired but not vitriolic, vivacious yet pleasantly restrained in class, asked to see her by appointment on a Friday afternoon.

Though tired, Pam agreed. In her mind's eye, she'd visualized a pleasant chat in which Mary Ellen would ask about the advisability of declaring a double major. She was a good student, not the best, but capable of doing well.

Instead, after entering the deserted TAs' office, Mary Ellen sat rather defiantly perched on the edge of her chair and immediately launched into a fiery-eyed diatribe.

Well, here goes, Pam thought, sitting back and picking up her pen to help absorb the blast. Bio majors were so damn uptight about A's. They'd badger you to death over a B+. Hoping to remain detached and unemotional, she started thinking strange thoughts.

A mini-movie, a cinematographic fantasy, the result of all her reading, ran through her mind.

Who do we have here?

The warrior-maiden. A modern Pentesilea, charging out of the trees, catching her teacher unaware as she trotted across the glade, helmet on the pommel of her saddle. The Amazon let out a blood-curdling yell and lifted her lance. "I'll get you, you bitch.

No long blonde hair streaming in the breeze, Clorinda style, on this warrior maiden. This was an all out red-haired hellcat ready to kill.

Lances broke on impact, horses stumbled. Each damsel-knight turned to face the other, swords drawn, moving in for the close-range slashes, the thrusts, the hacking, no longer any art, no fancy warding and parrying, but hack, slash, cut, stab, thrust, jab, mutilate, and maul.

"Well, I don't see what else I could've added in this essay section. What else is there? I think it's pretty complete."

Pam had assigned an essay on a passage in Dante's *Inferno*.

"Well"—it was a battle of "well's"—"you don't really tell me what circle he's in or talk much about the passage itself. You identify the figure and talk at length about him, but you don't analyze the passage linguistically or semantically. There's no mention of the contrapasso. Anyway, a B+ is a good grade. This is a good answer. It just isn't an A."

When it was over, though a victress, she felt victimized. She left her office wondering if academia was worth the pain.

Apparently the pain affected better souls than hers, including those of her professors. The second incident to mar her composure involved a junior member of the Comp Lit department, Conrad Helmstead, an untenured assistant professor in his early forties who'd been especially helpful to Pam.

A part-time faculty member in the Italian department, he taught narrative prose, ranging from seminars on Boccaccio and the short story in the Renaissance to survey courses covering the historical novels from Manzoni's *Promessi Sposi* to Pirandello's *I vecchi e i giovani*.

Conrad, as she called him in private, was a handsome fellow. Of medium height, always impeccably dressed, most often in professorial grays, he talked with the drawl of a Southerner at leisure.

In fact, however, like Pam, he was a native of Oregon, and had received his Ph.D. at the University of Washington in Seattle. Behind his measured speech, Pam recognized a drive that tended toward compulsion. His mouth would break into a big Tom Sawyer, country grin but, at the same time, his eyes, behind thick, black-rimmed spectacles, were tense. The paradox had always intrigued her.

Conrad's breakdown came as no surprise to his colleagues in the Comp Lit department and perhaps not even to his attentive students—especially those who'd read *Herzog* and recognized the same symptoms of overwork—but it was a shock to Pam. She knew him both as a man and as a teacher. It was her first eye-to-eye contact with severe burnout.

By his colleagues, Helmstead was known for his punctuality, his methodical determination, and his attention to detail. If the chairman asked the department for a cultural program dealing with Spanish, or French, or Italian civili-zation, Helmstead would come in the very next day with a detailed, ten-page outline covering history, literature, society, music, and three or four other areas of both high and low culture. Most of the other faculty members, meanwhile, would be talking among themselves as to the impossibility of really teaching well in English the culture of another country.

Professor Helmstead's breakdown, Pam learned from Sally and Jeff, who as usual knew all, manifested itself through a peculiar sexual eccentricity. On a Tuesday, two weeks before midterm exams, Conrad walked into Professor Anne Schobel's office, one of his Comp Lit colleagues, and unzipped his pants.

"Anne," he said. "I've just got to make love to you. I've wanted you for too long. Desire has been building up in me for a year."

It was nothing brilliant, erotic, or romantic, but Professor Schobel screwed him on her desk and, though flushed and puzzled by it all, didn't think Conrad was crazy. In fact, she was flattered she'd aroused such deep passion.

Helmstead, it must be confessed (as Sally put it), made it through three or four of the women professors in the Comp Lit department in one week before anyone suspected him or reported his bizarre behavior to the Dean.

Helmstead's mistake? Sister Maria Clara. How could a fellow be sane and attempt to screw a nun? Which is not to say, as Sally gleefully told Pam, that Conrad was unsuccessful. He was all too successful. Only later, when she saw the blood stains, did the good sister start screaming she'd been raped and that her vows had been broken against her will.

Pam knew Conrad would never force himself upon anyone. Undoubtedly the sister had been too overwhelmed by the request to contemplate resis-tance. When confronted, Helmstead pleaded innocence, but then added, enigmatically, by way of justification, "God spoke through me. I was his tool of revivification."

When they led Conrad from the building for his trip to the State Hospital, he was not, as one might expect, leering maniacally. Rather, with a smile of sweet forgiveness, as Jeff put it, he was singing a hymn, "Blessed Assurance," and, perhaps because he'd forgotten all but the first verse, repeating over and over, "Blessed assurance, Jesus is mine, O what a foretaste of glory divine."

When narrated to Pam by Jeff, over the giggles and additions of Sally, the details seemed humorous, but the case in itself was like one of Andrea Alciati's emblems, more complex than outwardly apparent and thus, for her, full of a significance that was clearly admonitory. It wasn't only anger that led to insanity, to paraphrase Seneca, it was excessive work, *immoderatus labor.*

In April, having visited Artie over Spring break, Pam received a job offer from New York University. It was one of four positions for which she'd interviewed between Christmas and New Year's Day at the Modern Language Association convention in New York. She was ecstatic and called Artie immediately. Just two weeks before they'd talked at length about getting together again and had wondered how to work it out.

"You said you were thinking of moving to New York, anyway," she told him over the phone. "For your writing. We can both live there now. Isn't that great?"

There was a moment of silence. She held her breath. She was afraid Artie would say, "No, it's not great. I've changed my mind. I don't like New York."

And then "Whoopee!" rang in her ear. "Wow! Fantastic! It's time we got back together. Let's go now!"

That was the summer of 1976. Five years, half a decade, had passed since their split. Both had grown up, as each admitted to the other. Both, in fact, sometimes felt old and world-weary. One more thing we have in common, Pam told him.

He said, "You know what I'm going to be playing in the car on the way to New York? Rod Stewart's 'Tonight's the night.'"

As a joke, she was about to say, "Who's he?" but then thought, no, Artie's likely to believe I really don't know.

I'm not that far lost in the woods of academia.

So, instead, she said, "I'm not really into disco but I'll be playing Donna Summer's 'Love to Love You Baby.' You know. Those lyrics you're going to have to live up to.

    'Do it to me again and again,
    You put me in such an awful spin.'"

They both laughed.

"Good one," he said.

Yeah, it was time to try again.

# Part Three • Homecoming
## (1976 - 1978)

# chapter 30

New York, for both, was a rotten apple. How many decades ago had it been green? After Chicago, where garbage cans were neatly placed in back alleys, and after Berkeley, where they were invisible, Old York, as they preferred to call it, struck both as a city drowning in garbage. Where did they put all that refuse? Surely New York alone could fill the Atlantic Ocean in little more than a year.

And the dog shit was incredible. It grew, like weeds in an untended lot, throughout the lower East Side. Soft piles, wet drippings, hard lumps, cylinders and domes, *merda* and *stronzo* (Pam's words), they all pollinated in the night, rising somehow through the cement sidewalks like forest mushrooms.

They looked for apartments in the Village for over a week before deciding it was too expensive. There was nothing near NYU that they could afford. Finally, though horrified by the area, they rented a one-bedroom apartment on the fourth floor of a high rise on Seventh Street between Avenue C and D.

They promised themselves that after Pam's job started in the fall they would move nearer the Village.

Still, despite the grimness of the neighborhood (they breakfasted looking out across a bottle-scarred empty lot at a row of burned out apartment buildings), despite the gangs of Puerto Rican youths who terrified them by their mere presence along the street (at night it was for both Artie and Pam a fearful gauntlet), despite the cockroaches, the garbage, the theft, the noisy neighbors, and the pollution, that summer in New York for them was like a third honeymoon, so much better than the second five years earlier which had resulted in their separation. Neither one worked. They lived off of savings, largely Artie's, and looked forward to Pam's salary in the fall.

In the heat, they made love often, especially the first month together. It was as if each felt the need to be rejoined to the other. *Physically.* Their efforts were so vigorous at first that it seemed all they did was sleep, eat, and make love.

Eventually they made their way out into the city. Excursions at first, however, only whet their appetites for each other, and they would rush home, stripping each other once inside the door, biting and sucking, often never making it to the bed. They jumped each other like cows in heat.

As the summer passed, they settled into assorted habits, varied enough to avoid boredom. They jogged together daily, took bike rides, saw the sights, visited the Cloisters, the museums, the art galleries, and bookstores, ate out in a host of ethnic restaurants, read books together, talked, took long walks, made love whenever they felt like it, and settled slowly into a warm companionship, a comfortable intimacy, which included squabbles as well as shared pleasures

As the summer advanced, the heat became overwhelming, especially for Pam, who'd come from the mild bay breezes of Berkeley. The humidity depressed her. She tried to prepare class plans while Artie wrote, she thought about research projects, but the effort of thinking tired hout.

"I miss having friends," she said to Artie one day, after moping around the apartment all morning. She felt guilty for accomplishing nothing. "We should try to meet some people. We're too closed-in here,"

As far as he was concerned, he didn't need anyone else. Pam satisfied his desire for friends. He preferred being alone or talking to her. Why complicate life with a bunch of other idiots?

"When school starts you'll meet a lot of people," he said, sitting at his desk, while she paced the room behind him. "You'll have colleagues who become friends."

Her silence bore down on him. "You could join a women's group." That put the burden back on her.

"I want us to have couple friends, too. We don't do anything to meet anyone."

Artie shrugged. "It's hard out of the blue. It takes time."

"It takes doing things! We haven't done anything where we'd meet people."

Artie took a deep breath. Why did he feel responsible for everything? It was as much up to her as it was to him to find activities. There had to be something they could do that he wouldn't mind.

"How about going to some of the poetry readings these cafés have?"

"I just don't want us to get stale."

"Stale! We've just gotten back together again! You need that much variety?" It was an accusation.

"Forget it."

His first impulse was to say, "Why?" and to continue the discussion. But then he decided it was simpler to accept her offer, despite the acid in her voice.

"Fine," he said, turning back to work.

The next day Pam returned to the subject during breakfast. "Maybe you're right."

"About what?"

"I should find my own friends."

"I didn't say that."

"I'm saying, I don't think we should do everything together."

"I thought we'd settled all this when we broke up the first time. Are we going to have the same fights we had then? I'm not trying to limit your freedom. We can live together and enjoy each other's company and still have different interests. I won't thwart your need for independence."

Pam finished washing the dishes. Artie had prepared a cold cereal of soaked bulgur, sunflower seeds, cashews, raisins, and grated apple. She dried her hands on the dishcloth and noticed it was already dusty with soot.

"It's not independence that bothers me. I want to share time together. I enjoy your company."

"I enjoy yours, too."

"But self-sufficiency matters to me."

"You are self-sufficient! My God, you haven't grown up in the kitchen your whole life. You've got a career. You'll always earn more than I do. Why're you worrying about that?"

Pam paused, sorting through words. "We've only been back together a few months, and I already feel what I felt the first three years of our marriage."

She saw that what she'd said had set badly with him. "Not the anger and frustration," she said, "but depending on you for all my emotional needs. I had friends in Berkeley—men and women—and I liked that."

Artie shrugged. "You can again."

"Being here alone, just the two of us, makes me realize if I rely too heavily on you for everything, what'll I do if you die?"

Artie stared at her amazed. "I'm barely over thirty."

"I know. Maybe I'm being irrational, but that's how I feel."

Artie laughed. "You're rarely irrational. Sure, I suppose I could get hit by a car tomorrow and die. Especially the way these taxis drive here. But you can't live your life preparing for the worst. You might waste twenty years worrying about what to do if a loved one dies rather than enjoying that person for the moment. What do you want? To have a successor lined up?"

She ignored the barb. "I want friends. People who'll be there when I need them."

"I'll be there when you need me, too."

Pam stared at him, standing above him across the kitchen table. Artie laid down the book he was reading. He interlaced his hands, chest high, and slouched back in his seat.

"You weren't there before," she said.

As soon as she said it, she expected him to erupt, to scream that that was a dirty blow. Instead, he sat there and stared back at her, his face frozen. Somehow this response of his was worse.

"I'm sorry," she said. She'd promised not to use that against him. They'd both agreed that the fault was mutual and that the break had been necessary and beneficial despite the hardships.

Artie shrugged. "That's okay. That was me then. I'm a different person now. We've made a commitment to each other, and I plan on sticking to it. You've got to trust more. Stick-to-it-ness is a trait we both value. You stuck to a hard academic program. I stuck to ..." He paused and they both laughed.

"What did I stick to?" he asked.

"You've stuck to your writing."

"In a way, but not like I should've. I've wasted a lot of time too."

"Maybe you needed that time."

"Probably. It's not easy going through life in mediocre jobs though." The implication was that Pam at least had a career. She wasn't drifting.

"Some people might envy you," she said.

"What if I'd gone on to grad school? Then I could teach creative writing and spend all my time writing."

Pam shook her head. "There aren't many jobs out there even for people with advanced degrees. You'd have to have a few novels published before you'd even be considered."

"Fuck it all, anyway," he said.

After they found the nearest delicatessen and a group of favorite cafés and restaurants, Pam and Artie set about exploring the area's bookstores. By August, they'd fallen into a weekly habit of a visit to The Strand on Broadway. They had lunch at Lescko's or the Odessa and then spent the afternoon wandering the aisles of The Strand. Pam would go downstairs to the Foreign Language section, while Artie drifted around the main floor, looking at half-price review books and then at the fiction section.

On day, downstairs, near the back wall, Pam found three volumes of De Ruggiero's *Storia della filosofia* and pondered buying the volume dealing with the Renaissance and Reformation. It was only two dollars. She held it for fifteen minutes, while she scanned the rest of the shelves devoted to Italian, and then slipped it back by the other two volumes.

Upstairs, Artie did the same with a Richard Brautigan volume on sale for $2.95 and then repeated the maneuver with a recently released spy novel.

With their savings dwindling, they limited themselves to the pleasures of touching dusty but life-filled used books, or running their fingers fleetingly over slick new volumes with dust-free dust jackets. The difference was like that between caressing a clay mug or fondling a plastic cup. One could drink from both but the clay mug seemed somehow to hold more life, more substance, more sustenance.

When Pam was assigned her office at NYU, she began more serious work, and Artie was left to wander the city or sit at home. He spent hours on the hard benches of Tompkins Square Park, sometimes writing short sketches, sometimes trying to draw, often lost in a daze. The periods of dazed withdrawal, he hoped, were times when his mind and his creativity recharged themselves.

His dad had always called him lazy. "Fuck, maybe I am."

Each day, approaching the park, he analyzed the mural on the side of the band shell. The woman's face on the left, in blue, with hair of white flowers. Who was she? A wind goddess? Music herself? The other angel-like figures held musical instruments. He would've liked to have thought of her as Spring, a modern-day offspring of Botticelli's Flora, but she looked too cold, although the park trees in the painting were in full leaf.

At night, going to pick up Pam, he would walk up St. Mark's Place, cross Cooper Square and Astor Place with its black cube, a lonely dice dropped by the giants of the universe one night, and then, if he was early, would amble up Eighth Street as far as Avenue of the Americas, stopping occasionally to look in the window displays of gift shops. Coming back, he would angle downtown to Waverly Place, turn left, and saunter by the elegant four and five-story walk-ups.

The first time he covered this route, he stopped in Washington Square before the arch, which, he saw to his surprise as he read the inscription, honored George Washington. And all this time he'd thought the square was built to honor Washington Irving. He wondered if the Cooper Union honored James Fenimore Cooper. He'd seen a plaque on an apartment building a few blocks away which claimed the site had been Cooper's summer residence.

Artie had convinced Pam that until they moved to a safer place she was never to walk home alone after dark. If Artie wasn't available, she should take a taxi. With Pam beside him the route seemed less frightening. Sometimes, at night, he walked it alone himself. He was scared for his life every time, but hated to pay a taxi.

Pam would say, to no avail, that his life was worth the fare. Seventh Street was especially bad between Avenue B and C. When he did have to return late alone, Artie found himself rehearsing imaginary confrontations. Was it better to speak only broken Italian, as if he were a foreigner?

One night, further west on Sixth Street, he heard someone behind him whisper "faggot." There were other pedestrians nearby so Artie didn't bother to turn and look. He could hear the tread of three or four guys. A few steps further on, in the middle of the intersection of Sixth Street and Second Avenue, the voice came louder. "Faggot."

Without turning to look, Artie angled kitty corner across the intersection. And then a shout, "Faggot!"

From there his imagination took over. He turned. "You weren't talking to me, were you?"

"That's right, faggot."

"Actually, I'm not a faggot. I'm happily married." (Why let technicalities cloud the issue. He'd been married; he was as good as married now.) "What made you think I was a faggot?"

"You look like one, faggot."

"I'm sorry to disappoint you, but I'm not a faggot."

And so on. A blasé conversation. He marveled later that in all his fantasies of violence, he himself took such a passive role. As if calm reason would be enough to protect him.

Sometimes, however, perhaps despairing of reason, he would resort to violence himself. For example, he redid the faggot episode. This time, near the end, after telling them he wasn't a faggot, he asked them to be kind enough to repeat, "You're not a faggot." When they refused, when one started toward him, he shot him in the chest, firing from his coat pocket. He riddled the fellow's body with four or five bullets and then watched the rest of the gang run in fright.

"I like symmetry," he'd tell the cops. "I put some holes in his body to match those in his head."

Maybe I'm lucky I don't have a gun.

In September, Pam met her first true friend in the city. She'd been introduced to her colleagues but had found no one with whom she was especially compatible. Instead, she looked elsewhere, finding Joanne Nelson by chance at the Village Women's Liberation Center. Pam had gone there to join a women's support group which met one night a week to share experiences and confront problems.

Joanne, a personnel office manager for a corporation headquartered in downtown Manhattan, lived in the Village and was active in the feminist movement. When Pam entered the center, Joanne was at the bulletin board, thumbtacking a notice there for an upcoming women's concert. Pam, unsure where she was to go for the encounter group, excused herself, and asked Joanne for directions.

"I'm going there myself," Joanne said. "I'm one of the leaders who's starting that group."

"Oh, do you have leaders in the support group?" As soon as the question left her mouth, Pam wished she hadn't asked it. Joanne ducked and bobbed her head. "Not really. Not once we get started. It's just that I and another woman are organizing this group. It's limited to twelve."

Pam didn't know if that meant it was full. "What happens if more than twelve show up?"

"No problem. We'll just split into two groups."

The meeting room was down a long corridor near the restrooms. On the way, Joanne stopped at a small office area and left a message for one of the staff administrators.

"Do you do a lot here?" Pam asked.

Joanne was striding energetically down the corridor. "I'm just a volunteer. I do spend a lot of time here though. I like helping women."

When they entered the meeting room, four other women were there. Pam looked at her watch. "Looks like we're a bit early," she said.

"I'll introduce you to all the old timers," Joanne said. "We're the core. We've all been in each other's groups before."

Pam wanted to ask why they were starting a new group, but Joanne was already introducing her. When Pam mentioned, in response to a question, that she was teaching at NYU, one of the women, an older lady in her forties named Helen, said her late husband used to teach history there.

Next to Helen sat Brandis, a woman in her late twenties, monstrously overweight. She, like Helen, was smoking, and ashes littered the front of her dress. She had a piece of chocolate cake on a paper plate which she was eating between puffs. She was so fat she had trouble both seeing the plate and keeping the food off her chest.

On the opposite side of the table, another smoker, Ester, a short stocky grandmotherly type, motioned for Pam to sit beside her. "This is Tu Lau," she said, pointing to a middle-aged Chinese woman. "She's the artist of the group."

Pam sat beside Ester, and Joanne took the end of the table. The smoke in the room bothered Pam. She was about to ask Joanne about ventilation when Joanne spoke up. There was a No Smoking sign taped on the wall.

"You remember there's no smoking during group," she said.

Ester pursed her lips. "Joanne, group hasn't started."

Three more women were at the door and Joanne motioned for them to come in. Ester looked at Brandis. "Brandis and I are going to suggest that we meet at my apartment. It's got central air. The smokers can sit at one end of the living room and the non-smokers at the other."

"We'll see," Joanne said cheerfully. "But no smoking now."

Brandis took a last puff and ground out her cigarette. Ester's, its filter lipstick coated, continued to smoulder on a thin bronze ashtray. The smoke was drifting toward Pam.

"I'm allergic to smoke," she said. "Maybe I should move to the other end."

"Oh no, honey. I'm through." Ester extinguished the cigarette. "You've got emphysema?"

"Asthma problems." That was as good an excuse as any.

"I've got emphysema," Brandis said, her breasts bouncing as she laughed, "and that doesn't stop me."

"That's nothing to be proud of," Joanne said. "You've also got a spastic colon."

Wow! And this is a support group?

By eight o'clock the room was full. Pam counted seventeen women. Joanne took charge and after talking about the structure of a support group and its purpose announced that due to the number of women present two separate groups would be necessary,

"I'll lead one," Ester said.

Joanne laughed. "Perhaps we could have one group for smokers and another for non-smokers."

Put me with the non-smokers.

Joanne went on. "I organized the meeting tonight, but I've decided not to lead a group. As you know, once we're set up, we supposedly don't have leaders. But someone always has to organize things, and I feel like I tend to take charge."

Everyone laughed.

"And Ester, our earth mother" (Ester beamed) "also ..."

"Go ahead and say it, dear," Ester said, smiling. "I know. I like to keep everyone warm under my wings."

"The question is," Brandis said, "how do we divide up?"

Another woman suggested they count off. "Odds go with Ester" (everyone laughed when Ester raised her eyes and looked heavenward) "and evens go in the other group."

"Some of us want to be together, though" Helen said. "I know I like Brandis and Ester. And Tu Lau's usually in our group."

Tu nodded. She had yet to say a word and Pam wondered if she knew English. She herself wanted to be in Joanne's group, but hoped to avoid Ester and Brandis.

"We'll send around a list," Joanne finally suggested. "Group A and group B. Sign up under one or the other and we'll see how it comes out."

Helen tore a sheet of paper off a note pad and drew a line down the middle. She handed it to Ester and Ester (Thank God! Pam thought) started it out circulating to the right. Pam would be the last to sign.

When the sheet reached Joanne, Pam was surprised to see her add herself to Ester's group A. The majority of women had signed up for group B. Perhaps Joanne was sacrificing to balance the groups. When the sheet reached her, Pam hesitated, pursed her lips, and wrote her name under group A after Joanne's. There were seven women in Ester's group. She hoped Joanne would control the smokers.

The rest of the meeting was devoted to finding a meeting place and time. Ester lived on Thompson Street near the Livorno restaurant. Her group would met at the restaurant.

When the meeting broke up, Joanne invited Pam for a coffee.

"Is there a café near here?"

"No, I meant at my place."

"Oh, that's nice. But maybe I'll drink tea, if you have any."

"I've got lots of tea. Come on, let's go."

"Do you mind if I call my husband from your place?"

She and Artie had decided to call themselves husband and wife in public.

"You got an uptight husband?"

Pam pushed the glass door open and held it for Joanne. "We were separated for a while and we're back together again. I just like to let him know where I am at night because he worries."

"Why don't you invite him over, then, and I can meet him. That way he'll feel less threatened when you're out with me."

Pam smiled. "That's nice of you." She actually meant nice of Joanne to say they'd be going out together. Good to be included so quickly.

"What's your husband do?"

"He's a writer."

"What's he write?"

"Short stories. I don't pry too much. I know he works on and off at a novel. He doesn't like me to read anything until he's completed it."

Joanne lived near the corner of Morton Street and Bleecker in a rent controlled building. Pam loved the apartment. It was small, with a bedroom the size of a large closet, but Joanne had paid a carpenter to build a frame to hold her bed near the ceiling. Underneath, she had a study area with a desk, small bookcase and typewriter stand.

"I take night classes twice a week," Joanne said, while they were waiting for Artie to bike over. "I'm trying to get my B.A. in personnel management. I can't move up any higher without the degree."

"How long will that take?" Pam asked.

"I guess I've got sophomore standing now. At the rate I'm going it'll take me ten years."

"How old are you?"

"Twenty-six."

"Gee. You're still young. I'm thirty. I feel old already."

"You've got a Ph.D. That's something!"

Joanne showed Pam the rest of the apartment—kitchen and living room—and then set about preparing some tea. They were chatting in the living room when Artie arrived.

"Hi!" Joanne called cheerfully, when she opened the door. "You must be

Artie."

He nodded, smiling, and stepped in. "Is it okay if I leave my bike out here in the hall? I forgot to bring the lock so I couldn't leave it on the street."

"You can set it inside if you wish," Joanne said.

Artie looked around. There wasn't much room. "It'll be okay out here," he said.

His first impression of Joanne was that she was a nervous type. Forceful too, however, and perhaps a bit abrasive. She seemed to address most of the conversation to Pam. Physically, she was athletic, well-built but stocky, with black hair clipped short, her face round and dominated by heavy eyebrows and a prominent nose. She still wore a thin retaining brace over her teeth.

For a while they talked about relationships. Artie and Pam related their history, and Joanne shared her experiences with a fellow from whom she'd recently broken up.

"We lived together three years," she said. "I liked him a lot. He was very energetic like me, had a great sense of humor, but we never enjoyed each other in bed. Finally we were making love about once a month and lousy then." She shook her head. "Larry works too hard. He owns a shoe store with his dad. Very generous but he just couldn't perform. I ended up feeling like I wasn't very attractive sexually."

"You have a fine build," Artie said, and Pam gave him a dirty look.

"Oh, no problem now," Joanne replied with a boisterous laugh. "It didn't take me long after we broke up to find out it wasn't me. I enjoy sex! It was Larry who screwed me up. He's a latent homosexual if there ever was one. He's living with another woman but he told me he prefers the company of men."

"Too bad you had to waste so many years," Artie said.

Pam nudged him. "What about me? I lived with you for three years and that wasn't so great!"

Artie frowned. "We had problems but not sexually."

"Not for you maybe, but what about for me?"

Artie shrugged. No use to fight it. No use to get in an argument, to start accusing each other, especially in public. "I guess we were just too dumb," he said after a moment's hesitation, trying to show he was man enough to accept his share of the responsibility. But, shit, it was hard to have his prowess questioned in front of a woman.

"I still like it daily," he added lamely and then decided to try to make a joke of it. "That's pretty good for someone almost fifteen years beyond his prime."

\* \* \*

In October, after Pam had been teaching a month, Artie found a notice taped to a light pole near Washington Square, announcing the formation of a writer's group. Pam had her group, so why not he? He jotted down the number on a grocery bag and called when he got back to the apartment.

A woman named Linda answered and told him they still had room for three or four people. The first organizational meeting would be that Saturday at her house. Saturday, Artie said, was a bad day for him, but Linda told him that the eventual meeting day would be decided by the group as a whole and that usually, from her experience, the day chosen was a weekday evening.

On Saturday, Artie climbed four flights of stairs to an apartment on Mac-Dougal Street. A young woman with hair drawn back in a pony tail opened the door. She wore no make-up but had nice features, finely refined cheek-bones, a pert nose, thin lips, ears pierced by gold earrings. She was dressed in a skintight black top and full-length skirt. As she led him down the hall, after introducing herself as Linda Aston, he noticed she wore ankle boots with white cotton lining along the top. She seemed rich. But then, everyone seemed rich to him.

Five other people had already arrived. They were sitting around the living room eating cheese and crackers.

"Who's the ceramicist?" Artie asked, picking up a vase to see if the base was signed.

"My husband, Michael," Linda said. "He's a patent attorney."

"Nicely done. I've taken a few courses in Chicago. I'm not quite this professional though."

"Michael did them years ago, actually. When he was at Yale."

Artie wanted to ask Linda if she worked outside the house as well, but she left to answer the doorbell. There were no kids in sight and nothing to show that Linda had children.

He sat down next to two fellows, one bearded and heavy-set, looked to be in his late forties, the other a short, nervous man, his black hair laced with gray, who spoke with an accent. John and Franco. They were talking about faculty members in the English Department at, Artie assumed, NYU.

Apparently one of the professors had gone in to the Dean to tell him of an offer he'd received from Stanford. The Dean, a crusty fellow near retirement politely listened, said "Good luck" when the fellow finished, and ushered him out.

John, the bearded guy, leaned forward and tapped his finger on the coffee table. "No! He should've made a counteroffer. That's no way to treat the foremost Milton authority of the time."

Linda interrupted at that point, calling the group to order before Franco could respond. She introduced herself, explained that it was her idea to start the group and that she was interested in meeting to read people's current work and to share constructive criticism. Before they picked a day and time and clarified how the sessions would function, she wanted them to go around in a circle with each person saying a little bit about him or herself and what they were working on. "I'm a short story writer myself," she explained. "I've published three stories in literary journals, but haven't had much success lately. I'd like to start a novel, but the form scares me. I'm not sure I have the persistence to finish." She smiled wryly, without opening her mouth, and looked at Artie to her left.

"Me next?" he asked and she nodded. He looked across the room at a young woman—Sarah, wasn't it?—then dropped his eyes to the floor.

"I'm near the end of one work which I call a novel but which is actually a collection of short stories, about one to two pages in length, three hundred and sixty-five in all. One a day for a year. I've sent it out to a few agents but it's not very commercial and no one wants to try to market it. I've also started a novel, several years ago now, but I can't seem to stick with it."

He looked to his left at Franco. Franco cleared his throat and explained hesitantly that he was a free-lance journalist from L.A. and that he'd recently moved to New York to live with a brother while he tried to complete a detective novel.

John was next. He was an assistant professor of English at Fordham, he said, interested in reading and discussing literature.

"Are you doing any writing yourself?" Linda asked.

John shrugged, shooting the cuffs of his shirt. He was wearing a sport coat. "I keep a journal with scraps and sketches. Nothing too serious yet."

Next to John sat a student at NYU, who was interested in both prose and poetry. She'd published quite a few poems and was working on a collection entitled "Hanging Gardens." Artie had missed her name so when she finished he asked for her to repeat it. "My real name's Miriam," she said blushing, but I go by Jeanne." She looked quickly at Artie. "It was the name of a favorite aunt of mine. She died when I was eleven."

Sarah spoke next. She was a red-head, shy eyes flickering behind oversized tinted glasses. She wore a white cotton T-shirt and faded jeans. Rambling, squeezing her hands, she said she wrote short stories of an experimental nature, none published, and an occasional poem.

Joyce, mother of three children, director of a child care center, spoke next. She was preparing a picture book of modern-day fables for middle-grade kids. Joyce was a tall, forceful woman, big-boned, weighty but not fat. When she spoke she shook her head, jangling the long brass earrings she wore.

Lost in thought for a moment, Artie missed most of the presentation of Boris, a gray-haired retired real estate salesman, with a beret in his hand, and a feisty growl to his speech. Apparently Boris was writing a biographical novel dealing with an obscure baseball player from the fifties.

Finally the ninth and last person, a woman named Barbara spoke. "I work for a career development program," she said, "and I meet a lot of people with problems. I've never written before, other than school papers, but I thought I might try to write stories based on what I hear in the office. Changing things, of course, so as not to violate anyone's privacy. I wouldn't be coming in with much at the start but I'd like to learn from the others." She crossed her legs, long and elegant, and lay one arm along the back of the sofa.

Artie liked Barbara's manner. She was sharply dressed in a dark gray dress suit, and had seemed initially stuck-up, but she spoke simply with a pleasant husky sound to her voice. Physically, she was the most beautiful person in the group, a brunette with cascading waves of soft curls, lightly made up, but with the features of a fashion model. Artie, with his gaps between upper dentals, envied her white and perfectly set teeth. Around her neck lay an elegant gold necklace.

The following ten minutes were devoted to the selection of a meeting time. Artie suggested Wednesday evenings (because Pam attended her support group on that night) and felt guilty when Linda swayed the rest to accept that day.

Linda, standing by the fireplace, also suggested that each week, as well as preparing something to read, they think about a topic of discussion in advance of the meeting. "Something like 'point-of-view' or 'structures of tension,'" she said.

Artie was about to ask what she meant by structures of tension, when Joyce, jangling her brass earrings, burst out with, "Oh, let's begin with structures of tension. That's such a fundamental point, especially for fables."

No one else spoke up, so Linda announced that concept as the topic for the following Wednesday.

"This first time," she said, "since we only have three days or so, I'll prepare something to say and then in the future we can all present our own ideas or assign a different person each week as facilitator. Okay?"

With that, the group broke up for socializing and Artie found himself stuck with Boris.

Boris, it turned out, used to run a restaurant before he got into real estate. He'd put his beret on, although, when talking, he'd alternately take it off and then replace it. Artie told him of his own experiences with the co-op and café in Chicago, and Boris talked of his restaurant operation, which was apparently quite elaborate.

"I used to hire chefs from France," he said, gesturing skyward. "I made trips to Europe every year to find out what was happening with French cuisine. My restaurant served gourmet continental food to the most famous citizens of the city. Everyone wanted to be my friend. That's where I met Ralph Gregorio."

"Who's he?"

Boris grabbed his arm, nearly spitting in Artie's face. "I told the group about him, weren't you listening? He's the baseball player I'm writing my book about. Tremendous guy, really an inspiration. We wound up selling real estate for the same broker. Now we're partners. He's got a story every kid should read. It's got all the angles."

Having listened to Boris until his eyes glazed over and his brain grew numb, Artie grabbed Franco as he walked past and asked where the bathroom was. Franco didn't know, but the question gave Artie a chance to excuse himself from Boris.

After going to the bathroom, Artie refilled his glass of wine and looked for a group to join. Barbara (the elegant career counselor), Sarah (he identified her as the red-head experimentalist), and their hostess Linda were standing around the fireplace. He was about to saunter over casually, when John Duchaska reintroduced himself, and asked Artie if they hadn't met before.

"I don't think so," Artie said, looking at John's distinguished gray sideburns which grew to just below the ear. "Unless perhaps at a talk at NYU. My wife teaches there and I occasionally go to a guest lecture. Most deal with foreign literatures though."

"Oh, what does your wife teach?" John reached into the pocket of his sport coat for a pipe and a bag of tobacco.

Shit! Artie thought. No one said anything about smoking. He hadn't thought of it earlier, because no one had smoked during the general discussion. Pam had told him about her problems. They both detested smoking.

"She's in the Department of Italian," he said, and then quickly rushed on, apologetically. "Smoke bothers me. Do you mind if I talk to you later."

"Oh sorry," John said, dropping the pipe back into his pocket. "I should've asked. I can wait."

"I wonder if there're other smokers?" Damn, he really could've been more subtle.

"There didn't seem to be, did there?" John said in a brisk and precise tone. He seemed to Artie to have a slight British accent, but Artie assumed it was merely the punctiliousness of an Easterner who'd attended the best of schools. For the rest of the conversation, which concentrated on his and Pam's background, Artie shifted about awkwardly, sensing that John, despite his apparent bonhomie, resented Artie's anti-smoking stance. John kept his hand in his coat pocket, apparently clasping the wood bowl of his pipe and seemed to be waiting to take it out again.

He was glad when John excused himself and walked off to get more wine. Taking advantage of the break, tired of desultory conversation, he found Linda, thanked her for the snacks and wine, and took his leave. It wasn't until he got home that he remembered he'd forgotten to ask what she meant by "structures of tension."

The following Wednesday Artie went to the writer's group with more trepidation than he wished. He'd taken along two of his recent sketches from *Nocturnal Emissions,* but he feared reading them aloud to the group. At home they sounded okay … but in public? They'd probably come across as amateurish and tawdry. As he soon found out, however, he needn't have worried. There were others all too eager to read their own things and not enough time for everyone.

Linda began the session with a short presentation. She was dressed more casually than the prior Saturday, now wearing gray cords and an Indian-print long-sleeved blouse with matching vest. Her hair was still pulled back in a pony tail but she wore long, gray, metallic earrings with Aztec designs and a cord choker-chain necklace with tiny blue beads. He admired the simplicity of her style. Someone had told him she was forty-one years old. He'd have guessed ten years younger.

Linda talked about the variety of structures in a literary work, from structures of feelings (static or kinetic) to structures of logic, where the meaning is carefully worked out in a story, and then devoted most of her time to what she called structures of tension, the contrasts and conflicts which keep a story or poem moving and which engage the reader's attention.

As the evening wore on, Artie grew progressively gloomier. He hadn't said a word in the general discussion and the academic turn to the conversation bored him.

John was given to theoretical abstractions and both Joyce, the writer of children's stories, and Linda seemed equally capable at handling critical jargon.

Artie was happy anytime Boris broke in. His comments were so buffoonish as to make everyone laugh. Boris would guffaw too, thinking, apparently, that the others were laughing not at but with him.

The only down to earth person with true intelligence (he exempted Boris from this last quality) was Barbara, the career development counselor. She was someone he could like, and she asked the questions he would've asked had he been more involved in the topic.

When the readings began, he was happy to see Barbara volunteer after Boris. Boris had read his first chapter on the childhood of his baseball friend Ralph Gregorio. Artie found it surprisingly well-written and interesting. Leave it to a salesman like Boris, he thought, to write a best seller.

Barbara read a sensitive story, which Artie enjoyed, about a young woman whose grandmother dies on the same day the woman begins a new job, and then Joyce, after an interminable introduction full of self deprecation, launched into a fable she'd written about an old king, faced with a dilemma of whom to leave his realm to. His offspring include two sons, both of mediocre intelligence, and a younger daughter, smarter than all of them. Joyce had only written the first half of the story and said she needed help with the resolution of the tale. She hadn't yet figured out how to end it. Was it better to show the daughter triumphant—winning the throne through her wit—or to depict her as capable of doing so, but as deciding in her wisdom that she didn't want to rule the kingdom?

The women in the group argued both sides until finally Boris broke in and suggested that the older son win out. "Violence always overcomes intelligence," he said when Linda protested that his response was chauvinistic. "That's just the way the real world works," he added.

John, empty pipe in hand, cleared his throat and suggested that Joyce was perhaps trying to be too topical. "The fable form requires age-old formulas to be effective," he said. "You're trying to force a modern content into it. If you want to write about the conflict within a woman when faced with the drive for power why not set it in modern times when it's appropriate?"

"Bullshit," Sarah burst out.

The room was suddenly quiet. Sarah, like Artie, hadn't said a word all evening. Her eyes flickered behind her tinted glasses and her face, framed by her red hair, was burning. Everyone waited for her to continue, but it seemed she couldn't unlock her lips. John broke the silence with an awkward chuckle and Linda said, "Well, it will be interesting, Joyce, to see how you do resolve it. I hope you can finish it by next Wednesday."

She was about to announce refreshments, when Artie spoke up. "Why don't we all take the basic plot Joyce has used and write our own ending. We can bring them next time, and see which is most effective."

No one seemed to like his suggestion.

Joyce finally spoke up. "I don't mind discussing possible endings," she said, "but I think I'd feel like my idea was being stolen if everyone developed it. What if someone else's ending is better than mine? I can't use it."

"I guess you're right. I was treating it as an exercise."

When refreshments were served, Artie made his way to the front window where Barbara was talking to John. He hovered by John's elbow, listening, embarrassed that John refused to acknowledge his presence, although Barbara turned to face both, John was asking her how she got into career development. When she finished describing exactly what she did, Artie managed to insert himself by asking, "What can you do for someone who doesn't have a career?"

Barbara laughed and said she ran workshops to help people identify values and skills. "You should take one sometime," she said.

"What do they cost?" He hated always being such a tightwad, but he couldn't resist the poor man's compulsion.

"I sometimes use a variable scale," Barbara said. "It's usually $75 for an all-day workshop. But we could discuss it."

"Wow," was all he could think of saying. Seventy-five bucks was out of his league.

Near the end of the conversation, he was sorry to hear Barbara say she wouldn't be attending any more sessions. "I overextended myself," she explained. "My job, my outside consulting, and my workshops are a little too demanding right now. By coming here, I lose the time I could spend writing. At this stage I think it's better I try to stick to that."

Artie nodded, while John said the group would miss her.

"I enjoyed your story," Artie said. "Keep at it."

** *

When the following week's session rolled around, he packed up some recent work and was about to leave the apartment when his resolve suddenly slipped away. Do I really want to go and sit through another two hours of critical bullshit? Sarah had chosen the correct word. He turned back from the door, took his jacket off, and called Linda.

"I won't be able to make it any more," he said quickly, unwilling to offer an explanation. "Thanks for your help and let the group know I enjoyed meeting them." And with that he hurried off the line, his ears burning. What an idiot I am sometimes. Can't even be nice enough to manufacture a good excuse.

Now, what to tell Pam?

She'd been happy he was meeting other people, all of whom he had described to her in detail. Happy he was doing something to further his writing. Shit! Didn't she realize writing was a lonely art? He accepted the truism because for him it was true. He didn't like groups. He preferred independence. Even if it meant being isolated in the boondocks, twenty years out of date. He would develop his own way and if it turned out others liked it, fine. If not, that was their problem.

And then he laughed at himself. That was a lie. He had fantasies of fame as fanciful as the next guy's.

Later in the evening, several hours after he'd told Pam of his decision, she sat slumped in a corner of the sofa, a glass of Sambuca on the lamp stand to her left, and on the arm of the sofa a Florentine leather bookmark in black with gold fleur-de-lis. She took a sip of the Sambuca and felt the glass stick to her lip. The coaster, visible beneath the stemmed-glass, depicted a Van Gogh, a scene of four boats on the beach and two with white sails uplifted, out on the water.

The pictorial details absorbed her eyes but not her mind.

The stickiness of the Sambuca, the sweetness on her lips, brought to mind her and Artie's first kiss.

Their first had been at the beach, outside Florence, Oregon, at Devil's Elbow. They'd walked along a promontory, scrambling through brush and over jagged rocks, until they'd found a large sloping boulder overlooking a tide pool. The tide was coming in and as they sat on the rock watching, the sun started its descent into the ocean. Waves shattered below them, sending crystal fragments dancing toward their feet.

Artie put his arm around her, and she turned to look at him, inviting the kiss, afraid, since so many months had elapsed since she'd first met him, that he'd be another kid like her high school boyfriend. She'd gone with him for three years and he'd never kissed her once. Not even at the Senior Prom!

And what happened with Artie? They kissed—she still felt the chagrin—and their teeth clacked together! After years of practice, not only on her arm in grade school, but with guys other than her boyfriend. Pathetic!

At least both laughed and kissed again, a little more successful after the first. Happy they'd passed the barrier.

How'd I get on kissing? That sticky Sambuca glass, that's what started it.

When Artie came out of the shower, she asked him what he was going to do to get out of the house. Was there something more important than the writing group?

"You wanna know what's most important to me?"

"That's what I asked."

Artie cracked his stiff neck. He was still on his feet, in the middle of the living room. He rubbed the base of his nose.

"My writing ... you ... red licorice."

"I'm glad you put me before red licorice. So, is that it?"

Artie crossed the room and dropped into the big chair. He stared at the ceiling a moment.

"You really don't need friends?"

Artie shrugged. "I don't care that much about friends. You satisfy me."

"That's not healthy."

"You been talking to Joanne again? She's the only woman in your support group I don't like. To lift women up, she thinks she has to put men down."

"Joanne's got nothing to do with it. I think maybe you expect too much from me."

"I don't keep you from having friends." He saw where this was going.

"You used to have friends," she pointed out.

"Sure. I always had friends in high school and college. Some even in Chicago. Acquaintances." He hadn't told her about Cheryl.

"But you don't anymore."

"I'm busy trying to write."

\* \* \*

That night, in bed, reading John Fowles' *The Magus* at Artie's request, Pam laid down her book and turned to Artie.

"I have to agree with you about Joanne. Her view of feminism's a bit whacky"

Artie jumped in. "She's the female side of exactly what she hates, the macho jocks. If she was a guy, she'd be talking about every woman's 'knockers' and 'Jugs.'"

"She's of a younger generation than you and me. She grew up after half the hard fights were won. She's just into being an equal, as good as men—"

"And as bad!"

"—in everything. If men enjoy women's bodies, why shouldn't women enjoy men's?"

"I didn't say they shouldn't. But she's so hypocritical. She picks on such picayune things." That he was referring to his own foibles he made instantly clear. "She makes me feel I'm not a feminist and I'm the most supportive person I know."

They both laughed at the inadvertent humor.

"Well, aren't I?"

Pam nodded. "I suppose so. Now, at any rate. But you weren't always."

"So? No one's conscience was raised when we were young. We grew up trained to be the same as our parents. She hasn't had to fight any of that."

Artie's complaint regarding what he called "pickiness"centered on Joanne's habit of correcting him any time he used the word "girl."

"It's getting so I'm calling ten-year old girls 'women.' I'm afraid to point out a girl playing. The first thing that comes to my mind now is, 'Oh, look at the young woman playing' and the kid's a three-year old."

Pam couldn't help laughing. She let Artie rant on, a half-smile on her lips.

"I referred to some of your students as girls and she blew up. I mean, shit!"—he was getting worked up now—"they're half my age. They're still in their teens!"

"Yeah, and when you're sixty, you'll be talking about forty-year old girls."

Artie frowned. Was she agreeing with Joanne now?

"Do you call my male students boys?"

"Sometimes I do. Now. If I say 'girls' I make sure the parallel is 'boys.' What'n hell is the parallel of guys, now? I asked Joanne once if she liked 'gals' and she said that was worse yet. I think guys and girls are on the same level."

"Nope." Pam shook her head, pulling the bedspread even. Artie had tossed it aside in his agitation. "Not for her. Why don't you just call both sexes 'guys'?

You do that half the time anyway."

"I saw this guy walking down the street! Like that? I saw this female guy talking to this male guy!" He glanced at Pam with a look between impish questioning and frustration.

For a moment she stared back in silence. "Perhaps you'd better just stick to woman," she said finally. "Now let's go to sleep."

Soon after New Year's Day, with 1977 stretching gelid wings preparing for its slow flight toward spring, with Pam back in school and busy teaching, Artie began work on a new novel. Over the Christmas holidays, he'd picked a title. Or two, at least. He wavered between *Catching Polliwogs* and *Ralph*, the latter influenced by Alberto Moravia's novel *Agostino*. Pam had asked him to read it, which he'd done in the original, when she learned he was going to write about an adolescent. But, shit! nothing like being intimidated by a great novelist.

He knew before starting that he had no chance of success. "After this one I'm going to go commercial," he'd say to himself and sometimes to Pam. "I'll pick a format, one of the commercial genres, crime fiction, and grind out a book."

Catching polliwogs meant a return to his childhood, to the days spent on his grandmother's farm in Ferndale near Bellingham. In the late 1940s, Artie's grandfather had built an earthen weir where the creek ran through a cleft in the valley and the year-round pond that formed in the swale soon burbled with bullfrogs and slippery polliwogs. As a kid, perhaps only five or six years old—Artie wasn't sure which—he'd go out to the pond by himself in the summer, find the raft and his tin can with the holes in the bottom, and spend hours lying on his stomach trying to fill a glass jar with pollywogs.

It was a memory, along with so many others from childhood, that freed him from the winter gloom of the Lower East Side. Or perhaps, he thought, it was another sign of approaching middle age. Sometimes he wondered what he was doing with his life and what he'd done in the past. It was nice not having a job, but also hard in a way. It meant he had no excuse not to write. And at the end of a day when he had only a page or two and many wasted hours in between, it was hard to justify not finding a job.

Sometimes, to help pass the time, Artie would accompany Pam to the university and read in the library or walk around the village or watch the students busy with social chatter on their way between classes. Occasionally, if he was either very bored or very energetic, he'd attend a lecture and listen to someone talk of church-state relations in Poland, or of the latest telescopes being built in the deserts of Arizona (perhaps, he thought, some of the desert heat would rub off the visiting astronomer), or of Ludwig Uhland and the Swabian romanticists. Now and then he'd even learn something he could use in his novel.

Winter seemed to stretch on forever. He noticed Pam was growing progressively gloomier. Almost every day now she told Artie she hated the city.

"If Chicago's like this, I don't see how you stood it for so long. So cold and gray."

"I hated every winter. Everyone just kept saying it takes time to adjust. Not sure I ever did. But at a certain point it takes less energy to stay than it does to leave."

He paused and looked out the kitchen window. The snow on the curb was black with soot and rubbish. Near the garbage cans dogs had left yellow pee marks, and there were piles of dog shit visible from the height of their apartment, four stories up. "Maybe we ought to go back to Oregon."

Pam looked at him and nodded. "I wouldn't mind sometimes. I miss the fir trees, the creeks, the lakes, the mountains. But then I miss the weather in Berkeley, too."

"Rain is better than this snow. I think I'm ready for a smaller town."

"It all comes down to finding a job somewhere. Not easy in my field."

Another day, Pam mentioned Europe. "We could go to Italy," she said. They'd just watched the late evening news, Nightline, with Ted Koppel, and there'd been a report from Rome.

"I'm never going back to live in Rome," Artie said. "That city did me in the last time I went there. Too big. Didn't help that it was a field trip with our art history professor from Pavia. I think we'd feel lost."

"You think New York or Chicago are small?"

"Okay, but there are smaller towns in Italy that are a lot nicer."

"What about Florence?"

He shrugged. "I prefer Venice."

"There's a grant I'm thinking of applying for that would allow me to do some research in Florence. If I get it, would you be willing to come? You can write there as easily as here, right?"

"Not really."

"*What?*"

"Shit! I don't care. Apply for the dumb thing. We don't even know if you'll get it. And if you do I won't have to find work."

"I don't want to apply for it, get it, and then have you say you're not going."

"If you get it, we'll go. You know how rusty my Italian is, though."

"You do fine around my colleagues," she said. "It might spur your creativity."

"I hope the grant's enough to live on. Nobody's going to employ me in Italy, that's for sure."

"Nobody's employing you here, either."

That ended the conversation.

# chapter 31

In the Spring of that year, to mark the anniversary of her third decade on earth, Pam learned that, indeed, she had won a fellowship from the American Society of Scholarly Research for six months, in the amount of $7,500, to conduct research on printing presses and the work of the *poligrafi* active in Florence in the early sixteenth century.

Pam knew Italian scholars had two classifications for writers. They were either *Minori* or *Maggiori*, minor or major. The people she had proposed studying were, for all practical purposes, *Minimi!* Less than minor, though, at the time, they were often the most famous writers in Tuscany. They were editors, scholars, critics, authors, and publishers.

The grant would begin in June and the university was allowing her to take a leave Fall semester without pay.

"Six free months," she crowed. "That's fantastic! I need the break."

The news would've made her happier if Artie's attempts at finding a publisher for his work were more successful. His first novel continued to be rejected. No one would look at *Nocturnal Emissions*. Even agents who read his one-page description of the book declined the opportunity to read it. "I can't even get anyone to *look* at it." And, later, after trying ten small presses, he told her, "Half the places are out of business, half say they don't have funds, half say they're only publishing poetry, half are into reprints only."

"That's four halves."

He didn't appreciate the joke.

Pam feared her success would only anger him more. When Artie fell into a blue funk, she tried to bring him out of it. "Don't take things so personal. All writers get rejection notices." Or, "It doesn't do you any good to get upset. Anger doesn't solve anything. Research some more markets. Use your head."

He didn't take that well either.

In late April, Pam and Joanne drove upstate together to visit two women friends who had moved to the country to homestead a small farm. Pam had cleared four days from her schedule.

Artie spent the weekend wandering around the city, visiting MoMA, catching a show at a theater near the village, eating out alone, missing Pam. He hadn't asked to go. He thought the separation would be good for them.

And in fact it was. On Pam's return, Sunday afternoon, they made love twice, with renewed enthusiasm, and settled down for a relaxing evening together. Pam was reading a library book, sitting on the sofa, while Artie wrote. They'd been peacefully silent nearly an hour when Pam spoke.

"You know," she said, "we never have talked much about it."

Had she been carrying on a conversation in her mind? With him or with the book? "About what?"

"I don't think I've dealt with my anger very well. We never have talked much about how I felt after you left. Back then, when we went to the counselor, we looked at our three years of marriage, not at my anger. I don't think I expressed it enough."

"Shit! When I came back you went crazy!"

"After we divorced, I kept a lot of anger in for a long time. I didn't even think I was angry! I didn't even think our split affected how I reacted to others that much. It's like a delayed reaction. We're back together and the anger's surfacing now."

Artie shrugged, trying to listen without being defensive, without starting an argument. Had she been talking to Joanne again?

"You're not giving up on us, are you?"

"Come on, Artie. You have more faith in me than that, right? We did decide to try again. That, to me, takes more commitment than the first time."

"But we decided *not* to marry again."

"You know why. It doesn't have anything to do with how close our relationship is, I'm just opposed to marriage. Philosophically, I think it's a lousy institution."

"It's just a state of mind," Artie said. "It's no different than just living with someone."

"It is to me." She drew her legs up to her chest, "I don't like the possessiveness that goes with it. 'My wife,' 'my husband.' 'I have a wife.' Why don't people say, 'I'm married to …' It's always a possessive verb."

"Come on. You're getting carried away by language."

"That's what feminism is all about. Language. You know— your troubles with Joanne. Girls or women."

"It's funny," he said. "All your 'independent' friends are getting married."

She'd told him one of her friends, Vera Lovati, had written from Canada to announce her upcoming wedding. Vanni and Gina Di Pietro had called from Berkeley to say they'd finally decided to formalize their relationship after living together seven years. And Kathy Wakinsky, one of Joanne's best friends in the city, a strong feminist, was getting married and moving to San Francisco with her husband.

"Marriage ties people together who shouldn't stay together. My parents for example."

He liked her parents. "Maybe, despite their fights, they need each other."

"Sure, like a dog needs a burr up his butt."

"Marriage doesn't have to destroy freedom."

"Look at all the women who give up careers for men. Look what it caused in our case—a lot of hardship and hurt. Marriage is a fucked-up institution. It's about control more than anything."

"People can be just as free inside a marriage as in a partnership. You bargain what you need in life. Careers and all. Look at us. We're bargaining how we're going to live together. Establishing what matters to each."

Pam laughed. "We're not married now!"

"Well, I feel like we are. It's just a piece of paper, a state of mind."

"It's a legal hassle. A person should be able to go down to city hall and just say, 'I'm dissolving my marriage,' and have it end just like it started. There's still a stigma attached to divorced women too. If you just live with a man and walk out, there's no stigma. You're not a divorcee. You're just a person."

Artie took a deep breath. "Okay, I can see it's easier to break up if you aren't married, but marriage provides economic security."

"I'm not saying marriage is bad for everyone. It's just not for me. I wouldn't expect any of your money, even if you earned more."

Artie laughed. "Fine. But how about me sharing yours if we split? I'm doing all the cooking and cleaning! Shit! I'd better get down and get a marriage license. I need protection!"

Their winter of discontent, it seemed, was running its course. On days when the weather was good, they were happy. On days when it was stormy, they tended to pick at each other. "Happily married again!" they'd both joke after these bouts. Their feelings toward New York didn't seem to improve. One evening, they were eating a dinner of lasagne and salad when a cockroach fell from a crack in the ceiling and landed on Pam's plate. She screamed in disgust and beat it into a pulp with her fork.

"God! We can't even eat without roaches jumping on our plates. I feel sick." She shoved the plate away.

"Throw it away. Get it off the table."

"You can wash the fork," she said.

"I'm not washing it. You wash it. Get a new one. Throw the stuff in the garbage."

"I've lost my appetite," Pam said. "You can eat all the lasagne for all I care."

Artie's fork was at rest in his hand.

Pam looked at the plate. "It looks like a dried chili pod," she said. "Want some spicy lasagne?"

Artie wrinkled his upper lip. "Ick! He was a great parachuter, wasn't he?"

They both laughed.

"I'm getting out of here," Pam said.

"We can't afford a nicer apartment."

"I mean out of the city. I'm tired of putting up with hassles. I hate this place. I feel like I'm going to be attacked in the street every time I come home."

"It's your job that's keeping us here. Besides, we're going to Italy soon. I came here for you. I can write anywhere as you say."

"We may be going to Italy, but we're also coming back. Back here! You know how hard it is to get jobs in academia. There may be nothing on the West coast."

"Let's do something else, then. Start a business. We can go back to Eugene."

"Eugene's economy is dead," she said. "We'd be better off in California. And it's warmer."

"California has too many people already. If we went to Berkeley to start an Italian caffè, we'd have too much competition."

"Well, I'm not going to Chicago."

"I never mentioned Chicago. But let's go someplace the Californians haven't gotten to yet."

"Like where?"

"I don't know. Are they in Idaho?"

"Is anything in Idaho?"

"The southern part of the state might be okay."

"I'd rather be in Oregon."

"Me too," Artie said. "That's why I mentioned Eugene. You'd be close to your family."

She nodded. "Let's clean up the table." She'd already scraped her plate into the garbage. "What if I could get a job in Italy?" she asked, her back to him as she put a jug of cider into the refrigerator.

Artie was at the sink, squeezing liquid soap on the dishes and running hot water over the salad bowls. The phosphorescent light flickered over his bent head. "I suppose it'd be okay—for a while." Could he keep busy in Florence? "But not for long."

# chapter 32

Pam memorized all the sights on the way to the airport, telling herself they might be the last things she'd ever see. Plane might crash on take-off. Once the were out over the ocean, her thoughts turned to the university. It was going to be hard to return there. Especially since it would be winter. Could she get a position elsewhere in the tight job market?

"Artie," she said, nudging him to distract him from an article he was reading. "This next winter is the last semester I'm teaching in New York. No matter what."

"Good. Fine by me. We can both find part-time jobs and I'll still have time to write."

She could tell he didn't like the pressure. But they'd agreed, since they'd lived in large part off his savings the summer before she started teaching, that he could have the school year free. Was he trying to extend that into the future? Letting a pattern develop? The grant was only going to provide support for another six months.

"I've always worked anyway." Artie said, hunching down in his seat. "Don't feel like you're the only one supporting us."

Pam was silent for a while. "I know," she said finally, almost to herself. "But one semester and that's it."

In Florence, having rented an apartment on the top floor of a restored building on Borgo Allegri, near the Loggia dei Pesci and the antique market, Pam and Artie settled down to work.

Pam, after two weeks of struggle in the Biblioteca Nazionale, found herself soured on the Florentine polygraphs. Should have picked the Venetians. Artie preferred Venice. She should have listened.

Too damn hot! But when she looked at the temps in *La Repubblica*, the highs in Venice were just as bad.

One day, instead of working in the National Library, she took a break and accompanied Artie to the Vieusseux Library in the Palazzo Strozzi. They spent the entire day reading magazines in the reading room, and the next day, Artie took her to the lending library of the Intercultural Foundation on Via Bernardo Rucellai. Artie had been told about the library, which contained a strong collection of novels in English, by the Rector of the nearby St. James Church, during one of his touristic jaunts soon after their arrival in Florence.

Instead of returning to the archives at the National Library, Pam spent the next month with Artie, reading mysteries and losing herself in the pleasures of light fiction.

On their way home in the heat, licking a gelato while strolling down Borgo degli Albizzi, Pam told Artie about her reading in the eighth grade. "My teacher, Mrs. Diderot, offered us extra credit and gold stars on a chart for each book we read and wrote a one-page book report on. I didn't care about the extra credit. I knew I'd get an A, but I loved those gold stars by my name. Jim Hetlidge always thought he was so smart and I wanted to show him. I'd hated him ever since the fifth grade, when he used to run behind me, flip my skirt up, and shout, 'I see London, I see France, I see Pam's underpants.'"

Artie laughed, twirling his own cone to keep the gelato from dripping.

"Anyway, I wanted to out-gold-star Hetlidge so I started reading a book a day. On the weekend sometimes I'd finish three or four books. I read everything I could in the juvenile section.

"By the end of the term, I had seventy-seven gold stars and the next person in line had fourteen! No one believed I'd read so many, but Mrs. Diderot had a one-page report on each."

"So, you had to come to Florence to return to your origins," he joked. "English literature. You should have majored in that, not Romance Languages."

"Then I wouldn't have met you," she said.

He had to admit she was right.

It was in August that Artie began to deteriorate. It started with their neighbors. Pam's and Artie's one bedroom apartment looked out over a courtyard, tall buildings on three sides, open gardens and small sheds on the fourth. Below them, on the third level, lived several Arab students. They liked to play loud music, which vibrated up and down the courtyard, and argued politics till three or four in the morning. Pam, at first, slept through it, but Artie lay in bed for hours, stewing. He pondered trying to communicate with Arabs in Italian and gave up. One of the guys had stopped by one morning to borrow an egg and they'd been constrained to use sign language. The Arab tried speaking English, but it was next to impossible to understand him. His Italian, worse than Artie's, was no help.

And so, he continued to fume and smoulder. What made matters worse was that when he finally fell asleep at four or five in the morning, he would be jarred from sleep at eight when the workers next door began hammering on the walls. Their landlady was having the apartment next to theirs remodeled. By law nothing could be done to the exterior of the buildings in their area, but the owners were free to restore interiors. The workers began daily promptly at eight, using sledge hammers to chip out brick walls. Occasionally the noise in the kitchen was so loud Artie and Pam rushed from the room to eat their panini and red-currant or cherry marmellata in the bedroom.

Within a week, Artie was a nervous wreck, muttering all night, swearing all day. "Why didn't Laura tell us that "distretto del popolo" meant noise?" he'd ask angrily. Their landlady, Laura Frigoni, had described the neighborhood as one "of the people." That hadn't sounded as bad as saying "the raucous district." Along Borgo Allegri itself, across from the park behind the day school, transvestites in red wigs roamed the streets by day and by night. They'd settled down in the midst of one of the city's more fabled areas. But hadn't Florence, like San Francisco, always been a city of gays? Pam told him even Dante's supposed teacher, Brunetto Latini, was probably a pederast. Dante did place him among the sodomites in hell.

From insomnia, Artie passed to a condition best described as *spaesato*, countryless. Isolated, especially when Pam finally started doing some serious research,, mentally unbalanced by anger, he began to rant at everything. "We can't even go to a show for entertainment," he'd scream. "These fucking Italians dub everything. God! I can't stand hearing someone do Clint Eastwood in Italian!" Cut off as if shipwrecked on a desert island, no news, no TV, no friends, no connectedness.

One afternoon, a dog began barking. It took Artie two hours to figure out where the sound came from. The dog's whining yap echoed from the buildings around the courtyard. Was it in one of the other apartments on the three built-up sides? The fourth side ran at least a block before it was enclosed by other buildings. Perhaps the dog was in one of the potting sheds? And then he spotted it. The puppy was penned in a wire enclosure behind a greenhouse. The fence ran beyond the edge of the shed, and Artie by luck happened to be looking in that direction when the puppy, a Cocker-Spaniel, stuck his head around the corner of the greenhouse.

An hour later, frustrated by the continual yapping, Artie opened the kitchen shutter and shouted at the dog. He was surprised to hear someone else respond. The voice came all the way from the far end of the U, a block away almost. An old woman on a balcony raised her arm and shouted agreement, as well as an imprecation in dialect. Embarrassed, Artie stepped back into the kitchen and closed the shutter.

The yapping kept up all evening. By bedtime, Artie was enraged. He strode through the apartment screaming he'd kill the dog and its owners if he had to. He grabbed a quart wine bottle, poured what was left into three glasses, and opened the kitchen shutters again.

In the twilight shadows, he couldn't find the dog but he could see the greenhouse. The owners of the dog, perhaps a new acquisition, had left him tied in their yard while apparently away for the entire day. Glancing around angrily, Artie saw other windows open in the heat, but no one was in sight. Across the courtyard, where two or three times that summer he'd caught a glimpse of a topless woman, he could see the light of a TV inside a bedroom. A man moved back and forth in the room. The woman seemed to be lying on the bed, watching TV.

Convinced that no one was watching, Artie swung his arm and let fly with the bottle. His aim was good. The bottle crashed through the top of the greenhouse, shattering glass with an ominously loud smash. Afraid he'd be glimpsed, Artie jumped back into the darkness of the kitchen—he'd doused all the lights before throwing the bottle. The poor dog was yelping in terror and Artie's own heart was beating in tune to the animals's cries.

Other voices were yelling now, shouting at the pup. Artie watched through the shutter as the family on the first floor ran into the courtyard looking skyward at the buildings around the base of the U. He hoped they thought no one was home.

Pam meanwhile, sitting in bed in darkness, was calling.

"Why aren't you in bed, Artie?"

"Can't you hear that dumb dog?"

"Well, shut the window, then. I was asleep."

"I've had to listen to him all day. I didn't get anything done. He's driving me crazy. Besides, it's too hot in here with the windows shut."

"It's too hot in here with them open," Pam said. "I'm dripping wet. "

Artie walked, nude, into the bedroom. He could see her white form in the darkness. "Why are you wearing that shift? You should sleep nude."

"I don't like the mosquitoes."

"I could start the Vape." The Vape was a small electrified box which emitted a vapor when a chemical tablet was placed in it.

"The fumes bother my breathing," she said, sitting up in bed.

"What'd we buy it for then?"

She didn't respond. He lay back, gritting his teeth. Pam was still sitting up. She swung around to face him, opening her legs. "Feel," she said.

He waited a moment, still fuming, and then reached out. Her shift was pulled up around her waist and she had no underpants on. Her body was wet. He got to his knees, bending to lick and suck her pussy. When he finished a half hour later, the dog was still yapping.

"I'm going to go crazy and kill somebody," he told her. "Either that or you're going to have to keep your legs wrapped around my ears all night."

"That sounds like fun," she said, but a half hour later when Artie got up to wander around the apartment, Pam was sound asleep. "Sic transit another night," he thought. One more day's march on the road to death. Death recently was becoming a fixation. Was he planning on killing his neighbors or himself? If I had a machine gun, he thought, I might go wild. One more madman gunning people down from a tower. Maybe they were insomniacs, too! If so, he couldn't blame them. At least not at the moment.

He began to broach the possibility of an early return. "I don't know if I can make it here anymore," he told Pam. "You're going to have a raving maniac on your hands."

Pam thought he was exaggerating. "You're just bored."

"I'm telling you, I'm going to wind up in a straightjacket."

"Come on, Artie, I need at least two more months. Can't you last till the end of October? We can leave a month or two earlier than we planned."

For another week Artie tried. He did everything he could think of to keep busy, to tire himself out so he'd sleep at night. In the evenings, after the traffic thinned, he ran north along the Arno from the Ponte alle Grazie near Santa Croce to the Ponte San Nicolò and from that bridge further north past the Ponte Giovanni Da Verrazzano to the Bellariva swimming pool. But even this distance, which exhausted him physically, failed to tire his mind.

By the end of the week, Artie was suggesting a temporary separation. Two months apart. He would leave as soon as possible for home and Pam would follow once she finished her work.

At first, Pam was reluctant. But she was just as reluctant to leave early and Artie was adamant. They discussed the idea for two days, each reassuring the other that the break was not permanent, that it was, rather, a sign of their maturity. They could exist as a couple and yet allow each other to continue developing as individuals. By the time they'd come to an agreement, the separation seemed almost a victory, a reaffirmation of their decision to live together as a couple.

"It means we can trust each other," Artie said. "We share a commitment to each other, but we can also accept each other's needs for a separate space."

"Freedom to pursue some interests apart," Pam added. "Have we used all the cliche's?"

"Probably, but I feel better already." He hugged her. "I'll be waiting for you when you get back."

Alone in Florence, Pam tried to immerse herself in work. Artie called from New York on his return to say he'd arrived safely. The apartment, however, had been broken into. "I don't understand why the person didn't take more," Artie said. "All that's missing, as far as I can tell, are the clock radio and the Polaroid camera. They didn't touch the typewriter. Must've been scared off. Joe says they came in from the fire escape. He replaced the window latch with a better one."

Joe was their neighbor down the hall on the same floor. They didn't know him well, but he'd agreed to look after the place for fifteen dollars a month while they were gone.

"I'll call you once a week," Artie said, "and we can write. I miss you already. I didn't think it'd be hard to last two months after we lasted five years apart, but now I'm not so sure."

"Try to keep busy," Pam said, attempting to sound cheerful, "and maybe it'll pass fast. I miss you too! I'm spending most of my time in the library. I've already been thinking I might be able to get the really important things read in a month or so. We'll see. But I'll write too."

In Artie's letters, which soon followed, he spoke often of moving away from New York. He broached the subject again on another phone call, wondering, if she wasn't able to get an academic job, what she'd think of them seriously trying to open a health food store or a soup kitchen in Oregon.

"We could settle in a small place like Cottage Grove," he said. "Or even in Eugene. The economy is shitty"—he remembered she'd raised that objection before—"but I think we could make it starting small. People still like to eat out."

Pam was noncommittal, but at least she agreed that New York was out.

"I want to get back to the West, too," she said, "but you never seem to consider California. I'm more likely to get a job there than in Oregon. I spent too many years studying to give up teaching so soon."

"We can keep our options open," he said. "Just keep it in mind."

Pam at night had no TV to distract her. The hardest hours were those after dinner before bedtime. Once or twice a week, she would try to invite one of the other women doing research to join her for dinner at a nice restaurant. Eating with someone else slowed her down, forced her to talk, extended the hours of companionship, delayed the lonely moments alone in the apartment.

She was grateful for Artie's letters. He wrote many more than she. Some days there would be two, even three, letters in the mail. She tried to write often, but her life seemed uneventful. She concentrated on her feelings for him.

When her letters reached Artie, he began to comment on her observations. "You know, Pam," he wrote at one point. "Maybe I've misinterpreted you. There's an expression used by Walter Van Tilburg Clark in *The Ox-Bow Incident* that I think applies to you. He's writing about a rough woman named Jenny Grier, big and tough as nails, a bit weird. She didn't always think things through, he says, but she did a lot of what he calls intelligent feeling. Well, I think that applies to you. I've called you too rational before, but I think it was me fighting my own feelings of inferiority that made me do it. I was blind to a lot of things, and it seems I learn more every day."

He also wrote to her about change. How does one maintain change in life and in love? Walker Percy's moviegoer was on to the "search," seeing those normal aspects of surrounding life as if for the first time. Artie instead, as he put it, was into the "escape," the attempt to break out of habitual practices by varying the expected sequence of events.

"When I was still young," he wrote, "I reacted physically. I ran from you, from responsibility. Now I realize that was a mistake. There are so many other ways I could've found newness within the relationship. I didn't try hard enough, maybe because I thought greener pastures lay beyond the fence. I know all this sounds trite, but I think I'm ready now to have us find the greener pastures together, to find them within ourselves. If as individuals we can find new things to interest us, why can't we do the same as a couple? In fact, we'd double our chances!"

The end result of the "search" and the "escape," he realized one day, was perhaps the same: to experience life rather than to glide through it as if anesthetized to the humdrum. Alone in New York, waiting for Pam, Artie made it a practice to force change upon himself. He wanted to open his eyes, to take more in, to flood his senses. The eyes were selective. He wanted to control more consciously their selectivity. He felt he'd been taught not only how to see, but what to see. It was time to start over. Was a return to one's origins a rebirth or a retreat from the world? He was determined to make it a rebirth.

When Pam pondered her return to NYU, she wondered if it was worth it. She realized she was losing interest in research, the pressure to produce scholarly article after article. A book every three or four years. She thought she knew why.

Two reasons. Maybe the change was just a way of preparing for the inevitable. She wanted to leave New York for the West coast and she knew that might mean no academic job.

Another reason? Overwork. She'd only taught one year full-time, but it felt like her sixth or seventh after all the classes she'd taught as a teaching assistant in grad school. The years of effort and strain in Berkeley had taken their toll. Few people had published as much as she at that stage of their career. She had seven articles by the time she left Berkeley. Most graduate students felt lucky if they had one or two. But the pressure could not go on building forever. It was time to release the steam cock, bobbing and hissing on top the pressure cooker of her mind. Freedom. Leisure. Rest. They seemed foreign words!

Knowing she might have to leave the profession, she found it difficult to stay motivated. Was the sacrifice worth it? She and Artie had already lost five years of their youth that could've been spent together. Oh sure, she knew rationally, they weren't lost. Much had happened, both good and bad. Still, sharing one's life, making a commitment, creating a loving relationship, didn't they both feel that was as important as writing a scholarly book or a novel?

Artie was right. There were other things more important in life than this drudgery. People for one. Health for another.

Living in New York, breathing the air, fighting the crowds, stunned by the noise—could she even do that for another semester? In her notebook she wrote "Ho deciso di piantare baracca e burattini." It was an expression she'd learned that week reading the newspapers. "I have decided to pack it in, lock, stock, and barrel." By chance, she counted the letters of the Italian expression. Thirty-five. Even the number was significant, midway through life. For her, of course, thirty-five was still a few years away. She wouldn't reach that milestone until 1982. Still, she thought, it doesn't hurt to prepare early.

But was it only an idyllic dream? Going back home?

For Artie it might work. He wanted to write in peace and quiet. He didn't mind working part-time at a lousy job. But wouldn't he run out of inspiration without the invigorating activities of the big city? And what would she do? The idea of starting a women's center appealed to her, but could she make any money doing that? It didn't seem likely. And she wasn't trained for that.

# chapter 33

After a week of hesitation, Pam made a decision. I'm going to do what Artie did. I'm flying home. Back to the nest. Or rather back to the tree where one could build a true nest. Not back home to New York. Back home to the West.

A stage of her life, she felt, was drawing to a close. And yet somehow things remained the same. Almost ten years ago she'd gotten married full of hope for the future, full of fond illusions which turned out to be false hopes. Now, after three years of marriage, after half a decade alone, both of which slowly wore away the sheen of youthful dreams, after another year and a summer together with Artie, struggling once again to live with another person, she found herself with idealistic fantasies for the future. Have I learned nothing? she asked herself. Am I just as naive as I once was?

Not really, she told herself. Her renewal of hope was accompanied this time by some measure of trepidation. What did the future hold? Would it be that easy starting over? Were the years spent gaining a profession, an education, wasted?

Going back to Oregon was a return in more ways than one. Wouldn't it be a return to the same grueling poverty of the early years of their marriage? What if neither could find a job? Were they really capable of starting a business on their own? All the millworkers and loggers were laid off; the railroad was slowing down; the economy was stagnant and getting worse. It didn't bode well.

Going back was also a return to their roots. Artie's family lived in Westville and hers in Eugene. If they settled in Cottage Grove, they'd only be twenty or so miles from her folks, and two hours drive from Artie's. It would be a return to the rain, to the winter drizzles that seemed to last two weeks straight, to days of clouds and grayness.

But at least there wasn't the cold and snow of New York or of Chicago. There were four seasons, not just two. And the rain brought its own pleasures and its own beauties: the fields of strawberries in early spring, and later the raspberries, blackberries, blueberries and boysenberries, all of which she'd picked, the rows of green beans, and year-round the tall forests of evergreen fir, the mountain slopes of the Cascades, the clear running streams which fed the McKenzie, brimming with trout, and the Willamette, rolling heavily through Eugene.

And the ocean beaches, she couldn't forget them, the rocky shoreline and tide pools teeming with marine life, the hidden coves, the lofty dunes, all were only two hours away. She envisioned Route F, the curving road leading from Eugene by Fern Ridge Reservoir, along the Siuslaw River, through the Siuslaw National Forest, to Florence, on the coast. Her heart leapt. Devil's Elbow to the north was where she and Artie had first kissed. And to the south were the dunes and Coos Bay where she lived for a few years as a child.

Somewhere over the Atlantic, on an Alitalia, jet from Milan to New York, she took out a pen and wrote a short spontaneous poem for Artie. Despite all her years of studying literature, it was the first poem she'd ever written.

I started smiling
five hundred miles away
coming home to you
flying at thirty thousand feet
just to see your face
waiting outside the gate
coming home to you
feeling high going fast
too slow
too many heartbeats away
can't wait to hear you laugh
can't wait to see you smile
coming home to you

But, after an ecstatic reunion at JFK, after grinning at each other all the way from the airport through the Queens to Manhattan, after staying in bed together all day and making love twice a day for the next week and daily for the week after that, Artie and Pam decided they would have to stay in the city until May. Pam felt an obligation to NYU and Artie realized they would need the money if they expected to start a business on the West coast. Plus it gave Pam a chance to find a university position.

When Pam went back to teaching in the winter of '78, Artie found a job in a small restaurant in the Village. He began working as a janitor there, cleaning up late at night after the restaurant closed and putting in about twenty hours a week. After a month had passed, he convinced the owner to add him to a weekend shift as a waiter, along with his janitorial duties. It wasn't long after before he was able to phase out as clean-up boy and join the staff as a full-time waiter. While his hourly wage was low, he received good tips and made enough for him and Pam to live off of. Pam's salary, nearly two thousand a month before taxes, went straight to their savings account. Their goal was to save a minimum of nine thousand by May and possibly ten if they budgeted well.

That winter, the Modern Language Association convention, where all the interviewing for university positions took place, was held in Chicago, and Pam attended, having arranged two interviews, one with the University of Washington in Seattle—her old friend David Palude was leaving for Michigan—and one with the University of Colorado in Boulder.

Rather than fly to Chicago, she traveled by car with two colleagues, sharing driving expenses, anything to save money, and Artie saw to it that in Chicago she stayed for free in the living room of Beverley Watson from the Food for People Coop.

In March, to her disappointment, Pam learned that the position at Boulder had fallen through, due to a lack of funding. The situation with Washington, however, remained open, though cloudy. Palude had written to her confidentially after the convention, telling her that the university had an inside candidate who they were favoring. The candidate was a woman with her Ph.D., a lecturer who'd been teaching part-time at the university.

Sure enough, a few weeks later, she received a form letter thanking her for her interest, but informing her that the position had been filled. Up to that moment, she'd secretly been hoping some university would offer her a position. She'd already let New York University know that Spring semester was her last. With the turndown from Washington she was out in the cold.

Jobless.

It was frightening, no matter how much she and Artie had talked of moving to Oregon and starting a café. Reality, when a necessity, was much harsher than her earlier vision of it.

Artie tried to bolster her courage. The cold winter grimness of New York helped. There was no way she would stay in the city another year. Whenever she was hesitant about the future, she tried to contrast Eugene to New York. It was a contrast not only between environments but between life styles, and she'd convinced herself that she needed a break from the pressures of academia.

A life in the country, in a small, laid-back city, with friendly neighbors, and a little café would, she told herself, do her wonders. There would be the pressure of earning a living, but, as Artie said, they at least would be working for themselves. "The only thing I'll miss," she told him, "are the free summers." But he pointed out that her summers had never really been free. There was always the pressure of doing research, of publishing yet another paper.

Artie himself was not immune to fear, despite the fact that he hid it from Pam. "Just think of all the experience I've had and am still getting now," he told her. "I've worked in a non-profit cooperative retail grocery store, I've run a café, and now I'm getting restaurant experience. The only hard part will be finding a good location and lining up suppliers."

Occasionally Artie talked about leaving a month early, so that when Pam finished school he'd have a living place already lined up and maybe even the business itself. Pam, however, asked him to wait.

"At worst, until we get something set up, we can live free with my folks in Eugene," she said. "That way we wouldn't go through any of our savings. And if you keep working till I finish, we'll have more yet."

Sometimes, in her darker moments, when she envisioned the café as a failure, she saw herself back picking strawberries, as she'd done in grade school. Could things ever get that bad?

Artie too found himself worrying about their future. How many people dared start a new life? Everyone talked about it, but few actually gave up their security to risk all on a crazy venture. The gamble sometimes made him giddy.

But he and Pam would be working side by side, their own bosses, making their living from their hands, living at peace in a setting where people lived simply, where life had meaning and was lived slowly, not rushed, as if humanity could not wait for death, but closer to the natural rhythms of the seasons.

For their vacations (when they could afford to take them!), he wanted them to visit all the cities they'd lived in as kids. They would find again Pam's house in Coos Bay, and Eugene would be there everyday to remind them of where they came from. For Artie, they could visit Portland, and Gresham, where he grew up. And Westville where his folks lived.

From there it was just a few miles to the Sandy River near Camp Collins or to Mount Hood. And finally they could drive up to Spokane, where his grandparents had their home. His trips there as a kid had always been a joy. Spokane was where he first saw "Howdy Doody" and "The Lone Ranger" on his cousins' TV. And where he went down the water slide at Liberty Lake, ate licorice ice cream, and visited more relatives in Fairfield, surrounded by immense fields of wheat and soy beans, thousands of acres, stretching as far as the eye could see.

Having reached the apartment, back after a short trip to buy groceries, Artie paused on the steps, looking around before going in. Had anything changed? Across the street loomed an abandoned building, burned out, and to the left a rubble-strewn lot, debris piled at the back. Half of the block was rotting away with age, the other half grimly hanging on to its last shreds of life. Some day, when it all decayed and fell to ruin, would grasses and shrubs sprout above the rubble? Would trees rise above the crumbled brick? Would there be a soft floor of pine or fir needles in ages to come? He hoped so.

On the day Artie quit his job, one day after Pam's last finals had been corrected, and they were both free, they whooped with joy, shouted "freedom" with self-conscious embarrassment , hugged each other, and went out to dinner to celebrate. "Time to revel!" Artie shouted, as they walked down the street, arms around each other.

"Now let's not get too carried away," Pam said "We've only got ten thousand three hundred and sixty dollars to blow."

Artie threw his arms to the sky. "Wow! We did it! Time to celebrate and then hit the road."

His comment on hitting the road sobered both of them.

"Tonight we celebrate," Pam said quietly, "and then tomorrow we get down to the serious work." And then she smiled. "Living."

"Earning a living," Artie corrected.

"Both," she said. "Living and earning a living together. On our own. Independent. It sounds nice but scary, doesn't it?"

The following day, a Saturday, they packed their possessions, sold several unwanted items in an impromptu sidewalk sale, and said their good-byes to friends. To save money, they were driving west in a Drive-Away station wagon. Their only expenses, other than a trailer Artie had rented to hold the rest of their possessions, would be gas and food. They planned on sleeping in sleeping bags in state parks and campgrounds most of the way.

Sunday morning, they rose early, just after three, neither able to sleep well. It was a May morning, still cool, the sidewalks wet and dark, scattered wisps of fog in the streets. Driving across Manhattan to Hudson Street and uptown towards the George Washington bridge, both were silent. The city seemed almost deserted, still quiet except for a few taxis and stray automobiles. When they turned on to the West Side Elevated Highway, Artie said, "Ten years."

Pam needed no clarification. He was talking about the past not the future. She'd been thinking the same thing. They'd started one life ten years ago and now they were starting another. Would it be more successful than the first?

As they crossed the bridge and began to pull out of the city, the sun rose behind them bright and yellow, it too heading west. Like them, going home.

# About the Author

Ron Terpening and his wife, Vicki, live in Tucson, Arizona. He is the author of the thrillers *Storm Track, League of Shadows, Tropic of Fear, Nine Days in October,* and *Cloud Cover,* as well as the Artie Crenshaw trilogy—*In Light's Delay, The Turning,* and *The Echoes of Our Two Hearts,* published as *The Hornets' Nest of Our Desires.* A professor emeritus of Italian Studies at the University of Arizona, he has also written numerous articles and books dealing with Italian literature, history, and culture.